PRAISE FOR NANCY STAR

"An extraordinarily moving, beautifully written novel, *Sisters One, Two, Three* is a searing portrait of a family haunted by tragedy and fractured by the toxic power of secrets. As the story progresses, we grow to know and love the fierce and eccentric Tangles, a family at once familiar and like no other. I was riveted from the first page."

—Christina Baker Kline, #1 *New York Times* bestselling author of *Orphan Train*

"With delightful wit and the prowess of an expert storyteller, Star offers profound insight into the maternal heart in this deftly braided tale of the utterly original Tangles. *Sisters One, Two, Three* begs to be read in one big gulp—and will leave you with a lasting understanding of the treacherous balance between love and autonomy."

—Lisa Gornick, author of *Louisa Meets Bear*

"Witty, compelling, and wise, *Sisters One, Two, Three* is the kind of novel I always crave but rarely find. Glory Tangle's relationship with her children, both as kids and as grown-ups, is as real as it gets. She's a fantastic character, a match for the surprises to be found in the perfectly evoked island setting of Martha's Vineyard. I really loved each of the three sisters, too, and was very nervous for all of them! Nancy Star, thank you so much for the hours I spent in these pages."

—Alice Elliott Dark, author of *In The Gloaming* and *Think of England*

"Nancy Star's gripping novel of mothers and daughters and sisters shows us how we can never escape our families—and why that may be our salvation. Full of surprising twists and deep emotional insights,

SISTERS ONE, TWO, THREE

ALSO BY NANCY STAR

SISTERS ONE, TWO, THREE

NANCY STAR

Published by Lake Union Publishing, Seattle

www.apub.com

Amazon, the Amazon logo, and Lake Union Publishing are trademarks of Amazon.com, Inc., or its affiliates.

ISBN-13: 9781503937468
ISBN-10: 1503937461

Cover design by Janet Perr

Printed in the United States of America

For Larry

PROLOGUE

Ginger Tangle had nothing against nature. She often stopped to notice the sky, clouds particularly, but also hawks circling and the dissipating puffy trails of planes. But today was different. Today, in the parking lot at the summit of Mount Washington, as she gazed at the granite ledges perched over sheer drops only inches from where her disgruntled teenage daughter stood, what she felt was hypertension. She could hear it, her heartbeat pulsing in her ears.

Yes, she had noticed the rough-hewn scenic overlook arrows, so quaint and welcoming as they pointed toward views that, yes, were expansive. But what held her gaze were the chasms. Had no one stopped to consider the possible outcomes of placing photo-op elevation markers and telescopes lined up like promises on top of boulders where the wind often turned hurricane force without warning?

Was Ginger worried Julia might get blown off by a sudden gale, or, worse, impulsively leap? No, it wasn't like that. But an overly bold and defiant skip to the edge? An eyes-on-the-phone clumsy stumble and fall? Accidents happened. Ginger knew this better than most.

• • •

The Mount Washington trip had been a last-minute addition to their New England college tour itinerary. An opportunity for family bonding, after what Ginger had predicted would be a long and difficult week.

Second thoughts had set in at once. Her research confirmed her gut. Her wilderness side-trip idea had possibly fatal flaws. She ticked them off for her husband, Richard. Moose on the roads, bear in the woods, and in the air, according to an alert on the CDC site bookmarked on her computer, mosquito-borne Eastern Equine Encephalitis. As if that wasn't enough, the weather on the summit was notoriously unpredictable. Snow squalls happened in July.

Richard saw it a different way. "A moose sighting would be awesome. You already packed bug spray. I checked the weather. It's going to be hot."

Day one of the college tour, Julia, tall and bony, all elbows and knees, exited their car like an awkward shorebird and announced, "No way." The sun peeking out from between the rolling mountains of Vermont made her red hair look on fire but her mood remained morose. "Middle of nowhere," she said, from a spot so beautifully landscaped it felt more park than parking lot. "Not going here."

Dumbstruck by the way the pink light hit the stone buildings, Ginger had pressed on. "Why don't you poke around a little before you decide? You never know. Worst-case scenario, you tell your friends at home I was mean to make you look." Ginger had realized her mistake immediately. Of course Julia would not be sharing this with her friends at home. This was the summer she'd dumped her friends in a trade-down for a boy named Nick.

Day two, on line at the snack bar of a large university in the middle of Boston, Ginger lost in thought wondering why the frozen yogurt machine was placed alongside the lunch offerings instead of the desserts, Julia had announced college wasn't for everyone. "Some people do better just being out in the world."

"You mean no college ever?" Ginger asked. "Or a gap year?"

Julia stepped off the yogurt line. "Just because you don't go to college doesn't mean you don't have a life." She headed toward the exit sign.

Ginger grabbed two bananas, paid for them, and followed her family out.

That night in their Boston chain hotel, Richard went to the front desk to track down the hypoallergenic pillows the room brochure advertised as available upon request, while Ginger lay in bed staring at the ceiling, a greatest-hits reel featuring Julia's boyfriend running in a loop through her brain.

Nick in high school: one year older than Julia. A senior. Did tech for the drama club. Also did music. Sound collage, Julia said, whatever that was. First choice for college, Ringling Brothers Clown School. Plan B if that didn't work out? There was none. Result of neglecting to find out in a timely way that the clown school no longer existed? A gap year.

Nick after high school: job right after graduation. Starbucks. Duration of employment, half a day. Reason for termination, according to Julia? Refusal to be fake cheerful. Other refusal, coming to the door to pick Julia up. Preferred parental avoidance technique, texting from the car.

Ginger's first sighting of Nick was on a stealth visit to his next job, at an independent coffee shop where fake cheer was not required. She assessed his appeal while on line. Tall, rangy, kind of good-looking, acne that might clear up if he'd keep his hair off his forehead, furniture tack–style earrings creeping up his cartilage—too unpleasant to look at.

When it was her turn to order, she asked for coffee with room for milk. Her generous interpretation of why Nick overfilled her cup so much that black liquid sloshed on the counter? The place was noisy and the boy couldn't hear. The time it took for Ginger to figure out what Nick meant, in dollars, when he rang her up and said, "That will be three hundred and fourteen cents"? Just under a minute. Duration of Nick's independent-coffee-shop job? Four days. Reason for termination, according to Julia? Owner had no sense of humor.

The hotel room door opened, startling her. Richard was back. No pillow. "Turns out they only have one kind."

"Thanks for checking." She reached for her eyedrops.

Richard sat down on the chair next to the bed. "Listen, I was thinking. About you and Julia. Maybe it would help if you backed off a little. Not saying it's your fault. Just—maybe if you back off, she'll back off." He shrugged and smiled. "Worth a try?"

She softened. This was how it went with them. Richard was a congenital optimist who got over things faster than anyone she'd ever known. She was a worrier with a dedicated pitfall-first view of the world. Most of the time, the combination made for good balance. But all the sparring with Julia was starting to wear her down. The balance was not holding.

Day three, a small liberal arts college in an idyllic Massachusetts town, another no-go. Mission unaccomplished, they piled into the car and set off for their fun overnight. Outside, the sun beat down, but in the car the mood stayed dark. In the distance the inn loomed from the mountaintop like something out of a horror movie.

Ginger had picked this inn because of its close proximity to good hiking, but it had the additional benefit—she'd learned from the colleague who'd recommended it—of being off the grid, neither cell phones nor Internet a match for the mountains of the Presidential Range.

Julia cursed from the backseat. Weak service discovered. "My phone has no bars. Does yours have bars?"

Ginger checked as if she didn't know. "Nope. But I think we'll survive. It's only for twenty-four hours."

"What am I supposed to do without a phone?"

Richard glanced in the rearview mirror. "Bet you anything they have Scrabble."

The innkeeper led his silent guests up a crooked flight of stairs to two rooms that felt perfect for slow cooking a roast. Ginger sat on the bed and fanned her face with her hands while Richard moved to open the windows.

The innkeeper stopped him. "No use doing that now. Mountain air-conditioning is you open the windows at night and close them in the morning. Open them now, it'll only get worse." He read Ginger's expression. "I'll find you folks a fan."

As soon as the innkeeper left, Ginger got up and opened the windows herself. But the hot breeze that lifted up the edge of the doily on the painted dresser brought no relief. She glanced across the hall. Too hot to bother closing her door, Julia lay collapsed on her bed. Ginger could see her daughter's dirty white sneakers splayed across the nubby blush coverlet.

Julia had no idea how much bacteria there was on the bottom of shoes. Few people did. Ginger knew this because in addition to being an elementary school nurse, she taught a night class at the Adult School—Nurse Tangle's Danger Class—and one of the topics she covered was

"Hidden Dangers: Shoes and Purses." Purses were the worst. The places women put them, first on the sink in a public toilet, then on the kitchen counter.

"Jules, take off your shoes," Ginger called.

Julia's feet came off the bed and her door slammed shut. A moment later it swung back open. She stormed into her parents' room. "Are you trying to kill me? The thingy on my desk says the Internet is down."

"That's annoying," Ginger said. "Want to—"

"No." This time when Julia slammed her door, it rattled the glass tray that sat atop the dresser doily in her parents' room.

At dinnertime, Ginger walked across the hall and knocked. "Jules? We're going down. Jules?" She pressed her ear to the door. Nothing. She turned the knob and made a mental note to warn her daughter that it was important to lock her door when she went away to college.

Sleeping, eyes closed, hair fanned out around her head, Julia looked sweet. Did sleep make everyone look sweet? *Was* she sleeping? Ginger put her palm in front of her daughter's mouth to feel for breath.

"What are you doing?" Julia pushed her hand away.

Ginger laughed at herself. "Making sure you're alive?"

Julia blinked and a scrim descended. "Not funny."

So this was how it would go. "It's dinnertime. Dad's waiting downstairs."

"Not hungry." She shut her eyes hard, the way she did as a child when she wanted something to go away.

"They stop serving at eight." Ginger scanned Julia's face for signs of an eating disorder but saw none. She checked her watch. "I'll call in twenty minutes. Try not to fall back."

"I'm not coming." She pulled the blanket up over her head.

"You look like a corpse. Can you even breathe?" No answer. "I give up," Ginger said—as if that was a possibility—and went down to join Richard at the table set for three.

In the morning, in the breakfast room on the screened-in porch facing the mountain range, Julia shoveled in her omelet—since when did she like spinach in her eggs?—pushed away her plate, and proposed a change in activity.

Except Ginger had already mapped out the route to the summit from the parking lot. She had even written down the number of steps from the tunnel to the first viewing platform. Plans like that were not meant to be discarded. "Change to what?"

"Swimming. That's what people do when it's hot. The housekeeping girl told me where to go. She's my age. She's so awesome. Look." She unfolded a trail map. "I got this at the front desk." She pointed. "Emerald Pond is the closest swimming hole. It's only a few minutes from where you park. The water is totally clear. You just climb up these big rocks and jump in. Even old people do it. It's deep," she added for her mother's benefit. "So we won't break our necks. And it's not the ocean." This was also for her mother. Ginger did not go in the ocean. Jumping into a mountain pool was something she could conceivably do.

Except for the part about the big rocks. "No. Top three causes of spinal cord injury? Car crash, gunshot, diving into mountain pools." This was more or less true. "It's a different climate on the summit. Even on a hot day it's cold. I guarantee you'll be happy we went."

Julia started to protest, but Richard interrupted. "Mom spent a lot of time planning this. How about we give her a chance? You never know. We might have fun."

It was a pale attempt at support, Ginger thought, but Julia agreed so she took it.

When they got to the parking lot, Richard turned off the car and Julia read the temperature gauge on the dashboard. "Only ninety-two degrees. Good work, Mom."

"This isn't the summit," Ginger said. "You'll see. It'll be cold up there." Outside of the car, she fished around in her backpack and found three hats, blue-and-green beanies she'd bought at a store in North Conway. She put hers on and handed out the others.

Julia held her hat like it was toxic, thumb and forefinger only. "What is this?"

Okay. Ginger would try it Richard's way. Back off. Ignore the bait. Ignore the question. "See the walkway? It's just past that bus."

Julia pressed her lips together. She pressed them so hard, they seemed to disappear.

"What?" Ginger heard the bite in her voice and tried again, kinder. "What?"

Julia turned to her father. "It's ninety degrees. I'm supposed to wear a wool hat that looks like the Earth. Mom snaps at me—*What?*—and then pretends she has no idea what's wrong."

It was a perfect and stinging imitation. "The hat is for wind," Ginger explained. "Summer weight. The man at the store said."

"The man at the store was deranged, and if you think I'm putting that on my head, you're deranged." Julia got back in the car.

Ginger felt Richard come close behind her. He gave her a hug and spoke into her hair. "Please, let it go." At work he was a bulldog, fearless and resolute, but at home Richard could not tolerate confrontation. This, Ginger suspected, was a side effect of his having lost both parents at a young age. Sudden deaths—car accident for his mother, heart attack for his father—preceded by garden-variety arguments about tracking mud on a clean floor and forgetting to pick up a rotisserie chicken for dinner, arguments where no one got a chance to make up. Loss and all that went with it was something Ginger understood.

She took off her hat. "Forget the hats." She stuffed it in her backpack. "Getting hats was a dumb idea."

Defiant, Julia put on her hat and pulled it down low. She crossed her arms. A minute later she took the hat off and got out of the car. She turned to her father. "I feel like I can't breathe."

"Are you nauseous?" Ginger handed her a water bottle. "Have a drink. It could be altitude sickness. We should head down."

"It's not the altitude," Julia said. "It's you. I can't breathe because of you."

That's when Ginger noticed the ledges. What was she thinking, picking a place like this?

Julia looked at her phone. "I'm going to the bathroom. I'll meet you on top. And don't worry, I won't get lost. There's signs everywhere. I couldn't get lost if I wanted to."

"Why would you want to?" Ginger asked. She felt Richard's hand on her shoulder. "Okay. Meet you up top."

They walked slowly through the short tunnel. Water dripped down the walls on either side. Children screamed nonsense words to make echoes. Ginger leaned into Richard and asked, "Did you know it would be this hard?"

He shook his head. "And we only have one. Imagine if we had two. Or three or four. How in the world did your mother manage with four kids?"

Pure instinct made Ginger turn around. She let out a soft moan. Julia was there. Right behind them. Listening.

"*Four* kids? Grandma Glory had two kids. You and Aunt Mimi."

Ginger felt her knees buckle. She quickly laid a hand against the wet wall to steady herself. Why had Richard said that? He knew this was a conversation she did not want to have. Now she had no choice but to answer. "I had a brother. He died."

"What? When? How?"

"We were little." Ginger took a breath. "There was an accident."

Richard added, "This is hard for Mom to talk about."

"Wait. You said Grandma had four kids. Who's the fourth?"

Ginger had worked hard to avoid this moment, but here it was. Now all that was left was the question of how much would be enough to share. "I have another sister. My baby sister. Your aunt. Aunt Callie. She left home young."

"Where is she now?"

Finally, something Ginger could admit. "I have no idea."

They walked in awkward silence, Ginger on alert for whatever might come next. When they stepped out of the tunnel, the light was blinding. Julia's cheeks looked hot.

"I don't get it," Julia said. "You're on me all the time about how I shouldn't hide things. How truth is the most important thing on the planet, blah, blah, blah. And now I hear I have an uncle I never heard of, who died in some accident you never mentioned, and an aunt who . . ." She was too mad to finish her sentence.

Ginger noticed a vein traversing Julia's forehead. "Take a deep breath, Jules."

"Am I going to end up like you? Oh my god. Am I already like you now?"

And Ginger laughed, surprising them all. Because it suddenly felt like a practical joke. When Julia was born, there was only one thing Ginger knew for sure: she would not raise her daughter in a family where what was true in the morning turned out, by night, to be a lie. Yet here she was, rivaling her mother in skills of deception.

The weather on the summit was exactly as predicted, even in the middle of a heat wave, freakishly cold. Ginger stuck her hands in her pockets and turned against the wind.

Julia walked around to face her. "Anything else I don't know?"

"That's it," Ginger said. "That's everything."

She wasn't lying. She was still a year away from learning the rest, that her brother's accident, the event she'd spent her entire adult life trying to pretend never happened, was not the only catastrophe on that perfect beach day those many years ago.

PART ONE
BEFORE AND AFTER

CHAPTER ONE

Ginger had no idea she was in trouble until her sister Mimi woke her up and told her so. This was not unusual. One or the other of the Tangle children—there were four in all—was often in trouble and Mimi was usually the one who knew why. If birth order had counted, it would have been Ginger, the eldest, who dished out the secrets of the world. But in the Tangle house, order came and went in fits and starts. Chaos was far more reliable.

"It's because you're thirteen," Mimi told her, adding a quick "Happy birthday!" before turning serious again. "Thirteen—everyone knows— is bad luck. So when you turn thirteen? Bad luck for a whole year. Nothing you can do." Information delivered, she darted across the hall to share this alarming announcement with Charlie, their eight-year-old brother, and Callie, the youngest sister, age six.

Now that her bedroom door was open, Ginger could hear the low growl of her mother Glory's voice on attack followed by the riled-up pitch of her father Solly's reply. The fight was a loud one, which was good news. The quiet fights were trickier. Sometimes the only tip-off was an onion smell, Solly's sighs filling up whatever room he was in with the sour gas of his agitated gut. With the noisy fights Ginger could scope it out and decide what was best, a targeted interruption or a keep-behind-a-closed-door distance. But it was impossible to know what was best with a fight she didn't even know was going on.

Mimi, done with sharing her news flash about Ginger's bad luck, skipped into their room, grabbed her pad, got in bed, and resumed her early morning project, making a birthday card. At least that's what she said she was doing. To Ginger, it seemed more like an excuse to crumple paper into balls, which she then tossed against walls, window, ceiling, and floor.

A stray ball bounced onto Ginger's chest. She was about to complain when her morning dream flashed back. "You were in my dream," she told Mimi. "You were with me in the kitchen and I was asking Mom if this year, for my birthday, instead of presents I could get my own room. Nothing personal," she told her sister.

Mimi shrugged—she didn't care—and then lobbed another mistake under Ginger's bed.

Ginger took the paper ball on her chest and crumpled it hard, making it smaller. "Then the kitchen turned into the basement and you weren't there anymore. I was alone and something was crawling on me and I couldn't see what it was and I couldn't get it off and I wanted to go back to the kitchen but the stairs vanished and I was stuck." She glanced over to see what Mimi made of this, but Mimi had vanished too. A moment later Ginger heard her clomping up the stairs, followed by the sharp click of her mother's heels on the floor in the hall.

"No," Glory was saying. "Gingie's not getting her own room and you're not getting her presents." She swept in wearing a fickle smile. "Happy birthday, your highness. Care to explain where I'm supposed to procure a private bedchamber for you?"

There was no point defending herself. *It was a dream* would not change her mother's response. Their house had three bedrooms, two parents, four kids. There was no attic, and the basement—dirt floor, crackled concrete walls—was unheated. It was the same in every other house on their block, modest Capes with a token patch of lawn that all the fathers mowed in a ballet of synchronized home improvement every Saturday morning, just as every June they celebrated summer by perfuming the air with tar as they walked up their driveways, buckets in hand, brushing on sealant to cover up cracks.

Ginger had heard their New Jersey neighborhood defined as mixed, meaning both policemen and firemen lived there. Neighbors were also teachers and people who sold things, like the man next door, Paul Clarke, who sold rugs, and her father, who owned a toy business selling overstock and seconds, or as Glory put it, junk.

She watched as her mother pondered the privacy issue. "Unless . . . the Clarkes do have that extra room." This was because, sadly, the Clarkes next door had only one child. "Want me to ask Evelyn if you can move in there?" She didn't wait for an answer. "I didn't think so." She pivoted and breezed back to the kitchen where, Ginger knew from Mimi, she was cooking up a *birthday surprise*.

"If you've got any luck at all"—Mimi said while throwing three balled-up sheets of paper against the wall in quick succession—"thirteen will go fast. At sixteen you get a party."

When the kitchen timer rang, Glory called up that the surprise was ready. Ginger stepped lightly on her way down the stairs so as not to leave prints. She stopped in the foyer to listen to what the argument was about. Consciousness-raising groups again.

"Why shouldn't I join a group? What are you worried will happen? You think they'll tell me to kick you out? Or make you clean? Maybe vacuum for once? Do you even know where the vacuum is?"

Ginger hurried to the kitchen and skidded to a stop on the linoleum floor. "Hall closet?"

Her father looked up, his brown eyes droopy as a basset hound's. Glory swiveled and beamed. "Look who's here." In one hand she held a long serrated knife, in the other a plate. Her birthday surprise rotation of baked goods was small. None were good, but today's—date nut loaf—was the booby prize. As usual, the loaf had come out of the tin in pieces, which her mother had tried with modest effort to mush back together into a solid form. The edges were black but Ginger knew, from experience, no matter how burnt the outside, the center would be wet with the taste of rum. Glory extended the offering. "Ta-da!"

"Thank you." Ginger took the plate, put it down, and smiled. She could smile even while gagging, but Mimi was a wild card. Mimi might decide to pretend to like the date nut loaf, or she might decide to stuff her face and then spit the mush out in her napkin while making retching noises. On a morning like this, when Glory's mood—Ginger could tell—was brittle, retching noises would not go over well. She scrambled for an idea. "Can I bring this to French class? Did you know Madame Olivier and I have the same birthday? Did you know she loves date nut loaf too?"

"No kidding. What a coincidence."

Ginger watched carefully to see if she was going to get away with her story. On the plus side, her mother liked the French teacher, who'd complimented her on her accent at parent-teacher night. On the minus side, Ginger had refused her mother's gift. She held her breath.

The knife went back in the holder. *"Bien."* Glory reclaimed the loaf and covered it up with foil. *"Voilà."* She handed it back to Ginger. *"Pour Madame."* She winked. "That wasn't bad, by the way. I give it an eight."

Ginger returned the wink with a halfhearted smile. She had only recently noticed that rating lies on a scale of one to ten was not something other mothers did.

"My turn." Solly handed Ginger a box. "First on the block, you're going to be with this one. James Bond Action Pen. Comes with its own pack of Vaper Paper. Runs on invisible ink."

"Invisible ink," Glory repeated. "Let me see. That must mean . . . you got a shipment of pens that don't work. Well done, Emperor of Duds." In company, Glory boasted that Solly was a toy entrepreneur, but at home she enjoyed needling him with pet names that were far less flattering.

The truth was, in the overstock business there were a lot of duds. Shipments of See 'n Say where the cows went oink. X-Ray Specs with only one lens. Pens with no ink.

"So they have no ink," Solly said. "Do I make a living? Do you have what you need?"

"Sure, King Con. Whatever you say."

Solly lumbered out of the kitchen to finish getting ready for work. Glory slid into the chair across from Ginger. "Okay, kiddo. You're thirteen now. There's things you need to know."

Usually, Ginger could feel it when one of her mother's bursts of confidences was coming on, and she could make it out of the room in time. But now and then she got caught off guard.

"For starters—you can write this down if you want—do *not* marry someone more than five years older. More than five years, you can get fooled. When I first met your father, he twirled me over to Roseland twice a week. So suave, I thought. Took me everywhere to dance. Even the Savoy, up in Harlem. Rumba, samba, fox-trot—he danced them all like a dream. You know he's six years older than me, right?" Ginger nodded and Glory nodded too. Then she snapped her fingers. "Abracadabra, twenty years later I wake up, and Mr. Dance Like a Dream has neuromas on both feet and a pair of orthopedic shoes that could fit the Jolly Green Giant."

Ginger closed her eyes and concentrated on chewing her Cocoa Puffs.

"Look at me, Gingie. You're thirteen now. Dreamtime's over."

Ginger opened her eyes in time to see her mother sweep out of the room to get last licks on her argument before Solly left for work.

• • •

The birthday dream of a room of her own must have gotten her mother thinking, because when Ginger came home from school, she saw the first bad luck of her thirteenth year had arrived in the form of a double-decker bunk where Mimi's bed had been. Callie's possessions now spilled from the bottom mattress onto the floor of what was suddenly called the Girls' Room.

"Why does Charlie get his own room?" Mimi asked even though Ginger told her not to.

"Boys and girls ought not to share bedrooms," Glory explained. "Buck up. You'll love it. You'll be up all night whispering secrets. I'm quite sure I'll regret the whole thing."

It was useless to complain so Ginger made the best of it with a roll of masking tape and a ruler, which she used to carefully lay down a set of double lines to mark her area. "My side is off-limits," she announced and then went back to her original afternoon plan, gathering her unruly hair on top of her head in a ponytail and sectioning it around two coffee cans to make it straight.

"You can sleep with me," Charlie told Callie, who was as unhappy as Ginger with the new arrangement. "You're still small enough to fit in my bed."

"Okay, good." Callie quickly gathered up her collection of stuffed animals. They were dogs mostly, different sizes and breeds. She called them her Arleys, having named them in rhyming tributes to her brother—Barley the Lab, Farley the Beagle, Marley the Schnauzer, and so on. In her old room, every night before bedtime, Callie would line up her Arleys and Charlie would read them a story. But when she asked her new roommate, Mimi, if she'd read to them, Mimi cut her off with a quick, "No. Way."

Arms full of Arleys, Callie walked out of the Girls' Room into the hall where Glory was waiting. "No more switching of rooms," her mother announced, and the subject was closed.

Later that afternoon Ginger noticed a tall stack of plates on the dining room table. But the family ate dinner in the kitchen. She found her mother fluffing the pillows from the purple sofa in the living room. This gave Ginger pause. The sofa, the plum velvet chairs, the piano no one played—the entire living room—was off-limits to them, except when company came.

"The Clarkes," Glory said, when Ginger asked. She bent down to brush a spot on the lavender plush carpet where the nap went the wrong way. "I thought it would fun, celebrating your birthday with the neighbors. And we have a special guest. Casper Diggans. Evelyn's brother. Did you meet him? Oh, I forgot. You didn't work there today." Ginger had a job as a mother's helper for Evelyn Clarke. She went over three afternoons a week, but because it was her birthday, Evelyn had given her the day off.

"Mr. Diggans came all the way from Boston. Your father and I went over last night to meet him. Talk about charming. Of course the Curmudgeon of Essex County doesn't agree. We were there for five minutes—Casper couldn't have been nicer—but that was enough for Solly Tangle to decide he disapproves. Be a peach, Gingie. Help me move my puzzle upstairs so we can set the table."

Jigsaw puzzles were Glory's hobby. She built them using upside-down game boards as the base so that if necessary, like tonight, they could be moved. The current puzzle, Big Ben, almost complete, sat on the board of one of Solly's favorite brainstorms—rebranding a shipment of misprinted Monopoly sets where every property was Jail, into April Fools' kits.

Ginger carried the puzzle and Glory followed behind, offering details about dinner. "I ordered Chinese. And I have a surprise planned for dessert. But I still need to work out the seating. Can't put your father next to Mr. Diggans. Maybe I'll put you between them. That might work."

"What doesn't Dad like about him?"

"Beats me." Glory shrugged. "It started before he met him. Evelyn told me, very nicely, 'Do not ask my brother about his job.' Apparently, it's some kind of secret. I told your father and his nose went right out of joint. Told me that's a hoity-toity thing to say. Is it hoity-toity to be a spy? That's what I think he is. Imagine. A spy next door."

Below them the front door opened. "Hello? Did everyone move away?"

"Yes, Solly," Glory called down. "We moved. We live on Mars now."

Solly chuckled. He must have had a good day. There was a moment of silence, and then he called up. "Eleven plates you got on the table? We got eleven people coming?"

"It's not hard to get to eleven when you start from six," Glory called and then turned to Ginger. "Will you go down and tell him it's just the Clarkes, Casper Diggans, and Ivan the Director. That's all."

This was a lot of bad news for Solly to take in. Paul Clarke, who he said was a bore with his constant lectures on wall-to-wall carpets; Casper Diggans, who he'd already decided he didn't like; and Ivan, the director of her mother's community theater group, who Glory quoted every night at dinner like he was her own personal fortune cookie.

Last night at dinner it was, *Ivan says a quiet exit speaks louder than a hundred words.* Glory had demonstrated that one, silently gliding out of the kitchen while the family strained to look enthusiastic. Looking neutral was always risky business around Glory, who could decide, in a blink, a darling daydreamer was really a pill. This wasn't a problem for Callie, with her *swoony smile*, or for Charlie, who could *melt a woman's heart with his fairy broom eyelashes.* Even Mimi got by, with her *Shirley Temple dimples.* Ginger was another story. According to Glory, Ginger had *a long face, not much you can do about that* plus eyebrows permanently knit into a worried slant. As for her own face, Glory boasted that people often stopped to say her eyes made Paul Newman's look gray, though Ginger had never seen that happen—maybe because it never had.

Glory joined them in the kitchen. "Why so glum?"

"Who's glum?" Solly asked. "I just don't know why I have to have dinner with the whole neighborhood."

"It's just Ivan and the Clarkes and Mr. Diggans. Who I think is darling. Today he volunteered to join the theater group. You know what a hard time we have finding men, Solly."

"See? That's what I mean." Solly tugged off his prescription shoes. "Who comes for a visit and right away joins a group? I don't trust him. I don't trust him for a minute."

"For the love of god." Glory headed toward the stairs, stepping around the children who'd gathered there to eavesdrop. "I need a vacation from this asylum."

"What's wrong with Mr. Diggans?" Mimi asked. "Is he a kidnapper?" They'd recently watched a public service announcement about kidnappers. "Does he drive a black car?" In the commercial a black car slowly cruised down a street while a voice cautioned all children watching to stay alert.

Callie moved closer to Charlie. "Is a kidnapper coming to dinner?"

"Nice going, Solly. Now you've got them scared of the neighbors." Glory continued up the stairs to her bedroom to put on her face.

"Don't worry." Solly gave Callie a pat on her head. "Mr. Diggans is not a kidnapper. It's nothing like that. Nothing to be scared of. Sometimes I meet someone, he rubs me the wrong way. Your mother meets the same person, she thinks he's peachy keen." He let out a sigh and disappeared into the den to see what Walter Cronkite had to say, leaving Ginger and her siblings alone with the scent of onions.

CHAPTER TWO

Being organized gave Ginger peace of mind. At work, the Band-Aids on the first aid shelf progressed logically from small circle to knuckle to knee-sized. At home, the mudroom cubby, which held suntan lotion and bug spray in the summer, was restocked on the first day of winter with Yaktrax boot grippers and Vaseline Intensive Care. With each thing in its place, Ginger could focus on what mattered: her mission to keep everyone safe.

First thing every school morning, Ginger would tape a flyer to her office door, every day a different safety tip. It might be "You Are the Boss of Your Body!" on Monday, and on Tuesday, "Sneezes Go in Your Elbow, Please!" At home, she turned a whiteboard affixed to the refrigerator into the family communications hub, with a daily post about the weather, "Sun is out. Lotion up!" and a question of the day, "Did you remember to brush your tongue?"

As a young child, Julia used to add pictograms, a crudely drawn hat or snowman next to the weather, a checkmark or heart next to the question of the day. As she got older, her annotations changed, first to "Yes," then "Okay," and one day, "Duh."

This past summer, Richard had suggested twice—first in a jokey voice, then in a more serious tone—that it was probably time to stop with the whiteboard. He reminded her that at seventeen, Julia found out about the weather the same way everyone else did, by checking her phone. Ginger disagreed. Not only did she believe Julia still liked waking up to her little notes, she was convinced her daughter would miss them if they suddenly stopped. At least that's what she thought *before* their Mount Washington trip. Now, a week after their return, Ginger woke up every day to find her messages had been erased.

"It's rude," she complained. "Ignoring it is one thing, but erasing it?"

"It was me," Richard confessed. He gave her a goofy grin, the kind he knew always made her smile.

Except now it didn't. "*You* erased it? You realize you erased our family meeting."

"Maybe it's time we gave up those too."

The suggestion startled her. Richard loved their family meetings. They were Ginger's idea—she organized the agendas—but Richard ran them, going through the topics in an orderly fashion, making sure everyone got a chance to voice their concerns, creating at least the feeling that decisions were reached by consensus.

"We can't give up the meetings now," Ginger said. "We need a meeting so we can apologize. So *I* can apologize. It's on me. I should have told her about Charlie and Callie. But how can I apologize if I can't get her alone in a room without Nick?"

"Just take her aside for a minute. And if Nick's there, so what?" He offered another smile. "And maybe ease up on the punishment. Maybe let her use the car again."

How was that a good idea? It was the first week of school and already Julia had missed curfew three nights in a row. "You're suggesting—what? We're supposed to just let her do—"

Julia walked into the kitchen and stopped. Her expression made it clear she knew they'd been talking about her.

"Morning," Ginger said, trying for a believable amount of cheer.

"Morning," Julia mumbled. She filled up a travel cup with coffee. "I'm getting a ride to school." She started out of the kitchen.

"Aren't you going to eat something?" Ginger got up and opened the refrigerator. "What about a clementine?"

"I'll pick up a bagel on the way."

Not a great choice, but Ginger let it go. "Jules," she said to her daughter's back. "We're having a family meeting tonight. Eight o'clock. Jules? Did you hear me?"

Julia left the room and the front door slammed.

"She heard you," Richard said. "She nodded. I saw it. She'll be here."

Ginger shook her head. "I don't think so."

Being right was not always fun—that's what Ginger was thinking right before Julia finally came home at eleven o'clock. Nick was right behind her.

Ginger stood up. "Sorry," she told the boy. "You have to go home. We're having a family meeting."

"You can stay if you want," Julia told him.

"That's okay," Nick said. "I'll go."

Julia saw him out. Their good-bye took ten minutes. When she came back, she sank into the couch. "Let the lecture begin."

"We're not here to lecture you," Richard said.

"I want to apologize," Ginger took over. "I should have told you about my brother and the accident and my sister. I have no excuse. I was wrong."

As if she needed to underline how much she didn't care, Julia let her neck go limp.

Her daughter looked like a marionette on break. Ginger took a breath and reminded herself that there were scientific studies showing people in comas could hear what was being said around them. Surely if a coma victim could hear, so could an oppositional teenager.

She continued the conversation, now directing her words to the top of her daughter's head. "In my family, growing up, there were things we just didn't talk about." Julia snorted and Ginger pretended she didn't hear it. "There are things that are still hard for me to talk about. But I'm here now. Happy to answer any questions you have. Everything is fair game." She waited but got no response. Even a snort would have been better than this. Silence. "Hello?"

Julia sat up and met her mother's eyes. "You don't get it. It doesn't matter. I'm not going to be living here much longer so I don't care. Are we done? I have a chem test tomorrow. I need to study."

"Then why were you out till eleven?" Ginger looked over at Richard, hoping for help.

"Go," he said. "Go study."

"Thanks, Dad." Julia ran upstairs and closed her door before her mother could veto the pardon.

Ginger shook her head. "That was not helpful." She whispered the next. "She's changed. Something's different. Could it be drugs? Behavior change is a big warning sign for drugs."

"I don't think so." Richard reached over and moved Ginger's hair away from her eyes. "Can you take a vacation from worrying about her? For one week. Just try it. See what happens. Because"—he motioned to the space between Ginger and Julia upstairs—"this isn't working."

Ginger might have taken offense at the implication—that Julia's behavior was her fault—except that Richard looked so sad. So she took the dare, a vacation from worrying for a week, meaning for one week she didn't say a single worry out loud.

At the end of the week, when Richard said, "Success! You didn't worry and nothing bad happened!" she smiled back, relieved to see him look so happy.

But Monday morning, first day at work after a week of not worrying, Ginger got a bad-news call from her friend Lydia, the nurse at the high school, about one of her favorite students—they weren't supposed to have favorite students, but all the nurses did. The boy, a sixteen-year-old, had gone to the hospital over the weekend after accidentally swallowing his magnetic tongue ring. "They got the magnet out," Lydia told her, "but they had to cut open his intestines. Poor kid almost died."

"No magnetic tongue rings!" Ginger wrote on the whiteboard that night before she went to bed. But in the morning her message was replaced by one written in Julia's handwriting, "Sleeping at Angie's. See you tomorrow."

"Did she leave yet?" Ginger asked as she sat down to her breakfast. "Did you see what she wrote?"

Richard looked up from the paper. "She's at zero period gym. And yes, I saw it."

"She thinks we're going to fall for *sleeping at Angie's*?" Ginger liked Angie, but she knew Angie had been dumped last summer for Nick, along with the rest of Julia's friends.

"Come on. What evidence do you have she's *not* going to sleep there?"

Ginger didn't need evidence. She had a built-in danger detector and Richard knew it. The problem was that even when she knew something bad was coming, she couldn't be sure of what the bad thing would be. What she was sure of was this: Julia was not planning on sleeping at Angie's. "We have to do something. I don't know how much more of this I can—"

Richard's phone interrupted her. He left the kitchen to take the call in private. Ginger hovered near the doorway but couldn't make out what he was saying. When he returned, he looked grim.

"What is it?" she asked. "Was it Angie's mom?"

"No. Work. New case."

"Oh. Boy or girl?"

"Boy and girl. Twins. Five years old. I don't want to talk about it. I have to go." He left to gather his things.

This was something new. Richard had used her as a sounding board for work for as long as they'd been together. His job was how they'd met. She was a new nurse—it was her second month at her school— when Orney, the gentle giant of a custodian who spent his spare time polishing doorknobs for no other reason than that the children noticed, walked into her office holding hands with a little girl named Ruby. The tears on Ruby's five-year-old face had only made her bruised eye more apparent.

"Go on," Orney prompted. "Tell Nurse Tangle what happened."

"I fell," Ruby said.

"Tell her what *really* happened."

"My mommy hit me."

The custodian stayed with Ruby, sitting at her side, big hand next to little, both coloring, while Ginger called the Abuse and Neglect Hotline. The intake worker on the phone gave the case a status of Immediate, so they didn't have long to wait.

Orney was one of the few people who knew what happened next, that the investigator couldn't locate Ruby's father, who'd left the family long ago, or the grandmother who'd gone away, location unknown, so Ginger stepped up, applied for, and was given provisional license for foster care. Later that day, Ruby's older brother told the law guardian assigned to them that Ruby had lied. His mother, the boy insisted, had never hit anyone. Because the children's stories didn't match up, Ruby was assigned her own law guardian. That was Richard.

They met for the first time when Richard came to interview Ruby at her foster home, Ginger's apartment. After Ruby was reunited with her grandmother, Richard made his next appointments with the girl in the office of her school nurse. One year later, when Ginger and Richard married, Ruby, by then in permanent custody of her grandmother, was their flower girl.

They continued to be short-term foster parents in the early years of their marriage, but as the number of Richard's cases grew, it got harder to decide which child to take. Often Ginger was made mute by the choices, weighing the needs of the daughter with the abusive alcoholic mother against the needs of the son with the schizophrenic dad. They were between foster kids when Ginger got pregnant, and after Julia was born they made the decision not to take in any more.

Ginger would not deny that listening to the things that went wrong in a family sometimes took her breath away and that, on occasion, when Richard shared details of a case of neglect, she'd gotten physically sick. But she didn't want *this*, for Richard to stop sharing altogether.

She followed him into the small den where he was packing up his computer. "Tell me about the case," she said. "I want to know."

"What's the point? It's just another horror story."

She recognized the tone. It was his courtroom voice, the one he used when the summation was over to signal that nothing more could be said.

"But—"

"No." He gave her a quick kiss on the cheek. "You have enough on your mind. Try and have a good day. Try."

It was during her ten-minute lunch break that she called Angie's mother, Shelley. Ginger and Shelley had been friends in that sort-of way mothers made friends, alliances formed when the girls were little, sharing information to prevent—well, no one really knew what they were trying to prevent. They just had a vague sense of dread about what was coming.

The scary *tweens* followed by the scarier *teens*. Pooling what they knew was their first line of defense.

As it turned out, by the time the girls reached high school, friendships had shifted and reshuffled more times than any mother could keep up with and soon the mother friendships faded too. It was still nice to catch up now and then when they bumped into each other in the supermarket or at the physical therapist. But it had been months—years—since Ginger had bumped into Shelley. If it was any other mother, she would have felt too awkward to call but Shelley was a worrier too. She'd understand.

Except, she did not. "Are you kidding? Julia is the most together of all of them. I'm thrilled she's sleeping over. I wish Angie brought home more friends like her."

Ginger wondered when Shelley had last spoken to Julia. "That's sweet. Of course I think she's great too. It's just she's got this boyfriend. And he's kind of a creep. So I wanted to make sure she really is staying with you. And not with him."

"Julia would never do that," Shelley told her, and then hurried off the phone.

It was just before dinner the next night when Julia texted. *Sleeping at Angie's again.* An emoji of a winking face followed. What that meant, Ginger had no idea. Against Richard's advice, she picked up the phone and made another call to Angie's mother. "Is it okay with you that she's staying another night?"

"Of course," Shelley said. "Julia's the best. And with her around, Angie's an angel. Last night, the two of them were so quiet Dick and I forgot they were even here."

Ginger hung up. "So naïve. Shelley has no idea the girls snuck out."

"You don't know that," Richard said. "Can't you give her the benefit of the doubt?"

Ginger shook her head. "I have no doubt."

She texted Julia three times that night and got zero responses, but she didn't report that to Richard. At breakfast she texted again. This time she admitted it. "I asked Julia if she wanted to come to my class tonight, but she didn't answer."

This would be the first night of the semester for Nurse Tangle's Danger Class. It was a popular offering at the Adult School. There were over a hundred classes in the fall session. Some, like Gluten-Free Cooking and Not Your Mother's Mahjongg, had enrollment spikes and troughs from term to term. But Nurse Tangle's Danger Class was always oversubscribed.

Richard was baffled. "Why would Julia want to come to your class?"

"I'm trying something new tonight. I'm going to start things off with a little talk about 'The Danger of Secrets.' I thought Julia might . . ."

Suddenly, she wasn't sure what she thought. That Julia might be interested? That she might be appreciative? She checked her phone. No text. She heard the front door close and looked up. Another first, Richard had left for work without a good-bye.

CHAPTER THREE

Ginger was setting the table when Solly called from the kitchen, "Somebody's bugs are here."

"The ants came?" Charlie ran to see them.

He and Callie had been double-team begging for a pet for a year. Charlie did the asking while Callie pretended to be the pet. For their first attempt, a dog, Callie panted as she pawed her mother, staring up with adoring eyes.

"How sweet," Glory said. "Want a lift to the animal shelter? I'm sure they'll be able to find a dog as cute as you a darling family in no time."

They tried a cat next, after Mimi told them cats were hardly any work. This time while Charlie asked, Callie purred and rubbed against her mother's leg.

Her mother shooed them both away. "Nice try but I'm allergic."

"Give it up," Glory told them the day Callie trotted over to her and neighed. "Bad enough I have to take care of *stuffed* animals. Every day I put them on the shelf. Every night they're back on the floor. We are not getting a pet."

But the edict had changed abruptly the night the family, gathered in the den, saw the commercial for Uncle Milton's Ant Farm on TV. Solly, who had a low tolerance for other people's pitches, waved the idea away with a laugh. "What kinda crazy idiot thinks people are going to pay money to bring bugs into the house?"

"If Uncle Milton is such a crazy idiot," Glory needled, "how come he's a millionaire? That's what he's making from *bugs*, Solly. Millions."

Charlie pounced. "Can we get one? Can me and Callie get an ant farm?"

Before Solly's grunt of displeasure was fully disgorged, Glory had answered for both of them. "What a darling idea. You most certainly may."

It took eight weeks for the farm to arrive and when it came Charlie was disappointed to discover that ants were not included. Instead, there was a coupon, and after he sent that in, another long wait. Now, of all nights, on Ginger's thirteenth birthday, the contentious ants had arrived. "Take them to your room," Ginger whispered to her brother. "Before the ant farm fight starts up again."

But it was too late. Glory had heard the commotion and breezed in to join them. "Is that a tube of darling ants I see?"

Solly rolled his eyes and moved to the den.

"We're bringing them upstairs," Ginger announced. "Go," she told her brother. He raced to the stairs with the ants, Callie and Mimi right behind him, but when Ginger tried to follow, Glory blocked her.

"Be a peach and put out glasses." She tapped her chin with her finger, nail glistening with fresh polish. "Who shall I seat where?"

Ginger cautiously relaxed now that she saw Outside Glory had arrived. That's how Ginger thought of her mother whenever company was coming. When it was just them, the family home alone, Inside Glory ruled the day.

The actual transformation of Inside to Outside was not pleasant to observe. It took about an hour with a makeup kit jammed with so many tools it no longer closed. For Ginger, the improvement in her mother had nothing to do with the change from ordinary-looking to movie-star beauty. She didn't care one way or another whether her mother's wavy hair framed her heart-shaped face, or that her lashes looked longer, or her eyes seemed a more striking shade of blue. But Outside Glory was so much easier to be around. With plain-faced Inside Glory, there was no telling what might set her off.

The doorbell rang. The Chinese food was here. Solly paid. Glory took the bag and proceeded to scoop the food out of the containers and into her best china bowls.

They were up to dessert—Scooter Pies with a birthday candle in each one, an idea Glory got from the newspaper and improved upon, she pointed out, by plating with doilies—when Mimi asked, "What happened to Ivan the Director man?"

Solly looked up from where he sat, stuck between Paul Clarke and young Thomas. In Glory's final seating plan, his usual seat at the head of the table was assigned to the birthday girl. Ginger hadn't been sure if she was supposed to accept his seat, but Solly nodded in a way that let her know she should. He nodded the same way a moment later when her mother presented her with a crown clearly meant for a young child. When she put it on, the silver headband dug into the skin behind her ears and the tinsel-fringed "Happy Birthday" sign shed glitter on her plate.

"Ivan's coming," Glory said. "His meeting in New York must have gone long."

As Ginger scraped the glitter off her Scooter Pie, she watched her mother lean closer to Mr. Diggans, who had resumed telling a story in a voice too soft for anyone else to hear. Ginger took a bite of dessert and turned to her father, who was getting a lecture from Paul Clarke about the proper way to maintain shag carpets. Her father's eyelids fluttered. He was falling asleep right at the table. "Dad?" she called over, but it was too late.

Glory had noticed. She stood up and clapped. "Okay. Adult time. How about you kids go upstairs. Show Thomas the ant farm, so he can see what a million-dollar idea looks like."

They didn't have to be asked twice.

They sat on the floor in a circle around the ant farm as if it were a campfire.

"Did you get any queens?" Thomas asked.

"You can't buy queens," Charlie explained and then made up the rest. "If you do, you get arrested. I wouldn't want them anyway. When you have queens, there's always war."

Mimi stood up. "Call me if it goes nuclear."

Ginger followed her into the hall. "Stop," she hissed. "You're going to get us in trouble."

Ignoring her, Mimi sat on the floor and pressed her forehead against the banister to listen to whatever story Glory was concocting now.

But their mother had the ears of a predator. "Girls?"

Ginger covered Mimi's mouth. Mimi pushed her hand away.

Glory went back to talking to her guests. "We actually met Milton Bradley once. Where was that, Solly? Was it the toy convention in Atlantic City?" Ginger and Mimi shook their heads. Their mother never went on business trips.

Solly changed the subject. "I think maybe Ivan the Director isn't coming after all."

"Who is this Ivan?" Mr. Diggans asked.

"He runs our theater group. Man's a genius. A lifesaver. Saved my life, at least." Glory proceeded to tell Mr. Diggans the story of her career derailment. Upstairs, perched beside the banister, Ginger and Mimi nodded at what was true and shook their heads at what was not. *Always wanted to be an actress.* They nodded. *First day in New York, got a job on Broadway.* They shook their heads. *My bad luck, show closed that week.* They shrugged. A show may have closed, but she wasn't in it. *Got a job as a personal shopper to support myself.* Double nods. *Sang in nightclubs on my days off.* Ginger wasn't sure but Mimi was. That part was made up.

"Quite a story." Mr. Diggans sounded impressed. "How did the actress and the toy man come to meet?"

"Dancing," Glory said and the girls nodded. "Solly was a cheek-to-cheek dream of a dancer, once upon a time. We considered a career together." The girls shook their heads. "But Solly decided he wanted a future in toys. Must have had a premonition about his feet."

"No one's interested," Solly said. "No one wants to hear."

"Sure they do. The real kicker," Glory confided, "is I didn't go back to acting because we wanted to start a family and then—nothing happened. Who knew it would take so long to prime the pump. Once I got going, different story. Shot 'em out—one, two, three, and four."

There was laughter and movement, and then Paul Clarke's voice. "Early day tomorrow. For those who work."

Mr. Diggans chuckled. "Touché." The front door shut. "What's big in toys these days, Sol?"

"Solly is quite the entrepreneur," Glory said. "Has a real eye for fads."

"It's not me. It's my four product testers upstairs. They're the ones."

"Not the older girls so much anymore," Glory corrected him. "You know how that goes. One day they're into toys. Next day, they're into boys."

"Eww," Mimi protested before Ginger could stop her.

"Girls?" Glory called. "How about you put a hold on the eaves-dropping and join the party. Bring everyone with you." It was not a request.

When Ginger got to Charlie's room, he was holding an eyedropper over the ant farm, telling another tall tale. "They can only get one drop a day. More than that, they'll drown."

Thomas stared, mesmerized. "How can that many ants share one measly drop of water?"

"Kidlings!" Glory called out.

Startled, Charlie's fingers closed hard on the plastic bulb. They watched as the eyedropper spurted all its water into the tank at once.

"It's okay," Charlie told a stunned Callie. "I ordered special ants. Extra-thirsty ants. Guaranteed not to drown. Right, Gingie?"

Ginger nodded and led them downstairs. When they got to the living room, they saw their father grinning at the door and the guests heading out.

"Too late. Party's over." Glory breezed past Solly and followed the Clarkes outside.

Solly's grin vanished. "What, you moving in with them now?"

Glory laughed gently—there was company, after all. "Did you forget? The *All My Sons* audition tomorrow? We're going to get Casper a script." She blew kisses into the room. "For your pockets," she sang out. "Special kisses. Last forever." The door clicked shut behind her.

Solly shuffled to the den and sank into his chair like a bad mood. Ginger herded everyone upstairs to get into pajamas. They reconvened in Charlie's room, to make sure none of the ants had drowned while they were gone. So far so good, but they decided they'd better keep watch for a while, just to be sure.

A slam announced Glory's return. It was Callie, rushing to get downstairs to share the news that the ants survived, who knocked over the farm, sand and ants spilling out in a rush.

"You go down," Charlie told Ginger. "I'll clean up."

Ginger stared at the mess sinking into the forest of avocado-and-gold shag carpet.

"I'll find them," Charlie insisted. "I'll find every ant. I swear."

• • •

When Ginger and Mimi got to the den, Glory closed the journal on her lap and let out a weary sigh. Being interrupted was one of the better-known burdens of her life. "Yes?"

Ginger sat beside her. "Did you get Mr. Diggans his script?"

Her mother looked surprised at her interest. "Matter of fact, I did not. Building was locked." She sighed again. "What I did get was news that Evelyn's going out for my part. Imagine. I mean, yes, I can use a break from memorizing lines. It's exhausting to get the lead every time. But we're talking about Arthur Miller. The man deserves a certain standard. Evelyn is my best friend but projecting? Too polite. Not to mention *Ann Deever* is supposed to be a knockout. I'm not saying I'm a knockout, but at least I don't have that little piggy nose." She lifted the tip of her nose to demonstrate. "Right up the nostrils, you can't help but look. She doesn't even realize." Ginger and Mimi nodded vigorously at the pity of it, a woman with no idea she had a piggy nose. Maybe they nodded too vigorously. "Where's Callie?" Glory looked around. "Where's your brother?"

Mimi turned them in without hesitation. "Cleaning up the mess."

After the vacuum cleaner went off, they heard Glory's bedroom door slam shut.

Ginger and Mimi found Charlie and Callie sitting, sullen, on the floor.

"She vacuumed up everything," Charlie told them. "Even the ants."

Callie lay down on her back and made like a dead ant, hands and legs in the air, tongue hanging out of the side of her mouth, eyes staring wide. She sat back up. "All gone." Her watery eyes were rimmed with red.

"The ants will be fine," Charlie assured her. "They're just taking a nap."

"In the vacuum cleaner?" she asked.

"You can get more," Ginger consoled them.

"There's millions outside," Mimi said. She looked a little guilty, which Ginger thought was appropriate considering she was the one who spilled the beans about the knocked-over ant farm. "I'll help you dig," Mimi went on. "To China if you want." She raced downstairs and might have gone out, right then, in the dark, but the phone rang. They all froze. A ringing phone always brought their mother. When she didn't appear, Ginger ran into the kitchen and answered it.

It was Evelyn and she sounded upset. "Can you put your mother on the phone, honey?"

They crowded together to watch as Glory put the receiver to her ear. Her face went pale. "A widow maker? He's gone? They called *you*?" She hung up, pressed her fingers to her temples, and silently climbed the stairs.

Solly went up after her but came back a minute later clutching the slim green Dramatists Guild edition of *All My Sons* in his stubby hand. "Your mother's not well." As Ginger followed him into the kitchen, he answered the question she hadn't known to ask. "Ivan. The director. Heart attack. Crashed into a tree on his way over here. Dead." He placed the toe of his oversized shoe on the step pedal of the trash can. The script landed with a thud. He moved to the den and turned up the volume on the TV.

One day in, and already Mimi's prediction was true. Thirteen was an unlucky year. And not just for her. Ginger could feel it, bad luck coming for them all.

CHAPTER FOUR

For years, Ginger had started each term of Nurse Tangle's Danger Class by opening the floor to parents and asking them to tell her their worries. It was from this survey of disquiet that she would create the semester's curriculum. She came up with this approach after finally noticing how often parents walked into her class with something very specific in mind. All it took was one news cycle about Ebola to make "What to Do When Lightning Strikes" seem like a tone-deaf topic. In the end, the topic didn't really matter. There were plenty of dangers to go around. As long as parents left her class with more information than they had when they arrived, Ginger was happy. But tonight she felt distracted, unsure that she'd be able to focus. Julia's extended *sleepover* had gotten to her.

With her whiteboard and collapsible easel under her arm, Ginger made a quick detour to the high school nurse's office. Her friend Lydia didn't teach at the Adult School, but she had told Ginger she'd be in the building to proctor a CPR test for the babysitting club.

Though they were both school nurses, Lydia and Ginger had completely different areas of expertise. As an elementary school nurse,

Ginger was proficient in nosebleeds and lice. High school nurse Lydia was the expert on eating disorders and bad boyfriends.

Ginger told Lydia her concerns. Julia was deceiving her. She wasn't where she said she was. Her friend, Angie, was colluding in the lie. The friend's mother was clueless.

Lydia shook her head. "I don't buy it. If the sleepover was bogus, there'd be clues. It's the saving grace of teenagers, how horrible they are at hiding their tracks. My opinion? She's exactly where she says she is. Let it be and it will pass."

As Ginger walked up the dim stairwell to the classroom, she tried to believe what Lydia said was true. But it didn't feel true. Lydia might know teenagers, but Ginger knew guile.

She found her room—this term they'd assigned her 302—and opened the door. The funky odor hit her at once. She glanced at the board—algebra equations—and diagnosed math anxiety. Putting aside her Julia worries, she got busy, trying to open the windows that all turned out to be stuck, fanning the front and rear doors to move around the stuffy air, and locating the wastebasket, so at least she'd know where it was if the smell made someone sick.

By the time she set up her easel, her worries about Julia had crept back, like water finding its own level, to their pride of place. She put the whiteboard in position, and as parents tentatively entered, tried to ignore the growing urge to take out her phone and text Julia again.

She was writing down parent-fears on the whiteboard—"Dangers of Recess," "Heroin in the High School"—when her phone vibrated. She took a quick look—it was her mother—and went back to making the list. The phone buzzed a second time just after the bell rang. She smiled as parents filed out past the whiteboard of warnings—"Candles and Fire!" "Common Household Poisons!"—and took the call. Glory. "Everything okay, Mom?"

"That's the first thing out of your mouth? *Everything okay* is your hello?"

Deep breath. "It's Tuesday night. I teach Tuesday nights, remember?" So much for the color-coded calendar she'd made to help her mother keep track of when she wasn't available.

"Then why'd you pick up? Did you know there's something you can jiggle on your phone so it doesn't ring? Julia showed me. Ask her. I'm sure she'll show you if you ask."

"I picked up because my class just ended. Is everything okay?"

"Again with the worrying. I'm fine. You're fine. Everybody's fine. I ran out of Metamucil is all, and I know you go by the drugstore on your way home. I'm trying to save you an extra trip. I was planning to leave you a message. You don't always have to answer."

"I know," Ginger said. "Okay. I'll get you Metamucil."

In the drugstore she replayed Lydia's words in her head. *Let it be and it will pass.* It wasn't bad advice. But the tricky thing about advice was how quickly it lost its power when the person who gave it wasn't present. She thought about this as she dialed Julia's cell. Was it true for her students? After she made them promise to *always, always, always* wear their helmets when they rode their bikes, after they nodded and repeated it back, did they walk out of her office and immediately forget what she'd said?

Julia's voice mail kicked in and despite the voice in her head urging her to hang up, at the sound of the beep Ginger spoke. "Just calling to say hello." That sounded ridiculous. "Just checking to see if you're coming home tonight." That sounded desperate. "I miss you, Jules." That probably wasn't good to say, either. She terminated the call and reminded herself, *If Julia was lying, there'd be clues.* But as she got in her car, she couldn't help but think, *What if there were clues and I missed them?*

Glory swung open the door. "What are you doing here?"

"Oh." Ginger hadn't meant to come back now. She'd driven over on autopilot. Her mother could do this to her, turn her from a nurse with a no-nonsense attitude into a person with neither will nor resolve.

Glory cocked her head. "I could have sworn on a bible you told me a hundred times you don't like to visit at night. Too tired, you always say."

Her mother looked different—small things, but Ginger noticed. Her wispy white hair had escaped from its usually well-secured bun. Her porcelain skin had been overpowered to a ghostly white. And though her eyes were still their usual fierce blue, her gaze was off, giving her the look of a slightly befuddled, retired dean.

"Something's on your mind." Her mother yanked the belt of her robe, pulling it tighter. "I can smell."

"You can tell," Ginger corrected her. "Are you sure you're okay?" She handed over the drugstore bag. "They had two flavors. I didn't know which you like, so I got both."

Glory peered into the bag. "I asked for this?" She set it on the hall table. "If you say so." It was tricky business, trying to figure out if Glory was attempting to be funny. "Long as you're here, might as well come in. Want something to drink? Don't be a grump."

Ginger followed her mother into the kitchen and sat down at the table, which was covered with pieces of the unsorted puzzle Ginger had given her last week. "What happened to the felt mat?" She'd bought the mat so her mother could roll up her unfinished puzzles when she wanted to use the table for something else, like eating.

"Beats me. Maybe it's with the teakettle."

Ginger looked at the stove. "What happened to the kettle?"

Glory shrugged. "Probably with the mat. That puzzle?" She nodded toward the table. "Too easy." This was her latest complaint, that the puzzles Ginger brought were too easy. The ones Mimi brought, hand cut from rare wood, works of art really, were expensive and impossible to do, but Glory didn't seem to mind.

The puzzle might be easy, but she'd made no progress since the last time Ginger was over. "Want some help?"

Glory shook her head and studied Ginger's face. "What's wrong? Nothing. You're fine."

Surprising them both, Ginger decided to share. "There's been some drama at home. With Julia. Boy drama."

"Oh." Glory sat down and moved around a few puzzle pieces. "I remember that. Boy drama." She shook her head. "Drama, drama, drama."

This was surprising to hear. Ginger could not remember a single incident of boy drama growing up. She had made sure not to have drama of any kind, and if Mimi had boy drama, she'd kept it to herself. Could Glory be referring to Callie? Was that what their big blowup was about—a boy? Ginger knew so few details. She'd left for college not long after Callie went away to boarding school and Mimi had left two years after that. By the time Callie came home, her sisters were long gone. Ginger and Mimi knew at some point there'd been a big argument, but what it was about was a mystery. "Can I ask you something?"

Her mother didn't flinch. "You know you can ask me absolutely anything."

That was laughable, but Ginger let it go. "Julia has this boyfriend and she knows I don't like him. We've been fighting a lot. Which made me think about you and Callie and the big fight you had. I know you don't like to talk about it. But what with Julia and all, I was wondering if you could tell me—was the fight about a boy? Is that how you and Callie became estranged?"

Her mother's fingers stopped their sorting and her eyes grew cloudy and dull. "What do you mean *estranged*?" Before Ginger could figure out how to respond, Glory stood up. "Where's my brush?" She rustled through several kitchen drawers and then disappeared down the hall.

When she returned, her hair was hanging loose. She scooted her chair around and sat so her back was facing Ginger. "I like to brush a hundred times before I go to bed but lately, I don't know why, I get to fifty and my hand aches like nobody's business." She gave Ginger a small silver comb. "Don't talk or you'll lose count."

Her mother's hair felt fragile as a web. Ginger counted to a hundred and stopped. "Done."

"You're a very good brusher, Gingie. Now, give me a kiss and go home."

Ginger leaned over and brushed her lips against her mother's soft cheek.

"Don't be a worrywart. Julia's a beautiful girl. And such an actress. Almost as good as me."

"Julia's not an actress."

"Oh, come on. Think positive for once."

In the car, Ginger experimented with thinking positive. "Julia will be there when I get home," she said out loud, smiling so her voice would sound like she meant it. But as she walked up the front path to her house, the positive thinking came to a halt. There was Richard— she could see him through the dining room window, framed as if in a photograph—alone at the table, computer open, legal pad beside it, pen down, mouth set in a frown, fingertips at his forehead, shoulders hunched in distress.

She locked the door behind her and went straight to him. "What happened? What's wrong? Is Julia okay?" She felt as if the room was starting to spin.

"Nothing's wrong." The pitch of Richard's voice, usually baseline conciliatory, now sounded defeated. "Nothing's wrong yet."

"What does that mean?"

He closed his eyes and sat so still that for a brief moment Ginger wondered if it was possible he'd actually fallen asleep. His eyes snapped open. "I don't know. Forget it."

"Forget what? You *don't know* what?"

He shook his head, got up, started out of the room. "Forget it. Really. It's been a long day."

"Something's wrong. I can hear it in your voice. Richard, what's going on?"

"Work problem. Neglect. Brutal. I'm tired. That's all. I'm going to bed."

She watched him slowly walk up the stairs in silence and tried to ignore the nagging sense that what he'd said was only partly true.

CHAPTER FIVE

The widow maker news about Ivan seemed to ricochet out of the phone and land, like a missile, on Glory's forehead. "Headache's a doozy," Solly told Ginger as he carefully plucked ice cubes out of a tray and laid them at the bottom of a stainless steel bowl, careful to preserve the silence. He added water and a towel and crept upstairs to administer the cold compress.

Downstairs, Ginger went into full doozy mode, disconnecting the phone, taping a "Do Not Ring" note on the doorbell, and setting out Charlie, Callie, and Mimi on the front step, as if they were milk bottles waiting to be picked up.

In the morning, while Glory slept in, breakfast was a silent free-for-all. Under Solly's distracted supervision, Mimi deconstructed packets of Hostess Sno Balls, Charlie flew peanut butter Space Food Sticks through the imaginary mouth hole of his imaginary space helmet, Ginger picked at the burnt edges of the cinnamon-sugar Pop-Tart she'd left in the toaster too long, and Callie made a messy party out of a can of Snack Mate and a bag of Bugles.

The *Daily News* obscured Solly's face, though whether he was holding the paper up to more easily read it or to block the sight of their carrying on, Ginger wasn't sure. The main thing was, he was managing. Managing to get them fed, to wrangle them into the car, to drop the right kid at the right school, and to get to work, all without disturbing their mother.

As for what would happen after school, who should walk home and who would get picked up, Ginger had no idea. But when she exited the white-brick building of her junior high at dismissal time, she saw, across the street, the familiar arm hanging out the window of their Chevelle Caprice, Pepto-Bismol-colored fingernails tapping out impatience on the sky-blue door.

"Doesn't Mom look better than ever?" Mimi asked as Ginger slid into the death seat.

Glory's eyes flicked to the rearview mirror. "Are you saying I looked bad before?" A contest broke out over who could come up with the best superlative to describe how great she looked before *and* now, but she ended it fast. "You trying to get my headache to come back?" They weren't, and no more was said. Not about the headache, not about the canceled play, and not about the deceased director.

Headache-free Glory, Ginger saw, had been busy. The velvet club chairs in the living room had been switched with the sofa. Drag marks on the den carpet showed the route the TV console had taken to its new spot, tangled vines of extension cords now straining to stay plugged in. The kitchen held the smell of meat, but all signs of food preparation had been erased. The porcelain sink gleamed. The floor was slick with Wood Preen. Empty jars lined the counter: Mr. Clean standing guard beside the Drano, the Glade alert beside the Bon Ami. At the back of her throat, Ginger felt the burn of bleach.

She opened the medicine cabinet and stared at empty shelves. "Where's the Luden's?"

"Expired," Glory called out. "Like everything else in this mausoleum. Come see my new puzzle."

Ginger joined her in the dining room. Big Ben was now boxed up, on top of the other finished puzzles piled against the wall in a tower of accomplishment. A new puzzle sat in its place.

"What do you think?" her mother asked. "It's Lake Lugano. Only one at Woolworth's I haven't done."

"Looks hard," Ginger said.

"A monkey could do it. I'm looking for gray corners, if anyone cares."

"We all care," Ginger swore. "But we have homework."

"Do I look like I'm stopping you?"

At dinnertime, Glory dealt out the harvest-gold melamine plates she used whenever Solly wasn't joining them. "Stuck at work. An emergency. Maybe the toy soldiers got drafted." She slid a rectangle of meat onto a plate and passed it to Ginger. "Put this on the front step."

The rectangle was Miracle Meat Loaf. The miracle was Solly didn't mistake it for a brick when he came home, just after eight. He gave a try at pretending the cold slab was tasty, even making noises meant to sound like pleasure, but Glory wasn't fooled. Her mood darkened.

The purging and rearranging continued. The next day when Ginger came home from school, she saw Solly's new shipment of one-armed Rock 'Em Sock 'Em Robots bagged at the curb for the garbagemen.

When she went over to the Clarkes' to work—it was a mother's-helper day—she told Evelyn what was going on. "She also switched the beds in my room. Now my sisters' bunk is blocking the window. I asked her why, but she won't tell me."

"It's because she's upset," Evelyn explained. The two of them were in the kitchen sitting side by side on stools, peeling carrots, Ginger's mother's-helper duties having recently been upgraded from watching Thomas, who'd just turned ten and pretty much entertained himself, to helping make dinner. But even watching Thomas watch TV was an upgrade from staying home.

That Glory had agreed to allow Ginger to accept the job in the first place was because of a combination of good luck and good timing. A group of women from the theater group were over, running lines, the day that Evelyn said, "You wouldn't by any chance be willing to let me borrow Ginger for a few afternoons a week, would you? It would be such a help."

"That's sweet," Glory had said, and then, after making a big production about needing time to think it over, she broke into laughter. "Be my guest." She smiled and winked. "Keep her as many days as you like."

After the carrots were peeled, Evelyn handed Ginger the knife. "Ever cut vegetables?"

"No," Ginger admitted. "But I'm sure I can do it. I'm very responsible for my age."

"Aw, honey." Evelyn let out a puff of air. Her eyes looked sad. "I know you are. Here, let me show you how to hold the knife." Her hand felt exactly as Ginger would have guessed, fleshy and soft. Glory's hand felt like a trap, the tiny wrist and delicate fingers making a fragile disguise for her steely grip.

At home, Glory was making carrots too, but hers came bagged from the freezer, every one the same size. When Ginger asked her why she thought Evelyn preferred carrots that were gnarly with the tops still on, Glory shrugged. "Beats me. Drives twenty miles to get them that way too. Imagine."

Back at the Clarkes' the next day, Ginger asked Evelyn why she drove so far for carrots.

"Oh, your mother loves to exaggerate," Evelyn told her. "I buy them right in town. You can tell your mother they have them up at the A&P."

Ginger did not tell her mother this because Glory had made it clear in her own wordless way that she was not happy her daughter was helping a mother other than her own. The only stories Ginger dared bring home were about things that were *un*pleasant, usually things that hadn't happened, like how Evelyn used a room freshener that made her gag, when the truth was Ginger loved the way the Clarke house smelled, of oranges and warm cookies—even when nothing was baking. It was after the bad reports got an icy reaction that Ginger figured out she was supposed to quit.

Evelyn was in the middle of demonstrating how to use a hand juicer when Ginger blurted it out. "I can't be your mother's helper anymore. It makes my mom unhappy."

"Aw, sweetie. That has nothing to do with you. She's going through a rough patch. Upset about Ivan. Upset there's no play. The theater group meant a lot to her."

Ginger smelled Mr. Diggans' cherry-tobacco pipe wafting in from the next room. He seemed to disappear into another room whenever she came over, but she could tell by the smell of his pipe he was there.

"Your mom needs a vacation," Evelyn confided. "That's all. I told her about a place and she's considering it. I bet she's already feeling better. You'll see when you get home."

What Ginger saw when she got home was a fright of cookbooks open on the counter, *Creative Cookery with Chicken of the Sea Tuna* and *The I Hate to Cook Book*, opened to the stained pages of Glory's favorite recipes. "Your father's coming home on time for once," Glory announced when she saw her. "So I'm making a feast."

The centerpiece of the feast was Tuna Tempter, a casserole of tuna flakes, condensed mushroom soup, and wagon-wheel pasta. Ginger watched her father eye the Pyrex dish with what looked like fear. She passed him the salt. That was the only way to get Tuna Tempter down: douse it with salt, close your eyes, and swallow.

He took the shaker and Ginger relaxed. Then he put it down and pushed his plate away. "I'll eat later." He patted his stomach. "We were so busy today, I lost track of time. Halfway through my corned beef, I saw it was four-thirty. So this I'll have for my midnight snack."

"Eat. Starve. I don't care." With a lurch, Glory pushed her chair back and stood up. "We have to go somewhere, Solly. If I have to look at these four walls all summer, I swear I'll—"

"Done." Solly smiled. "I already had the same idea. The Nevele. Connecting rooms."

Glory's eyes went dull. She could do that, make the light in her eyes flick on or off as if there were a hidden switch. "Place is a dump. What about where Evelyn and Casper go?" Her eyes switched back on. "The island I told you about. Martha's Vineyard. By Cape Cod."

"You want an island? Name one place the sand is whiter than Jones Beach." This was one of their perennial arguments, Jones Beach—Solly's childhood stomping ground—versus Glory's Jersey Shore. He offered a white flag. "You want the Shore? We'll go to Long Branch."

"You know who Evelyn saw on Martha's Vineyard once? Lillian Hellman. Lillian Hellman has a house there. I bet you anything she's friends with Arthur Miller. Imagine if I bumped into Arthur Miller and he heard what happened with *All My Sons*, how the play got canceled, how my career keeps going poof, up in smoke. It could change my life, Solly, if we went to Martha's Vineyard."

Ginger silently urged her father to agree. Surely he could see this was a good idea, going somewhere her mother would be happy. She watched him play with his napkin, unfolding it, refolding it, pressing down hard to give the paper a sharp crease.

He got up and threw the napkin away. "Where else? A place we both agree."

Glory strummed her fingers. "How about Portofino. On the Italian Riviera."

"Portofino Pizza on Route 46, maybe. But for lunch. For dinner, it's too crowded."

Glory sat so still Ginger wondered if she'd heard him. Mimi, who didn't notice that kind of thing, broke the silence. "What about Holland?"

Solly looked at her. "What do you know from Holland?"

"They have tulips." Mimi turned to Ginger. "Wasn't Holland before Portofino?"

Understanding slowly came and Solly made his way to the dining room. The children trailed behind him. He stopped when he got to the tower of puzzles, Big Ben boxed on top of Portofino, Portofino on top of Holland. "This is how you pick where you want to go? From a box?"

"Where I *want* to go is Martha's Vineyard." Glory twirled her wedding band and then grabbed Solly's hands. "There's a house Evelyn told me about. We can rent it for cheap. A darling house by a pond. Houses are a bargain there. People are scooping them up. Everyone in Evelyn's family's getting one. Maybe we should get one."

"You smoking funny cigarettes now?"

"Oh, never mind." Glory sat down and scanned the annoying clouds in the sky above Lake Lugano. "I'm looking for anything blue."

Ginger noted the sound of defeat. This was a rare win for her father. At least, she thought it was a win. But a few days later, when Glory pulled her into her bedroom, Ginger realized she'd gotten it wrong. The win was her mother's after all.

Glory shut the door. "I did it. I rented the house on Martha's Vineyard. Just for a month. Don't look at me like that, Gingie. You don't know how difficult your father can be. He thinks he hates adventures. Anything new, he doesn't want to try. So I have to ease him in. Once I ease him in, he'll come around. Pinky swear you won't tell him about the house yet." They linked pinkies. Glory pulled away hard.

"Now, here's the plan. Photographs of the house are coming in the mail. Once I get them, I'm going to put together a presentation. So your father can see how beautiful everything's going to be. But if he gets the pictures before I do, if he gets to the mail first, it's over. He'll hate the idea for good. Which is where you come in. You're going to intercept the mail and get it to me before your father sees it. Can you do it? Can I count on you?" Ginger nodded and Glory's eyes turned bright.

The photographs came on the worst day, a Saturday, when Solly was puttering around the house. But Ginger did her job well. She scooped up the mail from the floor in the front hall and managed to hide the hazardous envelope behind the living room drapes before her father passed through the room. Later, when he went to the bathroom, she retrieved the envelope and slipped it to her mother.

"Nicely done," Glory whispered. "A definite ten-plus." She buried the evidence underneath a pile of papers on her kitchen desk. After that it was a waiting game until Solly's favorite show came on. Then, envelope back in sleeve, Glory hustled Ginger to the pantry.

In Ginger's opinion the pantry was an awful choice for a secret meeting. For one thing, it was right beside the den, and for another, it had a thin vinyl accordion contraption of a door meant to be kept shut by magnets that had years ago lost their pull. Now, whenever anyone tried to close the door, it immediately retracted. If her father walked by, he could see right in, see them huddled close, staring at the snapshots of the house Glory rented behind his back.

Something about this had gotten Glory so excited she gave off heat, perfuming the small space with a mix of Albolene cleanser, Breck Shampoo, and Je Reviens perfume. Queasy, Ginger sat down, accidentally dislodging her mother's journal from the shelf behind her. It fell into her lap, splayed open, and she averted her eyes.

Glory's journal went up with her every night so she could write in it in peace before she went to bed, but during the day it might pop up anywhere. By now, Ginger had seen enough of it to know its contents.

Reviews of plays her mother hoped to star in, lists of cities she dreamed of visiting, and musings about her day. It was the last part, the musings, little glimpses inside her mother's mind, that made Ginger so uncomfortable her body would itch. Her policy now when she spotted the journal: Close it up. Look away. Move on fast.

As Ginger set the journal on a high shelf, Glory ripped open the envelope. On the other side of the wall her father was whistling to the theme song of *All in the Family*. If she could hear *him*, why did Glory think he couldn't hear *them*?

Her mother passed her a photo of a spindly chair. "That's an antique," she explained. Ginger nodded, noncommittal. Glory tapped the next picture, her fingernail polished to a new shade she called mauve. "Roses." She brought the photograph to her nose and inhaled the imaginary scent of the pale-pink flowers that spilled over a white picket fence. "Divine." She let out gasps of muted delight as she shuffled through the rest. *Porthole windows! Screened-in porch! California King!*

Solly's program broke to commercial. "Where'd everybody go?"

Glory stuffed the photographs back in the envelope, grabbed Ginger's arm, and whispered, "You know where my jewelry box is?"

Her mother kept her jewelry in a wooden puzzle box hidden in plain sight on her closet floor, but Ginger wasn't sure she was supposed to know this. "Closet?" Glory nodded and pressed the envelope into Ginger's hand.

"Think you can figure out how to open the box?"

Another thing Ginger was not sure she should admit. The puzzle box was a gift from a toy manufacturer in Japan. There were four steps to opening it, and Mimi had timed it so Ginger knew she could open it in under a minute. "I can try."

"Good. Put the pictures in the bottom compartment. Hurry. Go." She yanked open the accordion door. "I'm making Harvey Wallbangers," she sang out to Solly. "Be right there."

"We got drinks?" Solly said. "We got an occasion I don't know about?"

After the photographs were stashed in the puzzle box, it was easy to pretend the house on Martha's Vineyard did not exist. But that day-dream ended one morning when Ginger came down to breakfast and found Outside Glory in her favorite dress, a floral number that showed a peek of cleavage and emphasized her tiny waist.

"Look how beautiful." Glory opened her journal to show Solly pho-tographs mounted with black corners on one page, and on the other, an advertisement of a beach, cut out of a magazine.

"What do we got here?" Solly asked.

After Glory broke the news, she tried to soften the blow. "Just one month. Just July."

"I'm supposed to go away for a month when I got shipments com-ing every day?"

"You won't stay a month," Glory told him. She was smiling, but it wasn't real. "You'll come the first week and after that you'll come week-ends. With Paul Clarke. That's what men do, Solly. They come week-ends." Her face looked serene, and for a moment Ginger was tricked into thinking she was happy.

This time when Glory stood up, she rose so fast her chair toppled over. For a moment they all stared at it, the chair on its side on the floor, like some kind of kitchen roadkill. "If I don't get out of here, so help me god I will—"

"No." Solly cut her off. "We'll go. That's it. We're going."

And so it was decided.

CHAPTER SIX

They had just finished dinner—Richard was clearing the table, Ginger was loading the dishwasher—when the side door opened. After three nights at Angie's, Julia was back. No explanation, just a brief nod to her parents—what *that* meant, Ginger had no idea—and up she went, disappearing into her room.

Had positive thinking actually worked? Ginger gave it another try. "Do you think this means the Nick thing is over?"

The answer came in the form of a sharp rap at the front door. Richard answered it. The boy walked in, grunted hello, and went up the stairs, two at a time. Ginger heard Julia's squeal of delight and recalibrated. Was Julia home because Angie's mom finally realized she was being played?

It didn't matter. They had a new problem now. Without discussion or permission—was this a *permission* situation?—Nick set up semipermanent residence in their house. Now when Julia came home from school, Nick was with her. Every night at dinner, Nick sat down and joined them. And as if they were in some kind of reverse fairy tale, he stayed until just before the clock struck twelve.

Most nights, Ginger and Richard were in bed by eleven, but Ginger wouldn't fall asleep until she heard the sound of the boy clomping down the stairs. He wasn't quiet—it wasn't as if he was sneaking out—but sometimes she had to strain to hear the door close over the sound of Richard's snoring. It really was galling that Richard could drop off to sleep while the boy was still across the hall in Julia's room.

Ever the adapter, Ginger made accommodations. Cooking for four was not that different from cooking for three, and after she explained to Nick that they didn't wear shoes inside the house—a quirk of Richard's that she understood—he was pretty good at remembering to leave his disintegrating sneakers on the metal shoe tray near the door. The hardest part was watching Julia trail after him like a pet as he lumbered from their refrigerator to their basement to her bedroom. She'd made a brief attempt at declaring Julia's bedroom a "No Nick Zone" but surrendered that point after Julia replied, "No problem. We'll hang out at Nick's instead."

This wasn't the solution Ginger had in mind, and it gave her pause. Why *weren't* they hanging out at Nick's?

Nick gave her the answer. "We can go to my house now if you want. But my mom's home. It's going to smell." He turned to Ginger. "My mom smokes and the smell makes Julia sick."

At least there was that to be grateful for. Julia didn't like the smell of cigarettes. And while she was being all positive-thinking about it, she might as well also be grateful that so far Julia kept her bedroom door open and so far there'd been no appeals for the boy to spend the night. Those were her new lines in the sand, though the possibility of Julia crossing them hovered like a threat.

To minimize her distress, Ginger tried to make the sight of Nick go blurry. She could do that if she concentrated, turn the actual boy padding around her house into a vague tall shadow. And Nick, it appeared, had figured out a way to do the same with her.

Richard developed a different strategy for dealing with their unwelcome house guest, a combination of a *things could be worse* attitude and a sudden spike in late nights at the office. Dinner went back to a threesome, Ginger reduced to an appendage.

When the line in the sand was finally crossed—Julia closed her door with Nick inside her room—Richard wasn't home. This left Ginger standing her ground alone, in the hall, knocking hard on her daughter's door.

"Jules? Open the door." She knocked again. "Sorry, Jules, but your door has to stay open." She waited another moment. "I'm coming in." She gave them one more warning. "I'm opening the door now." She squinted, afraid of what she'd see.

What she saw was this: Nick and Julia sitting on the floor, backs against the bed, headphones plugged into the computer on Nick's lap, sharing earbuds so that each had one ear connected to the headphones and one ear that surely had heard her calling from the hall. Julia, oblivious to her presence, pointed to the screen. Nick laughed. Ginger squatted in front of them. "Why didn't you answer when I knocked?" She lifted the computer off Nick's lap.

Julia jumped up and the headphones split in half. "God."

"Door has to stay open. Understood?"

It was Nick who answered, "Sure."

She waited an hour to check. This time the door was closed but not latched, a technicality, really, but by then she was too tired to start a new round of battle, so she let it be.

When Richard came home, he was surprisingly unsympathetic. "What were they doing wrong?" he asked. "They were on the computer, right? How is that bad?"

She chalked up his brusque tone to another bad day at work.

That night, as she lay in bed waiting for Nick to go—his departure, she noticed, had now slid to one o'clock—Ginger decided this business of having the door shut but not latched was plain wrong. Same went for the new departure time. She made a list in her head of nonnegotiable rules and turned to share it with Richard. "You awake?"

His reply was a snore that sounded fake. Okay. It didn't matter. Her decision was made. She would handle this on her own.

The next night at half past eight—Richard at work as usual—Ginger was in the living room catching up on back issues of the *American Journal of Public Health* when she heard movement above.

Upstairs, her suspicions were confirmed. The door was shut but not latched. This time she entered without knocking. "Sorry."

Julia looked up. "What?"

"Sorry, but shut is the same as closed."

Julia shrugged and went back to what she was doing.

Ginger surveyed the scene. They were sitting on the floor. Julia's computer was on Nick's lap. Nick had on a new set of headphones—probably because the other set broke. Julia was cutting up a bedsheet. Before Ginger could figure out why Julia would cut up a bedsheet, her attention was drawn back to Nick. He was fiddling with a helmet. The helmet had wings sprouting from the ears.

Nick, she now noticed, was wearing something other than his usual torn shirt. He had on a jacket, military-looking, though what branch she couldn't place. The jacket was old, the material shiny, with maroon epaulettes, and on one sleeve, just below the shoulder, a crest with a bar and stars.

She glanced over and saw Julia was wearing an identical jacket, though hers had a pin on the lapel. It was the letter *S.* Ginger took a moment and put it all together. "You're wearing Salvation Army uniforms. Did you join the Salvation Army?"

"Very funny," Julia said, but she didn't look up.

"And why are you cutting up my sheet?"

"We bought the jackets today," Nick said. "Cool, right? Wait, that's *your* sheet?"

Julia set down the scissors. "I don't think you want to know the answer."

Ginger felt her cheeks flush. Julia was both wrong and right. She absolutely *did* want to know, but she also absolutely did *not*. "Door stays open," she told Julia. "Or Nick goes home."

She was back in the living room, eyes skimming over words in the magazine without taking them in, when Julia and Nick ran down the stairs and, without a word to her, retreated to the basement. When Ginger opened *that* door and brought down a load of laundry so small no one could be fooled into thinking it was worth washing, she found them sitting surrounded by toys. There was an American Girl doll, a doll suitcase, a doll cello, an old coffee can filled with markers, a decade of forgotten craft kits, modeling clay, glitter, string art. In the middle of it all was a garbage bag, which Julia seemed to be methodically filling with the remnants of her childhood.

Ginger deposited the laundry basket on the washing machine and headed back upstairs. As she passed them, she saw they were texting and laughing. Were they texting each other about her?

"You have to help me out here," she told Richard later, in bed, after she filled him in on what happened while he was at work. "Can you come home early tomorrow? Talk to her, maybe? See if you can find out what's going on? She'll talk to you."

Richard sighed. "Okay." He closed his eyes. "I'll try." He turned on his side, giving her his back. "But I really don't think it will help."

CHAPTER SEVEN

The house letter arrived; three single-spaced pages of instructions. Beach towels would be provided; they needed to bring linens. Windows should be closed each time they left the house; sudden storms could blow in without warning. The wooden pegs in the outdoor shower were coming loose; never use them. Glory read that part, twice. "Outdoor shower. Imagine."

As soon as the school year ended, Ginger's mother's-helper hours were expanded. But the Clarke kitchen was no longer a sanctuary because now, every day around lunchtime, Glory showed up, journal in hand, to find out everything Evelyn knew about Martha's Vineyard. Ginger didn't have to be asked to give up her seat at the kitchen counter. Her mother slipped onto her stool the second Ginger got off and the questions began: which beaches have the best sunset, which farm stand has the best fruit, which church has the best lobster rolls.

One week before departure day, Glory's planning ratcheted up and Ginger's duties got a downgrade back to watching Thomas watch TV. As she reluctantly made her way to the Clarkes' den, she heard her mother ask, "What about secret places? Any places where famous people like to go? Like Lillian Hellman, for example?"

Thomas turned up the TV, so Ginger never heard the answer to that one. But Thomas did explain the reason his uncle Casper wasn't around: he'd already left for the Vineyard. That's what the Clarkes called it, the Vineyard, or else, the Island, as if there was only one. He also explained that while Ginger's family was going up the following Friday and his family was supposed to go up the day after that, there was a problem with his family going. What the problem was, he didn't say, and Ginger decided it was best not to ask.

The day before they were to leave, Glory marched into the Clarkes' kitchen, opened her journal, and showed Evelyn what was written inside: one word too big for Ginger to miss, *KAPUT*, in the center of the page, block letters colored in with a black Bic pushed down so hard the paper at the top of the *T* was torn. Ginger lingered on her way to the den, listening in.

"That's all he said. The plan is *kaput*. Can't get away. Trouble in toy land."

Ginger could hear the curious tone of Evelyn's question and then the sharp words of her mother's answer. "Beats me. First it was, *a shipment went missing*. Then it was, some big-shot competitor went under and *the inventory is up for grabs*. Whole thing smells like rotten fish."

At home that night, with Solly still at work, Glory served them an early dinner, five foil trays of Salisbury steak and buttered mashed potatoes with a compartment of green beans, which they all, even Glory, passed over to get to the apple cobbler. "It's fine," she told them as she scraped out the last of the dessert from the ridges of the small square. "We'll go without him. Don't give me those puppy eyes," she told Callie. "He'll come when he can. Next weekend, I'm sure. Now go pack. Pack to blend in. Imagine the kind of person who has a beach house and bring that." They cleared their tins and scattered to pick out clothes.

While Charlie jammed T-shirts and shorts into a couple of sand buckets and then snuck out to hide the ant farm on the floor in the backseat of the car where Glory wouldn't see it, Ginger headed to the spidery storage side of the basement in search of a suitcase. She found Mimi down there too, lugging a green monstrosity of a valise to the stairs.

"Not that one," Ginger told her. "Take something smaller."

"But we're supposed to blend in, right? Only what do they wear? Should I bring my skorts? My peasant blouses? My huaraches? I don't know. *You* don't know."

Glory came to the top of the stairs. "Girls? Is something wrong?" And they both called up, "No."

Since she couldn't convince Mimi to pack light, Ginger evened things out by taking less herself. Although she had bought into the hope that her mother truly would be happier when they got to the rental house, there was no guarantee. Keeping things orderly and calm would at least improve the chances for a positive outcome. She took care of Callie's packing after she finished her own, grabbing what seemed a reasonable amount of clothes and squishing them in beside hers in the small suitcase she picked because it wouldn't impose on the other luggage in the car.

As it turned out, Glory didn't care who packed what. She also didn't care who left orange peels on the kitchen table, who asked for Bosco and didn't drink it, and who forgot to flush the toilet, again. Even when Solly came home and immediately fell asleep in front of the TV, her good mood stuck firm.

Departure day, it was rise and shine at the crack of dawn. Glory presented Solly with a buttered bialy toasted the way he liked it, nearly burnt, and kissed him noisily inches from his lips. Solly slid his arm around her torso and swept her into a dip and a spin.

"Aw, Solly." She playfully pushed him away. "You'll hurt your foot." She got his hat, stuck it on his head, and opened the door.

"Don't use up all the fun before I get there," he teased. "Don't forget to leave me the number. Don't forget to call soon as you're in the house so I can hear how nothing went wrong on the way. You're a good driver," he added quickly. "But the other drivers, I'm not so sure."

"I'll leave the number. But if I don't call soon as we get there, it might be because the phone isn't turned on yet. Don't give yourself agita," she told Solly, who'd stopped, halfway out the door. "The house letter said the phone's been off, but they're turning it on for the season today. It just didn't say what time."

"And if they forget?" Solly asked.

"Always with the worst. In that ridiculous scenario you'll hear from me tomorrow when Evelyn comes. Her house is close. Just past the dump and around the bend. Happy?"

"You call, I'll be happy." He gave kisses, top of the head, to each of the children, and then little kisses to Glory, one time so close they banged teeth, which made them both laugh.

They all watched as he trudged up the block to the train. As soon as he turned the corner, Glory clapped her hands. "Chip-chop. Put the suitcases in the car while I change."

She was zipping up her dress when she came outside. "What do you think?" She twirled around to show it off. "Darling, right?" The dress was new, blue, crocheted, and short. To Ginger it looked a poor choice for a long drive, but she nodded along with everyone else, doing her best to look convincing.

Glory hustled them into the car and then announced she had to scoot over to Evelyn's to get some last-minute instructions. As soon as she disappeared into the Clarke house, Mimi began complaining. "It's hot in the car. I'm going to die from heat."

Callie turned to Charlie. "Can you die from heat?"

"You can die from anything."

"I'm half-dead," Mimi said. Charlie got out and started digging in the dirt. "I'm three-quarters dead," she said, and Callie got out to help him. "I'm ninety-nine hundred and ninety-nine percent dead." She lay down across the seat.

Ginger saw the Clarkes' front door crack open. "Get up." She leaned out the window and called, "Get in." She took in the signs of her mother's mood change, shoulders hunched, eyes to the ground. "Sit up," she hissed, and this time Mimi listened.

By the time Glory got in the car, they were all sitting, hands neatly folded in laps. She gazed out the window. "Well." She rubbed her temples. "How do you like them apples?"

"What apples?" Mimi asked. "What happened?"

"What happened is Paul Clarke moved out last night. No warning. What do you think about that?" Ginger didn't know what to think. "Which means Evelyn's not going to Martha's Vineyard tomorrow. And Casper—well, what do you think he's going to do once he hears his sister's home, alone, abandoned." Again, no idea.

"Are they getting divorced?" Mimi asked. She sounded dangerously cheerful.

"I don't want to get divorced," Callie added quietly.

"Good god. Children don't get divorced. Callie, are those tears? You know tears are not for the car. Tears are for the privacy of your room with the door closed and the shades drawn."

"We have blinds," Mimi pointed out.

Glory, talking over her, didn't hear. "There's plenty worse things in the world than divorce." She looked in the rearview mirror. "Like having a bunch of glumsters stare at the back of your neck all day, for example."

They quickly rearranged their mouths into smiles that wouldn't fool a dog.

"We can stay home." Ginger tried to sound cheery. "There's fun things to do at home."

"I'd give that a two," Glory told her. "On second thought, a one-minus. You got to put feeling in your eyes. That's what good acting is about. If you feel it in your eyes, people will buy it's true."

Mimi opened the back door. "Come on. Let's go hide behind the couch until Daddy comes home. Then when he walks in, we can all jump up and yell, *Surprise! We're still here!*"

"Close that door right now." Glory turned on the engine. Hearing about Solly seemed to have decided things. "We're going. On vacation." The car bucked as she shifted to reverse. "And we're going to have fun. Loads and loads of fun. Agreed?" Her brood of bobbleheads nodded vigorously.

Suitcases and sand buckets blocked the back window, but that didn't stop Glory from accelerating down the driveway. She slowed briefly as she pulled out onto the street, sped up again to the corner, slowed as she made the turn, and continued, herky-jerky, to the highway.

The sea was calm, the sky was clear, the boat was big, the crossing smooth. Ginger felt sick.

"You got your father's stomach." Glory rooted around in her purse, dug out a packet of Ritz, and handed them over. "Don't inhale them. Nibble." She opened her journal and turned to the sea.

The crackers made Ginger queasier, so timing it with one of Glory's languorous blinks, she snuck them to Charlie, who raced with Callie to the other side of the deck to feed the gulls.

Mimi tugged at Ginger's sweater. "Want to play Spit? Want to play Spite and Malice?"

Ginger didn't want to play anything, so Mimi sat on the deck and took out her jacks. But something about this—the thump of the ball or the sweep of her hand—was annoying Glory. Ginger felt the heat of her mother's irritation seep into the air.

Her journal banged shut. "Even here? Sitting in the middle of the ocean, I still can't get a—" Without waiting to hear the rest, Mimi ran off in search of her brother.

Glory closed her eyes, and Ginger watched as her mother's slender fingers danced over to her gauzy kerchief, tucking in runaway strands of her honey-kissed hair. Her hand moved to her cheeks, then her neck, then her mouth. Ginger wondered what she was checking for and then what she was smelling that made her nostrils flare? Her subject swiveled, polarized sunglasses pointing at her. "For god sake, there must be something you can go do."

She joined Charlie and her sisters, and they all watched the gulls swoop and hover, hoping for more crackers. The boat glided through calm water. The sun painted freckles on their cheeks. The ferry turned and Charlie pointed to the dock. In the distance people were waiting, as if for their arrival.

Then Glory was behind them. "Everybody wave." She raised her arm and drew a slow arc, back and forth through the air. "See anyone waiting to surprise us? Come on, wave. Who wants to be the best waver?"

Competition between the siblings never ended well. Within moments Callie tried to get closer to the railing and Mimi yelled, "Stop it," and shoved her. Ginger was about to intervene but Glory beat her to it, her hand clamping tight around Mimi's wrist. Mimi made her legs go limp, feet dragging as her mother pulled her out of sight.

When a woman in a broad-brimmed hat hurried over to ask if everything was all right, Ginger didn't hesitate. "My sister gets seasick. If she doesn't get to the bathroom in time, she'll throw up all over the deck. One time when she did that, the smell was so bad the rest of us threw up too." The woman gave a weak smile and withdrew.

Like statues waiting to be brought back to life, they stayed where they were, even after the boat bumped the dock with a jolt. They heard her before they saw her—Glory rising out of the stairwell like a goblin. "Hurry up. Chip-chop. You're holding up the works."

On the vehicle deck no one spoke, not even when Glory hurried them past their car for the second time. "Good lord, someone stole it."

Mimi pointed. "It's right there." She slid in first, cheeks still burning red. Callie got in next, but she kept a distance in case what happened to Mimi was catching. Charlie scooted in last, leaving Ginger no choice but her usual punishment, the front.

Glory handed her a piece of paper. "Directions. You okay? Course you are." She brushed Ginger's hair out of her eyes. "Listen, kiddo." Her fingertips, moving quickly, felt light as butterfly wings. "You're my peach, you know that? My little bruised peach." She turned on a dazzling smile and drove off the boat ramp, onto the island of her dreams.

CHAPTER EIGHT

The November incident—Julia's Thanksgiving Rebellion—had a rehearsed feel about it that Ginger only noticed after it was over, when she and Richard were in the car on the way to Glory's. It was then, as she replayed their declarations in her head, that she realized Julia and Nick had taken turns talking, like characters in a play where the playwright decided to make all the dialogue of equal length. She imagined Nick timing it with his phone. Julia went first.

"Nick's mom isn't making Thanksgiving this year. She went to Texas."

"To visit my uncle Brian. He's my mom's brother and he's kinda sick."

"That's why she went. That's why I'm staying here. So Nick's not alone."

When they seemed finished with their explanation, Ginger told them she was very sorry to hear about Nick's uncle, but she didn't understand why that meant Julia wasn't coming to Thanksgiving.

"I don't even like turkey," Julia said as if that made a difference.

Ginger offered the obvious solution. "Nick doesn't have to be alone. Bring him with you. Grandma won't care. You can come," she told the boy.

They were in the living room, Nick and Julia squashed close together on the sofa, as if they wished they were one person. Nick, tall and gangly, knees rising high in front of him, fiddled with the small silver hoop at the edge of his unruly eyebrow. Ginger thought the hoop hole looked early-stage infected. She considered offering to check it out, but Nick interrupted her thoughts.

"Honestly?" He smirked and shook his head. "Your invitation? Doesn't sound like you mean it."

Emboldened, Julia stood her ground. "We're not going. Why do you even care? Thanksgiving in our family is a total fraud."

"What does that mean?" This was not the first time Ginger noticed it, that when Julia was with Nick it sometimes felt like they were speaking a language she didn't understand. She glanced at Richard, who shot her a *back off* look. Registered and ignored. "How is it a fraud?"

Julia used her fingers to count off the infractions. "No one ever says the truth. No one talks about anything real. No one wants to be there. Aunt Mimi's whole family hates it. Wallace told me when they go to their other grandma's they don't sit doing nothing all day. They can be on their phones or go outside. They can go on the roof if they want. It isn't so snobby and strict."

Describing a meal at Glory's as snobby was so off base it wasn't worth addressing. But the roof? "Have you gone up on the roof?" Richard shot her another unappreciated warning look.

"That's not the point," Julia said.

Ginger nodded. If the point was that the Popkins were more fun, she wouldn't argue. This was partly a matter of numbers. Mimi's husband, Neil Popkin, was one of six siblings, all of whom had procreated prodigiously. Because of this, Mimi's three boys, a dainty brood by Popkin standards, had twenty cousins, or maybe now it was up to twenty-five. The extended family included not just grandparents, cousins, aunts, and uncles, but great aunts, second cousins, first cousins once removed. There seemed to be enough of them to make their own country. The country of Popkin. Ginger believed, and Richard agreed, this was what attracted Mimi to Neil in the first place. He came with the protective shield of a clan.

Of course, Mimi would deny it. She was, or pretended to be, unaware of the benefit the chaos of the Popkin clan afforded her. Instead, she complained about how her house was always overfull, and given the size of her house, this was no small feat. Richard referred to the place as the Clue House, because it boasted a study, a library, and a billiard room. There was also a solarium, a media room, a dedicated closet for Neil's fly-fishing equipment, and a carriage house out back, which Mimi was currently using as a studio, now that she was an artist. Quilts were her current thing. Before she started quilting, she'd been a real estate agent. Prior to that she owned a children's furniture store. She'd also sold organic cosmetics and ran a small food cooperative. This was in addition to her volunteer work, heading up all the boys' booster clubs, spearheading the skate park, forming a committee to get rid of the geese in the pond near her house, and fighting to extend the hours of the public library.

By now, Ginger was used to the fact that none of her sister's pursuits lasted very long. Something was always wrong with them, eventually. It had been the same in college. Like a real-life Goldilocks, Mimi cycled through a big state school, a medium-sized university, and a small liberal arts college, transferring her way to her bachelor's. After that there was half a year of a master's in linguistics, two months of landscape architecture, and five days of a three-year midwifery program. The problem with midwifery was too many bodily fluids, plus night work.

As to how many infected tonsils and swollen adenoids Neil, an ENT, had to cure to support a house like theirs, Ginger had no idea, but she assumed it was a lot. Her own house was closer in size to the home they'd grown up in, *cozy* in her words, or as Mimi would describe it, *about a thousand square feet short of quaint.*

But no matter how big it was, Mimi's house was not big enough to handle the demands of the Popkin clan. Every relative—Ginger's tiny family included—knew that the spare key was under the green watering can at the back door. There was an alarm system that was never used because the house was never unattended.

Describing her lack of alone time was almost a sport for Mimi. Her weekends were jammed with mandatory family get-togethers and weeknights booked because no Popkin could have a birthday without a full complaint of relatives coming over for coffee and cake. And it wasn't just birthdays. There was always an occasion to mark. An anniversary, a graduation, a hiring, a firing, someone sick, someone sad. It was brilliant, really. With three boys and a job that changed so frequently, Ginger struggled to keep up, the Popkins were the final impenetrable layer of Mimi's hazmat suit, a tornado of activity protecting her from all undesirable parts of life, otherwise known as Glory.

Julia's observation—that Thanksgiving at Glory's wasn't fun—was a fair one. Ginger now regretted not trying harder to convince Glory it was time that she and Richard host it for a change. But her mother had been adamant. Thanksgiving, she insisted, was *her* holiday.

"How about I organize some games?" Ginger proposed to Julia. "The library is running a digital scavenger hunt. We could form teams. We can join online right now." Julia rolled her eyes. "Okay, how about charades? That would be fun. And if you're on Grandma Glory's team, you're guaranteed to win."

Her daughter let out an airy *hoosh.* "A scavenger hunt or charades? Really?"

"Okay, forget a game. Just come. If you want to go outside, go outside. Grandma won't care. She probably won't even notice. Going outside is not a problem."

"It's not a problem because *we* are not going." Emphasis communicated. Julia's position was clear.

"Sorry, Jules. You have to come. Not coming is not an option."

But apparently it was.

CHAPTER NINE

Glory leaned closer to the steering wheel. "Make a left where? And don't mumble. Project." According to her, navigator-mumbling was the reason she'd overshot the last two turns.

This time Ginger shouted out the instructions. "Make a left where the road splits. Over there."

Glory scowled but made the left. "I said pro*ject*. Not scream. Project and e-nun-ci-ate."

Ginger corrected her volume and enunciated. "Turn right after the clam shack."

"The what?" Glory scanned the unfamiliar landscape.

Mimi tapped her shoulder. "That thing." She pointed to a small gray-shingled building where a long line of customers snaked to the parking lot.

"A little notice would be nice next time." As Glory made the turn, the cars behind her honked, but she drove blithely on, past low stone walls surrounding meadows where sheep and horses grazed, as oblivious to her as she was to them.

Mimi leaned forward and jabbed Ginger in the arm every time she noticed something good. A pond with swans. A sign for afternoon pony rides. An honor farm selling sunflowers. In the far distance, Ginger made out the soft line where the horizon met the sea. The road zigzagged inland. The car coasted beneath a canopy of leaves, tree limbs wrinkled like alligator skin.

Glory slowed. "What next?"

Ginger enunciated. "Go past the store with the blue rowboat in front, and turn right after the climbing tree."

"That's what it says? *Right after the climbing tree?* No street name?"

"No." This answer seemed wrong, so Ginger tried another. "Yes?"

Behind them, traffic compressed—a pickup truck, a delivery van, a Volkswagen bus—as if the cars were now trying to nudge them along.

Mimi pointed. "There it is." Glory turned to look. The car swerved. More horns blared.

"For crying out loud." To avoid getting hit, Glory pulled into a snarl of bushes on the narrow shoulder and stopped. A branch poked through Ginger's window. Vehicles whizzed by, kicking up pebbles and blowing in a punishment of dust. "Let me see that." She grabbed the directions. When she finished reading, she let the paper flutter to her lap. This time, she stopped traffic in both directions as she pulled onto the road with a careful seven-point turn.

The sign for "Fisher's Hollow" was etched into a small piece of wood, the letters painted a faded green. "Excited?" Glory asked as she turned onto the road. The car dipped in and out of a rut. Ginger closed her eyes against the smells of manure, hay, lilies, and skunk. They lurched to a stop. "Well? What do you think?" The house was mostly hidden by a thicket of trees, but Charlie gave a two-finger whistle of approval anyway, which Callie and Mimi seconded with applause. Glory turned to Ginger. "What's the matter, your majesty? Not up to your standards?"

Because of the trees, Ginger couldn't make out much. The house was gray and weathered-looking. There were two round windows upstairs and a roof that looked like moss was growing out of it. None of this seemed right to mention. "It's beautiful," she said, and her mother smiled.

As they lugged their suitcases over the path of crushed shells past a parched flower garden, Glory picked out what she wanted to see. "Ooh. Beach plums. And those flowers? With the umbrella petals? Those are lady's slippers. Evelyn told me lady's slippers are murder to grow, but around here they thrive like nobody's business." She rustled around in her purse for a key.

Mimi skipped ahead and tried the door. "Open." She glanced down the hill. "What's that?" She raced off to investigate a large shed in a patch of trees.

Charlie and Callie ran after her.

This left Ginger to follow her mother into the house, where she hoped her skills as an early warning system could help determine how the rest of their day would go.

"Houses here can be very warty," Glory said as they toured through the rabbit warren of rooms on the first floor. "Evelyn told me people add on, pell-mell, whenever they can. Even a house that looks small from the outside can turn out to have wings."

Compared to their house at home, Ginger thought this house seemed big. But she kept her thoughts to herself. She really didn't know much about houses. Her mother stopped to take in the figurehead of a mermaid that was nailed above the entrance to the kitchen. Ginger was thinking the mermaid looked sad when Glory pronounced it *darling*. Apparently, Ginger didn't know much about mermaids, either.

According to Glory, there was a lot that was darling. The roses on the trellis visible through the kitchen window. The sea chest moonlighting as a coffee table in the living room. The blue glass bottles in the corner cabinet of the dining room, no two alike. And most darling of all, the master suite at the back of the house.

"Ooh. A California King." Glory bounced on the bed and kicked off her sandals. "White carpet." She dug her toes in the thick plush and nodded toward the drapes. "Let's see the view."

Ginger pulled the drape cord and, like Carol Merrill on *Let's Make a Deal*, revealed picture windows and a sliding door. Also revealed, outside, was Charlie digging a hole with his hands, Mimi raining dirt over his head, and Callie twirling as fast as she could. Ginger struggled to pull the drapes closed, but the cord was stuck. Mimi saw her and though no sound permeated the glass, Ginger could see her scream a warning. One more tug and the drapes closed. Ginger swung around, ready to defend her ill-behaved siblings, but Glory had seen none of it.

Her mother was at the vanity now, swiveling on a stool as she adjusted the three-way mirror. "The back of my head." Glory moved the mirrors to get a better view. "Imagine." She watched as her fingers fluffed up her hair. "It's like someone saw my dream and made it real."

The tour ended in the kitchen when Glory tried the phone. "Dead." She slammed the receiver down. "Your father's going to have a conniption. What am I supposed to do now?"

It was not a question that needed an answer. It was a statement that Ginger understood meant the good-mood portion of their first day was now over.

Charged by her mother with assigning rooms, Ginger corralled everyone inside. Since this house had no bunk beds, she put Callie and Charlie together in one room and Mimi with her in the other. To keep the calm, she let Mimi have the bed her sister decided was better. But even with the better bed, Mimi was not calm. Within a minute the vertical blinds were cockeyed, a wooden knob from the dresser drawer was under the bed, and the wall had fallen victim to the spindle chair, which went careening after Mimi experimented with how many times she could turn in a circle before falling.

Ginger ran her fingers over the dented molding while a chastened Mimi pleaded, "Please don't tell. I didn't mean to." A begrudging agreement was made. Mimi would lie still as a corpse in bed, while Ginger made things right. She repositioned the chair so the back of it blocked the molding and untangled the cord so the blinds hung straight. But as she was jamming the dresser knob in place, they heard familiar footsteps. Mimi didn't ask for permission; she darted across the room and threw her weight against the door.

"Don't come in. We're changing into bathing suits."

"For crying out loud. I'm your mother. What am I going to see I haven't seen before? And why are you changing into bathing suits? We're going to the grocery store." She gave up and moved to the next room. "How did that ant farm get here?"

Mimi skipped downstairs to report the newsbreak that Ginger's suit no longer fit. "Ripped," Ginger heard her sister tell her mother. "Exploded." She returned with two safety pins and a message. "You're supposed to hurry up. We have to go."

After Ginger finished pinning her suit together, she headed to the living room. She was in the front hall when she noticed the long tube tied with a red ribbon leaning against the wall next to the door. Attached was an envelope with her mother's name on it. She handed it over. "I guess we missed this when we came in."

Glory looked at it and beamed. "I thought there might be a surprise around here somewhere." She pulled off the ribbon and unrolled the scroll. "How darling. A map."

Charlie took the map and laid it on the captain's chest in the living room. "It's a treasure map." His nail-bitten finger followed a thick black line across the yellowed paper. "This must be the treasure." He tapped a roughly drawn *X*. "Careful," he told Mimi when she squatted next to him. "It's old. It could rip."

Glory finished reading her note and slipped it back in the envelope. "It *is* a treasure map. An old map to a secret beach. Compliments of Casper Diggans."

Mimi took a sniff. "Not old. Painted to look old. With tea. We did the same thing for Document Day. Wrote up class laws. Then painted it with Lipton's." She touched the map. "Still wet." She sniffed again. "Maybe it's coffee. What do you think? Coffee or tea?"

"Okay, that's enough." Glory reclaimed the map and put it on the kitchen counter to dry. "The main thing is it's a map to a beach where we're going tomorrow. Now, am I the only one around here who wants ice cream? Are the groceries going to deliver themselves?"

This time not having proper directions was no problem at all. Driving along country roads with the windows open and the ocean breeze wafting in was all part of Glory's dream come true. Soon everyone fell into a woozy silence. By the time the car bucked up over the curb of the parking lot of their first stop, the ice-cream stand, all the backseaters were asleep or faking it.

Glory squeezed the car into a spot next to an old red school bus, the words "Camp Jabberwocky" painted in cheerful script on the side. The bus was disgorging the last of a crew of campers. Some moved awkwardly, legs in braces; others waited to be helped into wheelchairs.

"Good grief," Glory muttered. "This is going to take forever. Be a peach, Gingie. Wake everyone up while I get on line." Ginger watched as her mother tried to scoot around a counselor who was struggling to give a teenage boy, legs hanging limp, a piggyback ride to the ice-cream stand. "Excuse me," Glory said. "Coming through."

The counselor, a stocky woman who looked to be in her twenties, turned around, wobbling as she did. The boy, hands around her neck, grabbed tighter. Both of them seemed to find this hilarious. Glory stepped back to avoid a collision while the counselor steadied herself.

"Maybe it would be easier if I just went and brought you your ice cream," Glory offered, sweet voice on. "I have a carload of kids with a bunch of free hands. They can bring ice cream back for everyone." She winked and whispered, "That way you can put him down."

The teenager yelled out, "No way."

The counselor laughed and said, "You mean *No way, thank you.* We like to do things ourselves," she told Glory. "Ready?" she asked her passenger.

"Yes, please," he answered, and both the counselor and the boy laughed again.

Glory smiled to seem good-natured and sped past them to get on line. By the time Ginger and her siblings joined her, she was chatting with an old man about the weather. "If rain makes your bones hurt, why in the world would you pray for it?"

"A little pain in the knee is no big deal. The island needs the rain. I pray for rain every night, but every morning I wake up to the same blazing sun."

"Cuckoo bird," Glory muttered under her breath as she took her place at the "Order Here" window.

When they got back to the car, a young girl, waiting to board the bus, held up her ice-cream cone and boasted, "I got this because I used the bathroom by myself!"

"Cuckoo bird," Glory said again, and slid behind the wheel.

• • •

There were more weather complaints at the grocery store, people in the aisles remarking about how parched the island was, how the beach sand had turned fine as dust, how the ponds were shallower than anyone's grandmother could remember.

"Wish I knew a rain dance," a woman said as they got on line to check out.

"I can do a rain dance." Callie moved into the aisle and did an imitation of a ballerina.

"Hold on, beauty queen," Glory said. "If it starts raining because of you I will not be—"

"So bad-tempered."

Glory swung around to face her scolders, two birdlike women standing close together on line behind them. Ginger tugged her mother's arm. "Not you. They're not talking about you."

The cashier agreed. "She's right, hon. They're talking about Miss Hellman. You know, the playwright?" She leaned closer. "Tina, over there? In the blue hat? Works for her. Part-time. Types her private correspondence and makes lunch. Woman asks for the same thing every day, and every day complains she doesn't like it. I don't know how Tina works for that dragon."

"Really?" Glory's eyes widened. "I think Tina is the luckiest duck in the world."

Tina, checking out in the aisle next to theirs, kept her eyes cast down as Glory leaned over to peer in her cart. "Lillian Hellman likes Corn Flakes? So do I. Gingie, be a peach and grab a box. I forgot to get one. Ask that man to show you where the cereal is." She nodded toward a clerk replenishing a display of corn right next to where Ginger stood.

"He won't hear her," the cashier said. "Tap him on the shoulder, hon. Then point to me."

83

Ginger tapped, pointed, and watched as the cashier used sign language to talk to the man. He listened, nodded, and motioned for Ginger to follow him. As she walked away, she heard her mother ask, "They hired a deaf man? That's so nice. Did he teach you to sign?"

"He didn't have to. Lots of us sign. Lots of deaf people on the island. We all just kind of pick it up. Comes in handy too. I have conversations in sign language with hearing people all the time. Great for telling secrets. If you signed, I'd tell you one now."

"Imagine," Glory said.

By the time Ginger got back with the cereal, the conversation about deaf people and weather was over and Glory had softened up Tina enough to confirm that Miss Hellman was on the island and guests were expected for the weekend.

"Is it Arthur Miller? Is Arthur Miller coming? I should warn you, I might faint if he is." Glory's eyes were shining bright. "Let me ask you, Tina. If a person wanted to bump into Miss Hellman, an admirer, like me—I wouldn't bother her, of course. Maybe a compliment, but that would be it—where would you suggest I go?"

But Tina was done talking. She snapped her purse shut and hurried out of the store.

The cashier handed Glory her change. "I seen Miss Hellman around a couple of places. Once up in Menemsha. Once down the road from Jungle Beach."

Glory took a quick breath. "Really? That's where we're going tomorrow. Jungle Beach."

Charlie snapped out of his supermarket stupor. "There's a jungle here?"

The cashier shrugged. "Jungle of hippies. Flower-power good-for-nothings. Ask me, we should load them and their truck on the ferry and ship them off the island for good. No jobs. No rules. No manners. No clothes."

"Why don't they have clothes?" Mimi asked on their way to the car.

"Another cuckoo bird," Glory said, but this time she didn't sound so sure.

Dinner was hot dogs and buttered corn, which they ate outside at a splintery picnic table under a pergola covered with flowering vines that were magnets for cartoon-sized bees. The bees touched down on the corn, moved to the rounds of tomatoes, and got stuck in the seeds of the sliced cucumbers. Charlie put himself in charge of batting them away, and Ginger cleaned up after him while Glory ducked inside at ever-shortening intervals to see if the phone was working yet. Finally, a cheer. "Hallelujah, dial tone."

Out on the deck, Ginger could hear her mother's side of the conversation. "For god sake, Solly. Why are you in bed worrying? Of course I'm fine. Everybody's fine. Why wouldn't we be fine?" There was a long pause and then, "I don't know. What more do you *want* me to say?"

Glory hung up, marched out, and gave Ginger instructions. "I'm calling Evelyn. You're in charge. Do not let anyone wander off. Or climb any trees. Or eat any of the berries from any of the bushes. If anyone goes to the pond, you have my permission to slap them."

"What pond?" Mimi asked, as soon as the screen door closed.

This time, Glory seemed to be mostly listening, and when she spoke, her voice was so low Ginger had to strain to hear. "Paul said what? How awful. Where will Thomas go? He's welcome to stay with us." There was a long silence, and then Glory's tone changed. "Why would I be offended? It makes perfect sense." The silence lengthened. Ginger stopped listening.

When the screen door reopened, her mother was holding a glass and her eyes were twinkling and damp. "Guess who's on his way? Little Thomas Clarke. Coming by himself to stay with his uncle Casper. For a whole month." She shook her glass and watched the ice cubes clink. "Woman is out of her bird." She sat down at the picnic table and closed her eyes.

Ginger could hear the sound of Mimi and Charlie arguing down by the shed. She watched as her mother's fingers slid to her temples.

"I'll take them inside," she offered, and ran to tell her siblings it was time to go in and play board games. "First one in gets to pick." She raced them to the house and then waited, so she was the last one in. As she passed her mother, Glory blew her a kiss.

Although there were a lot of games in the house, there was nothing they could actually play. Mimi's first choice, Monopoly, had no dice. The Ouija board had no pusher. In Clue, all the weapons were gone. When Glory finally joined them, Charlie was fiddling with the TV antenna, but that proved useless too.

Glory took one look at the snowy picture on the screen and sighed her way out of the room. When she came back, there was a slim phone book in her hand. She sat down and flipped lazily through the pages, as if it were a magazine.

"What are we going to do now?" Mimi wanted to know.

Glory didn't look up. "I haven't the foggiest idea."

"Time for bed?" Ginger suggested.

Her siblings clambered up the stairs, eager to get to their rooms before their mother stopped them. Unlike Ginger, they hadn't noticed Glory had lost interest in them. From what Ginger could tell, her mother didn't care one way or another whether they were there or whether they were gone.

CHAPTER TEN

Ginger rang Glory's doorbell and tried to give one more go at positive thinking, but this time all she could come up with were pipe dreams: Julia and Nick were kidding and would show up any minute; Glory forgot to tell them this year she was going to the Popkins' for Thanksgiving instead; maybe it wasn't really Thanksgiving at all.

The door swung open and her pipe dreams died. "Finally." It was Mimi. "They're here," she called into the living room.

After obligatory kisses on cheeks, Ginger shared the news that Julia was under the weather and not coming. There were mild noises of concern, and then everyone went back to what they were doing before Ginger and Richard had arrived, recoiling from a platter Glory was offering around the room, deviled eggs with yolks crusted over like warnings.

"Want one?" Glory offered an egg to Richard, but he declined. "What, are you all on the same cockamamie diet? Have an egg," she told Ginger. "You look pale."

Across the room, Mimi sent a signal to her sons, her thumb and forefinger together, moving—zip—in a straight line through the air.

The boys understood: *time to turn off your devices.* They shut down their electronics and let their mother herd them out of the living room. As with all holidays, the meal at Glory's was only a first stop for the Popkins. As soon as the main course was over, sometimes directly after it was served, Mimi would apologize and then hustle her family out for the next dinner, at Neil's mother's house—the fun dinner, Ginger now knew, where the boys were allowed on the roof.

As soon as she walked into the dining room, Ginger stopped. "What happened to the table?" Her mother's table, when opened, could comfortably fit eighteen. But today it was closed to its smallest size, cozy for a family of six. The plates, she saw, teetered, one atop the other. Napkins had been tossed helter-skelter. The centerpiece was an untidy jumble of silverware.

"I ran out," Glory said.

"Of what?" Ginger asked.

Neil knocked on the table and chuckled. "Might be a little tight here, Glore." Neil was a husky man who liked big things, oversized sofas, large cars, prominent noses. "How about we open this baby up? Where do you store the leaves?"

"Used to keep them in the closet. Till they were stolen. Imagine."

Of course later Ginger realized she should have questioned why Glory would think someone would break into a house to steal the leaves of a dining room table. But in the moment she wasn't on the lookout for signs of a diminishing mind. Her attention was turned inward—to unclenching her jaw and bringing her shoulders down from her ears, now that Glory and Mimi had moved on, without interrogating her further about the details of Julia's health.

Eager to get going, the Popkins quickly squeezed around the table, Neil taking the seat at the foot, Glory in her usual place at the head. This left Ginger and Richard, who'd hesitated, to sit slightly exiled, half a foot from the table, plates balanced on their thighs.

Sitting close to the buffet, Ginger could see Glory's cuisine had reached a new low. Overcooked asparagus dripped off the rim of a platter like clocks in a Dalí painting. And wasn't that the platter Ginger had tested for lead paint? There had been a bunch of them—serving dishes Glory picked up for practically nothing at garage sales—and to finally settle the argument over whether they were safe to use, Ginger had brought over a lead paint test kit. She was sure the asparagus platter was one of many that had failed. The large bowl beside it hadn't failed, but what was in it looked inedible. Breakfast sausages, possibly cold. Next to that was a casserole of stuffing that looked like a science experiment about dehydrated food.

"Oops," Glory called out. "Forgot the gravy." She disappeared into the kitchen.

Mimi swiveled to her sons to give a rush of instructions. "Just take a taste. You'll eat for real at Granny's. And don't use the gravy. And don't eat the sausages. Anything tastes bad, just spit it in your napkin when Grandma looks away."

"And stay away from that asparagus fish," Ginger said. "I mean asparagus *dish*."

Glory swept back in holding a bowl of cranberries and an open can of gravy. "*Now* we can start." She stood behind her chair. "Who wants to say Face?"

"Grace," Ginger corrected her.

"Thank you." Glory passed the cranberries to Troy, Mimi's youngest. "Try these. You'll love them. They're darling."

Troy put a cranberry in his mouth and turned to his mother. "These are *weally* hard."

Mimi picked one up and examined it. "Did you forget to cook the cranberries?"

"Why would I do that?" Glory turned to Troy. "They're not weally hard," she told him. "They're *really* hard. Can you say *really*?" She turned to Mimi. "I'll never understand why you insist on paying a stranger to help him when I could do it better for free."

"See what you started," Mimi said to Ginger under her breath.

Ginger knew Mimi was still mad at her for pointing out Troy's speech impediment in front of their mother. His problem wasn't the usual Tangle mangling which Glory and the sisters all had to a degree, though Mimi, through force of will, had pretty much managed to get over it and Ginger only slipped up occasionally, usually after her mother got under her skin. Troy's problem was more run-of-the-mill, certain letters in certain combinations.

Not surprisingly, Mimi had ignored Ginger's recommendation for a speech pathologist, opting instead for a doctor who'd written the definitive book on articulation disorders. No matter that the woman's office was on the upper east side of Manhattan, or that her only open time slot meant Troy would have to miss most of band practice twice a week. Getting Troy out of mandatory band practice was a small-potatoes problem for Mimi. That Troy would have to slink out of the practice room early while children made fun of his speech behind his back was not on her worry list. Unlike Ginger, Mimi did not have a worry list. The worst part for Mimi was dealing with this, Glory grousing about why she wasn't asked to help.

"I don't get why you schlep him into the city to see that woman," Glory complained. "All he needs to do is sing. Singing is the best cure. Troy, sing with Grandma. 'There once was a boy in the north country. He had'—come on Troy, sing with me—'he had sisters.'"

"No singing," Mimi snapped. "And *that woman* is a doctor."

"Oh, a *doctor*." Glory shrugged. "Troy doesn't need a doctor. He needs an actress. Who can pro*ject* and e*nunc*iate and sing. You know," she told Troy, "before you were born, I used to sing *and* dance. I was quite the actress."

"Good grief," Mimi said. "You were in a community theater group fifty years ago."

"Since when does talent have an expiration date? Anyway, didn't I go on tour last year?"

"Yes." Mimi nodded. "You toured all the best nursing homes in northern New Jersey." She turned to Neil. "What time do we have to be at your mom's?"

Neil was an excellent ear doctor, but he rarely listened. "Hmm?"

Glory grabbed hold of Troy's wrist. "I'm going to tell you a story." Like everyone else in the family, the boys knew this one by heart. "There was a woman in my theater group name of Shirley Gewirtz." Hunter, Mimi's middle boy, started lip-synching along until Mimi shot him a warning look and he stopped. "Not very good. Nothing to look at. Never got the leads. One day, changed her name to Sunny Worth. Sent out her head shots. Got hired for television"—she snapped her fingers—"like that. That's how good we were. Imagine."

"Shirley Gewirtz did one commercial." Mimi didn't notice that Hunter was now lip-synching *her* words. "For Lavoris. That's it. Her entire acting career. Halitosis."

"Not one of my problems." Glory stood up. The discussion was over. She fetched the gravy can and raised it. "Time for a toast. Isn't this darling? All of us here, together."

"We're not *all* here." Ginger immediately regretted having spoken. "What I mean is, just because Julia is home sick doesn't mean we should forget her."

"No one's forgetting her," Richard said quietly.

"Gingie's right," Glory said. "I forgot about Julia. I forget all the time now. I swear, if my head wasn't screwed on"—she twirled her finger in the air—"I would forget. I forgot what I would forget. Who got me started on this, anyway?"

A subject change was in order and Ginger quickly ran through possible options. Last week's splinter epidemic at school might work. She went over what happened in her head to make sure there was nothing in the anecdote she would regret. But before she could begin the story, Wallace, Mimi's eldest, broke the silence.

"Is that what happened with Aunt Callie? Did you forget her?"

"Wallace," Mimi hissed. "Why would you say that?" She and Ginger turned as one toward Glory, but their mother had vanished into the kitchen. "Who told you about Callie?" She looked at Ginger. "Did you tell him? Didn't we have an agreement that subject is off-limits?"

"Julia," Wallace interrupted. "Julia told me. And it's okay. I don't think Grandma heard."

"Thank god." Mimi glared at Ginger as if it was her fault that Julia and Wallace were friends.

In a way it was. Ginger knew being an only child could be lonely, so she did whatever she could to encourage Julia's friendship with her cousins. And she couldn't leave it up to chance. Despite being the same age, Julia and Wallace had little in common in their day-to-day lives. Julia went to public school, for one thing, while the Popkins boys went to private. And while Ginger insisted Julia pick a team or join a club after school—her daughter was not going to be one of those teenagers who roamed free all afternoon when school got out, getting in trouble—she did not curate Julia's activities like Mimi did with the boys, strategizing which ones would look best on a résumé. Even eating was different in the two households. Ginger shopped weekly at the supersized Pathmark, where she brought a list of staples like potatoes, chicken, whatever pasta and tomato sauce was on sale, and for a treat, single-serving bite-sized dark chocolate. Mimi, on the other hand, ducked in daily to Whole Foods to buy whatever struck her fancy, black-eyed peas pâté for a snack, organic beet-leaf pasta to serve with grass-fed bison bolognese.

To help the kids forge a friendship, Ginger pushed for the families to eat dinner together every few weeks. When dinner was at the Popkins' house, she was always relieved that Julia was polite even when it was a struggle to get down the goat cheese–oat truffle crepes Mimi presented as if they were jewels. At Ginger's house, the boys had no such problem. They were like gluttons, digging into the mashed potatoes and washing chocolate down with big gulps of milk that was not made of coconut, soy, or almonds.

"So is what Julia said true?" Wallace asked now. "We have an uncle who died?"

"I'm back," Glory sang out in case they didn't notice, and Wallace knew enough to stop talking. "Grandma coming round the mountain with the turkey. Who wants dark?"

Even though she preferred white, Ginger volunteered.

Glory speared an undercooked drumstick. As she passed it to Ginger, blood marked the trail. "Could someone get the seltzer? Before the tablecloth gets brained."

"Stained," Ginger and Mimi corrected her together.

Richard got a 2-liter jug of club soda from the kitchen and handed it to Ginger. Their hands touched for a second, and then Mimi grabbed the bottle. "I'll take that."

She poured the seltzer on the drippings, and they all watched the wet spot spread like a lie that could no longer be contained.

CHAPTER ELEVEN

Next day breakfast was Corn Flakes Lillian Hellman–style, which according to Glory meant two teaspoons of sugar sprinkled in each bowl. What made this Lillian Hellman–style, Ginger had no idea, but her mother had greeted them in a mood as sunny as her yellow halter-top bathing suit, and no question seemed worth the risk of unsettling her good humor.

After the rest of them got dressed for the beach, Glory hustled them to the car and told them their itinerary. The morning was for exploring. They'd stop for a look at the Vineyard Sound, the Nantucket Sound, and if there was time after that, some island ponds. After lunch, if all went well, best for last, they'd head to Jungle Beach.

"Why *best?*" Charlie asked.

"Why *last?*" Mimi added.

Why *if all goes well?* Ginger wondered to herself.

As usual, Ginger got the booby prize, front seat, and as usual, Glory drove like she was an actress sitting in the chopped-off half of a fake car on an old-time movie set, images of the world whizzing by as if on a screen. It was all, *look over there*, as the car swerved to the right, and *look at that*, as she overcorrected to the left. Anyone watching would surely assume they were a carload of drunken teenagers, and not a family with a mother who drove, forearms pressed against the wheel, as she inexplicably applied and then reapplied her lipstick every five minutes. Really, it was a mystery, how the same woman who could sit perfectly still, studying a single puzzle piece for minutes at a time, had to fidget constantly while driving. Suddenly a self-proclaimed expert on country roads, her hands fluttered like hummingbirds, to the radio looking for a better station, to her purse searching for a lozenge. Everything was urgent, her need for a tissue, for a nail file, for some Chiclets. And though she checked the rearview mirror frequently, communicating with glares or smiles to whichever child was or wasn't displeasing her, she seemed oblivious that they were all clutching their seats with white-knuckled grips.

Making matters worse, the drought had turned the unpaved roads bone-dry, so their car traveled in a cloud of its own dust. "Like Pig-Pen," Callie cheerfully observed, too young to understand the danger held in the equation of lack of visibility plus dreamy driver.

The road to the first of Evelyn's recommended beaches was only wide enough for one car to pass at a time. This meant oncoming vehicles would suddenly rise up, each in a cloud of its own dust, threatening to crash into them. The road's shoulder was a confusion of brush, hiding an infinite possibility of pitches and slopes down which a car might tumble. It all made for a game of chicken Glory seemed to have no idea she was playing. When a white Dodge Dart rose in front of them like a ghost, Ginger slid low in her seat, so as not to watch herself die in the windshield's reflection. Glory swerved into a bush just in time, and when the car passed, she swerved back onto the road, indifferent to the sound of twigs scraping the car door.

"Sit up, Gingie. Do you want to end up bent over like a question mark? Up, up, up. Books on your head."

Ginger sat up and pretended she had books on her head, which did help keep her from screaming. How could her mother not notice that a red Plymouth Fury was now hurtling toward them? The imaginary books tumbled. Ginger bit her lip and her tongue and screamed out, "Slow down!" The Fury veered off the road to avoid them.

"For the love of god, everyone knows it's the car coming off the beach that's supposed to pull over, not the car going on."

Ginger turned to see what happened to the Plymouth. "I think they went into a ditch."

"They're fine. How did you get to be such a worrier?" She fiddled with the radio, looking for something better. "I'm not a worrier. Your father, that's another story." The wind whipped up, grabbing a hodge-podge of trash and lost objects and tossing them about. Through the window Ginger watched a child's pink cloth bucket hat dance by followed by a picnic of napkins and then a crushed pack of Lucky Strikes. The road narrowed. Glory drove on.

When they reached the parking lot, everyone scrambled out and ran to the shore, relieved to have survived the ride. The beach, a narrow strip of sand facing a stretch of shallow water, was perfect for Callie. But Glory warned them not to get too comfortable. "We're not staying. We're just looking, remember? We have lots more to explore."

As the morning wore on, she hustled them in and out of the car, speeding too fast down narrow dirt roads, looking at—but not swimming in—ponds, sounds, and tidal pools. The sun got hot and then hotter, and they did the same. Callie needed a bathroom. Mimi was starving to death.

"What kind of explorers are you?" Glory pulled into a fry shack with a picnic table out front. "Imagine if Lewis and Clark stopped every time their stomachs growled."

● ● ●

At precisely two, hands glistening with grease from their fried shrimp and potatoes, Glory announced it was time for Jungle Beach. Ginger was back on navigating duty, though this time there was little to do. The treasure map showed one street, South Road, and one landmark, a stick-figure drawing Mimi decoded was meant to symbolize a farm.

"Should I keep going?" Glory seemed nervous about missing it. "Did we pass it?"

As Ginger scanned the landscape for any hint of a beach ahead, an acid-green pickup truck barreled up alongside them, a crush of hippies bouncing in the open cargo bed. She read the sign painted on the door in tangerine psychedelic script. "Look at the truck. It says *Jungle Beach*."

The driver honked and sped past them. A woman in the front seat stuck her hand out and offered a peace sign. The flatbed passengers waved. Then the pickup slowed and heaved onto a grassy shoulder ahead of them, the last in a line of cars and trucks parked there.

"I guess this is it." Glory bumped the car onto the grass and came to a hard stop inches from the back of the hippie truck.

The flatbed passengers were piling out in a swarm. They danced their way across the street together, and when they got to the other side, they all disappeared into what looked like a hole in a thicket of bushes.

Ginger glanced at her mother to see what she made of it, but Glory wasn't looking out the window. She was staring at her reflection in her compact, putting on a swipe of lipstick and then pulling a few hairs loose from under her hat to better frame her face.

She smiled, to make sure nothing was in her teeth. "Ready or not."

Ready for what, Ginger wasn't sure. But when she got out of the car, she followed her mother's gaze down the road and saw two figures, a lanky man and, beside him, a boy.

"Ship ahoy!" Glory called, waving her arms.

The man turned and waved back, matching her movements like a faraway shadow. It was Mr. Diggans, and as he got closer, Ginger saw the boy was Thomas Clarke.

"Thomas," Glory called out. "Aren't you a sight for sore eyes." Thomas stared at his feet, looking shy. "Be a peach," Glory told him. "Give us a hand unloading the car."

Mr. Diggans surveyed the gear in the trunk. "Afraid you'll regret it if you try bringing all that in. Bit of a hike ahead." He blinked, and Ginger noticed his eyes were set unnaturally deep in his face, like holes. "Let's see what you've got." He parceled things out so that everyone got something: an umbrella, straw mats, buckets and shovels, a couple of light chairs, some towels. The rest, he advised, would be better left in the car. "Unlocked is fine. It's safe. You can even leave your purse if you want."

Glory hesitated and then sang out, "Why not," and threw her purse in with abandon.

Mr. Diggans picked up the chairs and smiled, showing off his horsey teeth. "Ready to hike into the most beautiful beach in the world?"

And Glory answered, "We sure are."

The two of them walked side by side, laughter falling behind like scraps. When they crossed the road, Mr. Diggans headed toward the break in the bushes where the truck-people had gone. "The entrance is here. Duck when you go in. Single file. Thomas, you take the rear."

The bushes made for an overgrown tunnel tall enough so that only Mr. Diggans had to stoop as he walked. "Stay close to the person in front of you," he cautioned, leading the way. "Don't want anyone to fall into a boggy ditch."

"Watch out for skunks," Thomas added, and Ginger thought he sounded sad.

They walked single file until, a few minutes in, the path widened. The bushes over their heads parted so that now they could see sky, but thorny branches reached in from the sides.

"Bushes are biting me," Mimi complained.

"Hug yourself," Mr. Diggans advised, and flashed a smile to Glory, whose arms were already wrapped tight around the towels. The ground turned spongy beneath their feet. "Planks of wood ahead." Mr. Diggans stepped up onto something. "Here we go." Ginger heard his sandals tapping across a board someone must have placed over the boggy ground. "Watch out for splinters. No bare feet. Not yet. No bare anything yet." He gave Glory a wink and then continued up an incline. When they reached the top, the vegetation changed to succulents. Ground cover became sparse. The sun bore down. Ginger smelled the sea. "Here we are," he said. "Welcome to Jungle Beach."

Ginger heard a whinny and swung around in time to see a horse gallop out of the bushes a few yards down from where they'd just emerged. The rider, a young woman with long crimped hair, pulled the horse to a stop and leaned over toward Charlie. "Do you like huckleberries?" Before Charlie could answer, she handed him a basket, clicked her tongue, and took off, the horse trotting down to the far end of the beach and disappearing to the other side of the rocky cliffs.

By the time Callie broke the silence to ask, "What happened to her clothes?" Ginger's face had turned bright red.

"No one wears clothes at the far end," Thomas said.

Ginger looked toward the cliffs where the lady and the horse had gone. She could make out people now. Some walking, some throwing Frisbees, none of them dressed.

Charlie stood beside her and squinted. "Are those naked ladies?"

"Don't be ridiculous," Glory said, but her voice trailed off as she realized he was right.

"Ugh," Charlie exclaimed and turned around. "I just saw a naked man."

Mr. Diggans laughed. "Not to worry. Today, we're going the other way, where everyone will be fully clothed in the latest bathing attire." He kicked his brindle sandals into a huge pile of shoes that lay scattered on the sand like leaves and headed away from the cliffs.

"Tomorrow," Mimi told Ginger, "I'm not coming at all."

They followed Mr. Diggans to a large gathering of clothed beachgoers who were assembled in a sloppy circle of blankets and chairs.

"Come with me, Morning Glory. Let me introduce you around."

Ginger watched as he made the introductions. Here was his sister, Minty, and her husband, Bob, who had a house on the other side of the rocks. And here, for the whole summer, in the house just down from Minty's, were his cousins—Ginger didn't catch their names—whose husbands came up on the weekends, and here were some new washashores who'd just declared permanent residence.

She studied her mother's progress as she moved into the crowd, smiling and shaking hands, listening carefully as people introduced themselves, taking in names and details in that way she did, that seemed relaxed though Ginger knew she was working hard to memorize everything so that later she could easily recall it.

Many of the beach people, Ginger learned, hadn't come in through the bushes. They had walked over from houses hidden beyond the coves and cliffs, and they had left nothing behind. There were volleyball nets, fishing poles, clam rakes, even a folding table now set up with a gingham cloth on top, baskets of plates and cups competing for space with containers of food and bottles of wine.

Ginger staked out a spot at the periphery of the encampment. She was unrolling her straw mat when Mr. Diggans jogged over. "Would you like to meet Thomas's cousins?"

There was nothing wrong with the question, but Ginger didn't like that he'd asked. She still hadn't made up her mind about which of her parents was right about Mr. Diggans. "No, thank you." She glanced over to see if she was in trouble for being rude, but Glory was busy telling a story and when the group of listeners laughed, she tipped her head back and laughed too, up into the sky.

At dusk, the feasting began. The table was set with plates the color of seafoam and matching goblets, which even the Tangle children were invited to drink from, either apple cider or Orange Crush. Later, as the sun inched toward the horizon, the air became perfumed with sweet smoke, and people began drifting toward the cliffs where Ginger refused to look.

It was dark—she was half-asleep—when Glory tapped her shoulder.

"Time to go. Mr. Diggans has graciously offered to walk us to the car. Here." She handed each of them a small flashlight. "Compliments of Casper." She smiled and her eyes glinted in the moonlight. "Nice to have a man who thinks of everything."

CHAPTER TWELVE

Monday started as usual, a sloppy line of twitchy children snaking from Ginger's office door to the first water fountain, waiting for her arrival. The early birds were a hodgepodge of the anxious and the downcast, children sent by teachers who didn't have time or temperament to deal with morning tears, vague complaints, or the distress caused by a lost lovey. Before Ginger was a school nurse, she had no idea how often children lost things. What a hero she could be, just by saying, *Look—turn around. What's that poking out of your backpack?* Even big things, she learned, could disappear from a child's custody. She once sat, stunned, as a teary fourth grader confessed she'd just lost her cello for the second time.

Ginger was well aware of the difference between how she was perceived at school and how she felt at home. At school she was a reliable, efficient, clear-headed thinker. At home, she felt like a poster child for the derailed. In the past, she'd tried to apply her no-nonsense nurseness to her off-duty home life, but she never managed to make it work. This was how it would go: a boy at school would complain that he had to keep clearing his throat, and she'd confidently reassure him it was probably just a cold. If the problem persisted, she would call home and suggest the mother take him to an allergist. But if Julia complained of the same postnasal drip, instead of thinking *allergist*, Ginger would suddenly remember the mother she met at Field Day whose brain tumor had presented with exactly that symptom.

As always, Ginger dealt with the waiting children quickly, listening to their woes with practiced sympathy but not indulgence and then briskly pointing them back to their classrooms. When the first wave was dispatched, she began her morning calls. *This is Nurse Tangle calling to let you know Lila left her bear on the bus. This is Nurse Tangle reminding you to drop off a new EpiPen for Colin. This is Nurse Tangle calling to discuss what happened at recess with Luke.*

By nine o'clock the thermometer came out. The otoscope emerged around ten. At eleven the boy who was always constipated turned up, and right after him came the girl who pulled off a hangnail every day at lunch and made herself bleed. When the boy with the smelly feet showed up, she would talk to him about the weather—he liked to discuss types of clouds; cumulus were his favorite—while she sprinkled powder in his socks and then sent him on his way.

Throughout the day they'd come in clumps. The chronic complainers who had imperceptible sties or tender spots their gym teachers denied existed. The upset stomachs, the sore throats, the itchy heads. There were mundane tasks too: the students who came to get their eyes checked or to be weighed. But her specialty was the children with vague complaints. Not the children who lost things, but the children who themselves felt lost.

At lunchtime, Emmett came to see her. For a month, Emmett had come to school with a SunButter and dried kale sandwich, which he refused to eat. SunButter, the sunflower seed replacement insisted upon by peanut allergy sentinels, was not all that palatable paired with jelly. Who could blame Emmett for refusing to eat a sandwich of SunButter and dried kale? The previous week, Ginger had made a deal with him.

If he promised to take his uneaten sandwich back home with a note for his mother, he could have a yogurt from her small fridge. *Emmett seems reluctant to eat his lunch,* she wrote to Mrs. Samuels. *Maybe something plain for a while. Pasta or yogurt worth a try?* She thought she'd struck the right tone, but here was Emmett, back again. "How are you?" she asked him.

"Good. Do you ever take that clip out of your hair?"

Reflexively, Ginger smoothed back her hair and felt to see if the wide barrette at the back of her neck was still fixed in place. She wore her hair back at work for hygienic reasons, but she usually left the clip in when she got home because otherwise her hair tended to increase in volume throughout the day until it was out of control. "Sometimes I wear it loose on the weekend. What's up?"

"I want to turn in my sandwich but not for yogurt. My mom gave me a teaching moment about it last night."

"About yogurt?" The boy nodded. "Okay, well, what did you learn?"

"Yogurt is a milk product, and milk products are not a healthy food."

This was another daily challenge, keeping up with the slippery facts of the medical Internet news and the parents who consumed it. "Milk can be confusing," Ginger admitted. "Some people can't have any, some people can have a lot. Maybe your mom and I should make a milk plan. What do you think?"

Emmett nodded and laid his sandwich on her desk. "What can I have?"

With yogurt temporarily on the danger food list, she didn't have much to offer, so she switched with the boy: Emmett got her apple and turkey sandwich; Ginger got SunButter and kale. After he left, she closed her door—she tried to have ten minutes of private time for lunch—and took a bite. The taste and crunch was strange at first, but it wasn't bad. She was halfway through the sandwich when she heard the next group gathering in the hall. She wrapped up the rest for later, cleaned her desk with a Lysol wipe, and called out. "Next customer?"

Blisters. It was like an epidemic. Did no one's shoes fit properly? She quickly cleaned the affected area, applied a bandage, and answered the inevitable question. *No, I don't pop blisters. No, you definitely shouldn't pop it. No, not even your mom. No one should pop blisters ever.*

At four, she locked up her supply cabinet and headed to Glory's. Today, she planned on a quick visit, just a drop-by to give her mother a new puzzle and to see if she needed anything from the grocery store. But when she walked in the house, an odor hit her. "What is that?"

"Since when are you such a fussbudget? You didn't get that from me." Glory lifted the lid off the new puzzle—"Ooh, the solar system"— and spilled the Milky Way out on the table.

"Did you ever find that felt mat?" Ginger opened the refrigerator, where the smell seemed worst.

"Never been a fan of felt. Not at all flattering." Glory's fingers moved quickly as she turned the fragments of the cosmos star side up. Then she stopped. "I've done this one already."

"No you haven't. It's new." Ginger threw out a bottle of ketchup the color of sludge, a pickle jar with what looked like embryos inside, a dish of olives melting into brine.

"So snippy." Her fingers scuttled across the pile, hunting for straight edges. "You need a hobby. You'd feel better if you had a hobby."

"You're my hobby." Ginger slipped on a pair of marigold rubber gloves.

"I mean, collect something. Like I do. Like puzzles."

"Good idea." Ginger wiped up a puddle of liquid, origin unknown, from the top shelf. "What if I mark everything with a date? To help you know when it's time to throw things out."

"Sure, Madame Curie. Whatever you say." Glory stared at the puzzle. "Was this on the sale rack? Something's not right. Is it one of those seconds, like your father sold?"

"It's brand-new. The man told me. Are you feeling okay?"

"I'm fine. Stop worrying. Worrywarts get worry lines. You have a big one right between your eyebrows. Makes you look mad all the time. I don't have that. See?" She offered up her face and Ginger saw agitation. "Your father was the same. I told him all the time, stop looking for trouble, Solly. Look hard enough, you'll find it. And then where will we be?"

Ginger tossed a Tupperware bowl in the garbage. The thud caught her mother's attention.

"That's a perfectly good container. Why did you throw it out?"

"There was mold in it, it was warped, and it smelled. I'm just trying to help."

"So help with something I want." Glory thought for a moment. "Let's go somewhere."

"Like where? Want to see a play?" Ginger took out an ice tray and sniffed. Onions. She banged out the cubes into the sink. "We haven't been to a play in years."

Glory gave an indifferent shrug. "I was thinking more along the lines of Paris. I always wanted to go to Paris. Your father didn't, of course. Mister Stay-at-Home."

"Okay, Paris it is." Ginger pulled out the vegetable bin. This must be the root cause of the smell. She used a wad of paper towels to gather up the limp remains of unidentifiable food.

Glory narrowed her eyes. "Or the moon. Wouldn't that be darling? Going to the moon?"

"Sure. Why not."

"See? I knew it. You're not taking me seriously."

"I'm cleaning out your refrigerator."

"Sounds like *someone* woke up on the wrong side of the dead."

• • •

While the refrigerator shelves dried on the counter, Ginger went to the store to buy replacement food. But when she came back, grocery bags in her arms, she could smell the odor had returned. A disheartening mix of boiled beef, spoiled milk, bad breath, and musty skin, it seemed to be a part of the house now, coating the walls and the lightbulbs, activated every time Glory flicked on the switch. There was another smell too, an acrid odor, a warning sign Ginger couldn't place. She sniffed again. "Did you burn something?"

"You mean the teakettle? What a piece of nonsense. Your sister bought it. I'm sure it cost a fortune but—no whistle. How's a person supposed to know the water's boiling if there's no whistle?"

It was a fair point. "I'll get you a new one at the hardware store on my way home. With a whistle. I'll bring it tomorrow."

"As you wish. Now where are the corners?" Glory examined the puzzle and then gave up. "Long as you're going to town, can you make me an appointment to get my eyebrows done? At the nail place I like." Ginger nodded. "With that girl. What's her name? It's a month. May? April? Or is it a flower? Oh, it's syrup. It's Maple. I want an appointment with Maple."

"You mean, Mabel."

"Yes, but there's two of them. I don't want the new one. I want the old Maple. You know what? Long as you're going, better take the universe back. Tell them it's not right."

"Okay. Get kettle. Return puzzle. Eyebrow appointment."

"So huffy," Glory said as she put the puzzle pieces back in the box.

At the hardware store, Ginger bought a no-frills whistling kettle and at the shop across the street she found a puzzle of the Lady of Shalott, which the owner promised had just come in that morning. Last stop, she elbowed open the door to Utopia Nails.

"Nurse Tangle!" A woman at the manicure station closest to the door waved.

Ginger had no idea who she was, but that wasn't unusual. Grateful moms often said hello while Ginger struggled to place their faces and remember the names of their kids.

"Anne-Marie," the woman reminded her.

Recognition, slow to register, finally came. It had been years since the woman had a child in her school, and though she couldn't remember anything about the child, Anne-Marie was harder to forget. They came and went, these women, temporary fixtures in the hallways and the front office. Moms who organized teacher-appreciation luncheons and spring flings and acted like they were in charge of the school until their PTA terms were up, or their children moved on. Then they'd disappear, only to be replaced by others. Mostly their faces blended together and she couldn't tell them apart. But Anne-Marie, she remembered now, was one who stuck out. A woman with a certain kind of confidence that always put Ginger on edge. The type, she suspected, who had been in the cool crowd in high school and never gave up the craving to be admired as an adult. Ginger could still make out the ghost of Anne-Marie's cheerleader beauty—the good hair, the quick smile—but her face hadn't kept up. It was puffy, with eyes that were beginning to recede, lips that had thinned, and skin that had begun its gentle fall into jowls.

"How unlikely is this?" Anne-Marie's buoyant confidence remained.

Several facts came to Ginger at once. Anne-Marie had a son. A boy whose knees were permanently covered by large-sized Band-Aid tough strips because he always got in scuffles at recess. His name was Nick. She might not have put together Anne-Marie's Nick and *her* Nick—ten-year-old boys didn't always look familiar when she met them again at eighteen—if the girl sitting at the manicure station next to Anne-Marie hadn't just then come into focus. The girl struggling to make herself invisible. Julia. As far as Ginger knew, Julia had never had a manicure in her life.

"Oh. Well. Wow. Hi." Ginger tried not to sound too surprised, first that Julia was having a manicure; second, that she was having a manicure with Nick's mother; third, that the nails on the one hand that was finished were a freshly painted black.

"How great is this?" Anne-Marie wanted to know. "Now I can tell you face-to-face. Your daughter is amazing. I wish I had a daughter." She let out a laugh. "Who am I kidding? If I had a daughter, no way she'd be sweet like Julia. I don't grow 'em sweet. But swear to god, since Julia and Nicky started going out, Nicky's a different person. I love her. I love your daughter. I do."

"Thank you." Ginger forced a smile on her face and then noticed it, a tiny diamond stud in Julia's nose. "What is that?"

"Oh, don't worry," Anne-Marie assured her. "It's not a real diamond." Then she seemed to realize the stone was not the problem. "It's okay with you, right? Julia said you wouldn't mind. I never would have taken her to get her nose pierced if it wasn't okay with you." Anne-Marie smiled and there it was: the mother had the same provocative smirk as the son.

Ginger did not want to sound shrewish. "Well, it is a surprise." Julia looked away.

Anne-Marie lowered her voice. "Nicky doesn't know yet. He's going to be thrilled to bits. How could he not be, right? It's so adorable. Don't you love it?"

"Jules, can you step outside for a minute?"

"Now?" Julia pulled her hand out of the dish where it was soaking. The manicurist giggled and guided her hand back in. "Not done."

"Okay," Ginger said. "We can talk later. When you get home."

Ginger got in her car and, distracted, drove straight back to Glory's.

"Can't stay away, can you?" Glory asked when she answered the bell.

"Here's your kettle." Ginger handed it to her. "Here's a new puzzle." She turned to go.

"What about my appointment with Maple? What time did you make it for?"

"Didn't make it yet." Ginger didn't turn around. "I'll call them tomorrow."

"What a crab apple," Glory said, and shut the door.

Ginger walked into the house feeling so exhausted, she wondered if she might be coming down with the flu. To clear her head, she took a shower. When she got out, the phone was ringing.

As soon as she heard Mimi's voice, she knew something was wrong. "She's okay," her sister assured her, and then she explained. Glory got ahold of a new kettle, put it on the burner, turned on the flame, and fell asleep.

"Didn't the whistle wake her?"

"I guess not. The smoke alarm didn't wake her, either. Neither did the doorbell. Maybe her hearing is gone. Thank god a neighbor heard the alarm and called 911. The firemen broke down her door with an ax. One of us has to go over and get her. I don't know why they called me and not you." Ginger saw her message light flashing but said nothing. "The fireman told me she seemed confused. He said she shouldn't be on her own anymore. How can that be? She's not that old."

Ginger agreed. "But she's not that *young*, either. It can happen. Anytime." She sighed. "There've been signs. Which we've ignored. The question now is, what do we do about it?"

"Well, she can't move in here. Neil's already told me that would not be okay. Plus, we all know she'd be much happier living with you."

"Maybe," Ginger said. "It's just not a good time. I'm having trouble with Julia."

"Hello. Of course you are. She's a teenager. Now imagine she's a boy, multiply it by three, and welcome to my life."

"I'm having problems with Richard too."

"Oh." This gave Mimi pause. Through the phone Ginger could hear voices. *Mom? Uncle Eddy's here. Mom, Uncle Eddy's dog just pooped. Mom, I think Wallace broke my toe.* "Okay. I'll take her tonight. Just tonight. Can you bring her over? It's chaos here."

"Sure," Ginger said and quickly got off the phone before her sister could change her mind.

CHAPTER THIRTEEN

Beach emissaries appeared on their second day, girls, some as young as Callie, shyly proffering peaches, plums, and soda. But other than that token politeness, no one seemed curious about the Tangle children. They'd already been quickly sized up as just passing through and not worth the time.

For Ginger, this was a relief. From her position next to Mimi, on straw mats at the periphery of the crowd, she could keep a distant eye on the movements of the beach children. Like a single organism, they darted in and out of the water and then circled back to the blankets and chairs with intermittent regularity, all dripping wet and then all streaked with sand, all of them always hungry.

At first Ginger thought they were all related, but after watching for a while she figured out this was only because they'd spent so much time together it no longer mattered whose towel they used to dry off or whose sweatshirt they put on if they were cold. When someone complained of being hungry, someone else would grab the nearest bag of chips, and no one bothered asking if that was okay. As for which kid belonged to which grown-up, that didn't seem to make a difference either. Announcements were made to the crowd—*I'm going to the dunes* or *to the cliffs* or *to the water*—and answers came back in a chorus. *Okay, sounds good, have fun.*

The day the little girls came with their offering of peaches in a plastic bag, Ginger noticed Mr. Diggans watching and realized he was the one who'd sent them over. Later that day, Thomas stopped by—trailing a tail of boys—to invite them along on an expedition. "Gathering rocks. For the bonfire later. If you want to come."

Ginger declined for both of them, and when Mimi complained that she wanted to go, Ginger had to explain: "He only asked because Mr. Diggans made him."

On the third day when they met Mr. Diggans on South Road, he flicked a petal off the side of his Impala with his thumb and said, "Okay, Morning Glory. Your turn to lead the way."

Glory seemed unsure. "You'll be right behind me? You won't let us get lost?"

"I'll be close as your shadow." And he did stay close, even when Glory's pace quickened, her speed so brisk Callie had to run to keep up. At the tricky spot where the path split, Glory forged ahead without hesitation. And at the first plank of wood she hopped onto the board and balanced with her arms in the air, like a gymnast about to explode into a routine.

"No falling in the bog on my watch," Mr. Diggans called out, and Glory laughed, pretending to teeter before quickly righting herself and continuing on, graceful and sure-footed, all the way to the sandy beach. Mission accomplished, she turned and curtsied.

Mr. Diggans applauded. "Morning Glory, you could pass as a washashore. My guide services are no longer needed."

"A washashore? Me? What a darling thing to say."

After that, they hiked in on their own, always scanning for Mr. Diggans' brindle sandals at the shoe pile upon arrival. When the sandals were there, dark spots marking the indentations of his toes, Glory was giddy. When they weren't, it felt as if the sun had withdrawn from the sky.

Ginger continued to study her mother, watching as her chair moved deeper, every day, in small increments, deeper into the core of the crowd. Glory had made adaptive alterations. Her red lipstick was replaced by something pale that made her lips look like they were always wet and her mauve nail polish was off, swapped for a pale pink called *nude*. She was using her acting voice all the time now, with her not real smile, and her extra-high laugh. But every now and then, Ginger saw, her mother would sit perfectly still and Ginger knew, she was watching too, curious about these people who seemed to let nothing bother them.

Glory pointed this out in the car on the way back from a long day at the beach. "No one fusses about anything. Did you see that boy who came today? The one with the floppy hat?"

Of course Ginger saw him. The boy—he looked about her age—had walked in from one of the houses back behind the cove with Minty, Mr. Diggans' sister, and another woman Ginger assumed was his mom. His hat made him hard to miss. It was floppy and bright purple, with a giant green feather sprouting from the top like an antenna. It was big too, much too big for the boy's small head. But what caught Ginger's interest even more than his hat was what he did. The boy stood at the shoreline by himself all day, gathering seaweed. He'd pick up clumps from the sand or wade in and grab gobs from the water, and then very slowly he'd untangle the strands, carefully examining each one. He threw most of them back into the sea, but every once in a while, when he found a strand he liked, he let out a loud, "Whoop," and added it to his collection.

"I asked Minty what was wrong with him," Glory said. "Such an odd duck. Standing in one spot all day and letting out those whoops. But Minty said, *No, he's fine. A little different but fine. Collecting seaweed makes him happy. Entertains himself all day long. Nothing wrong with that.* And she's right. I watched him. Boy spent the whole day staring at seaweed, happy as a clam. And no one makes a fuss. Imagine."

The people who never fussed didn't even mind when the biting flies came the next morning. The insects arrived while Ginger was unrolling her mat and though the flies were practically invisible, together they made up a dark cloud that swarmed everywhere, up her nose, into her ears, and down the front of her shirt. But like her mother said, no one complained. It was just another excuse to have a good time. "Cover up," someone called, and a chorus followed: "Who needs a towel?" "Who needs a refill?" "Who's got the ice?"

Blankets were thrown and yanked over heads, and people made toasts with plastic cups beneath thin sheets. And when the winged invaders suddenly reconsidered their attack and left, disappearing in a gray cloud down the beach, the makeshift tents were tossed aside, more drinks were poured, and everyone went on as if the stinging midges had never been there at all.

When Glory, her golden hair an unlikely mess, noticed Ginger staring, she stretched out her legs, wiggled her toes, and said, "Is this the life or what?"

"Such good-natured people," she said on the way home that night. "No complain-o-grams. Not a sourpuss in the bunch. Have you ever seen anything like it?"

The Tangle children tried to make themselves good-natured, but no matter how much Glory wished they would become part of the blur of the beach children, racing in and out of the water, flushed and happy, bodies glistening with a dusting of damp sand, she was stuck being the mother of Charlie and Callie, who refused to do anything but dig a hole to China, and Mimi, who had come up with a rival project of her own, building a rock tower to the moon. Ginger irked her most of all, using her reflector not to improve her tan but as a shield in front of her face, so people would leave her alone.

The announcement came on the fourth day, in the car, on the drive to the beach. "Mr. Diggans is bringing us lunch today. Lobster. And don't tell me you don't like it, because you've never tried it." Her eyes checked the rearview mirror. "He'll have other things. It'll be a buffet. By the cliffs. Just us."

"Do we have to be naked?" Mimi asked. "Is *Mr. Diggans* going to be naked? I don't like him." She shrugged. "Can't help who you don't like."

"Tell me." Glory's calm tone was not to be trusted. "While *you're* building towers and *you're* digging to China and *you're* refusing to socialize, to whom do you imagine *I* am speaking?"

"Car!" Ginger yelled and closed her eyes.

The car coming toward them on Fisher's Hollow swerved just in time, and Glory jammed on the brakes. She pulled over to catch her breath and glanced at Ginger. Her eyes took in the out-of-control hair and constricting swimsuit. The three safety pins keeping it closed were not enough to hide that her suit was two sizes too small. "Heavens to Murgatroyd. When did those things pop out?"

"I don't know." Ginger crossed her arms over her chest.

"We'll have to do something about it. But not today. Today, Mr. Diggans is making us lunch." She pulled back onto the road and they traveled in silence to the grassy shoulder where everyone noticed—but no one said—theirs was the only car.

Mimi, first one out, checked for traffic and raced across the street before her mother could stop her. She waited at the shoe corral to make her report. "His sandals aren't here."

Glory marched down the beach with a steely gait. When they passed the woman and the boy with the floppy hat, she waved but didn't stop to say hello. Halfway to the cliffs she dropped her gear and brushed a loose strand of hair out of her eyes, leaving a dusting of fine sand on her forehead. With a sharp intake of breath, she lifted the umbrella pole high in the air and jammed it into the sand hard, as if she'd been practicing stabbing vampires in her sleep. She opened a chair and sat down with a sigh.

"Are you all right?" Ginger asked.

"For god sake. Do you want to worry both of us into an early grave?" She pulled her compact out of the beach bag, reapplied her pale lipstick, and stretched out her legs.

"I'm starving," Mimi announced.

Glory kept her gaze steady on the horizon. "Starve where I can't hear you. Gingie, take everyone to the water. You're in charge. Don't let anyone drown. We'll eat when Mr. Diggans gets here." She seemed to have no doubt he would arrive soon.

They marched in a sullen line to the shore and sat on the wet sand, kicking away clumps of seaweed as it washed onto their feet. Someone's stomach grumbled, but they couldn't figure out whose. Mimi stood up and turned toward their umbrella. "He's here."

When they got to the blanket, Mr. Diggans gave them each a small brown bag. "Martha's Vineyard fudge. Best in the world."

Mimi peered inside in case there was something else hiding. "Lunch is fudge?"

"Lunch. I forgot." Mr. Diggans sank to his knees beside Glory. "Can you forgive me?" He shook his head and put his hands to his heart. "A fool. That's what I am. A sorry fool."

But Glory did not want Mr. Diggans to be sorry. "There is no reason on earth you should be worrying about my children's lunch. Four of them, hungry all the time. They're like beggars, really. You should have seen the meal we had before we came. I'm surprised we fit in the car."

"Let me make it up to you. What about a picnic tomorrow. At sea? Do you like to sail?"

"That is absolutely not necessary," Glory said. "Do you have a boat?"

"I have friends with boats. What do you say, Morning Glory. We'll have a lunchtime sail past the grandest houses on the island. From a boat you can see everything."

"You don't by any chance know where Lillian Hellman's house is, do you?"

"What kind of washashore would I be if I didn't know that?"

"I can't go on a boat," Ginger told him. "I get seasick."

"I get seasick too," Mimi tried.

Glory laughed. "You do not. And I'll bring crackers for you, Gingie. You'll be fine."

Mr. Diggans begged forgiveness one more time, and they packed up their stuff to move to the encampment so that he could see who was around who had a boat.

The full crowd had arrived and soon talk turned to dinner. "We already ate," Glory said, to be a good sport. But when the fire got going, bowls and platters of food making the rounds, she relented. "Divine," she said of the skewered shrimp. "To die for," she said as she took another clam.

After dinner the crowd separated: adults in a sloppy circle on one side; kids gathering on the other. Ginger felt like she didn't belong in either group, but Mimi pulled her along to where the beach children sat discussing tomorrow's big event, the digging of the Cut.

"What's that?" Mimi asked.

"That's when they open the pond to the sea," Thomas told her. "Here, I'll show you." He gathered rocks and shells to demonstrate. "Say this pile of rocks is the ocean." He dropped a pile of rocks and then, a few inches away, made another pile of shells. "Say the shells are the pond." He went on to explain how in the morning a big digger was going to make a trench through the sand between the pond and the ocean. At first it would be a small channel, just a trickle of water from the pond to the sea. But the ocean current was strong, and the water was like a drill. "By tomorrow night the trench will be wide as a river. A crazy river with pond water zooming into the ocean and ocean water zooming into the pond. Like a river roller coaster with current going both ways."

"I want to go to the Cut." Callie stood up. "I want to ride on the river roller coaster."

"You can't," Thomas told her. The demonstration was over. "We're not allowed. We're not even supposed to know when they do it. They try to keep it secret. It's dangerous."

Callie grabbed Charlie's arm. "Can you take me to the river roller coaster tomorrow?"

"No." Charlie shook his head. "He just said it's dangerous."

Callie tried Ginger next. "Can you take me?" Callie was not normally a pest. Tagging along with her brother and sisters was usually all it took to make her happy. But now—was she finally growing up?—she seemed determined to get her way.

"Didn't you hear what Charlie and Thomas said?" Ginger asked. "It's not safe. We're not allowed."

When Callie moved on to try her luck with Mimi, Ginger asked Thomas why they made a cut in the pond if it wasn't safe.

Thomas shrugged. "Not sure. But when they don't, the water goes bad. If we went there now, before they open the pond, you could smell it. Smells like dead fish."

Callie was back. "Can we go tomorrow to smell it?"

Charlie and Ginger said, "No," and Mimi added, "You're acting stupid."

"Mom will say yes," Callie insisted, and she stomped off to give her mother a try.

"Don't worry," Thomas said. "No one will let her. Last summer someone drowned."

"Every summer someone drowns," a girl corrected him.

While the beach children reminisced about drownings and other catastrophes, Ginger glanced over at the circle of adults and was relieved to see that Callie, having been turned down, had moved on to doing an interpretive dance of what she thought swimming in the Cut might look like. The crowd, faces illuminated around the bonfire, watched in delight. A fragment of her mother's boasting—*dancing's in her genes*—flitted through the wind. A woman started singing a sea shanty, and Callie began to twirl. More voices joined in. Beach children wandered over to listen and dance with her sister.

"There was an old man in the north country." At first Ginger couldn't find her mother in the crowd. "Bow down, bow down." But then she picked out her voice. "He had daughters one, two, three." Glory claimed to have perfect pitch, but since she didn't know any of the lyrics, she sang half a beat behind, to blend in. "Love will be true, true to my love. Love will be true to you." The song ended in laughter, and it was time to go.

At the house, Glory, still glowing from the day, announced they could stay up late. They sat on the steps of the deck, counting stars and swaying like a bunch of drunken sailors. Callie asked them to sing the sea shanty song so she could dance again, but none of them knew the words, so they made up nonsense words instead. Ginger wished there was a way to make time slow down. Glory stood up and beckoned her. They both stepped out onto the dark of the lawn.

"There's going to be a bonfire at the beach tomorrow night. Adults only. How would you feel about babysitting for a few hours? For Thomas too. I'll pay you, of course. You don't mind, do you?" The phone rang before Ginger could respond. Glory ran in the house to answer it. Back on the deck, Ginger could hear through the open window the sharp edge of her mother's question.

"Tomorrow? As in, tomorrow, tomorrow? What time? You'll practically have to get up in the middle of the night to make that ferry. No, I'm just saying, why rush like it's an emergency?" Her voice went steely. "Of course I'm happy you're coming. Swear to god, I am being strangled by worrywarts." There was silence, and then the flick-flick, flick-flick of the porch light switching on and off, a signal that Glory wanted them inside.

In the living room they stood and watched her empty a puzzle box onto the table. She looked up. "What am I? A TV program? Are you waiting for the commercial to come on?"

"Can we go back out?" Mimi asked. "To look for shooting stars?"

Glory shook her head and started turning puzzle pieces right side up. "Stargazing is over. Your father's on his way."

CHAPTER FOURTEEN

The melted teakettle seemed like an indisputable sign that Glory's brain was melting too. It was time for triage. The talk Ginger intended to have with Julia about her nose ring, the closed bedroom door, and Nick's lengthening visits was tabled. Now, it was all about Glory.

It took a single overnight at the Popkins' for Mimi to offer to fund a full-time companion so Glory could age in place at home. Ginger, tasked with hiring someone, found the perfect candidate, a woman recently retired after twenty-five years as a kindergarten classroom aide.

The staying-home part agreed with Glory, but the companion part did not. Her critical thinking might be flickering in and out like a bad cable connection, but her critical talking showed no sign of decline. She fired the former kindergarten aide the second day. Whether the next three companions were fired or quit was impossible to puzzle out, and really, it didn't matter. The fact was they were gone.

It was Richard who lobbied for Glory to move in with them. That she was difficult was beside the point. For Richard, having a parent, even a difficult one, live long enough to get old was a lucky break.

Ginger agreed to a test run. After aide number five was hired, part-time, for when Ginger was at work, Glory moved into their home.

On her first night there, Glory went to bed at nine, woke two hours later confused, wandered into the bathroom half-dressed and came upon Nick, on the toilet. Both of them screamed and ended up at the foot of Ginger's bed, along with Julia, though by then all of them were laughing. Richard laughed too, but Ginger did not join in the merriment.

The next morning, Ginger woke up with a rash that spread, through the day, from neck to trunk and down her arms. Hives was the diagnosis. "Stress at home?" the doctor asked as he handed Ginger a prescription.

In an effort to keep the new part-time companion from getting fired, Ginger introduced Lorrine to Glory as their housekeeper. "Please try not to bother her while she's cleaning."

"Since when have I ever bothered anyone?"

At the end of her first day, Lorrine gave her report. "Your mother kept telling me to take a break from my *smudgery*. Also, she said I should get a hobby, like puzzles." Ginger explained about the family word mangling—that by *smudgery* her mother probably meant *drudgery*—and that no matter what she said or meant, it was best to just smile and agree.

Ginger thought Lorrine was working out fine until the end of the first week, when Julia told her otherwise. "Grandma Glory refuses to eat anything the lady gives her for lunch. And after lunch, Grandma sits on one side of the couch doing nothing and the lady sits on the other side of the couch and sleeps. Why do we even need her?"

This was disappointing to hear. "We need her because Grandma can't be home alone while I'm at work. I'll just have to find someone else." That's when it occurred to her. "How do you know what's going on at lunch? Are you cutting school?"

"God. We come home for lunch. I'm allowed to leave school for lunch."

"*We* come home?"

Ginger's rash spread to her back. The doctor called in an order for a stronger cream. Later, when Ginger struggled to apply the new ointment on the hard-to-reach spot between her shoulder blades, she realized that as recently as a week ago, she would have asked Richard to do it for her.

The next morning, before the alarm clock went off, they heard Glory in the hallway.

"Bathroom? No, closet. Where's the bathroom? Hello? Anybody here? Is there a bathroom in this hotel?"

Ginger turned to Richard. "This is not working. She's disoriented. I'm covered in a rash. Look." She lifted up her palms to show him the most recent territory to become covered by bumps. "I don't think I can take it if she stays."

The doctor called in an order for cortisone pills, and Ginger made another try at convincing Mimi to take Glory in. Mimi had the ideal setup, a carriage house at the back of her yard, which could easily be repurposed as an apartment.

Mimi was adamant. The answer was still no. Neil was convinced letting Glory move in would open the door for all future Popkins who were between jobs, or had changing marital status, or just wanted to be closer to the fun. "Up to me? I'd do it in a minute. But Neil says no, final answer." Popkins to the rescue once again.

Only one option was left. With Glory parked in the temporary care of a Popkin cousin for the afternoon, Ginger and Mimi shopped for a facility. They settled on the Meadows, a half-hour drive away. The final obstacle was selling Glory on the idea, but the intake nurse advised them on the best strategy. They were to tell Glory she was just coming for a visit.

And so it was that when they pulled into the entrance of the Meadows, a diminished Glory with a bright-red muffler wrapped around her neck, her belongings crammed into a single large Samsonite suitcase as white as her hair, Ginger pointed at the sign to her left which said, "Rehabilitation," and Mimi swiveled her mother away from the sign to her right, which foretold her future—"and Long-Term Care."

"You mean like a vacation?" Glory asked as they walked to the assisted-living wing.

"Kind of," Ginger said, and she opened the door to her mother's new apartment.

The studios in the assisted-living wing were all L-shaped, so a cot could be moved in if an aide was needed, temporarily. Everything, it seemed, was now couched in the language of the temporary. If an aide was needed full-time, Glory would have to be moved to the long-term wing, *temporarily*. There was only one final stop at the Meadows, and no one discussed it.

"You're not staying?" Glory asked when Ginger and Mimi put on their coats.

"I'll be back tomorrow," Ginger promised, and she and Mimi left, too tired and sad to speak.

At home, Ginger saw Julia and Nick had been playing house in the kitchen. An explosion of pots, strainers, wooden spoons, and bowls rose up out of the sink like a warning. A roast chicken sat on a cutting board, blood seeping out from the center cavity. She got the meat thermometer and stuck it in the thigh. "Jules?" She could hear they were upstairs. "Jules?" she called again.

Nick clomped down, loud as a horse. "Julia said to tell you we're in the middle of working on something. Hey, you found our chicken. Want some?"

"It's not cooked through," she told him and then noticed that the oven was still on. "When you're done cooking, you need to turn the oven off." She opened the oven door and put the chicken back in. She could feel Nick's confusion. She wasn't making any sense. "It's fine. Finish what you're doing. I'll watch the bird."

By the end of dinner, everyone was mad at everyone, Julia maddest of all. It was *their* chicken, she complained, bought with *their* money, and they wanted to cook it *their* way.

"But you didn't cook it. It *wasn't* cooked," was Ginger's first reaction, followed a moment later by, "What do you mean *your money?*" One of the consequences for Julia's missed curfews had been the loss of her allowance. Like Glory's new life in the Meadows, the loss was temporary, but the allowance had not yet been reinstated. "How do you have money?"

"I just do," Julia said, and when Nick gave her a look, she snapped at *him.* "I'm not getting into it with her now. Anyway, why is it so unbelievable that I know how to get money?"

"*Get* money? What, did you rob a bank?" Ginger turned to Richard. "Are you giving her money?" He shook his head.

"Let's go," Julia told Nick.

"Okay, cool." Nick got up and followed Julia to the basement stairs.

Ginger called after them. "Plates in the sink. You can't leave the kitchen like this."

Julia yelled from the bottom step. "We'll take care of it. Don't go insane."

"I don't know what they're doing down there," Ginger said to Richard as they cleared the table. "But they're up to something." She stopped. "You don't think they're working on a plan to convince us Nick should move in, do you? Because, no way. I draw the line. Absolutely not."

"No," Richard said, looking sad. He shook his head. "I don't think they're planning that."

This is how Ginger found out what they *were* planning: The morning after their chicken dinner fight, she padded downstairs, poured herself a bowl of cereal, sat at the table, and glanced out the window at the morning moon. Richard came down a moment later and they fell into their new routine, working out the arrangement of the newspaper sections so the pages didn't collide.

When the shower went on in the bathroom, Ginger looked at the ceiling and thought, *Julia's up early. That's odd.* Twenty minutes later, when Julia came into the kitchen, wet hair in a ponytail, face glowing and flushed, eyes wide-open and bright, Ginger thought, *She looks so beautiful this morning* and a moment later, *She looks like she's in love.* That Julia was clutching a shopping bag in one hand and a black North Face duffel in the other did not register, until Julia put the bags down.

Bags at her feet, Julia picked at her cuticles, her cheeks turning bright and then brighter red as she began her halting announcement. Nick was on his way over to pick her up. They were leaving today. Moving to Portland, Maine. Nick had friends in Portland who would let them stay for a while. She handed Ginger a piece of paper. "We're not definite about where we're going next, but all the cities on the list are cool about buskers."

"Buskers?" Ginger asked.

"Street performers," Richard said quietly.

They scanned the list together: Cambridge, Asheville, New Orleans, San Francisco.

Ginger looked up and asked, "What are you doing?"

"Moving. Moving out. Today. Now."

Ginger repeated the word *now,* though words had suddenly become nothing more than placeholders, with no meaning attached at all.

Her daughter's eyes, blue as Glory's, darted from the table to the walls to the ceiling to the floor, looking anywhere but at her stunned mother. "There's conditions."

"Conditions?" Another thing that made no sense.

"We're planning to stay in Portland until we get the performance all worked out. We've been doing it in the city, on the street, and in the subway, but it's not right yet."

Ginger's eyes moved to the shopping bag. The sheet and the helmet with the wings were peeking out from the top, and stuffed in on the side—it was just a glimpse of fabric—were the Salvation Army uniforms. "You've been performing in the subway in the city?"

Julia refused to meet her mother's eyes. "After Portland we'll probably go to Cambridge. They're totally cool about street performers there. Cambridge is where Amanda Palmer started."

"Who?"

"Street performer turned artist," Richard said.

Ginger wondered how on earth he knew that.

Julia interrupted her thoughts. "Doesn't matter." She was working hard to stay on script. "When we're ready to leave Portland, I'll send you a postcard about our next stop. I promise to let you know where we are—so long as you leave us alone."

"Pardon me?"

"You can't try to contact me. No more Facebook stalking. I shut down my page, as I'm sure you're aware."

No contact? Ginger tried to keep up. "What if there's an emergency?"

"There's not going to be an emergency," Julia told her.

"Probably not, but what if there is?" Ginger lowered her voice. "What if someone gets sick? What if someone dies? What if *you* get sick?"

"*God*. Why are you like this? No one's going to get sick." Julia sighed. "Okay, if someone gets sick, they should go to the doctor, and if someone dies, Dad, you can call Nick's mom. She'll know how to reach us. If someone dies."

"And then you'll come home?" Ginger pressed.

"*Stop.* I didn't say that." She turned to her father. "See what I mean? See how she is?"

"Okay." Richard's courtroom voice. "If something happens, which it won't, I'll call Nick's mom. She'll let you know. But we won't expect you home until—"

"Until I'm ready."

Ginger looked at Richard to see how this could make sense to him, but he was busy staring at his shoes. She felt lobotomized. Anne-Marie would know where Julia was, but Ginger wouldn't? If there was an emergency, Richard—only Richard?—could contact Nick's mom? And even then, Julia would not come home until—*she's ready?*

Standing her ground, Julia continued. "We want to be artists. We want to do performance art. But we can't if you won't leave us alone. I know it's hard for you, but you have to try. Because otherwise, if you come looking for us—either of you—if you send Aunt Mimi, or you call the police, or you call Nick's mom for no good reason, we'll move and we won't tell you where. It will be *poof.* Gone. Thin air." Her eyes looked fierce, but Ginger could see the rims were red, a wet film rising. Julia pressed her lips together, a tic she'd had forever. Seeing it made Ginger's eyes go wet too.

Julia regained her composure. "I sold my phone, so forget about calling. You'll have to be patient and wait for my postcards. Which I promise I'll send, so you'll know I'm okay."

"You sold your phone?" Ginger wondered exactly how a seventeen-year-old went about selling a phone that her parents had bought. She glanced at Richard and saw he looked surprised at this too. With a start, she realized this was the only thing that seemed to surprise him. Her body went heavy as stone. "You knew?"

Julia leaped to his defense, her anger wiping away everything else. "You can't be mad at him. He's been trying to talk me out of this for weeks."

Ginger mouthed, *weeks*.

"We were going to leave last night. I wrote you a note. But Dad said leaving a note was wrong. He said you deserved to hear it face-to-face." She crossed her arms. "So here I am. Face-to-face. If you leave me alone, you'll know where I am. If you try to find me, you won't." She pressed her lips together again and then added, "It's not forever."

For a moment, Ginger couldn't place how old her daughter was. Was she still a child? Could she do this? Could she just go?

And then, with his usual terrible timing, Nick pulled up in his rusted Saab and beeped and Julia ran out to meet him. By the time Ginger and Richard got to the curb, Julia's shopping bag and North Face duffel were in the back and she was in the front, pulling the door closed.

"Go," Julia told Nick. To her parents she said, "Bye."

In a voice too quiet for Julia to hear, Ginger asked, "Did you buckle up?"

It was Richard who replied. "She knows to buckle."

A reminder alarm started beeping. Nick turned the car off and hopped out. "Back door's stuck again." He tried to close it but the latch wouldn't hold.

Julia pulled her seat belt over her shoulder and it clicked in place.

Richard moved closer to Ginger. "I'm sorry. I thought I could talk her out of it. I wanted to tell you *after* I got her to change her mind." He reached for her hand.

Ginger let him take it. She could see the tendons in her daughter's neck flare out like wings. Julia was working that hard to keep her head from turning toward them. Nick continued to try and close the door, with no success.

"I thought if you knew, it would make things worse," Richard whispered. "I was wrong."

How could she be mad at him when she'd done the same thing herself? "It's okay."

Nick gave one last shove and the door latch held. He got back in and revved the engine. Ginger and Richard stood like a pair of cardboard-cutout parents, and Nick's old Saab—Ginger wished Julia had never told her the car had no air bags—took off with a screech to the corner. Then car, boy, daughter—was Julia really no longer a child?—disappeared.

CHAPTER FIFTEEN

First down the gangplank, there he was—Solly, clutching a large valise with one hand, struggling to balance a heavy wood-framed beach umbrella on his shoulder with the other. Her father, Ginger saw, had not gotten any instructions about blending in.

"A suit?" Glory backed up at the sight of him. "He's wearing a suit?"

This shouldn't have been a surprise. Ginger's father always wore a suit for traveling, no matter the destination. The Staten Island Ferry, Ratner's for lunch, monkey house at the zoo, according to Solly, *You go somewhere, you wear a suit.*

Eyes blinking in the sun, he found his family in the crowd. Grinning, he accelerated, nearly decapitating a woman with his umbrella as he passed.

"Oh, for god sake." Glory swiveled around so she wouldn't see more.

"So?" Solly said when he finally made his way through the crowd. "No fireworks to celebrate I'm here?" He seized Charlie's hand in a firm shake. "Look at you. Half a foot at least, you've grown. I don't see you for a week, you turn into a man."

"He's eight," Glory reminded him.

And Charlie said, "Next month I'll be nine."

Solly's delight was not easily diminished. His grin widened as he presented his wife with the umbrella. "For you."

Glory took another step back. "What'd you bring that for?"

"Didn't you tell me the umbrella you took from home is too flimsy? Like a toothpick, you said, it falls over. This?" He offered the umbrella again. "Solid wood. Weighs a ton."

"An elephant weighs a ton, Solly. You think I want to sit at the beach under an elephant?" She hurried toward the car and put a quick distance between them.

Solly heaved the umbrella, which seemed to have gotten heavier, back on his shoulder. "So?" he asked his children, who'd chosen to stay with him, where it seemed safer. "How much fun have I been missing?"

"Zero," Mimi said. "We don't do anything. Except for Charlie. He's digging to China."

Impressed, Solly whistled, but no sound came out, just air. "China. That's far to dig."

"I work on it every day," Charlie boasted. "Wait till you see how deep it is."

Solly tousled his hair. "You got another shovel? I can help you get there faster."

"I'm helping," Callie piped up. "We dig by the dunes. So the tide won't wash it away." She was proud to know this. "But I'd rather go to the Cut. Will you take me?"

"Sure," Solly said, having no idea.

When they caught up to Glory, Callie reported that her father was going to help Charlie dig to China, and after that, he was taking her to the Cut.

"Don't encourage them," Glory said, and when Solly moved toward the driver's side, she blocked him. "I'm the driver here."

Their father laid the umbrella across the laps of the backseaters, pointy end sticking out the window, and slid into the death seat. "This is nice. For once the scenery I get to see."

The car barreled along, and Ginger stared into the creases on her father's neck. Until now, she didn't know a neck could look unhappy. Her mother's neck was covered by a hat lifted off one of the iron pegs on the front porch. Somehow the hat managed to look unhappy too.

When they got to the house, everyone hurried in to change for the beach. By the time Ginger squeezed into her tight suit and rejoined her siblings, her mother was waiting by the car, lipstick back to red, a straight gash across her face.

"Solly? Are you coming? What is he doing in there?" When he emerged, winded, Glory took in his paisley swim trunks and white terry-cloth robe and winced before turning away.

"Are we bringing food?" Mimi asked as she got in the car. "Yesterday I starved to death," she told her father. "Yesterday, lunch was fudge."

Glory drove, hands tight on the wheel. "Take a good look at her, Solly. Does Sarah Bernhardt seem like she's starving to you?"

It took a very long time to get to the beach, and when Glory pulled into the lot, Charlie looked out the window and said, "This isn't where we go."

"He means this isn't the beach where he's digging to China," Mimi translated.

"It's a beach, isn't it?" Glory got out of the car and dropped her keys in her purse. "There's plenty of sand. Dig away." She pulled a lounge chair out of the trunk and started walking.

"We'll start a new hole," Solly said. "Maybe dig to Japan for a change. I know people in Japan. And won't they be surprised to see us pop out of the ground."

"That's okay," Charlie said. "I don't have to dig."

• • •

Glory sat in her lounge chair, hat low on her head, eyes closed. Mimi asked her father to come in the water with her.

"Who could say no to that?" He pulled off his shirt, revealing a torso white as bone, a dark patch of curly hair running in a line down his chest from his neck to his trunks.

Glory looked up. Her voice sounded calm, almost sleepy. "You can't do that."

"Why not? You need some kind of license to swim here?"

"You need eyes, Solly. What do you think that red flag is for?" She pointed to the flag they'd passed as they walked in. "Red means rough seas. There's no swimming in rough seas."

Solly looked at the ocean. "This they call rough? At Jones Beach, this is calm."

"Well, this isn't Jones Beach. They have riptides here, and the life-guards don't like it when people drown in riptides." She closed her eyes to make him disappear.

Solly had not come all this way to fight. He shrugged and moved on to the next task, getting the blanket ready. He had a system for this which he'd been perfecting for years. He methodically transported a big scoop of sand to each corner, mounding it just so to keep the blanket anchored. When he was finished, he stood up and clapped his hands to get rid of the excess dust.

Glory lurched up and brushed herself off. "Why do you have to send a sandstorm in everyone's face? Next time use rocks, like a normal person."

The day continued like a rock slide, downhill, and no one knew how to stop it. Glory's hat stayed low on her head, her mouth a flat red line, her eyes opened no more than a slit while Solly, clumsy as a bear, concentrated on rotating on the blanket—side, belly, side, front, side, belly, side, back—to get an even tan. At some point, he groaned his way back upright, got his transistor radio and earplug, and lay down, adjusting a pair of white eyecups so that the thin plastic strip sat straight across his nose. "Ahh." Finally, he was content.

Mimi kneeled beside him. "Can I sit by the water if I promise not to go in?"

Solly lifted up an eyecup. "Sure. Sit wherever you want."

Glory watched Mimi dart to the water. "You're letting her go alone?" Before Solly could defend himself, Ginger, Charlie, and Callie raced off to join their sister.

When the ocean presented a red-bellied jellyfish at Callie's feet, like a present, she jumped up and sat down closer to Charlie.

Mimi teased her. "Hey, Callie Claire. Do you know what makes a jellyfish stomach red?"

Charlie answered as he investigated. "Blood." He looked at his sisters. "I wonder whose."

Although they hadn't gone in the water, the tide had washed over their feet. Ginger examined herself—toes, heel, ankles—to see if she'd been stung. "Blood's not mine. Check if it's yours."

Everyone checked, but the blood wasn't from them. They stared at the waves crashing against rocks, sea spray shooting in the air. No one else was in the water that they could see.

"Maybe someone went out too far," Mimi guessed. "Maybe they crashed into the rocks. Maybe they're floating in the water now, eyes wide-open." She got up, grabbed the carcass of a horseshoe crab, scooped up the jellyfish, and tossed it so that it bounced off Callie's foot. "Did you know jellyfish can sting even when they're dead?"

Callie screamed and sprinted to the blanket, crying.

"Sorry," Mimi said quietly. They all turned and watched from a distance as Callie told her mother what just happened. When Callie finished, Glory stood up and started walking toward the path to the car.

When they got to the blanket, Solly was already packing up. "We'll come back tomorrow. Everyone will feel better tomorrow."

They were silent in the car, silent when they stopped to pick up pizza, silent in the living room where they sat, paper plates on their laps, eating dinner while Solly fumbled with the TV antenna.

"You're wasting your time," Glory said. "It doesn't work."

The snowy picture on the screen turned from blizzard to nor'easter. Ginger made out ghostly images of people, three of them, running down an alley.

"It's *The Mod Squad*," Mimi said. "That blob over there is Peggy Lipton."

"No it's not," Charlie said. "It's Linc."

"I'm living in a lunatic asylum," Glory said, and then, even though it was only eight o'clock, she stood and added, "I'm going to bed."

In the morning, as they sat eating breakfast, a steady drizzle of rain hitting the window, Solly told them a headache had come in the night. "Like a train wreck, your mother said it's exploding. So she's going to sleep in. But if we keep quiet, maybe leave the house for a while, by lunchtime she'll be good as new." As for what they should do now, he was at a loss.

They pitched in, coming up with ideas. First stop was the library. After that they went to town. Next came the carousel, and when they'd had enough of that, it was time for lunch. After lunch came ice cream. And in between it all, Solly stopped at pay phones to check on how the headache was progressing.

The rain stopped but the reports stayed grim. "It's like a vise," he said after they went to look at the swans. "Like knives stabbing her eyes," he said after they went on a pony ride. "Like an atom bomb," he said after they finished dinner. They were eating their second ice cream of the day when Charlie asked, "Can we go to the beach even though it's night?"

"Why not?" came their father's surprising reply. He took a long time consulting the map in the glove compartment before he picked their destination. "South Beach, it is."

They passed a small grocery store on the way and Mimi suggested they stop to buy flashlights, like the ones they used to come home from Jungle Beach. Ginger was in the front seat so she couldn't give her sister a warning kick, but it didn't matter. Solly heard nothing in the remark about Jungle Beach to give him pause. "Excellent idea," was all he had to say.

By the time they pulled into the South Beach lot, the sun was on the horizon. Minutes later the ocean turned invisible, save for an occasional flash of white from the breakers. Because Callie thought the night beach was scary, Solly carried her up to the nearby lifeguard stand, where, he promised, no monsters could get her. When Mimi asked him if she could put her feet in the water, another surprise. "Why not?"

They stood at the water's edge, mist tickling their faces, and looked up at the stars. Mimi said, "Maybe we should make wishes."

Ginger wished first, that their mother's headache would go away. Charlie wished next, that in the morning they could go home to New Jersey. Mimi changed her mind about the whole enterprise. "Wishes don't work."

They trudged back to the lifeguard stand, the top invisible in the dark, and Charlie pointed his flashlight. Solly called out, "Watch the eyes."

"We want to go home," Ginger yelled up and her father said, "Okay."

"I want to jump off before we go," Mimi shouted and another, "Okay," came back.

Mimi scrambled up the ladder with Charlie right behind her, both of them aware that at any moment permission might be rescinded.

It happened fast. One second Charlie and Mimi were arguing about who would jump first, and the next second there was a yell and a thud and Charlie was facedown on the ground right next to where Ginger stood. She waited for him to move but he didn't. Kneeling in the dark, she reached for the closest body part, his foot, and shook it. "Charlie?"

Her father clambered down the ladder, a noise like a sea lion coming from deep within his chest. She saw the flashlight lying in the sand and turned it on, the beam hitting Charlie's face. "Quit it," he said and sat up.

"Oy." Solly raced over. "You all right?"

Charlie nodded. "Except my arm. I can't move my arm."

The doctor at the hospital explained this was because his arm was broken.

When they got to the house, they scattered like vapor. They were in their bedrooms when Solly called upstairs. "Charlie. Your mother wants to see you."

The three sisters changed into their pajamas. Callie didn't want to be by herself, so Ginger let her slide into her bed, sandy feet and all. They lay silent for what seemed like a very long time before they heard their brother's footsteps climbing the stairs. He stopped in the doorway. "She's not mad. It's okay."

By the time they got up the next day, their father was gone.

CHAPTER SIXTEEN

Glory's favorite den chair moved with her to the Meadows, but though Ginger placed it next to the window, with its view of a small garden, Glory preferred to look the other way, out through her propped-open door into the hall. "Yoo-hoo!" she called to someone shuffling by. "Come and say hello. Don't be a stranger."

Her adjustment had been surprisingly easy, something Ginger attributed to the upgrade from full-time companion to full-time audience. "All the girls here love me," Glory reported, and Ginger understood *all the girls* meant nurses, aides, social workers, kitchen staff, lady hairdresser, lady doctor, and lady activity director. The activity director, Brooke, who'd been trying to start a theater group for years, loved her most of all.

"Brooke's a worrier like you," Glory said. "Told me it's impossible to put on plays on account of there's hardly any men. I told her we had hardly any men when they were alive and we managed."

"Yes," Ginger said, and then realized her mother hadn't asked a question.

Over dinner she told Richard this was happening a lot. "I zone out. I might look like I'm listening, but really I'm completely caught up in thinking about what I'm going to say when Glory finally remembers to ask about Julia."

"You're doing it again," Richard told her. "Making a problem where there isn't one."

Ginger felt the sting of blame in Richard's tone. He never said it outright, but she got the message. Julia's departure was her fault. While she conceded this was partly—even mostly—true, she would not take *all* the blame. They were supposed to be a team. And being a team meant what happened was on both of them.

"The fact is," he went on, "your mother would be thrilled to know Julia's out there trying to start a career as a performer. The family tradition continues."

Why did Richard not get that *the family tradition* was exactly the problem? Seeing Julia go was like seeing Callie leave all over again. And *career*? "Is that what you think Julia's doing? Starting a career?"

"I would say Julia is trying to live her life."

She didn't have it in her to argue anymore. The fights were too frequent now. Julia's departure seemed to have gotten into the bedrock of their marriage, finding cracks she'd never noticed before. How had she missed Richard's tendency to minimize things? And was she to understand her cautious nature had been irking him for years?

That night was the first of what soon became their new routine. Ginger woke around three to the sound of Richard leaving their bed to sleep on the couch. In the morning, he defended his change of location. It was because of how she reacted to his snoring, all the jiggling and poking in the ribs to get him to turn over. It bordered on violence.

"*This?*" She gave him a gentle shove. "This is violent?"

Richard seemed to have settled on silence as his preferred mode of communication, so it wasn't a surprise that silence was his answer now.

When he finally raised the idea of a break—just for a few nights at the Marriott downtown so they could both cool off—Ginger surprised them both by not trying to talk him out of it. Maybe a cooling-off period was what they needed. Maybe after a few days apart they would be able to talk things through without Richard accusing her of worrying Julia right out of the house or her firing back that Julia wouldn't have left at all if Richard had given Ginger a chance to help figure out a response with him, as a *team*.

Now, in addition to worrying about what to say if Glory asked where Julia was, she worried about what to say if Glory asked, *Where's Richard?*

As it turned out, neither topic was of interest to her. All conversation with Glory now revolved around her newly formed theater group. As Glory promised, the lack of men was not a problem. But the lack of people who could memorize lines was. "I finally figured it out," she boasted to Ginger one day. "We're going to specialize. Theater of the Absurd."

The excitement of the move to the Meadows fired up the faulty connections in Glory's brain, but not for long. Soon she was back to addled. One morning, an aide found her at the elevators, asking a visitor for help getting to the kitchen. The next day, a man found her in the parking lot, confused about where she'd left her car. After the first fall, it was clear she needed more care. Because there were no openings in the dementia unit, she was moved, temporarily, to a small room in the long-term wing.

Ginger stopped by every day after school to take care of whatever needed doing. She tidied up the odd things that appeared on her mother's night table, one day a small white box of chocolates—from whom?—another day a stuffed bear. She reviewed medication with the on-duty nurse and then, linking arms, took her mother for strolls, to the crafts center, to the library, to the chair yoga room. At the end of her visit, she'd deposit her in the lounge where a rotation of movies with Constance Bennett, Myrna Loy, and Cary Grant played on the TV in an endless loop.

But as soon as Ginger got back in her car, her thoughts would return to Julia, recalculating how long since she'd left—today it was four weeks—and wondering whether there'd be a postcard waiting in the mail when she got home. So far none had come, but every day she hoped a card was waiting. Some days magical thinking took hold and she hoped Julia would borrow a phone and send a text. So far: no card, no text, no magic, no luck.

At work she was focused, as always, applying healing salves to wounds, assessing pustules on rashes, taking notes during mandatory meetings about the new core curriculum, or helping to organize group gifts for the Spanish teacher's baby shower. But in her rare free moments, if there were no meetings to attend and no children to be seen, her mind would track back to Julia, always to Julia, wondering how she was.

To get through her days, she sacrificed her nights. No longer did she rotate like a rotisserie chicken in bed, hoping sleep would claim her. Now, when she woke with a start, no matter the time, her brain scrambling to locate the reason for her sense of high alert and distress, she'd get up and go to the computer. Google Earth—really all of the web—was her new best friend and her most vicious enemy. If she was in a hopeful mood, she would travel, virtually, through the streets of Portland. Streets with lovely names like Spring and Pleasant and Pine. Streets that sounded smart, like Oxford, or homey, like Kellogg. Zooming in on backyard swing sets and zooming out to study the neighborhood grid, sometimes a sense of ease would come over her because surely nothing bad could happen at the corner of Diamond and Pearl.

Other nights, when she woke anxious, she'd follow the cursor to Middle Street, to the squat red bricks of the Portland Police Headquarters or to the courthouse, where she'd examine the building so closely she could make out which windows had air-conditioner units and which units were reinforced with plywood planks. She'd check the online news after that to learn in real time about car accidents, assaults, and fires. Google Earth would then take her there, to the very spot where the incident occurred, so she could search, block by block, irrationally—these weren't webcams—for signs of Julia or Nick or their no-air-bag car.

Always, at some point every night, she'd end up watching videos of street performers. She watched performances in Portland and in Cambridge and in New York City and in San Francisco. She learned to distinguish between walk-by acts—musicians, mimes, living statues—and circle acts—puppet shows, break-dancers, magicians—though which kind of act Julia and Nick were doing, she really had no idea.

She watched the man who called himself a nihilist anarchist—he created puppets out of garbage and dead animals—and the man who offered to eat anything anyone gave him, for a price. There was a woman who painted cartoons on walls in abandoned buildings in front of an audience that consisted of her videographer and rats. There was a young boy—he didn't look like he'd been through puberty yet—whose specialty was sneaking into subway tunnels to do cartwheels inches from where trains passed by. A few of the performers struck her as actual artists. Some had concert hall talent, or great physical grace, or charismatic, expansive energy. But many more made her hyperventilate. So many panhandlers. So many mentally ill.

She watched as many as she could find, videos that were dark and grainy, shot in back alleys and subway tunnels, and videos that were professional-grade, shot at fairs and festivals. But no performers, no street dancers or festival singers, no sidewalk preachers or panhandlers were wearing Salvation Army jackets and a helmet and a sheet.

"You have to stop," Richard said, when he came home to pick up more clothes and found her hunched over her computer, still in her robe. "You're going to be late for work." Her first response was to bristle; he was speaking to her as if she were a child. But when she turned around and saw the tenderness in his face, she let it go. Maybe the temporary separation was working. Maybe they would be able to find a way to bring kindness back into their marriage.

That didn't stop her grief, though. It built up like acid reflux, a nagging irritation that grew to outright pain. Finally, in her nightly web travels, she stumbled upon a way to relieve it. The Portland Family Crisis Shelter posted a wish list every week, so now, every week, she sent a care package. She'd send towels or toothbrushes or shampoo—whatever they wanted—and as a bonus, she'd add a flyer with safety tips. *Insects to Watch Out For* or *How to Clean a Wound.* She knew this wasn't helping Julia. Julia wasn't living in a shelter. But at least she was doing *something*.

Because weekends had a yawning emptiness, she chose Friday afternoons, before her daily visit to Glory, to make the care packages. This week, night-lights were on the Crisis Shelter wish list, so she filled her shopping cart with twenty gender-neutral models of balloon bouquets and winking moons. It was at the last minute that she saw the Tinkerbells. Julia had a Tinkerbell night-light when she was a young child. Ginger still remembered the night it broke. Julia woke them up to say the light had gone out in the fairy's eyes. She'd refused to sleep in her room until the problem was fixed. It took Ginger days to finally locate a replacement.

These Tinkerbells looked completely different, but still, Ginger knew it was a mistake as soon as she grabbed them. The Tinkerbells, six of them, unnerved her as they stared from the shopping cart, and they unnerved her on the counter at the shipping store. Even after she'd left them behind, all boxed up and waiting to be loaded on the truck, she'd hurried, as if at any minute the Tinkerbells might come after her.

"Long time no see," her mother said when she finally got to the Meadows.

"I was here yesterday," Ginger said. Slipping off her coat, she sat in the chair by the bed. Her mother offered a pleasant smile, always disconcerting. Was it the smile that made her ask? Was it because the Tinkerbells had upset her? Or was she just so worn down she could no longer control the impulse? Whatever the reason, the question that had been much on her mind now came out of her mouth. "How did you handle it when Callie left home?" The smile vanished and Glory looked away, but Ginger didn't stop. "After Charlie died, how did you go on?"

Glory met her eyes. "Six one eight two four?"

"What?"

Her mother looked at her quizzically and then repeated the numbers.

Ginger felt woozy. Was this it? The next stage of Glory's decline? Digits? Had her mother's speech gone in one moment from normal to numerical? She'd heard of this but never observed it—sentences that held all characteristics of regular speech, clauses and pauses, intonations and questions, but were composed not of words but of numbers.

Or was this a ploy? It wouldn't be unthinkable for the queen of deflection to cook up her most creative duck-and-dodge scheme ever just to avoid Ginger's unwanted prying.

Her mother glanced across the room and repeated the numbers again. "Six one eight two four?"

"No one's at the door." It was disturbing to think that her mother was using number-speak to change the subject and even more disturbing to consider the possibility that the number language was the result of an episode of neurologic dysfunction. But it was also troubling that somehow, even when her mother spoke in numbers, Ginger completely understood—was it the tone?—exactly what her mother meant to be saying.

"Five four two eight ten?" Her mother pointed to Ginger's wrist.

Ginger looked at her watch. "I'm not late again."

Her mother's face rearranged into a scowl, and her gaze skipped to the top of Ginger's head. "One-fifty two-thirty four?"

Ginger checked to make sure her barrette was still in place. "I didn't do anything to my hair. Can you please go back to words?"

Her mother let out an exhausted sigh and lay her head back on her pillow. It was a new king-sized pillow, Ginger noticed. Mimi must have been here. This was how her sister made up for infrequent visits, by bringing things, a set of exquisitely embroidered pillowcases, a crisp new duvet cover, a scented diffuser—one time in a tinted glass bottle; another time in a dented tin, which Mimi made sure everyone knew came from a tiny store in the south of France.

Her mother started snoring softly and Ginger got busy, her long fingers tucking in the clothes that poked out of the dresser drawers as if attempting escape. The drawers had been like this for days now, slightly ajar and off their bearings. Inside were soft sweater sets in pastel colors, fine wool trousers with mother-of-pearl buttons, structured undergarments—some wrapped in tissue paper with tags on; others so old it was hard to tell which body part they were intended for. Ginger moved quickly, as if the clothes were hot to the touch.

Something red peeked out of the bottom drawer, and for a confusing moment Ginger wondered how the bathing suit she bought for Julia last summer had ended up here. Of course it hadn't. She'd returned that bathing suit the day she got it. It was a stupid impulse purchase made when she was still struggling to train herself to stop doing that, stop buying things for Julia because whatever she bought was wrong. Wrong size, wrong fit, wrong *idea*. But the color of the bathing suit was such a close match to Julia's hair. It was a whim, more magical thinking really, as if a present could change the atmosphere inside a house. She let go and the silky garment, a slip she saw now, slithered back into the drawer.

Her mother's eyes opened. She let out a whoosh of air, like a balloon deflating. And as if she'd just then decided number-speak was no longer necessary, she asked a normal question the normal way. "You going to visit me tomorrow?"

"I visit you every day."

"Hmm." Glory rubbed her hand. "It's been bothering me all of a sudden."

"Your fingers? Arthritis?"

Her mother closed her eyes again. "Good night, Gingie." She was dismissed.

In the hallway, Ginger bumped into Glory's social worker, Tracy, a woman of terrifying high energy who'd recently called a family meeting to discuss Glory's diminishing appetite. Ginger told her the real mystery was how *anyone* could digest in the Meadows Café, where no amount of exclamation points—Crepes!! Fricassee!!! Soufflé!!!!—could hide that everything smelled as if it was on the brink of going bad. And the food wasn't the only problem. In the Meadows Café, no opinion went undeclared. It was like a bingo hall gone berserk, residents shouting above the thrum of oxygen concentrators to share fragments of every flickering memory that popped into their heads. Add to that the sighing and the belching. It really was a wonder anyone ate anything at all.

For once, Tracy wasn't smiling. "Did your sister tell you I called?"

"No." Why hadn't Mimi told her?

"Oh. Your mom had a TIA. Your sister didn't understand at first—not being a health professional and all. She got scared. Thought a TIA was the same as a major stroke. I told her there's no need to worry yet. That a lot of times a TIA will resolve with no ill effects at all. I did suggest she stop in and visit, though. When is a visit a bad thing, right?"

So Glory's number-speak wasn't a ploy. And Mimi knew about it and didn't call.

"Bad timing, though," Tracy said. "Your mom being so excited about her performance. You should have told me she was an opera singer."

"My mom was an opera singer?"

"You're teasing me, right? Very funny. Well, I'm going to go visit her now. See if I can get her to sing. You know how sometimes people with aphasia can sing even when they can't speak?"

"Her words are back," Ginger said. "I just left her. She's herself again."

"Super," Tracy said. "You should come tonight. I think she said she wants to sing something from *La Bohème*." She hurried on to cheer up the next person on her list.

At the elevator bank, a woman in a wheelchair called over to her. "Hello, lady with the dog." She said this to Ginger every day now, and Ginger no longer bothered to correct her.

At Glory's house, she went inside to check on the progress of the painter. That was the division of labor: Ginger oversaw and Mimi paid. The kitchen, walls a clean creamy white, smelled of paint, but the painter was gone. No more work would be done in Glory's house today. She caught herself. This was not Glory's house anymore. That head-banging discovery came the day after Glory's move into the Meadows, when Ginger, attending to the mountain of her mother's past-due bills, came upon a statement for a reverse mortgage that neither sister knew anything about. She'd immediately called Mimi and shared the news that without consulting them, Glory had taken out a reverse mortgage, ten years ago, with the lump-sum option.

Mimi had been apoplectic. "That was the height of the market." She'd worked as a real estate agent just long enough to speak with authority. "Our net will be zero." It was odd how often Mimi complained about money. "After everything I've done." Sacrifices were recited. "I missed Wallace's Mock Trial finals two years in a row and—"

Ginger tuned her out. She had many techniques for escaping uncomfortable conversations. Her current favorite was to picture the medicine cabinet in her school office, reviewing what supplies she did or did not need. While Mimi fumed about the injustices she'd endured, Ginger pictured the top shelf. *Cold packs, hot packs, tongue depressors, gloves.* "She never thanked us for the TV." *Gauze sponge, gauze pad, tweezers, tape.* "After Neil and I bought her the dishwasher, she told us, *No thanks. It's easier to wash everything by hand.*"

As she walked out of the house she still thought of as Glory's, Ginger noticed how the late-spring sun hit her father's stone wall like a spotlight. Forever half-finished, the wall finally fit in, a perfect companion to the hanging gutters, weedy garden, and crumbling front steps. The rusty mailbox door creaked as she scooped out the leavings, a crossword puzzle magazine, a padded envelope from a theatrical makeup supply house, a catalogue with a brown paper cover that read, "Gloria Tangle, We miss you! Come back!"

Ginger got in her car and buckled the mail into the passenger seat so it wouldn't slide around. When she got home, the flashing light on her kitchen phone caught her attention. Her first thought, always, was Julia. The usual rush of disappointment followed.

Tracy, the cheerful social worker, was a fast talker on the phone, so Ginger had to play the message back twice to understand what she said. "I'm sorry for your loss. I'll call your sisters now."

"Sister," Ginger said to no one, and then sat, alone, digesting the news that Glory Tangle was finally gone.

CHAPTER SEVENTEEN

"How come we didn't go home with Daddy?" Mimi wanted to know.

Ginger kicked her sister's ankle. Couldn't she see that the night had not gone well? The evidence was right there, on their parents' bed: the comforter twisted like a rope, their mother's pillow crushed flat as a pancake while their father's sat like a puffy marshmallow, proof his head had been banished to the living room couch early on.

Glory acted as if she hadn't heard a thing. Her headache gone, she was on a cheery mission to get them to the beach fast. This meant finding Ginger a bathing suit that fit. "Which one?" She held up a black plunging one-piece and a mustard colored two-piece with a skirt. Since *neither* was not a choice, Ginger chose the black one.

As soon as she put it on, she saw it came with its own pointy breasts that didn't need her to stay erect. The rest of the suit hung slack on her slim frame. She came to show her mother it didn't fit, but after a quick once-over Glory announced, "Perfect." As if the suit had an opinion of its own, the straps dropped off Ginger's narrow shoulders and the top collapsed to her waist.

Glory took a second look. "That's nothing. Needs a little adjustment is all." This time it took five safety pins to do the job. "No muss. No fuss. Fits like a glove." She turned her back and Mimi poked the pointy breasts so that they went concave. Like a bird of prey—was it possible she *did* have eyes in the back of her head?—Glory swooped in and dragged Mimi outside. There was the sound of a slap and then Glory called through the screen. "Show's over. Time to go."

In the car Mimi's eyes were saucers of rage but Glory, driving fast as if they were late, made brisk work of Ginger's concern. *Barely touched her. Don't be fooled. She's tough as nails.*

When they got to the sandal spot at Jungle Beach, Glory breezed by as Mimi listed what everyone could see for themselves. "Huaraches. Earth shoes. Green thongs. That's it."

The chalkboard warned of high winds. A yellow flag snapped in the stiff breeze. They passed the leavings of the previous night's festivities. A shallow depression in the sand held the charred remains of driftwood. Discarded oyster shells sat in a heap. An abandoned sari was wrapped around the wood slats of a broken lobster trap.

"Looks like there was a party," Mimi observed. "Where is everyone?"

"Sleeping in, Columbo." Glory jammed the flimsy umbrella into the sand, the heavy wooden one having disappeared along with their father. "What did you think people do after a party?" She unfolded her chair, sat down, reapplied her pale lipstick, and used her pinky to fix a smudge no one else could see. With her mouth set into a soft smile, she opened a crossword puzzle magazine but didn't lift up her pen. The pages of the puzzle book fluttered in the wind. The umbrella jiggled like Jell-O.

"Look," Charlie called. "Someone worked on my hole for me." With his broken arm held close by the cast and his good arm overhead, Charlie jumped in. "I'm sitting in the hole," he called out a moment later. "Can you see me?"

Ginger turned and looked. "No. You're invisible."

He stood up. "Come in. There's plenty of room. Callie, jump. I'll catch you."

Mimi jumped in after Callie. "Hey, Gingie!" she called. "Am *I* invisible?"

"Yup." Ginger came to the edge of the hole and looked in. The hole was deeper now and wider too. It looked like a small excavation site, with sand piled up around the edges to make a low wall.

"Come on," Mimi said. "Jump. Mr. Diggans will never find us here."

That was all it took for Ginger to join them. But when she got in the hole, she found that even though it was wide enough for her to lie down in, sitting, her head poked out as if she were an oversized Alice in Wonderland.

Mimi broke the news. "You have to go. He'll see us if you stay."

"Don't worry," Charlie told Ginger. "I'm not done digging yet."

Ginger scrambled out, causing a minor avalanche, which Charlie applauded. "You made it wider. You made steps." Then he went to work, making the hole deeper so that when Ginger came back in, she'd be invisible too.

Mimi climbed out to check on her rock tower to the moon and Callie followed. But the tower had suffered the opposite fate of the hole: toppled. Only a few rocks remained.

"Did it fall down?" Callie asked. "Or did someone kick it over?"

Mimi shrugged. "Have to rebuild, that's all. Have to make it twice as high. Want to come with me? We need rocks with flat bottoms." She skipped to the shore to begin her search without waiting for an answer.

Callie turned to Ginger. "I don't want to go with her. I want to go with you. To the Cut."

"We can't."

"Why won't you take me?" Her pleading got louder. "Please? Pretty please?"

Even from a distance Ginger could see her mother's posture take on an angle of irritation.

"Please, please, please?" Callie begged.

"Stop it," Ginger hissed. "Let's go help Mimi."

While Charlie stayed behind to dig, Ginger stood guard at the shoreline, periodically cautioning her sisters to stay out of the water. Everything was under control until Callie started screaming.

"Monsters! Monsters are coming!" Callie pointed, screamed again, and ran to the blanket.

Ginger ran after her. As she ran, she saw the beach people had arrived. Mr. Diggans was now sitting next to Glory. Thomas was playing Ringolevio with his friends. But even the boy calling out, "Olly olly oxen free," stopped at the sound of Callie's screaming. Everyone's gaze, Ginger's included, went toward the group of people running from the cliffs, people naked and covered in mud. The monsters.

Callie let out one last terrified scream and burrowed her head in her mother's chest. By the time Ginger got to the blanket, Mr. Diggans was laughing.

He kneeled beside Callie. "Take another look. Those aren't monsters. Those are our friends. There's my sister, Minty, and her husband, Bob. Remember Bob? They took clay baths, that's all. With clay from the cliffs. Bravo," he applauded the clay people.

Her mother gave Callie a little shove. "Go on. Take a look." Callie tentatively untwined herself. "See? Are they monsters? No."

"Getting clayed is fun," Mr. Diggans told Callie. "It's like playing in the mud. Did you know grown-ups like to play in the mud?"

"No." Callie inched closer to the people she now recognized as human.

"It's like finger painting," he went on. "I bet you like to finger paint."

Callie nodded and looked at her mother. "Can I go to the cliffs and get clayed?"

"Not alone," Glory said. "Gingie, take your sister to the cliffs."

Ginger pretended she didn't hear her mother's instruction because she did not want to go to the cliffs. She did not want to be in a crowd of naked painted beach people, all of them laughing as if they were bewitched.

She watched as the enchanted crowd ran into the water, holding hands in a wide circle. They let go to dive under and then heads popped up, one and then another, out past the breakers, like seals. Laughing, they played catch with clumps of seaweed, which they then used to sponge off the rust-colored clay that had dried hard on their skin. When they finished, they swarmed out. With the clay washed off, they no longer looked enchanted. They just looked naked.

Ginger turned on her stomach and faced the other way. She'd never seen a naked man before. She'd never seen a man in pajamas, except in movies and on TV. Her father came down to breakfast fully dressed every day.

The wind whipped up. "We should go," she called to her mother. "It's too windy." The umbrella pole jiggled. "The umbrella's going to fly away."

"Have you ever seen such a worrywart?" Glory asked Mr. Diggans.

His thigh had moved so that it was touching her mother's. "I think she's lovely."

Ginger waited for her mother to make a remark about his leg, or about whether she was lovely, but Glory's mouth remained a line flat as the sand. Giving up, Ginger rolled on her back and closed her eyes. A moment later the sky darkened and she opened them. Mr. Diggans was towering over her. She sat up and averted her gaze to his feet. Impossibly, his toes seemed to have grown bigger. He had the feet of an ogre.

"Raspberries?" He kneeled beside her and offered an open container. "Picked them this morning. I hear you love raspberries."

"You're spoiling her," Glory called over and then, "Gingie, is he spoiling you?"

Ginger stood up, taking her towel with her. "I don't want any, thank you."

"Is she being rude?"

"Not at all."

Ginger peered into the container. The raspberries looked as if they'd been dumped in, the bottom ones crushed by the weight of the ones above.

"She's crazy for raspberries," Glory said. "The whole family is, right, Gingie?"

"We are," Mimi answered, and inserted herself between Ginger and Mr. Diggans. Despite her size, with her hands on her hips, Mimi made a stalwart barricade.

Mr. Diggans reached a long arm over Mimi's head and jiggled the container. "Go on. Take as many as you like." The raspberries didn't move.

To make him go away, Ginger picked one that still held its shape, but when she put it in her mouth it was overripe and she quickly swallowed it whole to be done with it.

Mr. Diggans' wide forehead wrinkled. "That didn't look good." She wanted to lie and say it was good, but she couldn't risk speaking because the berry was threatening to come back up.

"Let me try one." Mr. Diggans dipped a long finger into the container and scooped out a crimson gob, which he deposited in his mouth. "Ugh." He wiped his lips on the back of his hand. "She's right. They're awful." He wiped his hand on his trunks, leaving a streak of red. "Rotten raspberries was not my plan at all."

"It's the thought," Glory said.

He extended his hand to Ginger. "Forgive me?" His fingers glistened with spit.

She looked to her mother for guidance, but Glory's expression remained inscrutable so Ginger stretched out her hand and hoped that was right. She had no idea how long a handshake was supposed to last. It took two tugs to get her hand back.

"Yoo-hoo." Glory waved her crossword magazine in the air and brushed some invisible sand off her thighs. "Shall we finish?"

Mr. Diggans returned to her as if nothing had happened. Nothing had happened.

"We were here," Glory said, pointing. "Four-letter word for *shoe*."

"Clog," Ginger said, quietly.

"Beautiful *and* smart," Mr. Diggans observed.

"Why don't you go for a swim," Glory called over. "Before it gets too windy."

"It's already too windy," Ginger said. "They're going to change the flag to red."

"What are you, a psychic now? It's yellow. Everyone go with Gingie. She's in charge."

Charlie reminded her he couldn't go in because of his cast, so Glory let him stay and dig. Callie wanted someone to take her to the cliffs and to the Cut, but Ginger talked her into staying near the blanket by telling her they needed a brave volunteer for a special mission. The job was standing guard in front of Mimi's rock tower to make sure no one knocked it over. Callie accepted the assignment and like a little soldier, knees high in the air, marched back and forth, saluting people as they walked by.

Ginger followed Mimi to the sea. Glory called after them, "Don't go in far."

The wind picked up as they walked. Hats flew off heads. Tuna fish sandwiches turned crunchy and were abandoned. Gulls swooped in, making a party of the remains. But Glory said the umbrella was not loose, and the ocean was not rough, and the flag would not switch to red. So maybe people weren't packing up to leave and the sand wasn't getting in her teeth. Maybe her hair wasn't flying in all directions and the sky wasn't blue, and the water wasn't wet, and her family wasn't falling apart.

They sat at the water's edge and Mimi said, "Wouldn't it be funny if we got a jellyfish and threw it at Mr. Diggans and it turned out he's allergic and he got stung and dropped dead?"

"Hysterical." The blustery wind carried over the sound of a shriek. They turned and saw their mother chasing after the umbrella, Mr. Diggans right behind her. Glory ran the way she drove, her body moving forward while her head looked in the opposite direction. Both of them were laughing hard, oblivious to how the bobbling umbrella was threatening one family after another as it danced top over bottom along the beach, rising up over heads, touching down softly on sand, then up again to the next near-catastrophe.

A blustery breeze tossed Ginger's hair in a frenzy, blinding her, and then, as suddenly as it started, the wind dropped dead. She pushed her hair out of her eyes in time to see the umbrella fall like a missile, spear down, landing perfectly erect, to her mother's delight.

In the sudden calm she could hear Glory's laugh, heartfelt and real, as she ran with Mr. Diggans to where the umbrella stood. They both flopped down beneath it. A moment later they were up on their feet and Glory was motioning to her daughters while calling out instructions.

"I think she's saying you have to keep an eye on Callie." Mimi gave her mother a thumbs-up and they watched her disappear out of sight, to the far side of the cliffs.

Charlie was digging in his hole and Ginger was playing Spit with her sisters when Glory got back to the blanket. Mr. Diggans stood behind her, the umbrella perched over his shoulder, light as a twig.

Her mother's smile looked dreamy, and Ginger noticed her legs had been clayed.

Callie reached over and touched the red-brown streaks. "You did it. You took a clay bath. Can I? Can I get clayed?" She turned to her sisters. "Please take a clay bath with me?"

"No," Ginger said, and Mimi quickly seconded, "No way."

Callie experimented with defiance. Slowly, unsure how this would go, she took a step toward the cliffs. The family watched, amused. She was, after all, a little girl, the youngest of four, the one who made no demands. She continued, kicking sand, and walking ever so slowly, until Glory called out to put an end to it. "Callie Claire. You are not going to the cliffs alone. Now come over here and sit down."

Callie obeyed half of what her mother said, the sitting-down part. "I'm going." She scooted over an inch. "I'm going to get clayed, and then I'm going to swim in the Cut."

Glory laughed and turned to Mr. Diggans. "She wouldn't dare." Their heads tipped together as they went back to the puzzle.

Ginger watched her youngest sister who, like in a game of red-light green-light, moved toward the cliffs every time her mother's eyes went to the puzzle and then froze in place when her mother looked her way.

Mimi broke the bad news. "If she goes all the way to the cliffs they're going to make one of us bring her back. And it won't be me. I'd rather drop dead than go there."

"Then tell Charlie," Ginger said. "Tell him he has to take Callie to the cliffs right now."

"He won't. He'll say he's too busy digging."

Ginger disagreed. "Tell him Callie will get in trouble if he doesn't. He hates when she gets in trouble."

"Okay." Mimi got up. "I'll tell him he has to go, or else!" Problem solved, Ginger lay down and closed her eyes.

It seemed to take forever for Mimi to come back. When Ginger finally sat up to see if Charlie had agreed, Mimi was standing at the dunes doing nothing and Callie was nowhere in sight. It really was exasperating having Mimi as a sister.

Ginger called to her. "Did he go?" When Mimi didn't answer, she stood up and yelled, "Did Charlie go?" She walked over to where Mimi stood. "Did Charlie go with Callie?"

Her tone caught her mother's attention. Glory stormed over. "What now?"

"Callie went to the cliffs. I think with Charlie. But maybe alone." Ginger looked at Mimi but got no confirmation.

"What do you mean *you think*?" Glory asked.

Mr. Diggans joined them and looked toward the sea. "Would Callie go in the water without telling you?"

"She didn't go in the *water*," Ginger said. "Callie went to the cliffs to get clayed." She turned to Mimi. "Did Charlie go with Callie or not?"

Mimi didn't answer. When Ginger followed her sister's gaze, the tiny hairs on the back of her neck fluttered a warning. Her sister was staring at the sand where Charlie's hole was supposed to be but, impossibly, the hole was gone. It was as if the rules of the universe had shifted. How could a hole that big be gone? "Where's Charlie's hole?" Ginger slowly turned in a circle, and then reversed direction.

"For the love of god," Glory said. "You're looking in the wrong place."

Disoriented, Ginger turned around again, but everywhere she looked, the sand was the same: flat and level as a pond. How could everywhere be the wrong place?

"You're not looking where you should," Glory insisted, panic growing in her voice.

Mimi slipped her hand into Ginger's clenched fist. "I saw the sand go in. I saw the hole fill up." She paused and the rest came in a whisper. "Charlie's inside."

"What?" Glory sounded angry. But as she stared at the sand she finally saw what Ginger saw. The sand *was* the same everywhere. Flat, everywhere. Flat as ice. Her mouth gaped open and then, as if in slow motion, Glory's piercing scream echoed down the beach, slicing through the sound of families arguing about who had the tanning oil and if there were enough grapes to go around. The scream was followed by silence. The next wave crashed, and pandemonium.

CHAPTER EIGHTEEN

The first call Ginger made was to Richard. When he didn't pick up, she left a message. *Glory died. Can you call Nick's mom?* She felt a rush of adrenaline at the thought of Julia coming back, and then a flush of embarrassment. Her mother's death should not be reduced to a happy excuse for Julia's return. Besides, Julia had made her intentions clear. Ginger pictured her—cheeks red, face hot—appalled that the conversation had taken a turn to contingency plans in case someone died. Then she pictured Richard brokering the awful compromise. *If something happens, we'll let you know. But we won't expect you home.*

She crossed her hands, one atop the other, at the bottom of her neck, as if trying to shield herself from pain. Then she dropped both her arms. She'd know more later, when she spoke to Richard. Now it was time to call Mimi.

She tried her cell phone first, and when there was no answer, she called the house.

Troy picked up. "I think she's in the attic. I think she's looking for old clothes to cut up for a quilt. I think my dad commissioned one for his waiting room. I think—"

Ginger interrupted. "Troy, sweetie, could you go find her and ask her to call me right away?"

After that there was nothing to do but wait. To distract herself, she tried reviewing the contents of her supply cabinet. When that didn't work, she picked up a legal pad to make notes for her next Danger Class. The class was scheduled to be on "The Dangers of Recess," but what she wrote down instead was "The Dangers of Sand Holes." She started to cross it out—this was a subject that Ginger, well-raised in the art of deflection, had avoided discussing for years—but her pen stopped. Why *hadn't* she taught a class on this? She knew enough about them. She'd had a Google alert set up for *sand holes* for years. She kept close track of them, both where and how they happened and, of course, the aftermaths.

Just this July, a six-year-old boy died at a Massachusetts beach after digging a deep hole with a small plastic shovel. He was one of four sand-hole-collapse fatalities over the summer. They happened all around the country—in Oregon, the Bay Area, the Outer Banks, and at the Jersey Shore. They happened in England and Australia. She read all the articles and watched all the videos. The videos were strikingly similar, the brief shot of a school photo, a young smiling child, followed by a cell phone video of a doomed attempt at rescue.

New England Journal, she wrote on her pad. She'd come upon the *NEJM* study several years ago, a decade of sand-hole accident data—the youngest fatality, a three-year-old boy.

How had she never taught a class on this? Most parents had no idea a child happily digging one moment could be buried the next. And there were safety precautions. Easy ones. *Number one:* she wrote. *Check for holes on the beach. Number two: See a hole, fill it in. Number three: Never let children dig higher than their knees.* Her phone rang, and she put down her pen.

• • •

Mimi's reaction was pretty much what Ginger expected, acceptance followed by annoyance. "Of course. It's Thursday. Of course she would pick a Thursday."

Is this a bad day for Mom to die? Ginger thought. She didn't say it because she knew the answer would have been an unironic, *Yes*. Didn't everyone who knew Mimi know Thursdays were a nightmare for her? Thursday was Neil's late night, and despite a house filled with relatives, not one of them ever stepped up to offer help with the trifecta of getting Hunter to baseball, Troy to his math tutor, and Wallace to Mock Trial.

Since Mimi liked to be in charge of important things, Ginger decided to relinquish control and let her sister pick the funeral home. Her hope was this would get her sister off the phone before she asked the question Ginger wanted to avoid, but it didn't work.

"So, Gingie. How long do you want to wait to have this hulla-balloo? We need to give people a chance to get here, right?"

"People?" For a moment Ginger let herself imagine Mimi was referring to a minyan of Glory's old friends, men in loose-hanging suits and women wearing peds and pumps, rotary phone receivers pressed to their ears as they searched for something, anything, an eyebrow pencil would do, to scratch down the details of their friend's funeral. But of course that wasn't it. Glory had shed her friends years ago. By *people*, Mimi meant Julia.

"It's not a problem waiting," Mimi reassured her. "Are you getting her a plane ticket or are you going to drive there and pick her up? Is the boyfriend coming?" Ginger felt a surge of regret that she'd told Mimi anything about Nick. "Whatever. It's fine. We can wait. A few days. A week. It's not like Mom would care."

That part was true. The custom of quick burial would have held no meaning for Glory. Her religious practice consisted of two meals a year that were only vaguely related to Jewish holidays. In the spring she'd make a Passover supper, usually held on Easter Sunday, with a token tra-ditional offering to mark the occasion—freshly grated horseradish, for example, but no gefilte fish. In December she'd host a Hannukah party, where she'd serve latkes cooked so briefly the centers would still be frozen, and, if she remembered, applesauce from a giant jar which, after dinner, would retire to its primary purpose of growing mold. Lighting candles was not part of the program. *Too dripsy.*

"Neil's mother will have a conniption if we wait," Mimi was saying. "But she doesn't get a vote." She noticed Ginger's silence. "You *can* find Julia, right? She has a phone, doesn't she?"

Ginger had thought about this: if it turned out Nick's mom didn't have current contact information, Ginger would find Julia herself. Portland wasn't that big. Surely street performers knew where each other lived. She checked her watch. If she left now, and drove straight there, she could make it to Portland before dawn. She knew where to go, the neighborhood where buskers performed. She'd seen the streets in videos and surveyed the grid on Google Earth. She'd start when the sun came up, questioning fire-eaters and fiddlers and runaways. She'd ask anyone she could find if they knew of a couple who wore Salvation Army uniforms and did something with a helmet and a sheet. She stopped herself. It was amazing, really, how quickly her daydream went from Richard calling Nick's mom to Ginger picturing her daughter beside her in the car, coming back home for the funeral and deciding to stay.

But that would not happen. What would happen was that Richard would call Anne-Marie and Anne-Marie would call Julia and Julia would know her grandmother died. That was it. That would have to be enough.

Of course Mimi would find this impossible to understand. She hadn't been there when Julia left, so she never heard the steel in Julia's voice when she gave her ultimatum.

"Trying to get Estie Popkin to back down is never easy," Mimi was saying. "But I don't care. Waiting is the right thing to do." Because life had been kinder to Mimi, she still had the luxury of believing there *was* a right thing to do.

"Julia's not going to come for a funeral. We talked about it before she left."

"That doesn't mean anything. That was theoretical. Julia will change her mind the minute she hears the news. They were close, Julia and Glory. Don't you think she'll change her mind?"

Of course that was *exactly* what Ginger was hoping would happen. But feeding that hope would not make it true. "She's not coming," she repeated, and then a beep—call waiting—interrupted. "It's Richard. I'll call you back."

Before Ginger filled Richard in on the details of Glory's demise, she wanted to know if he'd reached Nick's mom. He had. "Anne-Marie said she can get the message to them tonight."

"Good."

"And . . ." He paused a moment and then went on. "I asked Anne-Marie to make sure to tell Julia we're not expecting her to come home. We just wanted to be sure she knew what happened with Grandma Glory. And that we both love her. No matter what."

Ginger nodded. "Okay." Her eyes were stinging. She wiped them with her sleeve. "Do you think Anne-Marie will say exactly that? Will she get it right?"

"She wrote it down," Richard told her. "She read it back. She got it right."

When Ginger called Mimi back and told her she and Richard both agreed it made no sense to postpone the burial, her sister didn't argue. They divided up the remaining tasks. Mimi would find a funeral home. Ginger would go to the Meadows to gather Glory's things.

"Keep your eyes out for an address book," Mimi told her. "I'll swing by the house after I'm done to check if there's one there. Case there's anyone else to call."

Ginger got off the phone fast, before Mimi could tell her which anyone *that* might be.

CHAPTER NINETEEN

The night of Charlie's accident, Ginger was struck by how part of what she remembered was hyperclear, as if everything had occurred a fraction more slowly than normal. The sky was crayon blue and the voices were sharp and people lurched around in jolts and starts. Other parts, though, were a blur, as if she was experiencing and forgetting in the same moment.

By the end of the day, this is what she could reconstruct: A man, long ponytail coming undone, ran from the far end with a metal spade. A woman, tie-dyed skirt, bandanna around her hair, loped behind him shouting to the crowd that there were more, plenty more shovels and buckets by the clambake pit. An older man, no shirt, deep tan, scar down the middle of his chest, called for volunteers to help get the gear, and then Mr. Diggans, face going from chalk white to beet red, yelling over all of them, his voice piercing through the chatter, *Stop. Stop. Right. Now.* His tone turned threatening. *Hands only.* She could picture the exact moment he said that, how everyone froze, confused, until he said the next thing, *Hands only until we know where the body is*, at which point several people began to weep.

Glory stood next to Ginger, leaning, listing, bare arm pressing into bare arm, and when Mr. Diggans said the word, *body*, her mother wobbled and then grabbed Ginger's hand, holding on tight, as if otherwise she might collapse.

Behind them, Ginger could hear the thrum of people talking and when she turned, she saw them, a ragtag crowd who'd run over from the far end with whatever clothes they could grab—some with nothing more than blankets loosely wrapped around their bodies—all of them watching her mother.

Glory started shaking, tiny shivers which seemed to pass right into Ginger's skin so that within moments both of them were standing and trembling together.

Ginger struggled and then finally got the words out. "I'm sorry." Though she still wasn't sure what had happened, she was sure it was all her fault.

Glory's reply was so quiet, Ginger had to ask, "What? What did you say?"

Mimi, standing on her mother's other side, translated. "Someone needs to find Callie."

It was Thomas, standing next to Mimi, who volunteered to get her. "Where is she?"

"At the far end," Ginger told him. "She went to get clayed. By herself."

As soon as Thomas sprinted toward the cliffs, Glory's trembling stopped and her hand loosened its grip and fell, useless, to her side. From where they stood, Ginger could hear fragments, words lashing over her, voices rising and falling with the wind. *Can't tell yet. Too risky. Careful now.* A lifeguard had arrived, but he was just a boy who stuttered as he radioed in the nightmare news, *sand-hole collapse*, to the person on the other end of his walkie-talkie. "Hurry," the boy said, and then, "please."

Ginger saw his eyes fill and imagined her mother chiding him to save his crying for when he was alone in his room with the door closed and the shades drawn.

Her attention snapped back to the crowd, now arguing about where it would be best to dig and where exactly the hole had been. Again, Mimi spoke up. "It was next to my tower." She pointed. "Where that rock is over there."

A dozen people spread out around the one remaining rock of Mimi's toppled tower to the moon. They dropped to their knees, digging like dogs, some of them sobbing.

In the distance Ginger made out two figures running toward them, Thomas and beside him a young girl. Ginger called to her mother. "Thomas has her." But her voice was drowned out by people shouting, *Stand back. Over here. Something moved.* "Thomas has Callie," Ginger called louder and she watched, stunned, as tears of relief streamed down her mother's face.

And then a hand grabbed hers. "Come with me." Ginger turned and saw Minty. Her other hand was wrapped tight around Mimi's wrist.

Ginger pulled her hand out of Minty's grasp. "I want to stay." She watched as her mother pushed her way into the crowd.

"Your mother wants you to come with me now."

"I want to wait for Callie." Ginger didn't mean to be yelling but she couldn't seem to get her voice to be normal. "Thomas is bringing her. I want to wait." Her words were carried by the wind.

Her mother heard and called back, "Go with Minty. Callie will stay with me."

"Why can't *we* stay with you?" Mimi asked and then everyone, diggers and watchers, went silent.

"Minty, take them," Glory yelled, and Minty let out a soft cry and yanked them hard toward the path through bushes.

This time when Ginger wriggled free of Minty's grip, she got as far as the edge of the crowd. She struggled to see through the scrum. There was a smattering of applause, and the crowd shifted just enough so she could make out a glimpse, disjointed images of Mr. Diggans' back and his arms. He was holding Charlie, crumpled and limp and impossibly small. "Move," she told the people blocking her, and someone did, and then she saw it, her brother waved.

"We have to go now," Minty said, and Ginger let herself be led away.

"It's going to be fine," Minty told them as they walked through the tunnel of bushes. "It's going to be fine," she repeated as they got into her car.

In the back of Minty's beat-up station wagon, Ginger and Mimi let themselves be lulled into a daze by the rhythm of the promise. *It's going to be fine.* They gazed out opposite windows. *It's going to be fine.* Their fingertips reached across the seat and touched. *It's going to be fine.* And Ginger repeated the words in her head, hoping that would help make them come true.

Up in their room, Mimi asked Ginger if she thought Charlie was okay and Ginger said yes. "Are you positive," Mimi pressed her, "or are you just saying that?"

"Positive," Ginger said, though she suspected Mimi could tell it was a lie.

They tried to think of ways to make time go faster so that Charlie would be home soon. That he might not come home at all had not occurred to either of them. It was after dark when they heard the front door open and voices whispering and the door clacking closed. Mr. Diggans, his voice friendlier than normal, told someone, "That's not the sun. That's the moon," and the person laughed. Callie.

Ginger and Mimi raced down, and Mr. Diggans rose to his feet. "Whoa. Ho. Hey. Sounds like the running of the bulls here. Why aren't you two asleep?"

"What happened?" Ginger asked, and Callie shrugged her shoulders. She didn't know.

"Upstairs," Mr. Diggans said. "It's way past bedtime."

"How come *she* gets to stay down?" Mimi wanted to know.

"Callie's going to sleep here." He tapped the couch. "She's frightened."

"Of what?" Mimi could not imagine.

Ginger felt herself shivering even though it wasn't cold. "Where's Mom? Where's Charlie?"

"Did Charlie break his other arm?" Mimi wanted to know. "Did he break his leg? That's good, right, to break a leg?"

"This is nonsense," Mr. Diggans barked, and Callie copied him, mimicking his gruff tone, "Nonsense, nonsense, nonsense."

"Back upstairs," Mr. Diggans shooed them. "Back to bed right now."

Mimi didn't want to sleep alone, so Ginger turned on her side and let her sister scoot into her bed. When Mimi started shooting questions, Ginger felt them like little darts on her back. "Do you think Charlie was scared when the hole caved in? Do you think his hair fell out? Do you think it went all white, like Cropsy?"

"Cropsy's not real."

"Mom says he is. Mom says Cropsy has white hair and chops up children who are bad. Is Cropsy real?" Mimi called to Mr. Diggans, who yelled back, "Be quiet."

Ginger thought it made no sense for someone to yell, *Be quiet,* but she got quiet anyway, so she wouldn't have to answer any more of Mimi's questions.

Soon the sweet scent of cherry tobacco drifted into the room, Mr. Diggans puff-puff-puffing on his pipe. Ginger turned to Mimi and saw the whites of her eyes wink on and off like lightning bugs. A tear leaked out, and then another, until there was a line of tears traveling like a tiny river along her sister's neat hairline.

"Why are you crying?" Ginger asked.

Mimi admitted, "I don't know. But I'm allowed to cry here." And they both turned as one to see if their window had shades.

After a few moments, when the scent of cherry tobacco faded—Mr. Diggans' puffing had stopped—Mimi asked Ginger, "Wouldn't Callie be less scared if she was sleeping with us?"

Ginger nodded and got out of bed. Together, they crept down the stairs.

They found Mr. Diggans asleep, head tipped back on the chair, pipe resting on a small dish he'd placed atop Glory's puzzle, making a wreck of the Taj Mahal. Callie lay on the couch, a blanket wrapped around her like a body bag. Ginger kneeled beside her and whispered in her ear. "Callie? Are you up?"

Callie sat up and waved. "Up, up, up."

Mr. Diggans' eyes snapped open. "What's going on here?"

"If she's scared, she should sleep with us," Mimi told him. "*We're* awake."

He checked his watch, a large complicated thing with dials and cutouts of the moon, and let out a long sigh. "I suppose that would be all right. I'm leaving early anyway. Meeting the first ferry. But don't worry. You'll only be alone for a little while. I'm picking someone up to stay with you."

"Who?" Mimi asked.

"*Poo-hoo,*" Callie echoed.

Mr. Diggans winced and rubbed his eyes.

Ginger took Callie's hand. "We're going to bed." And Mr. Diggans didn't stop them.

It took some time to arrange themselves so that they all fit in one bed, but eventually they found a way that worked, Callie in the middle on her back, Mimi and Ginger facing her like a pair of parentheses.

Callie fell asleep right away, but Mimi remained awake, pelting Ginger with more questions. "Where's Mom? Where's Charlie? Who's coming? Where's Dad?"

"Dad will be here soon," Ginger said, which was wishful thinking, and about everything else, "I have no idea," which was the truth.

CHAPTER TWENTY

Ginger had been driving to the Meadows to visit her mother every day for six months, but somehow this time she got lost, going south on the Parkway when she should have been going north, and after that missing the turn for the jughandle. When she finally arrived, it took three tries before she got her car between the lines of the parking spot, and once inside the building, she waited at the elevator for a full minute before noticing the "Out of Order" sign. She took the stairs two at a time and—how could this be?—got lost again.

It was on her second round circling the floor that she spotted Tracy, and it was only after Tracy stepped aside that she understood the reason she'd walked right past her mother's room. The nameplate on the door was now covered by a giant magnetic dove, someone's idea of closure.

Inside the room, erasure had begun. The bed was freshly made with a silk rose placed on Glory's pillow. Was this still considered Glory's pillow? Was it okay for her to be in this room? Was it okay that Julia wasn't coming home? Ginger sat down on the bed. Why hadn't Richard thought to ask Anne-Marie to tell Julia that it's good to be with family when someone dies? That mourning can be complicated. That pretending a death didn't happen can have all kinds of repercussions. *Stop*, she told herself. *Don't think. Stay busy.* This was how she got through her day. This was how she got through her life. She did what was required. What was required here? *Stand up. Open the closet. Take out the clothes. Put them in a bag.* What did *she* require? *Don't think.* That was key.

In the closet half a dozen velour tracksuits hung off kilter on metal hangers. Zipper jackets and elastic-waist pants in a rainbow of nursing-home colors: coral next to lavender, lime green next to sky blue. Such a soft blue, like a robin's egg, or the blue eyes of a newborn baby. *Don't think. Take the tracksuits off the hangers. Place them in the bag.*

There were clothes in the closet she'd never seen before. A red velour dress, with a dozen looped buttons up the back. A denim jacket with peacocks embroidered on the sleeves. Where would Glory have worn such things? *Were* these her things, or had the next person already moved in? But no—there was her mother's red ribbed robe puddled on the floor, as if Glory had melted away beneath it.

Inside one pocket of the robe she found a knot of tortoiseshell bobby pins. In the other, two hardened balls of used tissues. She tossed the remains in the tin wastebasket, where they fell with a thud. She surveyed the room. The drawers were jammed shut. The floor was streaked with water. A breeze from the open window blew a tumbleweed of white hair against her ankle. She hurried to the small bathroom where the air held the sting of ammonia and the toiletries awaited. Grabbing a tissue, she picked up a sliver of soap and a tall, sticky bottle of shampoo. She tossed things one by one—thump, the gnarly tube of toothpaste; whomp, the sticky roll-on deodorant; plunk, the crusty tub of hand cream. From the small glass shelf above the toilet, she scooped up a face puff, lipstick, blush.

Brooke, the activity director, stopped by to offer a carton for personal effects. In went the framed photographs of Mimi's children, one stacked atop the other.

It was in the final check of the room that she found the black marble composition notebook at the back of a bottom drawer. Written on the cover, in Glory's shaky hand, it said, "Notes to Self." Ginger cracked the book open, hoping for blank pages, but instead there was her mother's careful script. Her aversion to reading her mother's musings had not mellowed. She closed the book and considered her choices, journal in the box or journal in the trash. Dinah, the aide Glory said was mean, came in to offer condolences. Journal in the box.

"Sorry your mother passed," Dinah said as she offered a warm hug.

"Thank you for being so kind to her." As Dinah stepped away, Ginger noticed her calf. "Your leg is swollen. Have you had that checked out?"

Dinah looked down. "That? That's nothing. It's the phlebitis."

"Usually it's nothing," Ginger agreed. "But it can be serious. If it's deep in the vein, you never know. You could throw a clot. Have you talked to your doctor about it?"

"Well, not yet, but okay. Uh-huh. I will." Dinah hurried down the hall.

"Wait," Ginger called after her. "Sorry." She didn't mean to drive Dinah away. She didn't mean to drive anyone away. She just wanted to make sure Dinah had the right information. Richard called her an alarmist, but Ginger couldn't understand why everyone wasn't alarmed, all of the time.

Her leg started trembling. What was that about? Could grief make her leg shake? Or was it possible she'd been so busy worrying about Julia and Glory that she neglected to notice something was wrong with *her*? She quickly ran through a list of tremor diseases. Parkinson's, kidney disease, mercury poisoning. Could that be it? Could she have eaten too much tainted fish?

The problem was there were so many things that could happen and no way to predict which would be the one that actually *did*. At the last faculty meeting, she heard about another parent falling ill. A gluten-free vegan mother this time. Lately, it seemed like that's how it always went, the moms who juiced and cycled from one city to the next to raise money for diseases, suddenly diagnosed with ALS. If she got sick, would Julia come home then?

Stop, she ordered herself. She pictured her medicine cabinet at work. *Life Savers*. That's what she prescribed for children with clogged ears: two yawns and a Life Saver. *Altoids*. Those were for the sad children, who came in complaining of vague miseries but sometimes could be distracted by the sharp taste of a small mint.

Her leg was definitely trembling now. Okay, it was probably something mundane. Hypoglycemia, say, or a thyroid condition, or stress. Stress could cause all kinds of peculiar symptoms, and well, Ginger had been under an elephant's load of stress for a very long time.

What was strange, now that she thought of it, was that the quivering felt exquisitely specific. Her upper leg. Her upper thigh. Her right upper thigh. Why would stress only affect a person's right thigh? She concentrated on the sensation, just below the front pocket of her favorite pants. She pulled out her vibrating phone. "Mimi. Thank god it's you. I thought I might have mercury poisoning."

"What are you talking about? What took you so long to answer? Where are you?"

A simple task. That's what Mimi had to do. While Ginger was removing old tissues from the pockets of her dead mother's robe and throwing away Q-tips that still had her mother's earwax on them, Mimi had to make one phone call and go to an empty house to look for an address book which, even if it existed, they didn't really need.

"Ginger?" Mimi snapped. "Can you hear me? Hello? I can't believe this. Hello?"

"I'm here," Ginger said, but Mimi was gone and when Ginger called back, she got voice mail.

Hurrying across the Meadows parking lot, her foot came out of her clog and down she went, graceless as a goose. The box from Glory's room flew out of her arms, disgorging all manner of Popkins onto the macadam.

A man on his way to his car appeared out of the dusk. "You okay?"

"Yes. Fine. Sorry. Thanks."

As he helped gather the broken frames, he pointed at her palm. "You're bleeding."

She looked. "Just a scrape." She wiggled her fingers. "Everything works." She started toward her car.

The man touched her arm to stop her. "You forgot something. Over there."

She saw it immediately, peeking out from beneath her car, the marbled notebook, her mother's most recent journal. She thanked the man, who couldn't possibly know there was nothing she'd rather have run over, nothing she wanted less to kneel down and retrieve than the most recent written record of her mother's thoughts.

She tossed the journal on top of the broken frames, put the box in the trunk of her car, got in, and checked the rearview mirror to see why her face hurt. She removed a small pebble stuck to her cheek and was blotting her bleeding palm with a tissue when her phone vibrated again. This time she answered it quickly. "What's going on?"

"Callie's here," Mimi hissed, and her phone went dead.

Ginger sat for a moment and went over the facts. Julia was gone. Glory was dead. Callie was back. She leaned forward and checked the inky sky for signs of bad weather and then drove slowly through the moonless night toward the house she still thought of as her mother's.

When she pulled off the highway, the car behind her honked and she accelerated to the speed limit. The dashboard idiot light caught her eye and she wondered, *How long has* that *been on?* Before she could process what the icon meant, the car began to slow, this time on its own.

Another first. Ginger had run out of gas.

CHAPTER
TWENTY-ONE

Morning sun streamed in through the porthole window, warming the back of Ginger's neck. She peeled away from the wall and assessed the situation. Alone in bed, sisters gone, left arm squashed beneath her, numb. With effort, she heaved herself up and her fingers tingled back to life. Her foot searched for the floor and instead found something bony. She peered over the side of the mattress. Her foot was on her sister's leg; Callie lay on the floor in a fetal position, half of her body under the bed, still asleep.

The trill of Mimi's laughter rose from the kitchen along with the smell of pancakes. Ginger shook Callie's foot. "Get up." She jiggled her leg. "They're home." Another shake, harder. "Let's go."

Callie straightened, stretched, crawled out from underneath the bed, and rubbed her eyes. "Why?"

"Because it's morning. They're eating breakfast. Everybody's in the kitchen."

Everybody turned out to be Mimi and Evelyn Clarke, who was lifting a stack of pancakes out of a frying pan. Evelyn quickly slid the pancakes onto a platter, set it down, and came to give Ginger a hug. "How are you?" Another hug went to Callie. "How are *you?*"

"We're good," Ginger said, and Callie agreed, "Goody good."

"I'm so relieved." Evelyn wiped at the corner of her eyes. "Oof. I can barely speak." She waved the air and quickly shook her head, as if shaking off a troublesome thought. "How many pancakes? Two? Three? Four?" She offered the platter, and Ginger took two. When Callie couldn't decide, Ginger gave her two as well.

"If you want chocolate chips on top you can have them," Mimi said. "Or you could pour Bosco on top. That's what I did. You can have anything you want on top, right?"

Evelyn nodded, and wiped her eyes again.

"Where's Charlie?" Ginger asked. "Where's Mom?"

"At the hospital," Evelyn said. "She'll be back soon. Juice?" She started filling glasses without waiting for an answer.

Mimi quickly told Ginger what she'd learned so far. "Dad came on the same boat as Evelyn, but he went straight to the hospital. I don't know where Mr. Diggans went." She turned to Evelyn. "Is Charlie coming home today or are we going to the hospital to see him? I've never been in a hospital room. I hope we go there."

Evelyn put down the pitcher. "I'll be right back."

When Ginger found her, she was at the front door, holding it ajar, as if she'd needed air. A soft noise escaped from her mouth when she noticed Ginger watching. "I'm so sorry," Evelyn said as she opened her arms again.

"Sorry why?" Ginger let herself be held. She whispered the next. "What happened?"

"Aw, honey," Evelyn whispered back. "I shouldn't be the one."

"Please, I want to know."

Evelyn stroked Ginger's hair and then took her hand and led her to the living room, where the scent of Mr. Diggans' cherry tobacco still hung in the air like a cloud. As soon as she sat down, perched at the very edge of the sofa, Ginger knew, nothing good was coming. Evelyn was always crisply put together, with pressed clothes and hair tied back in a no-muss, no-fuss style. But today her oxford shirt was buttoned wrong and her hair had a crooked part that made it look askew. She was struggling with what to say, and worst of all, she didn't bother to dab away the tears that were now running in two wet lines down her face.

When she finally did speak, her voice was so quiet, Ginger couldn't understand her. "He didn't make it," she said. She repeated herself. "He didn't make it," and then, "He's gone," which was what Glory had said when Ivan the Director died.

Ginger waited to feel something, but her eyes stayed dry.

Evelyn stroked her cheek. "It's okay to cry. I've been crying all morning."

How could Ginger explain to someone who'd cried all morning that she had no feelings at all. She pinched her arm and still felt nothing. She stamped her foot on the floor, but her foot was numb. A moment later, the numb sensation passed. "I have to throw up."

And then they heard it, a car rumbling up the driveway. Ginger swallowed the taste of vomit and wiped the corner of her eyes where her tears had started to amass.

By the time Solly opened the screen door, they were waiting for him. Ginger thought her father looked unusually pale and slight, not at all how she thought of him. He hesitated for a moment when he saw her, and then, as if making up for lost time, quickly moved to give her a tight hug, arms stiff as fence posts at her back.

Glory remained outside on the top step, as if stuck. The sun was in her mother's eyes and Ginger could make out dark circles where her makeup had run. Her lips looked white and caked and her shoulders sat at an odd angle, as if her body had sunk down on one side. She seemed unable to do the simplest thing: walk into the house. Evelyn saw this, and fetched her, holding her by the elbow to guide her in, as if she were blind.

For a moment Ginger wondered if she *had* gone blind. At least that would explain why her mother walked past her without even noticing she was there. Solly took in Ginger's puzzled expression and moved next to her, laying a wooden hand on her shoulder. Together, they watched Evelyn lead Glory down the hall to the back bedroom.

And then Mimi and Callie were running out of the kitchen, Mimi hugging her father hard and babbling about how they'd stayed in their room all afternoon and how Mr. Diggans came and didn't want them downstairs and how they all slept squished in one bed. It took a while for her to notice her father wasn't listening. She stepped away and pulled Callie with her. "Where's Charlie?" Mimi asked, and Ginger closed her eyes.

"Not coming back," Solly said.

That wasn't enough information for Mimi. "Why? Where is he?"

Ginger quickly motioned up, toward the sky.

"In his room?" Mimi asked.

And Callie answered, "Heaven. Heaven, eleven."

"Not true," Mimi said. "Charlie waved at Ginger on the beach. He's fine."

"Okay. That's it." Solly hustled them to the door. "Come on. Outside." It was rare for him to tell them what to do, so when he did, they listened.

Outside, he pulled Callie close to him, as if she needed protection. "Your mother's not well. She hears talk like that, you'll make it worse. *Charlie waved. Charlie didn't wave.* It doesn't matter. He's gone. She's sick."

"Sick how?" Mimi asked.

He banged his heart with his fist. "Sick here." He reached over and rubbed a tear from Ginger's cheek with his thumb. Ginger hadn't even known a tear was there. "The doctor told her she can't have any talk like that now. She can't have any talk like that ever. Understand?" They nodded. "Tell me what I said."

"We can't talk about it now," Ginger repeated. "We can't talk about it ever."

"Good." He nodded. "I knew I could count on you."

"But . . ." Mimi was confused. "What is it we're not talking about?"

Solly put his finger to his lips. "Your mother could be listening. No questions." They all looked around. Glory didn't seem to be there, but how could they be sure? "What's done is done. Nothing will change anything. So." His hand went to his mouth, and his fingers did a little turn.

"He's locking his lips," Ginger whispered to Mimi, who was about to ask.

Solly's voice softened. "Tomorrow we'll go home. But at home, you're all going to have to be really strong for your mother. Can you do that? Be patient and strong?"

"I'm strong and patient," Callie boasted. "I'm patient and strong. I'm a strong patient."

"Stop it," Ginger said.

Solly pulled Callie closer. "Yes, you are. Strong as a skyscraper. All of you. You just got to stick close together. Like rubber cement."

"Like blubber cement," Callie repeated, as if this was a game.

Ginger gave her a shove. "Stop."

"Gingie." Solly's voice was pleading. "She's little. She doesn't know better."

"Sorry." She turned to her sister. "I love blubber cement too."

When they went back inside, Evelyn was waiting, eyes rimmed with red. Ginger watched as she stepped away with Solly and made a hushed report. He listened and shrugged and shrugged again, a staccato movement that got more and more pronounced until Evelyn reached over and laid a hand on his shoulder and the shrugs stopped.

Ginger slipped away so her father wouldn't know she'd been watching. He joined her in the kitchen a few moments later. "Evelyn wants to talk to you before she leaves. She's waiting outside."

Ginger found her standing next to an idling car.

"I wanted to let you know I won't be coming back to New Jersey for a while," Evelyn said. "But soon as I do, I promise, first thing, I'll come ring your bell." She laid her soft palm on Ginger's hot cheek. "Things may be tough for a while. But your mom is strong. Stronger than she knows." She took Ginger's hands. "She's going to be okay, I promise. But you have to promise something to me."

Ginger would have promised anything except she couldn't risk opening her mouth. There were just too many things that might spill out. She might plead for Evelyn to stay or she might beg for Evelyn to take her with her. She might even dare to ask if Evelyn knew what punishment Glory had in mind for her for letting the accident happen under her watch. That it hadn't been under her watch, she knew, would be no excuse.

Evelyn interrupted her thoughts. "Promise me you won't worry too much."

Ginger risked a nod. Evelyn nodded back, opened the passenger door, and slid inside.

Finally, Ginger found words that seemed safe. "When you get home, can I go back to being a mother's helper for you?" Tears were coming now, and Ginger had to squeeze her eyes hard to stop them. By the time she forced them open, the car had turned around. As it bolted down the driveway, she caught a glimpse of Evelyn, hands covering her face.

CHAPTER TWENTY-TWO

.It was only when Ginger tried to pay the gas station attendant who drove her back to her car that she discovered she'd left her wallet at home. She offered to come by and pay him first thing in the morning and then remembered tomorrow was her mother's funeral. She started to explain her frazzled state, but the attendant interrupted her. "Ma'am, this gallon's on me."

Back behind the wheel, it didn't take long for her thoughts to turn to Callie, but every time she tried to picture her youngest sister, she came up blank. Glory's prohibition against photographs had done its work. Her mother's reasons changed depending on her mood. Sometimes it was, *They're just dust magnets.* Other times it was, *I prefer to start every day fresh.* But now, with Julia gone, Ginger finally understood it. Her mother had banned photographs because the captured memories were painful to see.

She pulled up to the house and strengthened her resolve. Tonight was not the time for interrogation. For now, it wasn't important to know why Callie left or what kept her away. What mattered was she was back. As she walked up the flagstone path, careful not to disturb the deteriorating stones, Ginger wondered again how it was that Callie found out Glory died. Her best guess? Mimi tracked her down.

She stopped at the front door and saw her face reflected in the glass, her expression a billboard for worry. It was the same expression that drove Dinah scurrying down the hall with her phlebitis leg. The same expression that drove Julia into Nick's car, and then all the way to Portland. She could not risk driving Callie away too. She smiled and stepped inside.

The house grumbled its usual complaints. A pipe groaned from within the old walls. A floorboard creaked above her head. And there it was, the rocketing rhythm of Mimi's voice when she was telling a story. Her sisters were in the kitchen.

Ginger stopped. What should she say? What was a person supposed to say to a sister who'd been gone for—she paused to do the math, but the math was too painful—more than twenty-five years. A cabinet door slammed. Silverware clattered into the sink. A wave of dizziness swept over her. She slipped into the living room to pull herself together.

Strange, how the living room, which felt so abandoned after Glory moved out, now felt crowded with memories. When they were young, the room was off-limits—company only—but after Solly was gone, Glory took it over and made it her sitting room. Now it felt as if her mother had returned to reclaim every bit of it at once. There she was at the bay window, peering out to see who was stopping by the neighbor's house so late, and there she was on the velvet couch, adjusting the cold compress so it didn't sit so heavy on her eyes, and there she was, sitting on the club chair in a funk because the Norwegian Fjord puzzle Ginger bought for her turned out to have three—or maybe it was four—pieces missing from the boat.

The lights dimmed. Were her eyes going now? Possibilities presented themselves: infection, cataracts, macular degeneration, all of them ill-timed.

"Good god, what now?" It was Mimi in the hallway.

Ginger straightened. "Nothing. Something weird with my eyes. The light went dim, and then it got bright. I'm sure it's nothing."

"You mean like this?" Mimi slid the dimmer up and down, and above Ginger's head the high hats went dim and then bright. "As if I accidentally brushed against the switch, which in fact is what I did?"

"Oh. Thank god. I feel faint." Ginger touched her face. Her cheeks were damp. She moved her hands away and saw her fingers trembling. When she glanced over at Mimi, she noticed her sister was having moisture issues of her own. "Were you crying?"

"Absolutely not."

No crying in public. Glory had trained them well.

Ginger wiped at her eyes and then, at the same time, they asked each other, "Why didn't you tell me you found her?" Footsteps. The sisters moved apart.

"Here she is." Mimi's mouth turned up into a broad smile.

Ginger had carefully thought it through in the car; the best strategy for the reunion with her sister would be a slow approach, gentle conversation while she felt things out. But her body seemed to have a different idea, because now she found herself racing over and throwing her arms around Callie's back, surprising them both. They stood for a moment as if glued together, and then Callie shifted. It was a tiny motion, a quiver really, but enough to make Ginger step away. "I'm crushing you. I'm sorry."

"That's okay."

Mimi beamed. "Does she look great or what?" Impossibly, her smile got bigger, the tendons in her neck flaring so wide Ginger feared they might snap.

"She does. You do. You look great." Ginger didn't want to stare, but how could she help it? She couldn't find a remnant of the face she once knew. The woman who stood before her, in her late thirties with a lean body and freckled shoulders, was as unfamiliar as a stranger. Her eyes filled again, and not knowing what else to do, she lurched forward to give another hug, this time harder. Their heads touched, and she whispered, "Where have you been?" and then winced at her hungry tone.

Callie gently pulled away. "I'm happy to see you."

"This is super-duper great," Mimi cheered. "Together again. Forward march!"

"Are you here for long?" Ginger asked. "Where do you live? What do you do?" She needed to stop. But there was so much she didn't know. "I hope you're back for good."

"I'm back for now. One day at a time."

As if possessed, Ginger's questions kept coming. "How did you find out Mom died?"

Callie's face seemed to flatten. "Mimi just told me."

"Oh. You didn't know." Ginger reached out to embrace her again but stopped herself. "I thought that's why you came. Why *did* you come?"

"The lady at the place called me last night. She told me Mom was talking in numbers, and I should come see her. Just in case."

Ginger blinked as she took this in. *A lady had called.* "Tracy? The social worker?"

Callie nodded. The microwave beeped. "That's for me. I couldn't find the teaspot. Teapot," she corrected herself as she hurried to the kitchen. At least one thing remained unchanged. Callie still had what Glory liked to call the "Mangle Tangle."

• • •

They stood close in the front hall, whispering.

"No," Mimi said. "She didn't say a thing about where she lives. Nothing. Nothing about anything. I've been blathering on, telling her about the boys, about Neil, about you. She asked a lot of questions about you."

"Okay. We need to go slow. Let *her* be the one to tell *us*. I'm sure when she's ready to explain where she's been, she will. We just have to make sure we don't scare her away."

"Why are you lecturing *me*? You're the one giving her the third degree."

They heard the sound of a crash from the kitchen. When they got there, they saw Callie squatting on the floor, collecting the shards of a broken teacup.

"I'm so clunzy. I drop things all the time."

"I'm clunzy too." Ginger kneeled to help gather the pieces. "Family trait."

"Clumsy," Mimi corrected them both.

When Ginger dropped the shards she'd collected into the garbage, Mimi noticed her hand. "Are you bleeding?" She examined the cut. "Are you kidding me? Callie breaks a cup, and you bleed? How did you manage that?"

"I scraped my hand in the parking lot at the Meadows. It must have reopened. That's all. I'm fine." She grabbed some paper towels and sat at the kitchen table. "I was so excited to hear you came," she told Callie, "that I fell running to my car. Ridiculous, right?"

"I love to run too," Callie said, and then she went back to preparing her tea.

Making tea seemed to be a complicated process, and she did it with the focus of a monk. Could she be a monk? Ginger would not ask. Unless—what if Callie thought this meant she didn't care? What if she went back to her monastery and told the other monks she decided to return because no one in her family had been at all curious about her life?

"So." Ginger tried to keep her tone casual. "Mom said you were in a cult for a while." Glory had shared that, about her sister. She was in a cult, which some time later, she left. "But she never said which cult it was. Or where you went after you left."

Callie looked confused.

Mimi grabbed Ginger's hand. "Gingie, you're bleeding again. For god sake." She got Ginger's purse and handed it over. "You have a tourniquet in there? Or a big bandage at least?"

"It's because I'm a nurse," Ginger explained as she pulled out the zippered pouch she used as a traveling first aid kit, stocked with alcohol wipes, antibiotic ointments, and gauze.

"I know," Callie said.

"Oh." Ginger wondered how much Mimi had told her. "It's very warm in here, isn't it?" She touched her hot cheeks. "Or is it just me?"

"You," Callie said.

"It's not you," Mimi told Ginger. "It's not her," she told Callie. "You can't say things like that to Ginger. Do you remember that about her? How she's always worrying the sky is going to fall?"

Callie shook her head and went back to preparing her tea.

Even though she was sitting on the other side of the room, the smell of the tea was making Ginger queasy. She peeled off one of the plastic place mats stuck to the table to use as a fan but circulating the air only made it worse. "I think your tea is spoiled. Can tea be spoiled?"

Mimi's nostrils flared. "Smells like dog. What kind of tea smells like dog?"

"I can't smell anything." Callie put a mesh basket in a mug and sprinkled in the tea, a few leaves at a time.

"Quite a production," Mimi observed. "When I make tea? I don't even wait for the water to boil. Takes too long. If the boys see me at the stove, makes them automatically starving."

Ginger tensed. She knew how these conversations went. After the introduction of Mimi's boys, the subject would naturally turn to Julia. And she did not want to talk about Julia now. She went on the offensive. "Wait till you meet Mimi's boys. They're amazing. Practically men by now. Three talented young men. Mimi's talented too. She's an artist. Did she tell you?"

"I like to be busy, that's all. Busy makes for happy."

"She makes quilts," Ginger went on. "But she doesn't go to a store and buy fabric. She uses old clothes."

"It's a thing," Mimi said. "I didn't invent it. It's called upcycling."

"You do it well, is my point. It's your energy. Mimi has incredible energy. Before she became a quilter, she owned a store. Furniture for kids. Beautiful shop. I didn't even know she wanted a store and then, poof, one day there it was, open for business. That's how she is. One day to think it, one day to do it. What came before the store? Real estate?"

Mimi nodded. "Talk about a grind."

A timer rang and Callie took a measuring cup of water out of the microwave. She slowly poured it over her tea and said, "And before that, you sold jewelry out of your house, right?"

So they'd covered Mimi's work history too.

Callie carried her teacup to the table. As she got closer, Ginger covered her nose with her hand to block the smell. "I really think your tea's gone bad."

"It does smell foul." Mimi pried open a window and then held up the broken sash. "Come here, Gingie. You look green. Stand here and get some air."

With her face pressed to the screen and the soft breeze of the early June night hitting her cheek, Ginger's queasiness began to subside.

Something scrambled above her head, and she looked up. "Does Mom have mice?" That came out wrong. "*Did* Mom have mice?" That sounded worse. "Are there mice here?" There was more scrambling and then a bark.

"A dog?" Mimi had a long-standing fear of dogs she refused to admit. The dog they couldn't see barked again and Mimi let go of the window, which snapped shut like a guillotine, beheading a large winged beetle that had started a family on the sill.

"That's Echo," Callie said. "My dog. I left him upstairs. He doesn't like to be alone."

"You brought a dog?" Mimi looked outraged. "You know how allergic the boys are."

"She doesn't," Ginger reminded her.

Callie looked concerned. "Are the boys here?"

"That's not the point. I can't go home with dog on my clothes. Troy has asthma and we can't have anything with fur in the house." She checked her phone. "I have to go pick up Wallace." Her hand dug around in her purse for her keys.

"Before you leave," Ginger said. "We should talk about the funeral tomorrow."

"Right." Mimi reviewed the plans: "Limo's coming at one. Cemetery is an hour from the funeral home. After the burial we'll have a consolation meal at my house, which Neil's parents are arranging with the aid of a hundred or so of their closest friends. Afterward—"

"No," Callie interrupted her. "We can't do that."

"Can't eat?" Ginger asked.

"Nobody has to eat," Mimi said. "But there has to be food." She held up her keys. "Found them."

"Can't have a funeral," Callie explained. "Mom doesn't want that. She wants to be cremated."

Ginger took this in. "What makes you think that?"

"Doesn't matter." Mimi buttoned her coat. "Plans are made. Where do you want to stay tonight, Cal? Gingie's house is quiet. Mine is like a circus. Take your pick."

"I'll stay here, thanks. And we can't have a funeral. Mom told me. No funeral. She said I should insist." She turned to Mimi. "She said I shouldn't let you bully me."

"Mom called me a bully?"

Ginger was confused. "*When* did Mom tell you this?"

Above their heads they could hear the loud thumping of the dog's tail thwacking the floor. "Echo's upset. I should get him. Ginger, would you mind changing the arrangements? Mom told me you like to take care of things."

"I'm a bully, and Ginger likes to take care of things?" Mimi checked her watch. "I have to find someone to pick up Wallace." She left the room, cell phone pressed hard to her ear.

"Is Mimi always angry?" Callie asked.

"It's a lot to take in," Ginger said. "She's sad about Mom. And then you coming home? It's amazing. We couldn't be happier. But it's been so long. And it's confusing. Because we're the ones who've been here with Mom. We thought you and Mom were estranged. That you two didn't speak. So how could you know what Mom wanted?"

"The phone doesn't always work." Callie pressed her lips together, just like Julia.

Mimi speeded back from her call. "Okay. Wallace is taken care of. As far as cremation, that has got to be a misunderstanding. Glory is more a bury-me-in-a-cocktail-dress kind of gal. I'm going up to look in her closet to see what she's got. You want to come?" Ginger and Callie followed, but instead of going upstairs, Callie headed to the front door.

Ginger grabbed her arm. "Don't leave. We'll have Mom cremated. Mimi, we have to have Mom cremated, like Callie says."

"I'm not leaving." Callie picked up a backpack that was leaning against the wall. "I'm getting something." She reached inside and pulled out an envelope. "From Mom."

Ginger and Mimi silently followed her back to the kitchen. After they sat down, Callie pulled a sheet of paper out of the envelope and laid it flat on the table. Even from a distance, Ginger recognized the handwriting. It wasn't the compressed script of the elderly Glory, like the script on the cover of the journal now in the trunk of Ginger's car. This was Glory's handwriting before she got ill, all emphatic loops and flowery cursive.

It was as if a younger, healthy version of her mother had walked into the room. And as if she really had, all discussion stopped, and every head swiveled toward her words.

CHAPTER TWENTY-THREE

The trunk held sandy shoes jammed inside sun hats and bathing suits crumpled into sweatshirts. Suitcases had been hastily filled, dirty and clean mixed together. Charlie's things were nowhere to be seen.

Solly slammed the trunk and got into the car. Everyone sat, eyes straight ahead. He adjusted the mirrors, and Ginger stared at the back of her mother's hair. It was flat, the way it always went after Glory stayed in bed with a migraine. Callie noticed it too and reached over to fluff it up.

"Stop." Ginger pulled Callie's arm and fixed her hands so they lay clasped in her lap.

Mimi leaned forward and directed a question toward her father's ear, her idea of a private conversation. "What should I tell people when we get home?"

Solly stiffened. "Nobody's business."

"That's it? That's what I'm supposed to say? *Nobody's business?*"

"Say you don't know," Ginger told her when her father didn't reply.

"I *don't* know." Mimi sounded frustrated. "For *real*, I don't know."

Solly gunned the accelerator. Nothing more was said. Other than a request for a rest stop and telling the gas station attendant to "Fill 'er up," they made the trip home in silence.

That night, Ginger sat Mimi down and told her she had to stop asking what happened. It didn't matter that Charlie waved when they took him out of the hole. Charlie was gone. What mattered now was that their mother was sick about it, and if they kept going over what happened, she would stay sick.

As for what to do when people asked, that turned out not to matter because over the next few days, they both discovered, no one did. Mimi decided it was because everyone was too busy. It was the beginning of the school year, and people were racing from shopping for loose-leaf notebooks to getting haircuts and new shoes. But Ginger wasn't so sure. It seemed like a big thing to not notice, that a family who went on vacation with four kids came back with three.

When Evelyn finally came home at the end of the first week of September, she told Ginger she was right. "It is a big thing. Everyone noticed, and they're desperate for details so they can be sure what happened to you won't happen to them. My phone hasn't stopped ringing since I've been back. People want to know. They're just afraid to ask you."

"What do you tell them?"

"Nothing." Evelyn offered her a sad smile. "It's not my place to say." She was silent for a moment and then, as if she could read Ginger's mind, she said she was sorry but she couldn't use her as a mother's helper anymore. Thomas was going to stay with his father for a while. "Change of scenery," she gave as the reason and then seemed to regret her flippant tone. "It's complicated. Thomas felt so bad about what happened. And his father's just moved. Getting married—did you hear? To a very nice woman. Colleen. Not an evil stepmother at all. A widow with two children. Three now, I suppose." She took a breath and smiled. "We all decided this would be the perfect time for Thomas to visit. Now everyone can get acquainted. It's temporary, of course. I couldn't bear it if it wasn't temporary." She got quiet and Ginger didn't ask any questions.

But even if Thomas hadn't gone to stay with his father, Ginger soon realized she wouldn't have been allowed to work for Evelyn. It would have been too upsetting for Glory. That was the main thing now: making sure Glory didn't get more upset. With their return to New Jersey, her headaches had come back. She had one every day, incapacitating migraines that sometimes were so bad, Ginger could hear moaning from all the way downstairs. The only thing that brought relief was being alone, staying in bed, and switching up washcloths—a cool one on her forehead while a backup soaked in the bowl of ice water that took up permanent residence on her night table.

Ginger was sure the headaches were, at least in part, because of her. She wasn't sure exactly what her role was in the accident, but she knew accusations would be coming before long. Any minute now, they'd begin. That they hadn't started yet was confusing. Every morning she braced herself for the blowup. But her mother did not emerge from bed. Finally, Ginger asked her father his opinion. "Do you think Mom will be mad at me forever?"

"Mad at you? For what?"

She shrugged and met her father's eyes. "I know it was my fault. I'm sorry."

"Fault?" Solly's eyes shone bright, and then he wagged his finger. "No." He sounded angry. "You did nothing. I don't want to ever hear you say that again. Understand?"

Ginger didn't, but she nodded anyway.

When school started up, Evelyn came over every morning to help them get ready. Everyone except Callie, who refused to go to school. It was hard to know why, because Callie was on strike against talking. It took them a day to notice that because Callie had never been a big talker. How could she be when she had three older siblings to compete with? It was hard for all of them to get a word in edgewise, but Callie's solution was to make do with mime and playacting—sticking out her tongue if she was mad, stamping her feet when she wanted to demand attention. But on strike, she stopped even that.

Ginger didn't mind that Callie wasn't talking. In fact, she wished Mimi would give the silent treatment a try. What she did mind were the nightmares. Callie's bad dreams started the first night they were back, and it fell to Ginger to try and keep her frightened sister quiet. Most nights, she ended up bringing Callie to her parents' room, where she'd hand her over to Solly. Then, as if in a choreographed dance, he would slip out of bed, Callie would curl into his spot, Ginger would return to the Girls' Room, and her father would finish the night on the cushion of the thin foam couch in the den.

It was Evelyn who coaxed Callie into talking. She didn't get her to say much, but it was a start. "You can have a second Ring Ding if you want," Evelyn told her one night after dinner. "All you have to do is ask. Just say, 'May I have another Ring Ding?' and a second one—I promise—will appear, presto, like magic, on your plate."

When that worked, Evelyn moved on to encouraging Callie to give school a try. "Try for a day," she suggested, and when that didn't do the trick, "Try for a couple of hours," and finally, "Go for ten minutes. I'll be right outside, waiting in the car." Ginger gave a try at picturing her mother making that offer, but her mind went blank.

As soon as Callie went back to school, her night terrors stopped, just like that. Ginger didn't know why until Evelyn explained. Callie had been worrying about the same thing Ginger worried about: what to say when people asked about Charlie. But just as no one had asked Ginger, no one asked Callie. To Ginger it seemed like the whole world decided it would be better to pretend he had never existed at all.

Now they woke up every day to Evelyn in the kitchen plating whatever treat she'd baked the night before—muffins or banana bread—or cooking them a hot breakfast—French toast cut into hearts or waffles with sugar dusted on top. In the afternoon, Evelyn came back to cook dinner. Soon the house filled with the sounds of good cheer as they adapted to acting, if not always feeling, like everything was okay. Of course it wasn't okay, but at least with Evelyn in charge, sometimes entire days went by without a single cross word or choked-back tears.

At some point every afternoon, Glory would emerge, shuffling downstairs and offering a vague wave as she passed. It wasn't clear whether she'd come down to replenish her bowl of ice or was just curious to see what everyone thought was so funny. What was clear—Ginger could tell by the look on her face—was that she wasn't happy with this arrangement, her children under the spell of Evelyn's good-natured care.

It was the middle of October, the first of the crimson leaves on the red maple outside their dining room beginning to fall, when Glory's headaches stopped. Just like that, one day Ginger woke up and found her mother at the kitchen stove working the frying pan.

"Aren't you a sight for sore eyes," Glory announced as she doled out fried eggs, yolks hard, whites with crispy edges and the surprise crunch of a hidden shell. "Did you miss me terribly?"

Ginger and Mimi shouted back, "Yes!" while Callie, who still wasn't speaking much, gave a nod.

As for Glory's recovery, Ginger had several theories for how it came about. Maybe the doctor she saw for headaches finally figured out how to help. Or maybe it was the group she had decided to *give a go* at joining. Ginger had assumed this was a consciousness-raising group, until she overheard Solly tell Evelyn that every woman in the group had lost someone, except for one woman who lost twins. Whatever the reason, within a few days Glory went from cooking breakfast in her bathrobe to cooking dinner wearing a new dress, and with full makeup on.

"I have good news," she sang out as she passed the lamb chops. "Buddy has scheduled our season." Buddy Desadario was the new director of her theater group. "I'm not thrilled the first play is *Harvey*, of all things. But after *Harvey* we're doing *A Doll's House*. Nora." Her eyes brightened. "Imagine."

When Mimi asked if Evelyn was going out for Nora too, Glory laughed away the question. "Evelyn's not in the group anymore. Never had the right temperament for it. Besides, she's moving. It's too much house for her, all things considered."

Ginger, working hard to keep her expression blank, forgot to pay attention to her posture.

"Books on your head," her mother reminded her.

Several weeks after the news that Evelyn was moving, Glory asked Ginger if she was interested in helping their neighbor pack. "You don't have to," Glory said. "You're not her slave." She was sitting at the dining room table working on a puzzle, but it was slow-going. Over that fall, she seemed to have lost the ability to concentrate for long stretches. "Evelyn said she'll pay you. Where she gets her money, I haven't the foggiest." She glanced up and took in Ginger's pale face and stooped posture. Ginger's stomach had been bothering her ever since the day she heard Evelyn was moving. "You all right? Course you are. You can do what you want—help Evelyn pack or not. Makes no difference to me."

When Ginger walked into the Clarke house, Evelyn seemed to see the emptied rooms through her eyes. "I told Paul to take whatever he wanted, and I guess he wanted a lot." Shelves previously jammed with record albums and books had been purged. The few that remained collapsed in on each other. Photographs had been extracted too, leaving blank spots on walls, with hooks and faded wallpaper as placeholders. There were also big things missing, like the TV in the den and the stereo. "I don't really watch TV," Evelyn said. "Or listen to music. I haven't exactly been dancing around the house." The only thing that felt familiar was the smell of something baking. The timer rang. "Brownies," Evelyn told her as they moved to the kitchen. She pulled a tray out of the oven. "Let's let them cool while we work."

She had already done a lot of packing. There were boxes every-where—closed, labeled, and stacked against the wall. Open cabinet doors revealed a small pile of luncheon plates, a smattering of crystal glasses. Evelyn could have easily finished the job alone.

"Let me show you a trick." She got the lunch dishes and demon-strated how to pack, alternating sheets of newspaper with plates so that every plate was protected. "Want to give it a try?" After Ginger did, she proclaimed, "Exactly right. You're a natural."

Ginger packed carefully, but she knew no matter how slowly she wrapped the plates with paper, it would not be slow enough to keep Evelyn from going.

"I have to move," Evelyn said, as if reading her mind. "I can't stay here anymore."

Ginger didn't ask why. "You can come and live with us."

Evelyn laughed. "That's sweet. But I have a place. I'm going to be a washashore. On the Vineyard full-time. Thomas is going to join me soon as school ends. Don't know what I'd have done if Paul didn't agree to that."

"What will you do there?" Ginger had no idea what anyone did, except go to the beach.

"Work in my brother-in-law's business. He's a contractor. Remember Bob and Minty?" Ginger nodded and Evelyn repeated, "Bob and Minty. Dependable as daylight."

Bob and Minty made Ginger think of Evelyn's brother. "Will Mr. Diggans live here now?"

"Casper?" Evelyn laughed. "No. He's on the island full-time now. That's who I'm moving in with until Thomas comes. Then we'll move into our own place. Paul would not stand for it if Thomas lived with Casper. He hates him." She shook her head. "Can you imagine having someone hate your brother?" She suddenly remembered Ginger no longer had a brother. "Of course you couldn't. No one hated Charlie. I'm sorry. I shouldn't have brought that up."

"It's okay. I don't mind. No one talks about Charlie at all." It felt good to say his name out loud.

Evelyn looked relieved. "Good. All I meant was, it feels bad to find out someone you care about hates someone in your family." She stopped to consider this. "You don't think I hate your mother, do you? Because I don't."

Ginger couldn't imagine Evelyn hating anyone. "No. My father doesn't like your brother, either, but I don't know why." She wasn't sure this was okay to say. "Sorry."

"Oh, don't worry. I'm not surprised. It's like that with Casper. He means well, though. You know, your mom and Casper, they really are like two peas in a pod. The way they love to spin a yarn." Ginger felt on dangerous ground and said nothing. "With Casper, I can always tell. The story will suddenly drift into that other dimension. You know, everything is going along fine, it's just another story, you're barely paying attention, and all of a sudden the story changes course and you're sitting there thinking, *Wait a minute. That didn't happen.* But of course, you can't say that. You can never, ever say that. If you did, when you do, they just look at you like, what's wrong with *you.* Like *you're* the crazy one. *You're* the one who's out of your mind. You know what I mean?"

Ginger felt nearly paralyzed, because she did know. She knew exactly. It was as if Evelyn had gone into her brain and then said out loud every thought Ginger felt forbidden to think. But there was no way she could agree. Did Evelyn understand *that*?

"I guess some things probably are best left unsaid." She tore off a strip of packing tape and closed up the box Ginger had filled. "Hey, let's talk about the new people. The people moving in here asked me if I knew any babysitters on the block. Can you believe it? I told them, 'Are you kidding? Only the very best one who lives right next door.'"

"I don't think I'm allowed to babysit anymore."

"That will change." Evelyn got up on a stool. "How about you bring these home for your mom. A present from me." She passed down a set of champagne glasses. "I don't think I'll be toasting anything anytime soon." She remembered something else. "I have a gift for you. Come with me. I'll show you."

They went up to her bedroom, another place that looked purged, with open closet doors revealing empty space where Paul Clarke's clothes once hung.

Evelyn picked up a small round music box that sat on her dresser. "Found this in the basement. Paul gave it to me a hundred years ago." She wiped some dust off with her sleeve and handed it over. "Made me think of you. Turn the crank. It plays a song."

Ginger sat on the bed and turned the crank and listened to the scratchy tune and Evelyn sang along. "Beautiful dreamer . . ." Her voice was quiet and low. "Wake unto me." She couldn't carry a tune like Glory. "Starlight and dewdrops are waiting for thee." But she didn't seem to care. "Sounds of the rude world." She locked eyes with Ginger as she sang. "Heard in the day." And when Ginger's eyes began to fill with tears, Evelyn's filled too, as if in reply. "Lull'd by the moonlight have all pass'd away."

Ginger stared at the dented tin box. Even though it looked old, the colors of the children painted around the circumference seemed vibrant and alive.

"This will be *you* someday." Evelyn tapped the figure of a young girl driving a car. The girl's dark hair floated behind her head as if blown there by the wind, and her hands, covered in white gloves, held tight to the yellow steering wheel of the red convertible. Behind the car, puffs of smoke trailed like earthbound clouds. "You know I'm not leaving *you*. I'll write to you all the time. I'll write so many letters you'll wish I would stop. And someday, when you're old enough to drive"—she tapped the girl on the music box again—"you'll come visit me and Thomas. You're going to be okay," she promised. "You'll be better than okay. You'll be a wise, kind grown-up. You'll see." She stopped to think about it. "There's one of us in every family, you know. Human lie detectors. Geiger counters set to listen for the truth." Even though they were alone in the house, she whispered, "Your mother does the best she can. And she loves you, truly, in her way." She stood up and her face turned stern. "I want you to remember this. Nothing is your fault. Not what happened last summer. Not what's happening now. You're going to be in charge of the world someday, Ginger, but you're not in charge yet."

The doorbell rang. Evelyn set the music box on her dresser. They hurried downstairs.

"Look who's come to help us," Evelyn said when she opened the door.

Glory's mood wasn't good upon arrival, but the gift of the champagne glasses worked like magic. Her smile turned real as she held a glass to the window to admire its graceful shape. "These are actual crystal," she told Ginger, and then tapped the rim so Ginger could hear the ping that proved it. She carried the box to the door. "I guess this is good-bye." She and Evelyn touched cheeks.

Then Evelyn put her hand on Ginger's shoulder. "Do I get a hug?" When Ginger didn't move, she told her, "I'll be gone when you get home from school tomorrow."

Because Glory was right there watching, Ginger couldn't do what she wanted, which was to hug Evelyn so hard it might convince her to stay. She did manage to squeeze tight enough that Glory elbowed her and said, "Jeez Louise, Jack LaLanne. You trying to break her in half?" They all laughed at that. But as she laughed, Ginger felt her eyes welling with tears, so she excused herself, saying she had cramps, and ran home.

First one out of the house the next day, she noticed the top of the milk box on the front step was ajar. She swooped down and scooped up the music box before anyone noticed, and then tucked it in her jacket.

As her mother pulled out of the driveway, Ginger glanced back at the Clarke house and for a moment thought she saw a face peering out the living room window. But there was no one home. Evelyn's car was gone. The house was dark and abandoned. She quickly turned away.

CHAPTER TWENTY-FOUR

"No funeral." Ginger put down the letter. "That's what it says."

"Ridiculous." Mimi disappeared into the dining room, and Ginger heard her clanging around the liquor cabinet. "Every single bottle is empty," she reported when she came back. She opened the cabinets on either side of the sink. "Someone who loved Harvey Wallbangers has to have vodka somewhere." She moved to the cabinet opposite the stove and narrated its contents. "Matzo meal, tomato soup, Drano, Preparation H. Why are we paying attention to a letter written by a woman who was out of her mind?"

"What she means," Ginger translated for Callie, "is that Mom wasn't herself."

Callie nodded. "I know."

Mimi disappeared into the pantry and came back a moment later holding a Slinky. "Here we go." Her hands began to move, slightly up, slightly down, and the room fell silent to the *chin-ching, chin-ching* of the coils. "Right here." She stopped and the metal spiral settled, rearranging itself into two unequal halves. "Our inheritance. A Slinky and a letter from a lunatic."

"From someone suffering from dementia," Ginger corrected her.

"This was written before that." Callie pointed to the date at the top of the letter.

September, Ginger saw. September, two years ago. Two years ago, Julia was fifteen. She hadn't yet met Nick. She hadn't cut a day of school. Her worst transgression then? Texting at the table. Ginger turned to Callie. "Is that when you and Mom reconciled? Two years ago?"

Before Callie could respond, a door banged open upstairs. The barking dog was loose. They could hear him galumphing above and then careening down the stairs. His paws fought for traction on the wood floor in the foyer and then scrambling, he righted himself and burst into the kitchen. The dog, a springer spaniel, all white fur and liver-colored spots, ran slightly off kilter; his tail wagged so fast it looked comical. Of all people, he chose Mimi to explore first, skidding over and placing his head on her lap, gazing up at her with horsey brown eyes.

"Get that beast off me."

"Echo," Callie called. The dog turned toward her. "It's okay."

He wagged his way over to Ginger, who said, "He's beautiful."

"Thank you." Callie whistled softly and the dog came and lay down at her feet. "After the cremation, Mom wants a memorial service. Nothing big, just a short ceremony as we scatter her ashes. At the house or at sea. Whichever we want."

"What?" Mimi grabbed the letter. "How am I supposed to explain this to the boys? They know cremation is against our religion."

But Ginger was bothered by something else. "Why at the sea?" That seemed cruel. "And why at the house? We're selling the house. She knew that. She decided that. On her own."

Mimi narrowed her eyes. "Is that what this is about? Do you think you're getting the house? Because—don't shoot the messenger,

Callie—but Gingie's right. Mom took out a reverse mortgage behind our backs. Her house belongs to the bank."

"Oh. No. She didn't mean *this* house." Callie turned the paper over. There was more writing on the back. "She means the other house. The house on Martha's Vineyard."

Ginger shook off a chill. "That house isn't ours. We rented it one time. Why would she want us to scatter her ashes on someone else's property?"

"It's not someone else's. It's ours."

Echo's head was back on Mimi's lap, but this time she was too excited to notice. "We own a house on Martha's Vineyard?"

"We don't," Ginger told her. "That was a rental. One month. One time."

"I only know about now. We own it now." Callie looked surprised. "You didn't know?"

"Is it on the water?" Mimi was giddy. "I don't remember anything about that house. But if there's even a smudge of a water view, what a difference that will make in the sale."

"We don't own it," Ginger repeated. Just thinking about the house made her shiver. "Thank god."

"Really, Gingie? You're upset to find out you're part owner of a house on Martha's Vineyard? You could suck the joy out of a lollipop." Mimi left the room. More doors and cabinets opened and closed. A moment later she was back. "Coat closet." She held up a dusty bottle of Smirnoff. "Why didn't I think to look there first?" She glanced at Ginger. "Your face looks like chalk. Are you okay?"

"I'm fine," Ginger lied because no one wanted to hear the truth, that she felt unwell. Unwell and wobbly and out of body at the thought that Glory had wanted to own that house.

"How did she afford to buy it?" Mimi asked. Then she remembered. "Oh. The life insurance. Remember that? First time Mom ever gave Dad a compliment—when she found out there was life insurance. Of course by then, he was too dead to hear it."

It was odd how often this happened, Ginger and Mimi retaining different slivers of family memory. It was almost as if the recollections had been split down the middle and doled out: you get this, I get that, so no one would be privy to it all. Ginger glanced over and saw Callie washing her mug with great purpose.

Callie felt her staring. "I'm going back to the Vineyard in the morning." She began to dry the mug, rubbing so hard it looked to Ginger like she was trying to remove the glaze.

"Back?" Ginger asked. "Is that where you live? Is that where you've been?"

The mug was finally dry. Callie sat down. "If you want to come with me, you'll have to get here early. I'm leaving first thing."

"Bottoms up." Mimi poured herself a shot and drank it. "Tomorrow won't work." She poured another shot and offered it to Ginger, who declined. "Too much to organize. Plus, Gingie should really wait around here for a couple of days." She leaned toward Callie and whispered. "Has she told you about her *situation*?" She mouthed the next—*Julia*—and then stretched out her mouth in a grimace. "She can't go right—"

"I could go," Ginger cut her off. "If I wanted to. But I don't. I don't want anything to do with that house."

Callie nodded. "That's okay. Mom made provisions for what to do if the originals can't agree."

"What do you mean, *originals*?" Ginger asked.

"What do you mean, *provisions*?" Mimi asked louder.

"The originals is the four of us. I mean the three of us," Callie corrected herself. "Me, you, and Mimi. The provision is if we can't agree, we have to donate the house to the land bank. The lawyer has the papers. Donation isn't what Mom wanted. She didn't think you'd want it, either."

"Are you listening, Gingie?" Mimi said. "If we can't agree, we're supposed to donate the house to some bank. So pull it together. Your mother's dying wish is for us to go to the house one last time to toss her ashes. Are you going to ignore your mother's last wish?"

Satisfying her dead mother's wish was not something Ginger cared about. But she did care about Callie. Callie, who was sitting across from her now, finally, after all these years back home. Ginger did not want Callie to leave again. "You want us to come to the Vineyard to do this?"

"Yes."

"Okay. We will."

"What a relief." Callie smiled and there it was, the feature that had been hiding, the big smile of the cutest Tangle.

While Mimi shot back another drink, Ginger called the funeral home to change the arrangements.

The funeral home manager was like a petulant child. "Don't you want Mommy to be treated with respect?" But Ginger stood her ground.

"They'll keep her for tonight," she reported when she was done. "In the morning we'll have to stop over and sign a release. Then we have to go to the cremation society to sign papers there. The cremation society will arrange to pick her up." Her phone chimed—a text. She hurried out of the room, reading as she walked. It was Richard.

I'm home waiting for you. Where are you?

Richard had stopped texting months ago after he realized that even though Ginger knew Julia did not have a phone, she still got excited every time she got a text. Excited, and then disappointed. He must be worried to have broken his own rule.

She quickly typed back: *I'm with Mimi and Callie!! Be there soon.* She returned to the kitchen and told her sisters, "I have to go home. Do you want to come with me, Callie? Spend the night?"

"Thank you, but I'd prefer to stay here."

"You should come," Ginger said. "It'll be more comfortable." Then she saw it, the slight motion of her sister shrinking back as if to avoid being crushed. Was that what Ginger did? Make people feel in danger of getting crushed? "Never mind. If you want to stay here, that's fine. Mimi and I will swing by in the morning. We'll come early. We can figure out the rest after we all get a good night's sleep." She hurried off before she could make the mistake of pressing her sister again.

CHAPTER
TWENTY-FIVE

On the day the new people moved in, Glory made the announcement that she was going back to work as a personal shopper at her old store, the place where she worked when she was first married. "Part-time," she explained as she portioned out the Coca-Cola chicken: white meat for Solly and Ginger, thigh for Mimi, drumstick for Callie, wings for herself.

"Part-time is better than no-time," Solly said, going along. They rarely fought anymore because now Solly just went along.

"The man who runs the department, Mr. Freeze, says there's a good chance they'll need me full-time by the holidays." Glory crossed her fingers. "Let's hope." Solly crossed his fingers too, but Ginger didn't think he looked like he had any hope at all.

After dinner they moved to the den to watch TV. Tonight it was *Laugh-In*. As usual, minutes after the show began they all heard the gaspy snore that signaled Solly had fallen asleep in his chair. Glory got up and beckoned for Ginger to follow her to the kitchen.

"I've got news," she said when they were alone. "Great news. You're going to be a mother's helper after all."

For a second, Ginger allowed herself the thought that a miracle had occurred, that the new people were gone and Evelyn was back with Thomas, who needed more watching than ever.

Glory put an end to her reverie. "I mean for me. What do you say to being a mother's helper for your own mother? Is that a good idea or what?"

Ginger concentrated hard on putting feeling in her eyes, specifically the feeling that this was the best news ever in the history of the world. "It's a great idea!"

"You're my peach, you know that? Now, you're going to have to keep a very close eye on Mimi. I swear that girl lives to get into trouble. But she only does it for attention, so you have to try and ignore her, okay?"

Ginger had no clue how that was supposed to work, keeping a close eye on Mimi while also ignoring her, but she wanted to stay a peach, so she nodded as if the task was clear.

"Callie is another story. With her, you're going to have to be patient. She's going through a phase."

"What kind of phase?"

"A phase is a phase. What more can I say?" She sat down and motioned for Ginger to sit beside her. There were five chairs around the table now. Ginger didn't know where the sixth one went. It disappeared one night while she was sleeping, and in the morning when the sisters paused to figure out where to sit in the new configuration, Glory blurted out, "Enough with the assigned seats. Loosen up. Anything goes.

"We're in this together, kiddo," Glory told her now. "You and me." She laid her cool palm atop Ginger's hand, but only for a brief moment. Her tone changed to all business. "Okay, Pinocchio. We got to get our stories straight. If Callie doesn't feel like talking and someone asks what's wrong with her, what do you say?"

Ginger took a chance. "It's just a phase?" She could see that was wrong. "I mean, I'll say, 'Nothing.'" This time her mother cocked her head slightly, so Ginger knew she was on the right track. "I'll say, 'Nothing's wrong with Callie. What's wrong with you?'"

Glory laughed so hard it woke up Solly, who rushed into the kitchen to find out what was wrong.

"What do you mean *wrong*? Everything's great. It's a new day, Solly. Change is in the air." She stood up. "Now, if you two will excuse me, I've got a theater group meeting to get to." She made a slow exit and when she was gone, the room filled up with a familiar smell. Change might be in the air outside, but inside it was still onions.

Mr. Freeze's prediction came true. By early December, Glory was hired full-time. By the end of January she was named Personal Shopper of the Week, a title she held on to for months. This incarnation of her mother, the Glory who spent all day fussing over strangers, was a huge improvement over the previous one, the Glory who stayed in bed, or the one before that, the Glory who picked fights with Solly. Most nights now the family ate together in peace. Instead of Glory berating Solly for telling stories about his dull day, she regaled them with tales of *her* day: how she'd eased customers into sweater sets and miniskirts they swore they had no interest in trying on. How she won them over with compliments, easy to do, she explained, because she paid attention to what they said and what they wanted.

Audrey Hepburn would kill to have your bust, she'd tell one and to another she'd say, *You sure you're not Julie Christie's younger sister?* To win over her colleagues, she proposed department competitions, and when Mr. Freeze put her in charge of picking out prizes, she was careful not to win all the time. "Sometimes it's better to let someone else win," she confessed to her family over dinner. "People get very put out if I win three months in a row."

But win she did. A handbag or cardigan for herself, a hat or cashmere socks for Solly. The girls did well too: one or the other finding a surprise—either boxed or wrapped in tissue paper—on her pillow, a wool kilt, an argyle vest, a pair of white lace-up boots lined with fake fur.

There were occasional complaints. The other personal shoppers were cliquey. They didn't always appreciate her advice. They begrudged her talent for closing a sale. "What do they want me to do when someone requests me? Should I tell the customer no?"

For Ginger, listening to a little bellyaching was a small price to pay for the freedom that came with Glory's job. Now, between her mother's work and her theater group, she was hardly ever home.

But her father did not seem pleased. "Again you're going out? For one night, you can't stay in?"

"Wake up, Solly. The old days are over and good riddance to them. You know what Gloria Steinem says." Gloria Steinem had replaced Ivan the Director as the most quoted person at the table. "'American children suffer from too much mother and not enough father.'"

Ginger thought if her father had a choice, he'd vote to bring back fortune-cookie Ivan from the dead, rather than listen to fortune-cookie Gloria Steinem. But he didn't have a choice about this, or about anything. Far as she could tell, the amount of unhappiness in the house remained unchanged. It was just distributed differently. Glory bustled about practically beaming with delight while Solly napped or simmered in his chair.

The reason for his bad mood, according to her mother, was the toy business was in a slump. But since the slump seemed to have hit Solly's business alone, Ginger came up with another theory. The problem, as she saw it, was her father had stopped selling what he called "dumb toys." *Dumb toys,* she figured out, was code for any toy meant for a boy. Her father simply could no longer bear to be around Matchbox Superfast car sets, Power Play tabletop hockey, Moon Missile kits, or Skittle Pool. If her mother had been paying attention, if she was at least around, she might have pointed out these toys were not just for boys. Girls liked to play Skittle Pool and to build Moon Missiles. Look at Callie. She still liked lining up her stuffed animals and pretending to feed them, but she'd added the Matchbox cars she'd inherited from her brother into her make-believe games, giving her stuffed dogs lifts across the room to visit each other. Ginger now had to constantly leap up and kick the cars under the bed when she heard her father's footsteps in the hall. Callie remained oblivious but Ginger knew, if Solly saw those cars, he'd scoop them up and throw them out and no amount of moping would bring them back.

But Glory was not around much, and when she was around, she preferred the conversation to be about things like how few women looked good in harem pants.

Callie started wandering that spring. So while Solly was at work not selling dumb toys and Glory was convincing mothers-of-the-bride not to be afraid of wearing color, Ginger spent her afternoons walking the neighborhood searching for her sister. She quickly learned Callie's favorite hiding places: neighbors' yards, particularly those fenced-in for dogs.

Mrs. Budney was the first to complain. "Yesterday, your sister rang my bell," she told Ginger one afternoon. "Wanted to walk my dog. I told her, my dog died six months ago. Today she came back and asked if she could walk my cat. I don't have a cat. Is your mother home?"

"I'm sure she didn't mean to bother you," Ginger said. She didn't admit that hearing this was good news. At home, Callie had gone back to giving everyone the silent treatment. Bothering neighbors meant at least she was talking to *someone*. But Ginger knew enough to apologize. "I'm really sorry. My mom is at work, but if you want you can come back tonight."

She didn't expect Mrs. Budney to take her up on her suggestion but that night, right before dinner, she glanced out the window and saw their neighbor coming up the front walk.

"For god sake," Glory said after Ginger filled her in. "All right. What's done is done. Get that guilty look off your face. That's not going to help things."

Ginger tried her best to get the guilt off her face.

"That's worse. Try looking blank. Can you make yourself go blank?" Glory demonstrated a blank face, which seemed to make her soften. "It's going to be okay, kiddo. We can handle this." They were collaborators now. "You've got a little to learn, that's all. So watch and listen. Listening is key." She brushed the creases out of her camel-colored skirt and opened the door right as Mrs. Budney was about to ring the bell. This seemed to unnerve the woman, and Ginger wondered if that was the point.

"Mrs. Budney," Glory sang out. "It's been too long." And there it was, the change in her face, her frown lines gone and her internal light—it really was if she had a light inside—switched to bright. "Come on, come in. How've you been?"

"Very well, thank you." Mrs. Budney didn't ask how Glory was. Ginger had noticed this, that people no longer asked her mother how she was. "I don't want to be a bother."

"Bother? What bother? Come in. Have some tea."

"No, thank you. I'm here about your daughter." Her eyes flitted to Ginger. "The young one." She went on to recount how Callie asked to walk her dead dog and her nonexistent cat.

"Oh dear." Glory's frown line pulsed back and then vanished. "Sounds disturbing."

"It was." Mrs. Budney lifted her chin and Ginger watched as her mother, noticing the movement, echoed it, chin rising to the same angle.

"I know what loss feels like," Glory said. "And it doesn't matter what kind. Loss is loss. You loved that dog. You and your husband walked him all the time." Glory noticed a slight change in Mrs. Budney's face and corrected herself. "Of course, you were the main walker." Mrs. Budney nodded. Glory nodded too. She went on to ask how long they'd had the dog and how old the dog was when he died, and when Mrs. Budney described how the dog's arthritis affected his gait, Glory rubbed her own hand as if she could feel the dead dog's pain in her fingers. Before long, they were at the kitchen table sipping the tea the neighbor hadn't wanted, and by the end of the dazzling performance, Mrs. Budney was considering a proposal that they chip in and get a dog together.

"Would that be insane?" Glory asked, laughing at her own idea. "Two neighbors, sharing a dog? Joint custody? Obviously, Callie would take care of the dog after school—she really wants a dog—but during the day, I'm not home. That's why we can't get a dog." She paused. "Ever since last summer." She cast her eyes to her lap. "I work now."

"I'll take care of it during school," Mrs. Budney volunteered. "I don't work."

The next thing Ginger knew, the two women were making plans to go to Connecticut to visit a beagle breeder who Glory said got first place at the Westminster Dog Show two years in a row. "Ever watch that?" she asked Mrs. Budney. "I try and watch every year."

As soon as Mrs. Budney left, a trail of cookie crumbs marking her path to the door, Ginger asked when the dog show was on. "I've never seen it. Can I watch it with you sometime? Or is it on when I'm at school?"

"What are you talking about? How do I know when it's on? Anyway, I don't have time to discuss dogs. I've got to make a fruit basket for that Buddinski before she starts bad-mouthing your sister up and down the block." Fruit baskets were one of Glory's solutions for handling prickly people. She modeled them after baskets she saw in catalogues, but hers had lots of crumpled tissue paper on the bottom so they looked abundant, even when there were only a few pieces of fruit.

Mrs. Budney and Glory never did go on a trip to see the breeder in Connecticut or anywhere else. But Ginger did have to take Callie over to deliver a fruit basket and apologize, and when they returned from their mission, Ginger got a stern lecture about keeping Callie in sight after school from now on.

Keeping Callie in sight at all times was a challenge. She seemed allergic to staying inside. When Mimi offered to share the job of bodyguard, Ginger accepted. It made sense, four eyes being better than two. It didn't take long for her to realize what a mistake *that* was. Adding Mimi's eyes only made things worse. Mimi had all kinds of ideas that didn't work out well. There was the misguided walk to town, which ended with them all getting kicked out of Woolworth's for making a mess of the puzzle department, and after that, the failed attempt at keeping Callie happy by showing her how to climb the oak tree on the front lawn outside their house.

"You'll get a great view of the whole neighborhood," Mimi had promised her.

That it turned out Callie's ankle was strained, but not broken, made little difference to Glory. "You're letting me down, Gingie," she said, after calling her into her room. "I thought you were responsible. Was I wrong?"

"No." Ginger debated how much blame to give to Mimi. "It's just, Callie won't listen. She barely talks." She could read in her mother's face that this had been a mistake to say. Before she could take it back, Mimi ran in to join their discussion.

"I know what the problem is," she said. "The reason Callie doesn't like to talk is because of what she saw. Right?"

Glory cocked her head. "What did she see?"

"I don't know." Mimi looked like she was regretting what she said. "She saw what she shouldn't have seen." She started to back out of the room, but Glory blocked her.

"What are you talking about?"

Mimi surrendered. "It's about what she saw last summer. When she was with you and Charlie. At the hospital." She shrugged. "That's what people say."

"Which people?" Glory sounded more curious than angry.

"My teacher. The lady down the block. The mailman. Everyone. *Don't know what she saw, but whatever it was she shouldn't have seen it. What was it? What did she see?*"

The color seeped out of Glory's face. "I never should have taken her to that horror show of a hospital." She sat on her bed and seemed to deflate. "You can't imagine." Ginger and Mimi sat down on either side of her and leaned in to buck her up. "If I told you what happened, you wouldn't believe me."

"I would believe you," Ginger volunteered. "I always believe you," by which she meant, she always tried.

Her mother shook her head. "No. I'm not supposed to think about that." Her spine straightened and her eyes came back to life. "And neither are you. Next time someone asks you what happened, or they want to know what's wrong with your little sister, don't respond. Put your fingers in your ears if you have to." She plugged her ears. "You can even hum." She hummed and tried to look lighthearted. Then she dropped her arms, got up, took her brush out of the drawer, and started counting. "One, two, three, four . . ." She slowly ran the bristles through her hair. "You know the best way to get your hair shiny, right? Brush a hundred times. A hundred times a day."

The girls nodded.

"About that other thing, forget it. That's the best idea. Just forget it. I've already forgotten it. Remind me why you're here?"

"Sorry," Ginger said, and she and Mimi fled to the uneasy sanctuary of their room.

CHAPTER
TWENTY-SIX

Richard followed her up the stairs. "Her room's a mess," Ginger warned him. "I want to get it ready."

"For what? Julia's not coming home for the funeral."

"It's a scattering," she reminded him. "And we don't know that for sure. I didn't think Callie would ever come home and now here she is." They stopped in front of Julia's door. Ginger had shut the door months ago when she realized no matter how hard she tried, she couldn't help but look in every time she passed by.

Richard opened the door and peered into the chaos. "Her rug is soaked." He stepped inside, careful not to trample the minefield of clothes which lay on the floor exactly where Julia had dropped them. He shut the windows. "Why are these open?"

Ginger didn't share the reason, that the windows had been open since the day Julia left, since that night, when Ginger got out of bed at three, or maybe it was four in the morning and, without intention, walked into Julia's room, climbed into Julia's bed, lifted up the comforter, and pulled it over her head, breathing in the scent of her daughter's raspberry Herbal Essence shampoo. She didn't tell him then and she didn't tell him now, how the smell of the bedclothes had made her jump, how she'd pushed off the blanket and leapt out, how she'd raced to open those very windows, first one and then the other, taking in deep open-mouthed breaths, trying as hard as she could—and for reasons she still could not explain—to get her daughter's smell *out* of her nose.

That night, when Richard woke up, he thought it was the sound of water filling the bathtub that disturbed his sleep, not the sound of windows opening and of Julia's track medals, hanging on ribbons from curtain rods, clanging together like broken glass.

When he found Ginger that night, standing in the bathtub filled with water, still wearing her robe, he'd asked if she was all right. The question seemed so ridiculous, she didn't bother answering. Wasn't it clear she was not all right? He'd struggled for a moment, trying to figure out what was called for. Then he rolled up his pajama bottoms, stepped into the tub, and embraced her. That was Richard. In the end, he always did the right thing. He got in the tub and embraced her. But he rolled up his pajama bottoms first. As far as she could tell, in the weeks that followed Julia's departure, he hadn't lost a moment's sleep.

Ginger brought in a stack of bath towels from the linen cabinet and they got to work, laying the towels on the soaking carpet. Her glance flicked to the medals still hanging from the curtain rod, to the collage on the wall beside the bed—superhero women in poses of power—to the clock radio that flashed the wrong time—collateral damage from a recent storm—and to the photograph of Julia on her desk. *She looks so happy,* Ginger thought, and then, with a start, realized who'd taken that picture, that the rapturous smile on her daughter's face was there because she was looking at Nick.

Richard spread out the last of the towels, and when he was done he put his hand on top of hers. Together, they pressed down, tamping hard to absorb the moisture. When the towels were soaked, they gathered them up and dumped them in the tub. Then they went to their room and undressed without speaking. Silently slipping under the blanket, they curled toward each other, tender and gentle, two twisted spoons, moving closer at the same moment to make love.

In the morning there was the usual moment of confusion, followed by dread. Something happened. What? She opened her eyes and took inventory. Julia was gone. Glory was dead. Callie was back. Someone was breathing into her neck. Richard.

"You okay?" He pulled her closer. She nodded and he slipped out of bed.

The day proceeded, dreamlike. She made the necessary calls: first to her friend, Cheryl, who agreed to sub for her; then to the principal to let him know her mother had died and she needed time off.

Richard made breakfast, eggs perfectly poached. While they ate, he offered to stay with her; he could get someone to cover for him at work. Ginger told him no. "You should go in. You might want to save your favors in case you want to come for the scattering."

"Of course I'm going to come."

Their good-bye was tender, but promised nothing.

When Ginger and Mimi got to Glory's house to pick up Callie, they found she'd already left. A note on the kitchen table told them she was taking the noon ferry out of Woods Hole. Another note gave them her cell number and the address of the Vineyard house, *in case they forgot.*

Mimi was mad. "It's not right. She swoops in, tells us what to do, and then leaves the mess for us to clean up." She tried Callie's cell, to vent. When Callie didn't answer, Ginger felt relieved. Having Mimi yell at Callie would not make anything better.

"We don't have that much to do," Ginger said. "The main thing is we'll be together for the scattering. That's what's important, right? The three of us together?"

"What's important is selling the house. I googled last night. Real estate there is crazy. I wish I could remember more about the place. Distance from water is everything." She left serial messages on Callie's voice mail. *How far is the house from water? Does it have a deck or porch? Is there a view from the roof?* But Callie did not pick up.

At the bank, Mimi signed to gain entry to Glory's safety deposit box without mentioning her mother had died. "Easier this way," she whispered to Ginger, who'd had no clue Mimi had become cosigner for Glory's accounts right before the move to the Meadows. Now they huddled in a small privacy booth and examined the loot: six silver Kennedy half dollars in a beaded change purse. The financial news didn't improve when they learned the balance of the savings account. "Fifty dollars and change," Mimi muttered as she drove to the Cremation Society.

Ginger concentrated on ignoring both Mimi's disappointment in Glory's bankbook and her obsession with the prospect of selling their surprise inheritance home. She knew anything she said might start Mimi on her usual tirade about the impossibly high cost of private school for three kids, or the exorbitant price of sleepaway camp these days, or the fast-approaching combined total of three college tuitions. By now Ginger knew, almost to the dollar, the outrageous cost of upkeep on their pool, the fees at their tennis club, the yearly total of the not-so-secret support she and Neil gave to multiple Popkins in various degrees of need.

She stayed silent as they drove, letting the questions Mimi shouted into Callie's voice mail turn into a hum. *Hummm*—Is the road paved or is it dirt? *Hummm*—Are the toilets regular or compost? *Hummm*—Are the homes of the nearest neighbors within view?

At the Cremation Society, Ginger signed the authorization form while Mimi grumbled her way through the urn catalogue. After much deliberation she settled on a faux clamshell that the cremation staffer, worn down by Mimi's inquiries as to durability versus dissolvability, concurred was the most perfect of all of the urns, the definite best choice for a scattering at sea. The same staffer then broke the news that it would take three days for the filled urn to be returned to them. When Mimi balked, the woman interrupted her. "Okay. Okay. We'll aim for two."

At the end of the day, when Mimi wondered aloud whether they should both wait for the urn or whether one of them should go ahead to join Callie, Ginger quickly volunteered to go. Driving alone to Woods Hole seemed a far better choice than spending four hours in a car with a put-upon Mimi.

"It makes sense for me to go ahead," Ginger told her, and Mimi seemed happy to agree.

The next day, when Ginger reached the ferry terminal, she found a chaotic scene. One of the ferry slips was closed for construction. Two ferries had been canceled due to mechanical problems, and the next boat due in had been delayed by fog. Because now there wouldn't be room for all the cars that had reservations, Ginger followed directions and parked at a satellite lot and then called Callie to let her know she was going on the boat as a walk-on. This time Callie picked up her phone and promised to meet her on the other side.

It was only as Ginger reached the gangplank that she realized how much she did not want to go on board. She did not like to travel over water and she did not want to step on the sandy shore on the other side. But, of course, she got on anyway because that's what was called for and Ginger always did what was called for.

The boat was crowded and by the time she boarded, there were no more seats. She found a space against a wall in the lower cabin and turned away from the window so she wouldn't see the water. As the ferry began its slow departure from the dock, her knees buckled slightly. She pinched her ear hard so she wouldn't faint.

"Poor thing." The woman standing next to her looked concerned. "The color just drained from your face. You want a Dramamine? I can ask the purser if he's got a Dramamine. Or you can try going up a deck. Higher you go, better you'll feel."

Ginger thanked her and headed for the stairs. But the next deck had the snack bar and reeked of soggy hamburger rolls and scorched soup. The sea got choppy and the snack bar staff began to put away anything that could slide, but passengers at the tables still popped open Tupperware containers filled with pungent food from home. If Ginger stood there, she would surely get sick. She hurried to a narrow stairway leading to the upper deck. She didn't realize till she reached the top step that this deck was outside, everywhere open to the sea.

The wind howled, sending her hair snapping over her face. Someone called, "Mom?"

Sweeping her hair away out of her eyes, Ginger whipped around and saw a girl. Tall, gangly, long hair, same age as Julia, same kind of T-shirt, cutoffs, worn-out sneakers. But she wasn't Julia. Behind the girl, a woman, her mother, replied to her call with a sharp, "What?"

"Never mind," the girl said, and they both disappeared down the stairs.

It happened several times a week now, Ginger saw Julia, and then realized she was wrong. Sometimes these girls looked like Julia but just as often they didn't. Apparently looking like Julia wasn't necessary. As long as there was some tiny similarity, her brain would make the leap. So if, out of the corner of her eye, she saw a girl with hair that was long and wavy but *not* dark red, she'd still think *Julia*, and if the girl had dark red hair cut into a matronly bob, *Julia*. Recently, a tall girl in a puffy orange vest turned around and Ginger thought, *Julia*, until she realized this Julia was a man.

The first few times it happened she would calm herself by listing the differences—too tall, thin hair, wrong color eyes, brown skin—but that reminded her of how Glory used to sort people, *heart-shaped face, fairy-broom eyelashes, Shirley Temple dimples*, so she stopped. The habit was hard to break. *Too many freckles,* she thought now.

As the wind whipped up, Ginger slipped on the rain slicker she'd brought along in case the weather turned foul. She pulled the hood up over her head, but a strong gust, like a practical joker, pulled it back down. Around her, the few remaining passengers, tired of having their bodies battered by the sudden gale, retreated indoors. Crab-like, she moved, one hand over the other, down the narrow steps.

Back inside, the flat-screen TVs on opposite walls played on. Café smells hung heavy in the air. Greasy fries, a Tupperware of curry, the burnt clam bits at the bottom of the chowder pot. Ginger found the bathroom and got sick as quietly as she could. When she was finished cleaning her face, she cleaned the sink and then wiped the mirror with a paper towel because she'd noticed spots that might or might not have been from her. She returned to her place at the wall as the chains clanged, the ropes got tossed, the boat bumped into the dock.

Still feeling unsteady, she slowly rolled her bag down the ramp, and blinked in the sudden and surprising sun. There they were, Callie and Echo standing against the primary colors of a perfect Vineyard day.

"What a trip," she reported. "Terrible traffic to Woods Hole. Two ferries were canceled. The water was so choppy they shut down the snack bar."

"It's sunny here," Callie said. "I'm parked a few blocks away." Echo tugged at his leash. "Okay," Callie told him. "Let's go." She set off at a slow jog. Ginger, hurrying alongside, struggled to keep up as she pulled her luggage along behind her. When they got to the car, Echo jumped into the front seat, but Callie made a quick gesture so he moved to the back.

Minutes later they were out of town, tourist shops replaced by a landscape of rolling hills and stone walls.

"I need to make a quick stop." The car lurched as Callie turned down a dirt road.

Ginger caught a glimpse of a sign, the word "Parking," carved into wood, letters painted red. Her stomach dipped. "Here?"

Callie nodded as she pulled into a spot and turned off the car. "Echo can't come with me. Dogs aren't allowed on Charlie's beach. Will you stay with him?"

Charlie's beach. "Where are you going?"

Callie got out, slammed the door, and leaned through the open window. "It's not far to the shortcut. I'm a fast runner."

"Shortcut to where?"

Callie commanded Echo to lie down and then motioned for him to stay and the dog obeyed. "I won't be long."

"Wait," Ginger called out, but her sister had taken off at a sprint and was gone. She sat for a moment, unsure of what to do.

When her phone rang, she quickly checked to see who it was. Richard. "Hey—everything all right?"

The line was thick with static. She had to strain to listen as Richard explained that Julia had just called his cell.

"She's okay," he quickly added. "Anne-Marie tracked her down and told her about Glory. She's sad but she's okay."

Ginger let out a soft noise. Of course this was good news. It was a relief to know Julia was okay. That was the important part. Not that it was her father who she'd chosen to call. "Did she cry? Is she coming for the scattering?"

"Didn't cry. Isn't coming."

"Okay." Ginger took this in. "What did she say when you told her Callie was here?"

"I didn't."

"Why not? You should have. You need to. She'll come home if she knows Callie's here. I'm sure of it. You have to call her back and tell her."

"Gingie, no. She doesn't want me to call back. She told me she borrowed some random person's phone. Look, this is hard for both of us. But you should know, Julia told me she's grateful we sent her the message through Nick's mom. We're doing the right thing."

How Ginger had come to be surrounded by so many people who thought there *was* a right thing, she had no idea. Something nagged at her. "Then why did she call? Did something happen? Is she sick? She's not pregnant, is she?"

Richard groaned into the phone. "She called because she's worried"—the phone started to break up—"you."

"Me? What about me?"

"She's worried about *you*. She called to make sure you're okay." The line went dead.

Ginger put down her phone. Echo sprung up and nuzzled her neck. She turned and pet the dog, and as she did she said out loud, "I have to find a way to make this right. For Julia and for me."

CHAPTER
TWENTY-SEVEN

By the time they approached the second anniversary of the accident—
this would be the last year Ginger kept track of time *that* way—Glory
was working six days a week and had a loyal customer base of well-
heeled women who refused to let any other personal shopper help them.
This left Solly, his work hours shrinking, to field the calls from school.
Callie's wandering had taken a turn for the worse when she made the
discovery that the front door of her school was open and unattended all
day long. This meant she could leave whenever she liked.

Through a combination of geography and luck, the first time it
happened, Ginger caught her. The geography was that Callie's school
was at one end of the same long block as Ginger's. The luck was that
Ginger was in Earth Science, where gazing out the window was normal,
when she saw her sister Callie skipping by.

Feigning a bathroom emergency, Ginger left through the rear classroom door and kept going, right out the side exit of the building. She
caught up with her sister a block away. When she explained to Callie

that she had to stay in school all day like everyone else, her sister didn't protest, and when she returned her to her third-grade classroom, her teacher seemed relieved. As for Earth Science, Mr. Michaels, droning on about *the cooling of magma* when she walked out of his class, had only progressed to droning on about *the solidification of magma* when she returned, and his granite face showed no sign that he found her extended bathroom break concerning.

Both assessments, however—that the third-grade teacher was relieved and that Mr. Michaels hadn't noticed she was missing for most of his class—were wrong. Mr. Michaels was livid, and beneath the third-grade teacher's facade of relief was rage.

Solly was mad as well. "Two principals I got to see because Callie went to get fresh air?"

To help smooth things over with the principals, Glory brought each one an extra-large fruit basket, with cherries and chocolate bars hidden among the apples and pears. It seemed to do the trick. But the next time they got called for Callie leaving in the middle of the day, the mandatory meeting was with Miss Mackeral, a guidance counselor who did not succumb to Glory's charms.

"School's a lunatic asylum," Glory said when they got home. "That Miss Mackeral looks like a prison guard. That's where she should work. Jail."

"The school *is* jail," Solly piped up. "The problem is they don't give Callie what's interesting to do. No wonder she wants to fly the coop. If I went there, I'd fly the coop too."

"You know what, Solly? You're right." Glory unbuttoned her most recent prize, a kelly-green raincoat. "Actions speak louder than words. I don't know why I didn't think of it sooner."

"Think of what?" He sounded a little alarmed.

"A fresh start. That's all she needs. A new school. You know, I read you can enroll your child in any public school you want, long as you pay tuition. Which we can, now that I'm working."

"I don't know. How much is tuition?"

Glory didn't answer. She was busy flipping through the yellow pages, writing down the names and numbers of all the elementary schools in the surrounding towns. "One of these schools is going to be a lucky duck, getting Callie as a student in the fall."

After several nights at the kitchen table with a calculator, Solly worked out that in order to pay tuition he would need to supplement their income, so he started taking on odd jobs on the weekends. Now they never knew where he might pop up. One day he was across the street, mowing a lawn. Another day, there he was, bulbous shoes balancing on the rungs of a ladder as he cleaned out muck from the gutter of a house around the block. One Sunday, on a trip to the mall, Glory pulled into an Exxon station, called to the attendant to check her oil, and there he was, Solly sticking his head next to her window saying, "What? No hello?" Now, along with the smell of onions, her father carried with him the faint odor of gasoline.

It was the doctor who suggested her father get a hobby to unwind in his spare time, but the one Solly picked wasn't like the projects other fathers did. It wasn't replacing rotted fence pickets or battling the crawl of ivy that kept displacing the mortar from the brick.

Solly's project revealed itself first with a primitive sketch on a napkin, and shortly after that, with a delivery of rocks deposited in the driveway. After that he began, one stone at a time, building a wall along the front perimeter of their small patch of lawn. Ginger fretted about her mother's reaction, but when Glory came home from work and saw what he'd started, all she did was cross her arms and say, "Why so piddly, Solly? Why not bigger rocks?" from which Ginger deduced the project had already been approved.

Once the base was finished and work on the upper wall began, Ginger wondered if her mother actually saw the wall at all, because surely if she did, she would have made him stop. Instead she let him go on and so, legs astride the metal folding chair he'd dragged to the sidewalk, Solly continued cementing stones, one atop the other, into narrow jagged peaks that from a distance looked like piles of dripping sand.

It was summer, two years after the accident, when Solly called everyone into the den to watch the evening news. Ginger was the only one who came. She made herself comfortable on the floor, leaning against her father's chair as Walter Cronkite spoke to the nation.

"Good evening. President Nixon will announce his resignation tonight and Vice President Ford will become the nation's thirty-eighth president tomorrow."

"Get your mother."

Ginger found her mother in bed, journal on lap, pen in her mouth, thinking.

"Mom is busy," Ginger reported after Glory shooed her away. "She'll come soon."

Solly nodded. Although Ginger had never heard him say a single nice word about the president, it was clear from his pallor this resignation was a big deal. She lay on her stomach, head resting in the V of her hands, and watched as Dan Rather continued the report: "According to his staff, unless the president has a sudden change of head and heart—"

"Tell your mother she has to come now," Solly said.

Her mother was on the phone, but Ginger pressed her father's case. "He said you *have* to come. The president is resigning." Glory cupped her free ear, which Ginger understood meant, *Stop interrupting and leave me alone.*

"She'll be here in a minute," Ginger lied. She returned to her position on the floor and noted how grim Dan Rather looked as he shared the news.

"On a Potomac cruise aboard the yacht *Sequoia*, his daughters urged him not to do it. He agreed to reconsider."

"Will he?" Ginger liked the idea of a president who listened to his daughters.

"As of this hour," Dan Rather answered her, "he has not changed his mind."

Suddenly, this was all Ginger wanted, for the president of the United States to change his mind because of his daughters. "Do you think he might change his mind?"

Her father grunted a reply, which Ginger understood meant, *Shh. I'm trying to hear.*

"Last night," Dan Rather continued, "at a family dinner upstairs in the White House, some of the family was in tears."

This was almost impossible to imagine, the family of the president of the United States in tears. "Does he mean watery eyes or actual tears going down their cheeks?" This time when her father didn't answer, she turned around. She noticed right away that his eyes were unfocused, but it took several moments for her brain to sort out the rest.

As the medics lifted Solly's body onto the stretcher, Richard Nixon declared, "I have never been a quitter." As they carried Solly out of the den, Richard Nixon said, "In passing this office to the vice president, I do so with a profound sense of the weight of responsibility that will fall on his shoulders tomorrow."

"He fainted. That's all," Glory insisted and the president said, "As he assumes that responsibility, he will deserve the help and the support of all of us."

When the medics finally got her to understand her husband was dead, Glory's knees buckled. They offered to take her to the hospital but she declined, so they helped her to the couch.

There was much clattering—first the gurney's wheels got stuck on the molding in the threshold of the den, and after that it banged into the wall in the narrow front hall—but finally, Solly Tangle's corpse left the house.

Without being asked, Ginger went to the kitchen and filled a bowl with ice water. She came back and placed a cool washcloth on her mother's pale forehead. "Heal the wounds," Nixon said as Glory stood up, letting the washcloth fall to the floor. "Put the bitterness behind us," he beseeched the American people, as she headed for the stairs. "Rediscover those shared ideals," the president implored, as Mimi and Callie called from the kitchen, where they'd been hiding, "Is it safe to come out?"

"Yes," Ginger told them. They sat together, three sisters huddled close, crying freely, as Richard Nixon promised the return of their strength and their unity as a great and free people.

Later that night Ginger considered calling Evelyn because, surely, Evelyn would want to know. But though Evelyn had promised she'd write, she never did. And Ginger, who had no idea how to go about looking for someone, knew better than to ask.

At the funeral she met many people she'd never heard of and a few she rarely saw. From her father's side there was Clara, his sister who lived in Chicago. Clara was the one who sent dollar bills in birthday cards every year, the one they had to call to say thank you, which was awkward. There were also the cousins who lived on Long Island who felt so terrible they never visited that Ginger ended up comforting *them*. From her mother's side there was only one person, Glory's Aunt Ida, a tall, thin woman who sat by herself for the entire funeral with a look of such terror on her face, no one came near her.

By the time they got home from the cemetery, one more chair had been removed from the kitchen table, though by whom Ginger had no idea.

Glory did not wallow. At the end of her first week as a widow she went back to work. The sisters did their part, trying not to look too sad in front of her, and also not to look too happy. But at night, when they were alone in their room, one or the other and sometimes all three would slide under the covers, to muffle the sound of their sorrow.

In September, Glory surprised them by announcing Callie was not changing schools after all. This came after a long meeting with Miss Mackeral, the guidance counselor prison guard who Glory succeeded in turning into an ally. Ginger suspected this had something to do with her father's death. The latest sad event seemed to change how Callie was seen, from being a problem child to being a girl in need of rescue. Accommodations were made, a kind teacher selected, class friendships socially engineered. None of it worked. Callie continued to leave school in the middle of the day two or three times a week.

By January of that year, Ginger, Callie's self-appointed search and rescuer, was labeled a chronic cutter. The punishment was afternoon detention. This presented a problem. If Ginger wasn't home after school to distract her, Callie would roam the neighborhood, no matter the weather. Ginger solved the problem once she realized no one got detention for staying home sick. The first few times she faked it, but after a while her stomach cramps felt real.

Glory had no idea Ginger was playing sick, but she did notice she wasn't eating much and cautioned her to watch it. "Gaunt cheeks are not becoming on a long face."

Soon after that, Mimi joined in, the two sisters working out a schedule of alternating sick days so that one of them could always be on watch for Callie. It didn't take long for Miss Mackeral to figure out their scheme. The consequences were swift.

"You heard me." Glory paced back and forth in the small den. "You're over the limit on absences. You have to repeat the year. All of you." The girls stared into their laps. "Warden Mackeral says you're bad for each other. Says I should split you up. I asked her which one of you she wants to adopt, but she wasn't amused. As if one girl in trouble wasn't enough. Now I got an epidemic on my hands." She went on to rail about Mr. Freeze, who'd blown his top when she told him she had to miss work for another school meeting. Ginger wasn't sure which problem was upsetting her more.

Her mother's solution was to ask Mr. Freeze if she could go back to working part-time. But her former champion was no longer interested in making accommodations for her chaotic home life. These were tough days, he told her. Newark stores were shutting down. Widow or no widow, one troublemaker at home or three, part-time was not an option. And if she continued to miss work, full-time would be at risk too.

Minders were hired to watch the girls after school, but none of the women could manage to keep up with Callie's expert disappearing acts. And so the next incarnation of Glory Tangle arrived: a woman in charge. With no one to consult or convince, she made swift plans.

"Your father was right. They don't give Callie enough to do. That's why she walks out of school all the time. She likes being outside better, and they haven't come up with a single reason for her to stay in. Who can blame her? But I found a place. A very good place." And with that, Callie was packed up and shipped off to a boarding school in Massachusetts that specialized in young children with theatrical talent.

Ginger wrote Callie a letter the day she left, but Glory put the kibosh on mailing it, quoting from an information packet she'd received from the school. "Families aren't supposed to send letters before a student is acclimated," she explained. "Letters from home to unsettled students can make homesickness worse. They say to wait—to let Callie write us first."

So Ginger waited. But just like with Evelyn, no letter arrived.

When parents' weekend at the boarding school came around, Glory explained that Callie wasn't ready to see her sisters. "Too hard on her. Besides, you know how it is when the three of you get together. It's like a tornado. Someone always gets hurt. So you concentrate on you, and I'll concentrate on her. I'm counting on you, Gingie," she added later, when they were alone. "I don't think I can bear it if one more thing goes wrong. Pinky swear, nothing more will." Ginger pinky swore and Glory left and nothing went the slightest bit amiss.

When Glory came back from parents' weekend out of sorts, Ginger asked if she'd done something wrong. Her mother shook her head so Ginger braved another question. "Did Callie?"

"Listen to yourself. Isn't a person allowed to be down in the dumps? I mean, with all I've been through."

Any mention of Callie seemed to bring the same response. The message was clear: the only way to keep their mother out of the dumps was not to mention Callie at all.

Ever the trouper, Glory bounced back. She kept her job, but Mr. Freeze lost his. Her new manager liked the idea of part-time so Glory cut back her hours. When her theater group got the opportunity to go on tour, she managed to convince her new boss that it would enhance her value to her clients if she took time off to work as an actress. Every time she left to go on tour, she made Ginger pinky swear nothing would go wrong at home. And nothing ever did.

For a while, Ginger and Mimi continued to talk about Callie when they were alone, wondering what her school was like, if she had any friends, if she thought about them as much as they thought about her. But one day Glory overheard them.

"Your sister is fine. This endless harping about her has to stop. Understand? Not another bird."

"Another *word*?" Ginger asked.

Glory's hands went to her temples. "I really don't think I can stand this anymore."

It had been challenging when Ginger and Mimi had to learn not to mention Charlie in front of their mother, but their years of practice paid off now. With Callie's absence, the silence came easier. Ginger had an advantage. College was coming into sight. She focused hard on making her time at home as painless as possible. Everything was going along fine until Mimi asked when Callie was coming back for Christmas break.

Glory answered in a voice both calm and threatening. "I'll say this once and never again. In acting school they go on trips during breaks. Right now, they're in Canada cheering up people in nursing homes. I'm done with questions. I mean it. One more and, swear to god, I'll lose my mind for good."

So it was that by the time Ginger left for college, she had completely absorbed the idea of a new composition of her family, this time with Callie erased.

Her first night of freshman year, Ginger and her roommate Randee stayed up until dawn telling each other the stories of their lives. Randee, a perky blonde from upstate New York, started them off with a benign question. "How many brothers and sisters?"

Without missing a beat, Ginger looked her in the eye and answered, "One. My sister, Mimi. That's it. Just one." The lie slipped out easily, and Ginger was happy to let it become true.

PART TWO
FROM NOW ON

CHAPTER TWENTY-EIGHT

Echo's anxious breath filled the car as he paced the narrow backseat. When his whining increased to a high-pitched frantic bark, Ginger got out. She needed air. The dog immediately settled. A moment later he was up again, poking his head through the open window, barking.

."Fine," Ginger told him. "I'll look for her. But you can't come. Callie said you're not allowed on Charlie's beach." She shook off a chill. "I'm not going on the sand. I'm just going as far as the path." Her tone seemed to satisfy him. He thumped down on the seat, head on paws.

"I can't believe I just had a conversation with a dog," Ginger said to no one.

As she walked to the path, Echo tracked her movement with his eyes.

• • •

The path to the beach was made of thin slats of wood, which the wind had dusted with sand, like a sprinkling of sugar. Head down, Ginger hurried. The path climbed in a gentle grade and at the highest point, when the wood slats stopped, she stopped too. Ahead of her, the sand snaked through high grass. Beyond the grass it spread out like a threat.

Her gaze skipped to the sea where, amid ribbons of teal, navy, and aquamarine, she could make out the bobbing heads of children in the surf. Their bellies slapped hard on boogie boards while their parents stood guard at the shoreline with watchful eyes, as if they could stop the waves with love. She scanned the water—no one was in trouble—and looked toward the cliffs.

Had it been a trick of memory? Were the giant rocks that loomed so large, the red-tinted fortress past which she and Mimi so stubbornly refused to go, nothing more than this: a few narrow towers of compacted earth with enough space between them for a car to drive through? Was Callie there now, behind this disappointment of a cliff?

A noise caught her attention. Was it a dog? Was it Echo barking? No. That was impossible. There was no way she could hear him all the way here, not with the noise of the ocean and the wind. She pictured him anyway, Echo barking himself into a frenzy, jumping out of the car to look for her, landing wrong, whimpering and hurt. She turned around and hurried back.

Callie was sitting in the car waiting, her hands on the wheel.

"Were you at the cliffs?" Ginger asked as she got in. "The cliffs are so small. I remember them as huge."

"They *were* huge. There's been erosion." Callie started the engine. "I didn't go that way. I went in the other direction."

"What were you looking for?"

Callie swiveled around to check behind her. "Didn't find it. But I got in a run. I needed a run." She slowly backed out and Ginger saw a flicker of a look she recognized, the lost look she knew from the faces of the children who didn't fare well.

She wanted to reach out and touch her sister, wanted to tell her it was okay to feel sad, that feeling sad when your mother dies is normal. She wanted to say, even a happy reunion with a sister could feel strange if the sisters hadn't seen each other for years. But she didn't say any of it because she got it. This thing she did, her empathy and concern, turned out to have the unfortunate consequence of driving people away.

"It's not far to the house," Callie said as she pulled out of the lot. Minutes later, she turned down a rutted lane. The car bucked into a narrow gulley and then rocked onto steadier ground. Gnarly bushes scraped against the doors as if in protest. Echo nuzzled Callie's neck and she made another turn. Tires crunched on crushed shells and pea gravel. Callie pulled into a clearing and parked.

"The house is up that path." She pulled Ginger's bag out of the trunk. "You can take either of the upstairs bedrooms. We can go to the market and get food later. You might want to clear out the shed for the boys. Mimi left a message that they're coming for the scattering. They can sleep in the shed if you clear everything out. Julia can stay there too, if you want. If she comes. You don't have to do it today."

Ginger nodded. "Okay."

"Everything that's in the shed can go to the dump. I mean the Dumptique," Callie corrected herself.

"Dumptique?" Ginger repeated.

Callie got back in her car. Echo jumped into the front seat. "I'll see you soon."

"Where are you going? Let me come with you."

But it was too late. The windows rolled up with driver and dog both sealed inside, and Callie drove away.

The house she didn't want to remember was nothing grand. Just a gray shingled Cape with blue trim and a large screened-in porch that jutted out from the front like an afterthought. As she walked up the path, a tendril poked through a fence picket, tickling her ankle. Why hadn't she thought to wear socks? She grabbed a granite post for balance and checked to see what kind of plant had touched her. Three things were guaranteed to give Ginger a rash: Glory, Mimi, and poison ivy. Glory was gone, Mimi wasn't here, and poison ivy should have been easy to avoid. She'd taught hundreds of students to memorize the warning: "leaves of three, let it be." How had she forgotten to be vigilant?

She counted the leaves on the vine next to her foot. Four. Good. Then she noticed something beneath the tangled tendrils. What? She looked closer and saw a flat stone, half-covered by vegetation. She pushed the vine away with the toe of her shoe and saw words sandblasted on top. The rock confirmed ownership. This was "The Tangle House."

A hummingbird, chest plump and iridescent, hovered, dive-bombed her face, and flew off. She continued past a sad-sack garden: blue hydrangeas, branches dipping down; lady's slippers, petals shivering in the breeze; pale-pink tea roses spilling through slats of a broken trellis. Ginger was no gardener, but she knew these flowers because they were identical to the ones Glory planted at home. The New Jersey flower bed had been put in all at once in a frenzy of planting not long after Solly died. At the time, Ginger thought it was meant to be a memorial to her father, and in a way it was a perfect stand-in for him. Always a disappointment, the hydrangeas bloomed a purple Glory complained reminded her of rotting plums, and the roses, sweetheart pink when she put them in, turned, overnight, to the rubbery tint of pencil erasers. As for the lady's slippers, Glory had to order new ones every year from a specialty farm in Vermont because no matter how carefully she tended them, they didn't last a week.

It was odd how Glory persevered in her garden, giving it attention she gave to no other species in her life. Inside the house, they could go without breakfast with no consequence, and when the occasional houseplant Solly gave her—pass-along Christmas gifts he got from suppliers—died of neglect, Glory could be spotted smiling as she smacked the pots with her palm to empty out the last of the dried-out dirt. But the front garden was tended with care. Over time a treasure trove of Pinky balls accumulated beneath the wilted leaves of the sickly plants, Spaldeens gone astray during street games and abandoned because even the neighborhood bullies knew better than to tread on Glory Tangle's garden.

The front door clacked against the warped wood frame. Was this why Glory got irritated with how their doors closed at home? *They slam shut like a vault,* she'd complain to the handyman. Phoosht, *every time, like I live in a jail.*

As Ginger made her way through the house, dim memories flickered back to life. The warty rooms, which Glory explained were added year by year, the master bedroom added to the back, a porch tacked on to the front. In the living room, there was the painted captain's sea chest, and in the dining room, the cabinet with the collection of blue glass bottles, no two alike.

The kitchen, she noted, was clutter-free. No stacks of newspapers, magazines, restaurant menus, mail; no baskets of bills or bowls of overripe fruit. Everything had a place. She opened the refrigerator and saw a single glass bottle of milk, a white porcelain bowl with three blue-speckled eggs, a stick of butter still in its foil wrapper, a fat-free yogurt, two green apples. A large glass canister next to the sink was filled with tea leaves. This was where Callie lived.

The two bedrooms on the second floor were smaller than Ginger remembered. But there was the porthole window, and there, the skylight, and there, of all things, the spindle chair. She laid her suitcase on the floor next to the bed near the window in the room she'd briefly shared with Mimi and began to unpack into the balky bottom drawer. The knob came off in her hand. A door opened downstairs.

"Gingie? Callie?"

She hurried down and found Mimi in the hall, an oversized suitcase at her side.

"Did you know the phone doesn't work?" Mimi asked. "And my text didn't go through."

"How did you get here?"

"I know. Amazing, right? That awful woman from the Cremation Society called right after you left. They got Glory done faster than they expected. Richard convinced me to fly. What a little plane. He's worried about you," she added. "Being alone."

"I'm not alone. I'm with Callie."

"Practically the same thing. Where is she?"

"Out. Looking for something. She wouldn't say what."

Mimi didn't appear concerned. "Come look." She headed to the dining room, holding a shopping bag in her arms. "Come see Mom." She lifted out the urn. "It's hideous, I know. Good thing Mom is too dead to see it." She placed the urn in the middle of the long oak table. "There. Centerpiece of attention. Now, listen." Change of tone, change of subject. "We need to be on the same page here. Callie has to move near us. I mean, god, she has three nephews and a niece she's never met." She turned to the sound of car wheels on pea gravel. "You have to back me up." Mimi swiveled and greeted Callie with a cheerful, "Here I am!"

• • •

The sisters convened in the living room, three chairs set in a triangle of discomfort; Echo, last one down, put his head across the top of Callie's feet.

Mimi pulled out a folder from her oversized purse. "Here's the good news."

"What are we doing?" Callie asked.

"I got us a realtor. Krissy. She's in your singing group, Cal. She's coming for a walk-through in the morning." Mimi surveyed the room. "Place looks pretty good, all things considered. We'll have a better sense after Krissy comes, but I think it'll show well. And here's the best part. I found a house for you, Cal, right around the corner from Gingie. It's perfect."

Callie looked confused. "I have a house. I live here."

"Course you do," Mimi said. "But forward march. You've been alone long enough. Time to move near us." She glanced at Ginger's hands. "Again with a rash? Gingie gets rashy whenever she's upset. Which seems to be all the time. I assume she told you about Julia."

"We're not talking about Julia now." Ginger sat on her itchy hands. "I had no idea you were living here, Callie. You must have thought it was awful we never tried to get in touch. Did Mom know you were here all this time?" Callie nodded. "Why didn't she tell us?"

Callie shook her head. "Can't explain." Suddenly Echo leaped into her lap, taking her off guard. As if to apologize for surprising her, he started licking her face and didn't stop until, laughing, she gently pushed him away.

"Forward march," Mimi reminded them. "We have a lot to do. We've got the scattering to arrange, and we've got to figure out what needs to be done to get this house ready to show."

"You can't decide to sell the house." Callie was firm. "The originals all have to agree to a sale. And I don't agree. I live here." She stood up. "I have to go. I have some seminaries to check out before dark." She whistled to Echo. "There's only two left." She opened the door.

"Seminaries?" Ginger asked. "Why?"

"Don't wait for me for dinner. After the seminaries, I have a concert at the Tabernacle." She moved to the front door, Echo right behind her.

"Are you looking for someone to lead the memorial service?" Ginger asked. The front door banged shut. "Are there seminaries at the Tabernacle?" she called through the screen. Callie's car started up. "Can I come?" It was hard to tell if Callie shook her head or if she was just turning to watch for trees as she backed up the car and drove away.

"Why does she keep leaving?" Ginger asked. "It's like she doesn't want to be in the same room with us. You think she's angry we never came to see her? Maybe she doesn't believe we didn't know where she was."

"She's not angry. She's just . . . Callie." Mimi lugged her suitcase to the stairs. "Why do you always make lemons out of lemonade?" She bumped her bag up a step. "Let's concentrate on getting the house in shape. The realtor's coming at nine tomorrow. Have you seen the pond? I know there's a pond out there somewhere."

"Mimi, we can't sell. Callie lives here. Why doesn't it bother you that we didn't know?"

"Because, forward march. We knew she lived somewhere. What's the difference where it was? I would have thought all that mattered to you is that now we're all together."

Ginger went on alert. "Did you know Callie lived here?"

"No." Mimi let out a groan. "Well, mostly no." She sat down on the step. "If I paid attention to every story Mom told me, I would have lost my mind. I worked very hard *not* to pay attention. I still do. And it's harder than you can imagine. I try to look disinterested all the time, but for some reason I'm the person people like to tell things to. Marriage on the rocks? I'm the first to find out. Bad blood test? Guess who gets the call? My opinion? Talking to me is one step away from talking to a tree. But apparently people like talking to trees."

Ginger refused to be distracted. "Did you know Mom was in touch with Callie all this time?"

"No. Maybe. I don't know. You left first, Gingie. Mom would have preferred it the other way around, to be left with the good daughter, but better than nothing, she got me. So, yes, she talked to me. Or at me."

"What did she tell you?"

"Who knows. I trained myself to not listen. The minute she got that cuddly tone in her voice, that *you are my very best friend* thing she did, I'd shut down. You never did that?"

"I did," Ginger admitted.

"Okay. So you know. Probably half of what"—she gestured toward the urn and lowered her voice, as if Glory's mashed-up ears might still work—"over half of what she said was made up, and we didn't always know which half. My solution? I treated it all like it was made up." Mimi whispered the next, as if it was a secret. "When she talked about Callie—which luckily wasn't often—that was the worst. I could tell there was something she wanted me to know—*us* to know. The second I heard *Callie* come out of her mouth, I doubled down on not listening." She got up and started dragging her heavy suitcase up the stairs. "Aren't family reunions fun?"

Ginger's phone buzzed—a text from Richard. *Are you okay?*

Yes, she texted and then added, *miss you a lot.* She quickly pressed Send before she could decide whether saying that was wise. "Cell service is working," she called to Mimi. "If you need to make any calls."

When Mimi came down, Ginger had just finished googling "Tabernacle in Martha's Vineyard." "Callie's in a concert tonight in Oak Bluffs. It starts in an hour. We should go."

Mimi tossed over her car keys. "Be my guest. I'm exhausted. And if you go, oh my god, I'll be alone for the first time in years. Don't take it personally, but I can't wait."

● ● ●

The GPS in Mimi's rental car gave Ginger several choices for routes to the Tabernacle. She chose the shortest one, on a road that wound beside the ocean. Richard would have been surprised. He was one of the few people who knew the reason for her aversion to the sea, even if he didn't understand it. After all, it wasn't like the ocean was responsible for Charlie's accident. But even though he didn't understand it, Richard stepped up and over the years whenever invitations came, to rent a beach house with friends, or to go to the beach for the day, he'd be the one to say, "Thanks but we're not beach people. We like mountains. Mountains and national parks."

It wasn't a problem until Julia was older, bored with national parks and mountains, disinterested in visiting cities her parents claimed were cool—Montreal, it turned out, was not cool if you went with your parents. Julia wanted to go to the Shore, like everyone her age. She wanted to hang out at the boardwalk with friends. It took a long time but eventually—it was inevitable, really—she asked, "*Why* aren't we beach people?"

Of course Ginger didn't answer. She had perfected the art of not answering certain questions. It was right after that when Richard started taking Julia to the beach himself. The last time the two of them went, the summer before Julia left with Nick, Ginger had promised her, "I'll come next time for sure." Another thing Ginger looked back at with wonder, that she used to believe there would always be another chance.

She navigated through the crowded streets of Oak Bluffs and parked near the ferry. She was hurrying up Beach Road when she felt a nudge behind her knees. She swung around and saw Echo. The dog shook, spraying her with seawater. And then Callie was at his side, out of breath and agitated. "He went in. I told him not to, but he did."

"He seems okay." Ginger turned and looked out into the twilight, at the ocean. For once, she could see nothing wrong. "The sea is calm."

"It's not. See where the waves are crashing? Right at the shore? That's called *shore break* and it's dangerous. The riptide is fierce, but people get fooled, like you just did. It looks calm, but it isn't." She kneeled down and gave Echo a hard rub. All was forgiven. "I have to go. I can't be late." She took off at a jog and then stopped. "Aren't you coming?"

"Yes." She had to run fast to keep up with her sister. But Callie stopped every few blocks to make sure she didn't leave Ginger behind.

CHAPTER TWENTY-NINE

The Tabernacle was an open-air structure with wrought iron arches, colored glass windows, and a copper roof topped by a cupola. It sat in the middle of a small green surrounded by a circle of gingerbread cottages.

Ginger remembered coming to Oak Bluffs years ago. That's where the old carousel was, where Solly took them the day Glory stayed in bed with a headache. She remembered riding the carousel for hours, and then, when they were done, leaving to explore another town. They never came here, to this enclave of storybook houses. Ginger would have remembered it, tiny cottages decorated with figurines and stained glass windows, homes so close together she imagined a resident of one could pass a cup of sugar through an open window to the other without either neighbor fully extending an arm.

She passed a cottage with a hand-painted sign that said, "Alice in Wonderland," and another that said, "Wizard of Oz." But even the plainest were well-kept, with colorful trim and deep porches that overlooked postage-stamp gardens made lush by abundant flowers.

As she followed Callie past tourists snapping cell phone pictures of people on porches, their rocking chairs turned so their backs were to the street, her sister told her, "Don't say hello. If their chairs face away, it means they don't want to be bothered. They'll turn their chairs facing out if they want to chat." As if to prove her point, at the next house they passed, the chairs faced the street and a man sitting in a pink rocker tipped his hat. "Nice to see you back, Callie Claire."

"Who's that?" Ginger asked.

"A friend." Callie sped up to a path that bifurcated the small park encircling the Tabernacle. By the time Ginger caught up, she was wrapping Echo's leash around a tree trunk. "I could take him inside, but some people get offended. The concerts are for everyone, but it is a church." She checked the leash to make sure it was secure and motioned for Echo to lie down. "I won't be long." He lowered his head onto his paws but his eyes followed her, brows alternating, as she moved toward the open-air building.

At the entrance, a woman pressed a slim weathered songbook into Ginger's hand. Ginger passed it to Callie, who took it and said, "Thanks. I left mine at home."

"I didn't see you there, Callie Claire." The woman put the books down to give Callie a hug.

"Sorry I'm late." Callie slipped off her jacket to show that she was wearing a white shirt and khakis. "I'm all ready, though."

"You are such a dear. But tonight's Community Sing. Our concert's not till next week. Besides, you shouldn't be worrying about that now." She gave her another hug which Callie took, though her arms stayed stiff at her side. "You need anything, you promise to call me?"

Callie nodded and then gestured for Ginger to follow her in. They passed rows of open seats on rustic benches in the back, which is where Ginger would have sat if Callie hadn't said, "Not there." With purposeful strides, she led them to the front of the pavilion, where the seating changed to straight-back wooden chairs. To Ginger's eye there were about a hundred of them, almost all occupied. Callie stopped next to a man in green pants and a bow tie chatting to a group in the front row.

When he saw Callie, his face opened into a wide grin. "Callie Claire is back! So good to see you." He noticed her companion. "Let me guess. One of the sisters. You would be—Ginger. Am I right?" He extended his hand. "George. Pleasure to finally meet you. Sorry about your mother. One in a million, she was."

Ginger smiled and shook his hand. "Thank you."

"I should thank *you* for lending her to us. She was a kind soul. Had the soul of an angel." He placed his hands on his heart.

Ginger cocked her head. Was he confusing her with someone else? Had another mother died? Would it be impolite to set him straight?

George checked his watch. "Okay. Better get this show started." He gestured to seats in the front row. Callie took one on the aisle and Ginger sat beside her.

George climbed the stairs to the stage and adjusted his mike. A piano player joined him. They consulted, head to head, and when they were done, the piano player looked toward Callie and gave her a tip-of-the-hat salute, which she returned with a backward wave.

"Do you know everyone?" Ginger asked.

"No. I know the people I sing with. They're very kind."

George tapped his mike and the crowd quieted. "Welcome, welcome. You'll have to bear with us tonight. New sound system. Hope you're in a patient mood."

There was laughter and a smattering of applause.

"A few announcements." The system cut in and out, chopping off words, but no one seemed bothered. Ginger followed along as best she could. It was something about a cleanup at the Campgrounds, and the date for Illumination Night, and the newly expanded hours for the museum. A screech of feedback made everyone groan. Somewhere someone made an adjustment. George's voice boomed out. "Better?" The crowd applauded. "Before we get started, I want to say a few words about one of our community chorus patrons, Glory Tangle. Her dear Callie Claire is with us tonight, along with her sister, Ginger." He gestured toward them and the crowd applauded.

Ginger turned to Callie. "Patron?"

Callie stared straight ahead, and Ginger noticed she was clenching her jaw. As soon as the applause subsided, her sister's mouth relaxed.

"I'll do my best," George announced, "to get Callie Claire to stay to the end so you can offer your condolences. 'Swiss Navy' will be our last song tonight, Callie Claire. Will you wait?"

Someone nearby called out, "Stick around, Callie," and when Ginger turned to see who it was, she saw Callie was uncomfortable with the attention.

"Tonight," George told the crowd, "a challenge. Sea shanties. Are you up to it?" The crowd's applause confirmed they were. A screen descended. "How do you like this? No more excuses for not singing along. Lyrics, compliments of Glory Tangle." There was enthusiastic clapping and the music began. Text scrolled down the screen. "The words to this one have been changed a bit. Chalk it up to the Mangle Tangle. Your mother did have a unique way with words." He directed this toward Callie.

Ginger leaned over and whispered, "Did Mom send them a big donation or something?"

But the singing had already started and Callie, with her chin up, sang along, full-hearted, with the crowd.

"There once was a boy in the north country. He had sisters one, two, three." Ginger recognized the tune as Glory's dishwashing song. Her mother often hummed it, but sometimes she sang with made-up lyrics, nonsense words strung together, gibberish, or so Ginger thought until now. "Love will be true, true to my love. Love will be true to you."

The song ended and the crowd applauded itself. George applauded too. "Happy to see everyone brought their energy tonight!" George moved them along to "Kookaburra," in a round, with an admonition to "stand up or at least do *something* when you say the first half of the word. You *do* know what the first half of *Kook*-aburra is, don't you?" When that song ended, George motioned for everyone to stand. "This is an offering in memory of our dear friend and patron, Glory Tangle."

Ginger watched as all around her parents shuffled, pulling collapsed children to a stand and setting sweatshirts, purses, and water bottles on the floor. George waited patiently until everyone, Ginger included, was up. Callie was the last to stand. George signaled to the pianist as words flashed on the screen. This time when the crowd sang, Callie did not join in.

"Fading light, dims the sight. And a star gems the sky, gleaming bright. From afar, drawing nigh, falls the night."

The great open-air room fell still. George let his hands fall to his side. He waited—he was patient and willing to wait for a very long time—until everyone was seated. Then he put his hands to his heart and offered a nod to Callie, which she returned with a backward wave.

"All right. Let's go. As promised, 'Swiss Navy.'"

The mood of the crowd turned buoyant as they performed their favorite song with practiced gestures, stamping feet as they "marched with the infantry," pointing fingers as they "shot with artillery." When they stood for the final chorus, Callie stood up and kept going, hurrying down the aisle and out of the front of the Tabernacle.

By the time Ginger caught up to her, she was untangling Echo's leash. "Sorry," she said. "I needed to get out. Fresh air." Echo, happy to be released, jumped on top of her. Wobbling, Callie laughed, and then righted herself. "Okay, boy. Let's go for a run. Come on. Back to the car." He pulled at his leash, eager to get going, and Callie called to Ginger, "See you later," before disappearing around a corner.

Ginger hurried through the dark streets of Oak Bluffs to the car. The town was busy, the night filled with the sounds of children laughing and their parents calling for them to keep up. In the distance, she heard the low roar of waves hitting the shore and the thump of cars coming off the ferry.

Twenty minutes out of town, driving slowly through the pitch-black of the up-island night, a buck leaped in front of her car. Ginger jammed hard on her brakes and stopped, just in time. The buck vanished into the woods on the other side, but Ginger didn't move. A moment later, a doe sprang out of the trees and, face illuminated by the car's headlights, stared at her as if stuck. Ginger switched off her lights, and the shadow that was the doe bounded to join its mate. A second later, there was a rustle of leaves and two young fawns sprinted, fearless in their determination to join their mother.

Ginger sat shivering at the thought that if she hadn't stopped and sat there, hadn't waited, she could have killed them all: father, mother, fawns. Her thoughts switched to the images she tried so hard to avoid: Julia, dreadlocked and dirty in a park. Julia, hungry and hurt on the side of a road. Then a memory came. Julia in the parking lot at the summit of Mount Washington, arms crossed over her chest, telling her mother she couldn't breathe. Couldn't breathe because of *her*.

A car flashed its brights in her rearview mirror and whizzed past. Ginger drove on, not much faster than a sleepwalker.

CHAPTER THIRTY

Mimi's soft leather driving shoes were parked at the foot of the stairs. She'd gone to bed. *Good,* Ginger thought. She'd rather talk to Callie by herself.

As she walked to the back bedroom to wait, she recommitted to her decision. If she wanted to have an honest relationship with Callie, she had to be willing to ask the question. The question would hold no judgment. They were both young, Callie was just a child when she went away. A child who had seen something she shouldn't have. It was possible, likely even, that Callie would have no memory of what she saw. But the only way to know was for Ginger to ask.

To make it easier, Ginger would share first. This was what she did at work when she wanted to help her timid students open up. She would tell a little boy she was hungry, and then the boy would admit he hadn't eaten any dinner the night before. She would tell a girl she was feeling sad because her mother was sick, and the girl would confide that her mother was in the hospital and might never come home.

So tonight, Ginger would tell Callie about Julia. And she would share what she had realized at the Tabernacle. She'd been hoping for the wrong thing. Ever since Julia left, she'd been hoping her daughter would snap out of it and come home, admit that leaving was a mistake. But watching Callie at the sing-along, surrounded by a community that cared about her, Ginger found herself with a different hope. The hope that Julia would find what Callie had, that no matter where she ended up, she'd create a good life, surrounded by people who loved her.

It was surprising to see that so many people loved her sister, considering how hard Callie was to love. And it wasn't only that she was odd. She'd been odd for a very long time. But she was odd now in a different way. Ginger had noticed it the very first day of their reunion, and she noticed it every day since. Callie could accept an embrace, but she couldn't return one. She could answer direct questions, but she never offered more than what was asked. What was it? Depression? She ticked off the warning signs. Appearance, sleep habits, feelings of hopelessness. Ginger didn't think so. Anger? That Ginger and Mimi hadn't tried to find her in all the years she'd been here? How had Glory managed that, made it so that she and Mimi didn't even try?

She looked around the room. Memories were everywhere. Glory breezing into the master bedroom for the first time, swooning at the clean-line whiteness of it all. There'd been the bed—*California King!*—and the walk-in closet—*cubbies for shoes!* The carpet, now an industrial wall-to-wall the color of dried leaves, then white as snow—*like walking on a cloud.*

In the bathroom Ginger could practically hear her mother's voice, the long-ago exclamation: *Two sinks! Two mirrors! That darling crocheted hat for extra toilet paper! Toilet tissue,* she'd corrected Ginger, who hadn't said a thing.

The California King had been replaced by a single twin bed made up military-style, a taut paisley coverlet in a muted mix of burgundy and browns spread on top; with the big bed gone, there was now room for Callie to set up a reading chair with a table and lamp, and a study area with a bleached-oak desk, and above that, shelves. Ginger ran her fingers along the spines of the notebooks lined up with perfect posture, and then across the boxes—puzzle boxes, she saw upon closer inspection.

Her eyes skipped to a pile of papers on the desk next to the laptop, xeroxed flyers with a fringe of phone numbers on the bottom. She picked one up and read it. "Callie's Dogs. Limited Availability. Affordable and Trustworthy. References Upon Request." Her sister had a business taking care of dogs.

The flyer slipped out of her hand and floated to the desk, and when Ginger retrieved it, her fingers brushed the keyboard and the laptop came awake. A screen saver cycled through photographs of dogs at the beach. There was Echo and then others: a wet golden retriever, a small white dog with matted fur, a muscular black dog with a tennis ball in her mouth. As the image changed again, Ginger glanced down and saw a slim book on the floor—a song booklet from the Tabernacle.

She picked it up and flipped through, stopping at a page with the sea shanty they'd sung earlier that night. There were lines crossed out—"There was an old man in the north country. He had daughters one, two, three"—and above them, in Glory's careful script, new lyrics were written in. The words they sang at the Tabernacle: "There once was a boy in the north country. He had sisters one, two, three. Love will be true, true to my love. Love will be true to you."

The song suddenly seemed so sad. Ginger closed the book and put it down and the screen saver, done with dogs, flashed on to an image of Callie. Younger—in her twenties, Ginger guessed—in her pristine Vineyard kitchen. How long had Callie been here? How often had Glory come? Before the questions could sink in, the next picture came up, Ginger at home with Richard and Julia, just a little girl. Then it was Mimi and Neil in their parklike backyard with their boys and several Popkin relatives horsing around behind them. Images flashed by. Ginger and Richard on their wedding day. Mimi holding newborn Wallace, newborn Hunter, newborn Troy.

It seemed so unfair. The facts fell like weights. Glory had a ban on all photographs in her home while Callie had Ginger's family as her screen saver. She knew nothing of Callie's life while Callie knew all about hers. Exhausted, she lay down on the bed and watched the pictures cycle through and then cycle through again.

She woke with sunlight on her face and the sound of someone in the kitchen.

Mimi. "I was wondering where everyone was. You and Callie have a sleepover?"

"No. I was waiting for her in her room. I guess I fell asleep. She's not here?"

Mimi shrugged. "Haven't seen her." She opened a container of coffee, took a sniff, and recoiled. "This smells like it's a hundred years old. I already threw out the one that smelled a thousand years old." She glanced at Ginger. "What's wrong? Did something happen last night?"

Ginger sat down at the kitchen table and checked for her barrette, but it was gone. "It was strange." She worked out a knot and twirled her unruly hair into a bun, which immediately came undone. "Callie is friends with half the island. Everywhere we went people knew her, and Mom, and us. I mean they knew *of* us. Did you know Callie has photographs of us on her computer? And our families? Me and Julia. You and Neil and the boys. We're her screen saver."

"That's sweet." Mimi opened more cupboards. "I can't function without coffee." She felt Ginger's stare. "What? Are you unhappy I want coffee or are you unhappy we're Callie's screen saver? That means she cares about us. Come on, Gingie. Forward march. We're together now. We need to stay together. If you have to worry about something, worry about that." She opened the freezer, but it was empty. "I'm going to get coffee. Want anything?"

Ginger shook her head. "She could be dog-sitting. I saw flyers in her room. That's what she does. She has a dog-sitting business."

"See? Dog-sitting. Nothing to worry about." She sighed and sat down. "Look, two things about Callie that haven't changed. She's always been different and she's always been happiest out and about. Don't blow this up into something it's not. I'm going to get coffee, and I'm going to assume by the time I get back, she'll be home." The door clacked closed behind her.

Always been different. Ginger turned the phrase over in her mind. She thought about how it would go today if there were a family like hers, where a young child died in an accident. One thing was for sure: if a six-year-old student under her watch was hauled off to a hospital during a family catastrophe and ended up witnessing her brother's death, Ginger would refer that child to a therapist. Post-traumatic stress disorder. That was it. Ginger's retroactive diagnosis. How had she missed it? Callie had all the symptoms after Charlie's accident: nightmares, difficulty sleeping, changes in behavior, emotionally numb. But there'd been no such diagnosis then and no one to suggest taking Callie to a therapist. Easier to label her a wanderer. A child who acted odd for reasons no one would explain.

She tried to recall if she and Callie had ever spoken about the day their brother died. But of course they hadn't. None of them did. That kind of talk was forbidden. Just as later, it was forbidden to say anything about Callie's behavior. *She likes to explore.* That's how Solly used to put it. *Explores the world like a regular Christopher Columbus. Was Christopher Columbus so terrible?*

Ginger laughed, remembering that. And then her memory skipped forward to the night, Solly long gone, when Glory broke the news that their sister had joined a cult.

"Decided just like that." Glory snapped her fingers. "I told her, it's a terrible idea, but she's eighteen, so of course she thinks she knows better than me. What am I supposed to do when she tells me the cut isn't dangerous? Tie her to a chair?"

Ginger had corrected her, "Cult," and then studied her mother's face. Had Glory been thinking out loud? Had she forgotten Ginger and Mimi were with her? Or was the ban against talking about Callie now lifted? Ginger weighed the odds and risked a question. "Which cult is she in? There are so many."

Glory seemed to wake up to her mistake. "What are you talking about? It's nothing of the sort." The topic was closed. "Who wants to play Spite and Malice?" When neither Ginger nor Mimi made a move to get the cards, Glory's tone turned caustic. "Or are you going to insist on continuing this conversation? Because if you do, I am perfectly happy to climb onto the roof right now and jump off." She lurched up, as if she actually was going to do that, right then, go to the roof and jump.

"I'll get the cards," Ginger said, and never mentioned Callie's name to her mother again.

The first time Richard met Glory, at a dinner she made to impress him, he brought Callie up. "You ever consider trying to kidnap her out of the cult?" At the time, Richard had clients who were doing just that, arranging to kidnap their child from a cult. He was trying to be helpful, Ginger knew, but still she kicked him and held her breath.

He got away with it because Glory liked him. She'd liked him from the start, liked the way he looked and liked the way he laughed at her jokes. She'd told this to Ginger in the kitchen that night. "Such a good face. Chiseled. Shows character. Good eyes too. Light up like fire when he hears something funny. Sign of a keeper, Gingie. Don't let this one go."

His questions continued. "Would you like me to find you a deprogrammer? I know a good one."

"Gingie told me your job is to save children. Makes my heart want to burst." Glory lowered her voice. "Unfortunately, between you and

me, not every child can be saved. Some butterflies need to fly free."
Ginger watched it register on her mother's face that her metaphor had
failed. "You are so darling. But there's nothing you can do for Callie.
She's not in a cult anymore."

This was news to Ginger. "Where is she?"

Glory shrugged. "Prefers to live elsewhere. Prefers to be left alone.
Prefers we stop discussing her." She drilled her eyes into Ginger's, and
then she got up and disappeared into the kitchen, returning a moment
later with a platter of what looked like melting snowballs onto which
she'd dribbled a sauce that was an unfortunate shade of yellow. "*Voilà!
Le* Floating Islands."

The porch door clacked closed, Mimi announcing her return. She
juggled a container with three cups of coffee in it and a bag of beans.
"Don't look so disappointed." She put everything down on the counter.
"Callie's not back?" Ginger shook her head. "Well, I brought one for
her just in case." She pulled a sheet of paper out of her back pocket.
"Look what was on the bulletin board at the store." She handed Ginger
a flyer. It was a copy of the same flyer that was on Callie's desk, except
this one had a note pasted across it like a warning. "Closed Temporarily
Due to Family Emergency."

"So she's not out dog-sitting."

"We don't know that for sure," Mimi said. "Maybe someone called
and begged."

A knock at the door put an end to their discussion. "Hello? Hello?
Krissy here."

As Mimi walked by to let in the realtor, Ginger got a glimpse of her
face. This was a first: Mimi was worried too.

CHAPTER
THIRTY-ONE

The fringe of coin-shaped medallions at the end of the realtor's orange scarf caught the morning light, and the clutch of tiny silver bracelets on her wrist jangled as she held out the plain white box to Ginger. "Chilmark Chocolates. Has Callie taken you yet?" Ginger shook her head. "She will. I see her there all the time. She's a chocolate fiend like me. This chocolate"—she nodded toward the box—"amazing. Plus the kids they hire . . . you can't imagine. You might think they have disabilities, but no matter how long that line gets, no matter how annoying the customers are—and by August, trust me, they are *all* annoying—those kids never lose their cool. They close at the end of August." She tapped her ample stomach. "So I make up for it in July. Chocolate for breakfast. My guilty pleasure. May I?" Ginger nodded and Krissy picked out an apricot half-dipped in dark. She proceeded with the usual questions: "You the older sister? You the middle?" Her last question was about Callie. "She here?"

"No," Mimi said with fake cheer. "She's out and about."

"We don't know where she is," Ginger clarified. "I was with her at the Tabernacle last night, but we left in separate cars. I came home and she didn't. I'm actually worried that—"

"She always worries," Mimi cut in.

"Visiting a dog," Krissy said. "That's my bet. Your sister does not love every dog owner, but she loves every dog. And the dogs are crazy for her. Someone was just telling me how they were walking their dog last week and the dog took off. Bolted. Turns out he smelled Callie driving by in her car. Amazing." She directed the next to Ginger. "Don't worry. She's got a lot of people looking out for her."

"See?" Mimi said. "Everything's fine. Shall I take you through the house?"

"I'm ready." Krissy helped herself to another chocolate. "I've never been upstairs."

"Good a place to start as any." Mimi gave the realtor a double-dimple smile.

Ginger bowed out. "You don't need both of us to show you around. I'll go get started on cleaning out the shed."

"She means *guesthouse*," Mimi told Krissy. "The boys are going to go crazy when they see it. I'm renting a couple of bunk beds for when they come. Guarantee they won't want to leave. You know you should try to find a buyer who's an artist. I'm a quilter, and what I wouldn't give to have a space like that for my studio. Guesthouse or studio, or both."

Krissy scribbled notes on her pad. "Did Callie happen to mention if she wants to stay up island or is she open to moving down island if we can find the right place?"

"Neither," Mimi told her. "Callie's moving near us."

"That's what we're hoping," Ginger added. "We don't know if she will."

"I wouldn't count on it," Krissy said. "Callie's a real island girl."

"Time will tell." Mimi was not going to get bogged down on this now. "Let's walk through the house, and then look at the pond. I know it's in the woods back behind the guesthouse. I'm sure we can find it."

Krissy made another note. "Ponds can be good or bad. Depends. But I need to see it. Nothing's worse than listing a house with a pond and finding out it's degraded into a puddle."

Ginger immediately started thinking of all the things worse than a pond degrading into a puddle, but instead of sharing them, she excused herself to change into cleaning gear. An old shed was an ideal environment for rodents.

Krissy followed Mimi into the upstairs hall bathroom, where she proceeded to run through her home-inspection checklist: "Let's flush the toilet. Can you turn on the shower?"

Ginger went into her room to change. To protect her ankles from any ticks that might have found their way into the old shed, she tucked her pant legs into her socks. To protect her neck, she popped up her shirt collar. She found a pair of rubber dishwashing gloves under the sink and put them on. Then she collected buckets and cleaning supplies from the laundry room. She was balancing a broom, a mop, a bucket with cleaners and bleach in it, and another with sponges and rags when she met up with Krissy and Mimi in the front hall.

"Wow," Krissy said, taking in Ginger's getup. "You look ready for some serious cleaning. You expecting mold?"

Ginger hadn't thought about mold.

"There's no mold," Mimi assured the realtor. "This is how Gingie looks when she cleans. She tends to overdo. Right, Gingie?"

Ginger nodded and offered a weak smile. "There's just a lot of junk inside, that's all. Callie told me everything in there can go over to the dump, or—is there a place called the Dumptick?"

"The Dumptique," Krissy said. "It's a store across from the dump. A giveaway store. People bring all kinds of stuff there. The ladies who run it will take almost anything. I've seen chairs without seats. Torn coats. One person's garbage is another person's treasure. And everything's free, so who can complain?"

"What a great idea," Mimi said. "I'll come with you, Gingie. Maybe I can find some more clothes for the quilt. I'm making a quilt in honor of my mother," she told Krissy. "Now let's go find that pond." She led the realtor outside and they both disappeared into the woods.

The shed, nestled in a grove of mottled trees, seemed to be simultaneously growing out of the earth and swallowed up by the woods. Lichens and moss collaborated to make a perfect camouflage. Ginger wished she had a face mask. She had a full box of them in her supply cabinet. At work she wore them—to protect the kids—if she had a case of the sniffles. Here she was thinking more about rodents. Rodents carried so many diseases. Leptospirosis. Tularemia. Babesiosis.

She pushed open the shed door and a puff of dust blew into her face. Covering her mouth with her sleeve, she stepped inside. Dim light struggled to get through windowpanes painted with pollen. She flicked the switch, but the naked bulb hanging from the ceiling did little to improve things. She made her way around the perimeter of the room, opening windows as she went, for light and air.

Hulking objects, old and rusted, clattered against each other as she passed. The little sunlight that managed to come through the opened windows put a spotlight on the dangers. Pine walls dark with damp, wide-planked floor rotted at the edges. The air was perfumed with a mix of earthworms and, yes, mold. There was no visible evidence of rodents, no droppings she could see, but just in case, she switched to the kind of shallow breathing she taught anxious children who were scared of thunder. Julia used to be scared of thunder. *Keep busy. Don't think. Clean the shed.*

She dragged out the big things first: a child's wooden desk, the steel frame of a fold-up cot, a bent beach umbrella, an old Radio Flyer wagon. Smaller objects came next: water guns, a scuffed wooden box, a metal trap that smelled like skunk. By the time Mimi and Krissy returned with their report that they'd found the pond, and—good news—it was not a puddle, Ginger had removed almost everything from inside.

"Is Callie's car back?" Ginger asked, and Mimi shook her head.

"You guys," Krissy said, "you have nothing to worry about. Bet you anything Callie ended up dog-sitting last night. Probably out now taking a bunch of dogs for a run. She has a great business. Never takes on more than she can handle. Turns clients away all the time. Drives people crazy. She's *the* go-to dog lady, not that Callie thinks about herself that way."

Mimi beamed and her dimples deepened. "We're very proud of her."

Krissy promised to get a listing number together in a couple of days, and Ginger told her not to rush because they weren't ready to sell.

"We *are* ready to sell," Mimi corrected her as Krissy got in her car. She waved as the realtor drove off and then helped load boxes into her rental car for their run to the Dumptique. "We *are* going to get Callie to agree. She *will* move near us." While Mimi harped on about the inevitability of the move, Ginger pictured her supply cabinet. *Bactine next to Betadine. Cold packs next to eye rinse.*

"Sand toys," Mimi said.

Ginger swung around and saw that her sister had stopped loading the trunk and was now rifling through a box. "It's just junk. Come on. Let's finish up and go."

"I remember this." Mimi held up a plastic mold in the shape of a semicircle. "This was for making moats around sandcastles." She lifted out a large rectangle. "What was this one for?"

Ginger recognized it. "That is what's left of Uncle Milton's Ant Farm." She let out a rueful laugh. "Who would have thought the ant farm would outlive the ant farmer."

When the shed was empty and Mimi's car was loaded with the last of the boxes, Ginger swept the floor and washed it twice—the second time with bleach. Then they set off for the Dumptique.

Mimi drove past Beetlebung trees and honor farms selling honey and sunflowers, and Ginger scanned the landscape, hoping, ridiculously, to see Callie and Echo running by or, even more ridiculously, Callie and Echo and Julia. She turned to her sister. "At what point do we call the police to report Callie as missing?"

"She's an adult," Mimi reminded her. "If she was a minor it would be—" She stopped herself.

Ginger assumed this was because Mimi was thinking of Julia. Julia had been a minor when she left, and because of that, Mimi thought Ginger should have called the police right away. She wasn't the only one who expressed that view. Several people had suggested it: *Call the police. She's a minor. They'll bring her home.*

Of course, they didn't think it through, didn't consider what would happen next. If Ginger and Richard had dragged Julia home, two months later when she turned eighteen she'd be free to leave for good.

"What would *you* have done?" Ginger asked Mimi now. "If Wallace told you he was moving and that if you looked for him he'd disappear forever." She braced herself for a harsh answer, because of course Mimi was sure that would never happen to her. She could practically hear her sister thinking it. *Wallace would never do something like that.*

But Mimi sounded neither harsh nor sure. "I don't know, Gingie. I honestly have no idea."

There were two signs ahead, one pointing to the dump, the other to the Dumptique. Mimi parked, and as they walked in silence, she took hold of Ginger's hand.

CHAPTER THIRTY-TWO

The Dumptique was crammed with a little bit of everything a person might need in a day. Ginger saw a drawer labeled "Wooden Spoons," another that said, "Outlet Covers," a third that said "Scissors and Shears." There was an aisle just for dresses, one for blazers, one for towels. Small bins on tables held nail files, doorknobs, and buttons. Large bins held cereal bowls, alarm clocks, and coils of fabric belts. A wall of ripple-paged paperbacks faced shelves of hardcovers swollen by damp.

It was a place of purging and claiming. A young mother looked for a raincoat to fit her growing son. An old man wanted mugs for unexpected guests. A teenager in expensive sneakers was prowling for a vintage T-shirt. A college kid tried hard to convince his trailing mother that the blender he was scavenging for was for breakfast smoothies only.

Overseeing it all were two women: one who sat behind a folding table; the other circulating through the store directing people. "Socks are in the bin next to the scarves. For ladles, turn right at the flashlights."

When Ginger asked the woman behind the table—name tag Dee—what they should do with their donations, Dee directed her to pull the car around the back and unload. Small items were to be placed on the folding table near the door, large items stacked beside the tree.

They had just unloaded the last of it when Dee joined them. Like a judge at a dog show, she walked past the offerings with a slow, appraising gait. She pointed and nodded, "Yes, yes, yes," and shook her head, "No and no." Mostly it was "Yes."

"Moving in or out?" she asked, as she continued. "Yes" to the dented metal fan. "Yes" to the shadeless lamp. "No" to the clam rake, too rusty and missing half the teeth.

"Cleaning out," Ginger said. "Our mother died."

A quick breath in. "So sorry. What's your name?"

"I'm Ginger. This is Mimi. Our mother is Glory Tangle. Was Glory Tangle."

Dee looked up over her half glasses. "You're the sisters. How's Callie Claire doing?"

Ginger flashed Mimi a look. This is what she'd been trying to explain.

"You're just cleaning out, right? You're not selling. Your mother always said she couldn't bear thinking about Callie having to live somewhere else. Although, now that Casper is . . . Oh dear." She shook her head. "It's all so sad."

"Casper Diggans?" Ginger hadn't thought of him for years.

"Ignore me," Dee said. "I was talking to myself. Sometimes I do that. I don't even know I'm saying things out loud. What else you got?" She surveyed the remains, a battered box the size of a large attaché case, a carton of soil-encrusted garden tools, a stack of old puzzles. "Yes" to the garden tools and the puzzles and "What's this?" when she got to the battered box. "I think there's something carved under all that dust." She took a rag out of her back pocket and wiped away the pollen. "Well, look at that."

Ginger leaned in and made out a vague design, possibly a woman holding a flute. Possibly snakes coiled at her feet. "It's a tree," Mimi decided.

Dee tried to open the box but couldn't.

"Look on the side," Ginger advised her. "There might be a latch hidden on the side." She had never seen this box before, but she recognized the style. It was a puzzle box, just like the ones her father got from his favorite distributor in Japan.

It took a moment, but Dee found the latch. When she moved it, they all heard the click of the lock releasing. She lifted up the lid and sighed. "Empty. I'm always hoping to find hidden treasure. I'm not picky, either. Gold coins, jewels—anything would be fine with me." She peered inside. "Nice lining. See?" She passed the box so Ginger could see the soft scarlet velvet inside.

The box felt heavy in Ginger's hands. She shook it and heard something shift. "There's another compartment." She used her finger to measure the depth. "See how shallow it is here?" She put her finger on the outside to show the difference. "There's a false bottom."

"Wow." Dee was impressed. "How'd you figure that out?"

"My sister has two superpowers," Mimi explained. "Worrying and opening puzzle boxes."

It took less than a minute for Ginger to find it—a narrow slat camouflaged by the grain of the wood. When she slid it over, they heard another lock release. "Opens from the top *and* the bottom."

"I have a good feeling about this," Dee said. "Can you wait while I get Rita? Rita gets so mad when she misses out on the good stuff."

It was too late. Ginger had already turned the box over and opened the bottom compartment. "Sorry." She showed Dee and Mimi what was inside. "Just an old newspaper."

But Dee was more thorough than that. "Maybe underneath?"

Ginger lifted up the paper. Underneath was more of the same. She flipped through the pile. All of it was the same, the same front page of the same edition of the local paper, pages yellowed, print faded but still readable.

"Hey, Dee?" Rita called over. "Can you come here and help me decide about this coat?"

Dee excused herself, leaving Ginger and Mimi to examine the newspaper alone. They didn't need to look beyond the front page to know why it was there. They recognized the date at once: July 11, 1972. The story was above the fold, alongside a yellowed photograph of a large crowd on a wide beach.

Mimi picked up the top copy and read the article out loud. "Two boys were buried in a sand-hole collapse yesterday. Beachgoers, scooping out sand with hands and plastic shovels, finally pulled the boys out."

"Two boys?" Ginger repeated, and they both read the rest.

"Why don't they say the other boy's name?" Mimi asked.

"They don't say Charlie's name, either." Ginger thought about this. "Maybe they were rushing to get the story in before they went to press. Another boy. I had no idea. Did you?"

Mimi shook her head.

And then Dee was back. "I'll take the box. You can bring the newspapers to the dump."

"No." Ginger grabbed the puzzle box and held it close. "We're keeping it."

"Up to you."

As they drove across the field to the dump, Ginger tried to picture the beach children they'd met that long-ago summer, but she couldn't conjure up a single face. "Who do you think it was?"

Mimi shrugged. "I have no idea."

They threw the rejected junk into the appropriate receptacles and got back in the car.

"Do you think Mom knew who it was?" Ginger asked. "Do you think she knew the other mother? Do you think they stayed in touch?" Mimi shrugged again.

This was strange to think about, that all this time there'd been another family who'd gone through the same thing, had the same bad day, and then the same awful night. Suddenly, Ginger remembered Dee's comment about Casper Diggans. "Do you think Casper Diggans is still alive?"

Mimi thought about it. "He'd be about a hundred by now, so no."

But Ginger did the math in her head. "He'd probably be in his eighties." She looked out the window. They passed a nondescript house. "He could be living anywhere. Do you think he's here now? On the island?"

"Why do you care? You didn't like him the first time around."

They pulled into the driveway, where Ginger noticed, but did not point out, Callie's car was still not back. Mimi went up to fetch her quilting bag so she could get to work on her tribute-to-Glory quilt. Ginger checked her phone to see if she had service. When she saw she did, she started googling.

There were three Diggans on the island that she could find. Two were in Vineyard Haven and one was in Chilmark. On the second try she found the one she wanted.

CHAPTER THIRTY-THREE

After Ginger identified herself, there was a brief silence. When the woman on the other end of the phone spoke again, her voice was muffled, as if her hand was over the receiver.

The next voice on the phone was clear. "Hello. This is Thomas."

A memory clicked into place. Casper Diggans' nephew, her neighbor Evelyn's son. "Thomas Clarke?"

"Wasn't sure you'd remember me. Been a long time."

"Of course I remember you." She tried to place when exactly they'd last seen each other and with a start realized it was the day of the accident. She last saw Thomas when he was coming back from fetching Callie, back from the far side of the cliffs.

Mimi burst out of the kitchen, talking loudly into her cell. "Yes, ballads. Mournful ballads. I assume you have some in your repertoire."

"Are you here?" Thomas asked. "On the island? With Callie?"

"I'm on the island," Ginger said. "That's Mimi you hear in the background. Callie's out. I don't know where. That's not why I'm calling—but she isn't, by any chance, with you?"

"No, sorry. You know how Callie is, though. She feels cooped up if she's inside too long."

"Aren't mournful ballads the whole reason people hire bagpipers?" Mimi asked. "Hold on. I've got another call." Ginger could see her sister was in her element, multitasking beyond what ordinary mortals could manage. "Yes, a scattering at sea. Have you ever catered a scattering? Can I put you on hold? I disconnected my bagpiper and he's calling back."

"Sorry?" Ginger realized she hadn't heard what Thomas just said.

"I was just saying how Callie sometimes gets it in her head that she has to go for a run, right away, or all of a sudden she'll decide there's a dog she needs to look in on at that exact second, and off she goes. She kind of keeps her own schedule. You said there was something else?"

"No," Mimi barked into her phone. "Lobster rolls cannot be on cold buns. You can? Toasted *and* buttered?"

"I have a question. It's out of the blue, I know." Ginger struggled to drown out Mimi's voice. "I have a couple of questions, actually." She stopped, because, where to begin?

Mimi paced in front of her, checklist clutched in her hand. "Hydrangeas." She had moved on to the florist.

"Would this be better in person?" Thomas asked. "I'm not far. I can come over now, if you like."

From where Ginger stood, she could see Mimi's list was long. When her sister was done with the florist, she was going to call about renting tables and chairs, and the next thing after that was confirming the captain and the boat.

"Maybe I can come to you," Ginger suggested. "If you're not too far. Are you walking distance?" She could feel Thomas hesitate. "Or we can talk later, if that's better."

"No, no. Come here. That's good. It's a bit of a hike, but it's a beautiful one."

Ginger scribbled down directions and then went upstairs to change into hiking clothes. She had brought bug repellent and hiking pants but, worried that was overkill, had left both in her suitcase. Now, as she pulled them out, a blue-and-green Planet Earth beanie came with them. Julia's beanie, from their Mount Washington trip, was hiding in the suitcase all this time. She put it on and went downstairs to tell Mimi she was going to see Thomas Clarke.

Mimi, negotiating with the bagpiper, waved her away. "Okay. Whatever. I heard you." And then back to the bagpiper, "Absolutely not. I am not paying for four hours."

By the time Ginger reached the main road, she was sweating. She took off the Planet Earth hat, but kept it pressed against her nose for several minutes, inhaling a dim hint of the berry scent that was Julia's favorite shampoo. Now, when she thought about Mount Washington, all she could do was wonder at whatever made her think it was worth it to have an argument over a hat.

The sun beat down as she kept a lookout for the sign to the old brickyard, which, according to the directions, was just beyond the second fork. After the second fork, she was to turn right at the old farm stand. Did *old* mean abandoned or was there a newer farm stand nearby? Why hadn't she thought to ask Thomas how long this hike was supposed to take?

With Julia's hat in her back pocket she walked on, thinking about the days before Julia left, how worried she was about Julia's closed bedroom door, how sure she was that Nick's smile, when he walked in the house, was a smirk. Was it?

A rogue branch tickled her cheek and she quickened her pace. The sun grew hotter on her nose. Her eyelashes picked up sweat from her cheeks. The trees thinned. She tasted a hint of salt in the air. The path spilled into a parking lot. Without intending to, she had walked to the sea.

At the head of the lot, a teenage boy wearing bathing trunks and an official-looking shirt sat on a low beach chair. He noticed her approach and stood up. "Welcome to Great Rock." He sounded like he'd been trained to say this. "Did you drive in?"

"No." She started to explain and then noticed he held a binder and a pen and was waiting to write something down. "You're not asking because you're curious."

"No." He shook his head and smiled and his face changed from some idea he must have had of professional seriousness to his normal state of open ease. "I'm supposed to keep track of who drives in and who walks in. We run out of parking fast. I hate turning people away. I really appreciate people like you, who walk in."

"I didn't really mean to walk in," she told him with a laugh. "I'm actually lost. Do you know where Blackberry Hollow is?"

"No, but I'm sure I can find it." He pulled out his phone to check and then apologized. "Sorry. No cell service. Comes and goes. Pretty annoying. I've seen the road, though, I'm sure. I don't think it's far. Long as you're here, you should grab a look at the water. The storm the other day swept away all the seaweed and pebbles. Looks like the surface of the moon down there. Really awesome. Won't last, either. Happens just a couple of times a year. Worth a look." Done with his ambassador job, he sat down and opened his book. It was, she saw, *The Great Gatsby*. He noticed her take in the title. "My girlfriend told me I *have* to read this. *Have* to. So . . ." He shrugged and lifted up the book to prove he was doing what he was told.

And Ginger wondered, did his girlfriend's mother ever think *he* was smirking? If Ginger had tried to get to know Nick, would Julia be walking beside her now?

"She's down there," he said, pointing to a staircase made of railroad ties.

"Julia?" Ginger felt as if she'd been slapped. How did he know her? When had she arrived?

"Mariah. My girlfriend. According to Mariah, this is the best beach on the island." He glanced down and took in Ginger's pants tucked into her socks. "I went through with a brush cutter this morning," he told her. "Part of my job. Keeping the path clear. It's clear now, straight to the beach." He went back to reading. His duty to report on the conditions of the trail was now done.

"Maybe I will check it out," Ginger said. "Just a quick look."

"Awesome," the boy said without looking up.

The path descended in a gentle slope and then steepened. At the bottom, a wooden staircase led to the sand. As she stepped off the last tread, she began to shiver. *It's just the breeze*, she told herself. She hurried past several unoccupied blankets and stopped at a group of large rocks facing the shoreline. She climbed onto the biggest one and tucked her feet into an indentation in the stone. Then she faced the sea.

Spine checks. She needed to schedule those before the school year was up. It was easy to get through the boys quickly. Large gangs of them would stuff themselves into her office to get checked together. But the fifth-grade girls were modest. No matter that she'd perfected her technique, lifting up the back of their shirts so that no one else could see, or that she used a practiced patter to distract them: "Your hair looks beautiful today" or "Your sweater really matches your eyes." Most of them still felt awkward about their bodies and if they *had* to see her, which they did, they preferred to see her alone.

Julia had beautiful posture until she met Nick. Nick was tall and slumped and wouldn't you know it, soon Julia was slumping too. Ginger knew she should not point this out. She remembered exactly what it felt like to have her posture criticized. But she hadn't been able to stop herself. The result was as expected. The day she said something about Julia's posture, it suddenly took on a more pronounced and quite intentional curve. She shook away the thought and watched the waves crash on the shoreline.

Shore break. That's what Callie called it. Ginger sat up straighter and stared at the ocean, ready for anything. A moment later she slumped, like Julia. Being ready was really no help.

A large rock jutted out of the sea directly in front of her, the top like a bald head with a fringe of seaweed hair. A trio of cormorants landed and huddled close, leaning hard against each other as if that would keep the waves from sweeping them away. Farther out she could see the giant boulder that gave the beach its name. Great Rock. At first glance she thought the shapes on top of the giant rock were cormorants too. Then one of the shapes uncoiled. It was a boy.

There was a group of them: five teenagers perched near the front of the rock, which rose high, at least twenty feet above the water. The teenagers stood, flapping their arms, preening, like birds about to take flight. Then, no warning, one jumped in.

It wasn't safe. She stood up and watched the others hurry to the edge, watched them peer into the water. She was too far away to hear them, too far away to see their expressions, but their bodies telegraphed distress. Of course she knew CPR. She was a strong swimmer, certified as a lifeguard in swimming pools. But she did not go in the ocean. She had not dipped in a toe since she was thirteen years old.

She scanned the beach, but there was no one else there. Just the teenagers' empty blankets and discarded towels, and too far away, up the stairs, up the path, the boy on the lawn chair reading *The Great Gatsby* for his girlfriend, Mariah.

A head popped out of the water, the diver, a boy. He bobbed and splashed. They were just having fun. He motioned and called to his friends to dive in and join him. A second boy did, and then a third, and she sat back down. They were having fun, and she was ready to save them. She laughed, and the cormorants, surprised, flew away in a rush.

When she looked back at the rock, there was one person left, a slight figure, the only girl. Mariah. The girl, Mariah, moved to the edge of the rock and stopped, as if considering whether or not to jump in.

"Don't," Ginger said quietly, but the girl was too far away to hear. Ginger's fingers felt inexplicably cold as she imagined it was Julia standing there. Julia would have jumped in fast just to prove her mother wrong.

Ginger heard the echo of her voice. *Do not jump off rocks. Do not stay out past twelve. Do not slump. Do not smirk.* It was inevitable that after a while, everything else would fall away and all Julia would hear was the *not, not, not* until Julia herself disappeared.

With perfect form, the girl, Mariah, knifed into the sea. When her head popped up, her friends applauded, the water exploding with their exuberance.

At the unoccupied blanket next to her, two seagulls fought each other over a bag of kettle corn, pecking, pushing, fighting to get to the bounty inside. Then, as if an alarm had sounded, they flew off at once, leaving the pockmarked bag behind.

In the parking lot on Mount Washington, when she stood in crushing silence beside the hot car as Julia stuck the Planet Earth hat on her head, Ginger wished they could take a break from each other. She didn't take it any further than that. Just a fleeting wish she admitted to no one, not even Richard. A wish, she knew, mothers were not supposed to make. And somehow it was that wish—of all the wishes she'd ever made, and she had made many—that one foul, half-thought, careless wish that had come true.

Her shoes felt heavy as she trudged back across the sand. She was almost at the steps when Mariah emerged from the water.

"Hello," the girl said, and then smiled before running off to get her towel. That was all, just hello, and then, as seawater dripped down her chin, a smile.

The smile made Ginger mute. It wasn't only that Mariah seemed about the same age as Julia, or that she looked so beautiful, with the same flushed-cheeks look of being young and in love. It was that Mariah had done exactly what Julia would have done, all Julia ever wanted to do: jump off a rock with grace and abandon and walk out, just fine, from the sea.

Ginger hurried up the stairs to the path. When she passed the boy on the low chair, he looked up and asked, "You okay?"

She wiped her eyes with the back of her hand and said, "Yes, fine, thanks," and then added in a whisper, "Just a little sad." She quickened her pace so that she would be beyond the bend before the sweet boy had a chance to ask her, "Why?"

CHAPTER
THIRTY-FOUR

When Ginger passed the huge boulder with the stack of bricks on top for the second time, she realized the trail she was on was a loop that she'd now gone around twice. She proceeded slowly after that, scanning the woods on either side for the turnoff she'd missed. Fifteen minutes later, there it was again, the rock with the bricks piled on top.

Humiliated. That's how she'd feel if she had to dial 911 and tell the dispatcher, *I'm lost in the Menemsha Hills. I don't know where.* She imagined the embarrassment of a helicopter search, of hearing the motor of the engine overhead, of waving to be seen in the dense brush. But even humiliation was not a possibility. The intermittent cell service was currently in the "no bars" mode. Her last-ditch idea, to make her way back to the beach and beg a ride from Mariah or one of her friends, turned out to be equally futile because now the turnoff for the beach seemed to have vanished as well.

She sat down, leaned against a large tree trunk, and began berating herself for a myriad of failures. Failing to bring water, failing to bring a map, failing to bring food, failing to dress appropriately for hot weather. She proceeded on to bigger failures: failure to work harder to make things right with Richard, failure to work harder to give her daughter more space to be herself. Her thoughts stopped at the sound of motion from deep within the trees. She jumped up as a pony pulling a carriage burst out of the woods.

The woman in the driver's seat made a clicking noise and the pony stopped. "Didn't mean to scare you. Sorry."

"That's okay," Ginger said. "I'm just jumpy. Jumpy and lost."

The woman's felt riding helmet and sunglasses obscured her face. "You look lost." She yanked on the reins, and the pony begrudgingly gave up on eating the low foliage. "Where do you want to be?"

"Blackberry Hollow. Do you know where that is?"

"Sure do. And you're right. You are very lost." She pointed to a metal ledge behind her seat. "If you want a lift, climb on. Not exactly built for passengers, but I haven't lost anyone yet."

Ginger eyed the small space between the wheel hubs. It did not look at all safe, but her lack of orienteering skills gave her no alternative. She climbed aboard.

The woman, Holly, showed her where to stand and how to grip the waist-high metal bar so that it wouldn't knock out her teeth when she had to duck under a branch, or ram into her chest when they ran over a stump. "Don't worry," Holly said when she saw Ginger's wary look. "It's not far. Maybe five minutes, if I can keep this crazy pony from nibbling on the scrub oak." She gave another soft click of her tongue and the pony took off at a gentle trot.

After a few minutes the path narrowed and the pony slowed to a walk. Holly glanced back to make sure her passenger had come through the brambles okay. "You visiting Thomas?"

"How did you know?"

"I'm a genius. Also, it's the only house on Blackberry Hollow. He your caretaker?"

"No," Ginger said, and then, "I don't know. I'm just visiting. My sister Callie lives here."

"You're Callie Tangle's sister?" Holly leaned over and patted the pony. "Callie likes Wilma. Not so much my other pony, but who can blame her. He's not likable. She loves my dogs too. I got four Welsh springer pups right now. Echo started out one of mine. Sweet dog. Lean right"—Holly shouted and then—"hold on," as she made a sharp left. She pulled the carriage to a stop. "Thomas's place is just ahead. Tell everyone Holly says hello."

"I will. Thanks. Can I pay you for your trouble?"

"Do I look like a taxi?" Holly and her pony disappeared back into the woods.

Ginger hiked up the road in the direction Holly pointed. She could hear traffic in the distance, cars and trucks whizzing by out of sight beyond the ridge. The air smelled of pine, hay, and exhaust. In the distance, she could make out a pitched roof. Solar panels caught glints of sun that ricocheted into her eyes. It seemed like all the insects of the world had arrived, conspiring to buzz around her head. The trees thinned. Her back felt wet with sweat. The sun beat down hard. Her feet were blistered and her mouth parched, and now, little flashes, like lightning bolts, were appearing in the corner of her eyes. She felt faint. Time skipped forward. She didn't remember walking up the steps to the house, but here she was, standing at the front door. She didn't remember knocking, but she heard a woman's voice. "Coming." Time skipped again and the woman was in front of her, calling in an urgent tone, "Thomas!"

Ginger watched as if from above. The woman seemed familiar. She wanted to ask her name. But when she spoke, the words that came out of her mouth were, "I'm feeling unwell." Her hearing was the last thing to go. There was the tapping of someone's feet as they ran and then a thud, which she somehow understood to be the sound of her own body hitting the floor.

• • •

When she came to, she was sitting in a chair across from a woman whose long gray braid was draped over the front of her shoulder. The woman held out a glass of water. "Take her to the hospital," she said. "And don't just drop her off, Thomas. Wait with her till they've seen her."

Ginger sat up straighter. "I'm okay." She took the glass and drank the water in big gulps, stopping only to reassure them. "Just dehydrated. Thank you." When the glass was emptied, the woman went to get more. "Thanks," Ginger said when she returned. She finished the second glass and put it down. "That's better. I should have brought water. I'm such an idiot. I never thought I'd end up lost. I'm sorry for the bother. I really am fine."

"Your color is back," the woman admitted. Then, as if she'd been waiting to make sure the danger had passed, she put her hand to her mouth and gasped. "Look how beautiful you are."

It was the hand Ginger recognized first, the strong hand, and then the wide face, the kind eyes, the nose, slightly turned up at the end. "Evelyn?" She stood up fast and grabbed the back of the chair for balance.

Evelyn reached a hand to steady her. "Oh my," she said, and then, "Oh my," again.

"Why don't you two sit outside for a bit," Thomas said. "It's cool in the shade out back."

Evelyn agreed and led Ginger by the elbow through the house to the patio outside the kitchen door. She waited till Ginger sat before slowly lowering herself into one of the wrought iron chairs set around a small café table. Ginger noticed a shiver of pain cross her face.

"Be a dear," Evelyn told Thomas, "Get us some lemonade from the fridge. And something to eat, if you don't mind." Her eyes followed her son as he went inside. "He's so good to me." They sat in silence.

Evelyn stared into Ginger's eyes, searching. "Do you hate me? It's okay if you do."

"Why would I hate you?"

Evelyn lifted a shoulder. She couldn't quite manage a full shrug. "When you didn't write, I assumed"—she studied Ginger's face—"you didn't get my letters."

Letters. Plural. "No. I didn't get any letters."

Evelyn sank back in her chair. "I wondered about that. I asked your mother once. Didn't want to upset her. Kept it casual. *Haven't heard from Ginger. Did she get a chance to read my letter yet*—like that. Your mother was hard to fool. Got offended immediately. Told me if she was going to be a thief, she'd go for diamonds, not stamps. I should have known. She didn't really want us to stay in touch." And then she remembered Glory was gone. "Sorry. I don't mean to speak ill of her. Your mother was a fighter. She had a ferocious will. If she believed something was wrong, she'd fight like anything to make it right."

Thomas came out with a tray. He set it down and asked his mother if she wanted a pillow. She shooed him away, and he took it with a look of genial exasperation.

"Fusses over me endlessly," Evelyn confided after he'd gone in. "I'm perfectly fine. I've got old bones is all, and there's nothing he can do about that." She took a sip of lemonade and Ginger noticed the tremor in her hand. "Thomas tells me you have questions."

Ginger decided to begin with the newspaper in the suitcase. "We had no idea there was someone else in the hole. We thought Charlie was the only one who"—she forced herself to finish the sentence—"died. And the article didn't say who the other boy was."

"Oh, that article. *The other boy.* You can't imagine how many people thought Thomas was the other one in the hole. For the longest time after, we'd be going about our business, and people would run over and grab him, like he was back from the dead."

"Who *was* it?"

Evelyn picked up her glass but her shaking was worse now, so she put it back down. "No one told you." She seemed to be struggling to understand. "You don't remember anything?"

"I remember a lot. I remember people digging, people crying, people trying to help. But I don't remember the kids. Other than Thomas." It was unnerving, how Evelyn was looking at her now. Despite the heat, Ginger started shivering again. "What don't I know? What happened to the other boy?" She couldn't imagine what could be worse than what happened to Charlie.

"There was no other boy." Evelyn folded her hands.

"Thank god. That would have been too much to bear."

But Evelyn didn't look at all relieved. She reached across the table and placed her hand on Ginger's. "It was your sister. Callie was with Charlie when the hole collapsed."

"No," Ginger corrected her. "Callie was at the far end, on the other side of the cliffs, getting clayed. Thomas went to get her. I saw them coming back. Minty wanted me to go with her, but I wouldn't go until I saw Callie." Much was a blur, but not that. That memory was clear.

Evelyn nodded. "Thomas told me he went to get her. But he never found Callie because she wasn't there. You must have seen him walking with one of the cousins. Thomas told me he came back from the cliffs, from looking for Callie, right when she was pulled out of the hole." She dropped her voice. "They tell me when the hole collapsed, Callie fell in on top of Charlie." She dabbed at her eyes. "Charlie was buried beneath her." She whispered the next. "He didn't have a chance."

For a moment Ginger was still. Then she asked, "How long? How long before they got her out?" She knew every factor that affected prognosis. She'd spent years parsing this out from the news stories she read about sand-hole collapses. What she'd learned was that nothing, not the density of the sand or the temperature of the air or the expertise of the doctors or the equipment at the hospital mattered as much as *duration without air.* How long the child's brain was starved of oxygen determined life or death or damage.

"I wasn't there," Evelyn reminded her. "They got her to the hospital in time."

And then Ginger remembered it, the moment she looked back at the beach and saw Casper carrying a body. A body limp and small, an arm that reached out to give a fluttery wave, a delicate hand that confused her. She remembered thinking, *Charlie looks so small, his hand like a little girl's.* Because it *was* a girl's hand. It was Callie's hand. Glory didn't take Callie with her so that Charlie would wake up to the cutest Tangle. Callie had been *admitted.* "And the hospital discharged her. They wouldn't have sent her home if she wasn't okay."

"It was a different time," Evelyn pointed out. "Callie seemed okay enough. You saw how she was. You see how she is. What did *you* think?"

"I thought"—Ginger corrected herself—"we thought, Mimi and I, we were led to believe Callie had a bad reaction. From being at the hospital. From seeing something when Charlie died."

"He didn't die at the hospital. He died in the hole. With Callie on top of him."

"Did she suffer brain damage?"

"We didn't ask so many questions then. Callie, anyone could see, she wasn't the same. But no one talked about *diagnosis* or treatment. Your parents tried to do right by her. They really did. But no one knew what the right thing was. And there was a lot of anger. Finger-pointing. At your mother. At your father. At Casper. At me."

"Why you?"

"I'm the numbskull who suggested your mother come to the island in the first place. And I'm the one who introduced her to my brother. Casper tried to make up for what happened. He did. He took very good care of Callie when she came. Looked out for her until she could look out for herself. After that, he stayed on as caretaker. Really, his whole life was about caring for Callie. Until he couldn't. Then Thomas took over."

"Caretaker of the house or caretaker of my sister?"

"The house." Evelyn thought about it. "Maybe both."

Ginger let this sink in. "How did Callie end up here?"

"I'm still not sure I understand everything that happened. I know after your father died, your mother struggled. Trying to take care of Callie, and you and Mimi. What was it she used to say? *When you were together, you girls were like a tropical cycloon.*"

"Cyclone? Typhoon?"

Evelyn shrugged. "Something like that. Casper was the one who came up with the idea about moving. He thought all of you should move here. That Callie would have an easier life. The house Callie lives in, your house, that was Casper's. Went from my mom to him, and then he sold it to your mom. For Callie." Evelyn wiped at her eyes.

"But we didn't move here. Just Callie did. Why?"

"Your mother's the only one who could have explained that. I didn't understand. No one did. Minty and the rest of them, they thought she was awful, sending Callie here and keeping you and Mimi with her. There came a point I couldn't say your mother's name out loud in front of them."

Thomas interrupted. "Mimi just called and asked me to tell you she's been worried to death and if you don't come home now, she'll call the police. I think she was kidding, but I'm not sure. If you want a lift, I can take you. I have to go that way anyway to check on a house. Marauding turkey on the loose."

Evelyn reached over and tapped Ginger's hand. "Go ahead. Go see your sister." She stood up, holding the table for support. "We'll talk again soon." They embraced for a long moment, neither wanting to be first to let go.

• • •

In the car Ginger asked Thomas when he took over as caretaker for the house.

"I've been helping my uncle for a while," he answered. "It's about a year since I've been doing it on my own. Uncle Casper didn't want to stop. Even after he turned eighty. But then he fell. Broke his hip. After that, something changed. He wasn't the same. Been in a wheelchair ever since. Still, working till eighty—that's not too bad, right? We just moved him to a place in town. His mind, it's going. Not fun to watch." He blurted out the next. "I was there. The night they had the big fight about Callie coming. I wasn't supposed to be, but I was there."

"You remember it?"

He nodded. "I'll never forget it. It was a big deal. I was out in the backyard on the tire swing. Tire swing's still there. I check on it now and then—make sure the rope's still good. Callie is a big fan of that swing. But that night, it was just me, alone on the swing, when all of a sudden a pack of adults comes marching out on the deck like someone called a meeting. They were rough on your mom. And on Uncle Casper. Your mom, she didn't say anything. Not at first. She just took it. I was sitting on the tire swing trying not to move, trying to make myself invisible. But I couldn't make myself deaf. They were shouting all different reasons why Callie coming without the rest of you was an awful idea and your mom just sat there. When she finally did speak—it was dark by then. I couldn't see her but I could hear—she said, *Callie's like a flower. A special flower that needs to be transplanted somewhere it can grow right.*"

Ginger struggled to take this in. "But we didn't all move. Did she explain that?"

"No. No one explained, not to me. But things were crazy. For years after the accident my mom and my aunts would drag me and my cousins to all the town halls to give out flyers to the summer people. The summer people would be lined up to get beach passes, all vacationy, wearing sun hats and smelling of coconut oil, and my mom and aunts would shove flyers in their faces about how dangerous the beach was. We didn't win any popularity contests. I mean, here's the town trying to get people to go to the beach, giving out brochures for restaurants and for how to get a clamming license, and along come these wild women yelling, *Danger, danger. Don't let your kids play in the sand.*" He let out a rueful laugh. "At the time, us kids, we didn't understand. I get it now. They were just trying to make sure no one else went through what your family did. You know, Callie is like a sister to me. My mom and Uncle Casper were like second parents, when Glory couldn't be here."

"How often did she come?"

"Depended. Sometimes a weekend. Sometimes a week. Summers she'd come longer. Where did you think she was when she was here?"

Ginger laughed. "I don't know. I'm still trying to figure that out."

"I guess the accident turned everything topsy-turvy. You know, your mom used to kid around that Callie didn't really need her. That she just tolerated her. And Callie would agree. I guess it was true. Callie never did know how to lie." He pulled into the driveway of the Tangle house and turned to face her. "You ask me, Callie turned out pretty good. Maybe your mom knew what she was doing, after all."

Mimi came running out of the house. "Finally. I was about to send out a search party."

"I told you where I was going. You remember Thomas, right?"

Dimples on, Mimi extended a hand. "Nice to see you. Want to come in? I put up coffee."

"I'd love to," Thomas said. "But I have to go check on a house down the road. I can stop by after, if that's okay."

As soon as Thomas drove off, Ginger filled Mimi in on what she'd learned, that it wasn't a boy who fell in the hole with Charlie. That it was Callie. Suddenly, she noticed Callie's car was back. "Is she home?"

Mimi swung around and saw it too. "She must have come in while I was upstairs."

They rushed in the house, calling out their sister's name, but there was no answer. When they got to Callie's room, they stopped at her closed bedroom door.

Mimi was about to knock when she heard something. "Listen."

Ginger listened and heard it too, a muffled voice from inside the room. The words were impossible to make out, but the melody was familiar. She heard a laugh and her stomach clenched at the sound of Glory.

CHAPTER
THIRTY-FIVE

The sliding door to the backyard was open, the glass streaked where someone had cleaned. Ginger noticed wadded paper towels and an empty bottle of Windex in the wastebasket. She stepped to the door and called out. "Callie?" She slid the door closed. "Gone."

"Look who's here." Mimi stood in front of Callie's desk; the laptop was open and Glory's face filled the screen, a video of their mother frozen, midword.

"Callie must have just been here watching this," Ginger said. She pressed a key and Glory came to life.

"We can go over this as many times as you need. You are an excellent memorizer, Callie Claire. Am I right? Course I am."

Ginger clicked back to the beginning and there she was, her mother, white-haired and frail.

"Sit where I can see you, Callie Claire. Over to my side. Can you see me?" Glory smiled. "Goody, goody good."

"Callie's not here," Ginger told the image on the screen because in that dizzying moment her mind failed to sort out that Glory could not be Skyping in for a chat because Glory was dead.

"Listen." Mimi turned up the volume. "You can hear Callie in the background."

"Do you have your notebook, Callie Claire?" Glory asked.

"I don't need it," came Callie's muffled reply.

"Course you do. There's nothing wrong with writing things down. It's a scientific fact. You write things down, you remember them. Not just you. Everyone."

"Okay," Callie said. "I'll write things down."

Ginger stared at the screen. "When was this made?"

"You sure that's pointing at my face?" Glory leaned in closer. Her forehead grew distorted. "Is that thing set up right?" The image jiggled. An arm—Callie's—stretched across the screen to fix something. "That's better."

They were in the kitchen, Ginger realized. The kitchen in New Jersey. She tried to place it in time. Her mother's white hair was in disarray, and her eyeliner had been applied with a shaky hand to only one eye. "This must have been right before we moved her into the Meadows. Callie was in New Jersey. And Mom didn't tell us."

Glory smiled. "Bored of me yet?"

Callie's voice, offscreen. "I'm never bored."

"Course you're not. Now, remember. Once we make this thingama-jig, you can listen to me whenever you want. Over and over is perfectly fine. But do it in private. Remember we talked about privacy? Maybe you should write that down in your notebook. That way you'll never forget. Do you have a pen?"

Offscreen: "I don't forget anymore. I don't need a pen."

"Everyone forgets, sometimes. Go get a pen. I'll wait." Glory closed her eyes and counted to ten. "Got it? Goody, goody good. Now, when I talk about privacy, it's not because your sisters don't love you. Believe me when I tell you, they love you a lot. Stay there. I'll be right back." She moved out of sight, but Ginger could hear her singing. "I know you're in here. Can't hide from Glory. Oh, my, what happened here?" She came back and smiled at the camera. "Better?"

"Fresh lipstick," Ginger observed. "Eyeliner on the other eye."

"Let's go over what you are *not* going to do. Remember, you can go over this as many times as you need." Glory blinked hard twice, what they used to call "eye hugs." This was the moment where the video had been frozen when they first came in. "You are an excellent memorizer, Callie Claire. Am I right? Course I am. Now about the house. Stay in it. Be firm no matter what the sisters say. They'll have plenty to say. Especially Mimi. But she'll come around. If the choice of who gets the house is you or the land bank, believe me, she'll pick you." She smiled, proud of herself.

Ginger glanced at Mimi, who was watching through narrowed eyes.

"She means well," Glory said. "It's just Mimi thinks I'm not fair. Nothing you can do. Been that way since the day she was born. If she starts up with the *It's not fair* business, just sing a song in your head. Not out loud. Out loud doesn't work as good. Try the 'Swiss Navy' one. Song's perfect for getting into the brain cracks. Pushes everything you don't want to think about out. Not just you. Works for everyone. Keeps the brain crisp." Glory cleared her throat and started singing, alternating shoulders thrusting forward to a beat no one else could hear. "'We don't want to march with the infantry. Ride with the *binfrantry*.'" She stopped. "Do the motions. That's what makes it fun." She looked disappointed, and then smiled. Callie must have finally done what she'd asked. She started moving too—standing up, stomping her feet—but since the camera couldn't follow her, all that Ginger saw was a flash of her mother's stomach, of her hips, of her neck. "'We don't want to fly over Germany.' Okay, now you try. Just in your head." Settling back in her chair, Glory stared out with piercing eyes. "Are you singing?" She joined in, singing silently, exaggerating the movement of her lips so Callie could see what the words were. "'We're in the Swiss Navy.'" When she was done, she applauded. Then she turned serious. "It will make me very happy to know you'll be living in this house with your brother. His memory, I mean. And don't worry. If you need help with the house, you have Casper. He'll always be here for you. Well, not always." A look of distress passed over her face, but she shook it away. "Otherwise, ask Thomas. What a sweet boy, that Thomas is. A real lifesaver."

Callie said something Ginger couldn't understand.

"I know you think you can." Glory's voice turned softer. "But everything doesn't always go exactly how we want. Sometimes emergencies happen and we need a backup. Not just you. Everyone. That's what your notebook is for. Backs up your brain. Remember what we learned? How we don't forget what we do every day?"

"I don't forget things."

"When you're stressed you do. Which is normal. Everyone gets stressed. And you're lucky. You have Echo." She stopped and listened to something Callie said. "Normal life span, twelve to fifteen years. What is he now, eight? So he'll be around awhile. You remember what to do when it's his time to go? Course you do."

Offscreen, Callie answered, "Ask Holly for a new dog."

And Ginger realized, "Echo is a service dog."

"You have Holly's number in your book, right? Goody good. And you're not too shy to call her? Good. You have to promise you won't get shy about your words again. Do you promise?"

Ginger turned up the volume, but they could not make out Callie's answer.

"So what. You get a little tongue-tied. Who doesn't. Talk anyway. And sing. Singing keeps stress away. You must not let yourself get shy about using words, Callie Claire. You don't want to ever lose your words again. I will never forgive that school-witch, making you self-conscious about talking. Well I fixed her, didn't I? Every family has its quirks.

Ours is we mix up words. That's what Tangles do. End of story. Mission accomplished."

"She mixed up words to cover for Callie," Ginger said.

Mimi's eyes narrowed further. "I sometimes catch the boys doing that."

Glory smiled, revealing a piece of toast stuck between her teeth for eternity. "We both did a good job, didn't we? I always said, being an actress comes in handy, even when you're not on the stage. We could have gone to Broadway, you and me. With your face, plus how good you are at memorizing? We could have had quite the careers. I guess we did, in a way." She raised her chin, daring the world to argue the point. "If you get down in the dumps, you remember that. We turned out to be a couple of excellent actors. You know what they say. Pretend everything's fine, everything *is* fine. And I'm not lying when I say that. I'm no liar."

"Hah." Mimi coughed out a laugh.

"Hold on a sec," Glory said. "Don't move." She got up and disappeared, but Ginger could hear her singing her way into another room. "Almost ready. One more second. Here I come."

"New dress," Ginger observed when her mother came back.

Glory sat down and smiled at the camera. The toast was gone, but a smudge of lipstick was on her tooth in its place. "Okay, let's talk about food. I know you think you have it all worked out. But still, remember, *three meals a day*. Even when you're not hungry. It's not your fault if you forget. That's what happens with people who lose their sense of smell."

"Why can't she smell?" Mimi asked.

"Happens sometimes with brain injuries."

"Remember what to do? Course you do. Go by the clock, Callie Claire. Eight is breakfast. Noon is lunch. Four have a snack if you're hungry. Six is dinner, hungry or not. What?" She leaned toward where Callie was sitting. "I know you can take care of yourself. I know. You've told me. You don't need me. You tolerate me."

Ginger couldn't make out the words, but Callie's tone was reassuring.

"Perfectly fine. Doesn't bother me a bit. Nothing bothers me. I'm like you. Self-sufficient. Put me in a room where I can sit and write my plays all day with no one interrupting? Happy as a clam."

"Plays?" Ginger repeated and Mimi shrugged. No idea.

"In this house? Never could get a minute to myself. So much tumult. But do I dwell? No. Water under the bridge." Glory suddenly looked alarmed. "That's an expression. You know I don't want you jumping off bridges. Doesn't matter if you're a good swimmer. You don't always know if something is safe or not." There was the muffled sound of Callie talking. Glory nodded. "Yes, you used to swim like a fish. But you think I can do everything I used to? Your father and I used to dance like a dream. I came this close to being a Rockette. Now, I kick a pebble out of my way, I topple over. Just how it is. Promise me Callie Claire, no more jumping off the Oak Bluffs bridge. And no swimming in the Cut. What did the doctor tell us? You have an urge to do something, you're not sure it's a good idea, what do you do?"

A soft voice answered, too quiet for them to hear.

"Correct. You put that note under your pillow and you sleep on it. Every morning, you check. If there's a note, you read it and decide. That's called *not being impulsive*. Especially if you get stressed. Not just you. Anyone can make bad decisions when they're stressed. Something to remember when I'm gone." Callie mumbled something. "Of course I'm here now. What I'm talking about is someday. Someday when I'm not here." Glory sighed, and seemed to deflate. "Of course, you can always visit me on your computer. Or in here." She tapped her head. "Memory." She seemed to be struggling to maintain her composure. She shifted, moving closer to the screen, and pulled a tissue out of her sleeve. Now Ginger could see the spidery lines around her lips and the broken capillaries in the crease of her nose.

Glory swiveled away, patted her cheeks and eyes with her tissue, and swiveled back. "Remember, when I'm gone you'll have your sisters. And don't worry. It'll be fine with all of you together. Everyone's all grown up now. Transplantation took. Every one of you bloomed. You're one big beautiful bouquet." Her stare hardened. "Your sisters will do anything for you." And then she seemed to sink into her chair. "I don't know how I got myself into this predicament." She turned away and dabbed her eyes, and offscreen Callie said something. "I'm fine. You know me. I'm always fine." She straightened her spine. "Far as the sisters go, just remember, Mimi is as stubborn as a bloodstain. Came that way straight out of the womb. And Gingie has skin like a peach. Bruises if you look too hard. Nothing you can do about it." She sighed and her mouth twitched. "Was every decision I made the best?" She got very still. "Maybe not." She shook off the thought and looked away, and when she looked back her eyes were wet again.

"Pay no attention to my eyes." She sniffed, hard. "Dry as dust in this house. Eyes tear up every time I *brink*. I'll be fine. We Mangles are always fine." She wiped her eyes with the side of her hand and smiled. "I got to ask Gingie to get me drops. Gingie loves to do errands. You need anything at all, Callie Claire, just ask her. Makes her happy. I don't know why. Girl has a marshmallow for a heart. If you have a big problem, get Mimi on the horn. What a fighter. Like a bulldog. Never gives up. She's like me that way. And if Mimi says no, ignore her and ask again. She'll come around. She may be tough on the outside, but inside, another big heart. Both of them, all of you. My three bighearted girls. Ooh." She waved her hands in front of her face as if she needed cooling off. "Better stop. Getting *dripsy*."

Her hand touched her mouth three times, little kisses, which she blew into the air. "Kisses in your pocket, Callie Claire. Special kisses. Last forever." She touched her hand to her lips again, and then looked over where Callie was sitting. "Enough?" The screen went black.

CHAPTER THIRTY-SIX

They watched the video a second time. When it was over, while Glory blew kisses for Callie's pocket, Ginger glanced up at the bookshelf above the desk, at the notebooks lined up like soldiers. Notebooks that reminded her of the ones she'd used in elementary school. She pulled one out, handed it to Mimi, and pulled another for herself.

She ran her hand over the cover—an embossed illustration of two girls, heads hidden beneath bonnets, exchanging daisy bouquets—and then opened it. "Are these the plays she was talking about? Mom wrote plays?"

"They're her journals," Mimi said, skimming. "From when she toured with her theater group."

Ginger read a couple of paragraphs. "This isn't real. This didn't happen. Listen. 'Today we performed at the Lake Lugano Concert Hall in Schenectady.' Lake Lugano? In Schenectady?"

"There could be a Lake Lugano there. We don't know."

"Okay, but you think this is true? 'The hotel was once a palace. The bathroom sink is made of gold. Every night we dress for dinner. That's the rule. Men have to wear white tie and women wear gowns. With long white gloves. Imagine!' A palace in Schenectady? And gowns? Mom packed gowns and long white gloves?"

"It could be. It's possible."

Ginger didn't think so. She read from the next page. "'Today, I was late for rehearsal because I called home, and wouldn't you know, Mimi had just started a fire in the oven. I told Gingie, do not let her cook anymore.'"

"I remember that," Mimi said. "I made us TV dinners and put it on broil instead of bake, and there was a fire in the oven. That happened."

"Okay. That part's real. But listen to what she says next. 'Lucky for Gingie, I didn't have time to stay on the phone and be mad because the butler was standing there, waiting to draw my bath, and I didn't want to be rude.' She had a butler waiting to draw her a bath in Schenectady?"

"Mom was the queen of exaggeration. What else is new?"

Ginger flipped forward and read some more. "'This theater is like a church. It's got a domed ceiling with an actual mural painted on it. Like Broadway, only better.'"

"That could be," Mimi said, though she sounded less sure.

"Here's the theater at the next stop. 'Like a tiny jewel box. Like a church. With a mural on the domed ceiling. Like Broadway, only better.'" She flipped through, skimming. "Every theater in every town they went to is the same. Same curtains, same ceiling, all of them, like Broadway, only better." She skipped ahead a few pages. "'Tonight was formal dinner before last dress. The chef made a coq au vin like you can't believe. When he came out to meet us, he asked me what movies I've been in. Imagine! He thought I was a movie star. And he is not just any old chef. He used to be a chef for the Queen of England. Imagine. The queen's chef thought I was a movie star.'"

"She loved to embellish."

"Really? Which part is true? The theaters are like Broadway? The queen's chef complimented her?" She flipped to the end and read another entry. "'Last night we got the news. Richard Nash is coming to our performance! The actual playwright of *The Rainmaker* is coming to see me. This is it. My life is about to change.' Okay, here she switches. Back to reality. 'Callie is doing very well. She can make her own meals now and she washes her own clothes. Who knew she'd turn out to be my most self-sufficient? She told me she's got a plan to start a business. A real entrepreneur, like her father. Imagine. Busy all the time, planning her business taking care of dogs. I hardly ever see her, but I don't mind. I'm content to sit in this lovely chair on this lovely deck and write to you, my darling journal.'" Ginger closed the book. "She was here. That's why the people in the Tabernacle knew her. Not because she was a generous patron who sent them a check in the mail. She attended those concerts. She told us she was going on tour with her theater group, told all those stories about summer stock. But she was here. Sitting on the deck outside. Making things up." Ginger glanced at Mimi and her shoulders sank. "You knew?"

"No. No. But—she might have tried to tell me." Mimi sighed. "You were in college, okay? Callie was at her *special acting school.* I was stuck, finishing high school. I tried to stay out of the house as much as possible. Especially when Mom got weird. I mean, unusually weird. One night, out of the blue, she apologized to me. It was all crazy talk, about how she wasn't where I thought she was. It didn't make any sense. I thought she was drunk."

"You didn't ask her to explain what she meant?"

"Really? When you were alone with Mom and she got all, *Let's tell each other what's really in our hearts,* what did you do?"

"Got out of the room. Fast as possible."

"Thank you. Which is exactly what I did. Can't tell you where I went, but I got out of there fast as I could. Next time I saw her? Makeup on, perfumed wrists—like it never happened—she tells me she's going with her theater group to Niagara Falls. I never questioned it." She slumped in her seat. "What was wrong with me?"

"Why would you question it? It was such a relief when she went away." Ginger pulled another book off the shelf, a later model, this one with a hand-tooled leather cover. She opened it and read. "'I miss those two girls. I think about them all day long. Imagine what it would have been like if we could have been together. I'm going to call them. Both of them. Send them kisses. Kisses for their pockets. Special kisses last forever.'" Ginger closed the book.

Mimi took the last journal off the shelf and skimmed it. "No theater group touring here. This one's all real. 'What a horrid day. All that nonsense with the Cut. I wish I was allowed to read the notes Callie puts under her pillow. But no, I'm not to interfere. I'm to leave her alone so she can learn to be independent, self-sufficient, self-reliant. What good is self-reliance going to do her if something dreadful happens at the Cut?'"

"The Cut," Ginger said. "Didn't Mom say something about that on the video?" She tracked the video backward and stopped it.

Glory's worried face filling the screen. "'No more jumping off the Oak Bluffs bridge. And no swimming in the Cut.'"

"Callie was always a good swimmer," Mimi said. "What was Mom afraid of?"

"I'm not sure," Ginger said. "But I think we better figure it out."

By the time Thomas came back from his client's property, the pack of aggressive wild turkeys now scattered in the woods, Mimi was sitting on the couch, laptop open, complaining about how Google had let her down. "I got a fashion blog, a movie, what to do if you get cut from your team, how to care for a cut finger. It's useless."

Ginger explained to Thomas. "We just watched a video Mom made for Callie where she warned her to stay away from the Cut. We're trying to understand what she meant."

Thomas nodded. "That drove Glory crazy, Callie always wanting to go swim in the Cut. Here. Let me show you." He borrowed Mimi's computer and pulled up a short video. "Friend of mine made this a couple of years ago. This is what it looks like the day they open the pond." He turned the screen around, and they watched the image of a giant digger cutting a small trench in the sand.

"That doesn't look dangerous," Mimi said. "It's a foot wide. You could step right over it."

"True." Thomas took back the computer and pulled up another video. "Here's the same trench twelve hours later. What would you guess? Maybe fifty feet across now? The water did that. They always wait to open the pond until the moon is either full or new because that's when the tide is strongest. With a strong tide, the water acts like a drill." He pulled up a third video, three people on horseback fording what looked like a raging river. "This is the same place, at the end of the day. *After* the pond's had a chance to calm down."

"That's calm?" Ginger asked.

Thomas nodded. "That's why kids always want to go the first day. Water zooming in two directions like a river going nuts. It's something to see. And not only because of the water. The fish go crazy too. You get hundreds of herring racing out of the pond and then, like someone rang a dinner bell, the big fish show up with their mouths open. It's a great day to be a fisherman. The fishermen always seem to know when the pond is going to be opened. And on top of the fishermen coming out to get the stripers and the blues, and the stripers and the blues coming out to get the herring, you get the birds. They come for the fish too. And where there's birds, there's birders. Meanwhile, the water is crazy with riptides."

"You told us about this," Ginger remembered. "But why do they do it—open the ponds—if it's so dangerous?"

"Have to. If they didn't, with all the leaching septic tanks, it'd be bad for the oysters, bad for the fish, bad for the birds. It does get crazy at the Cut, though. Even the day after they open the pond. It's like a party. A real blast, except for when it goes bad."

"Bad how?" Ginger asked.

"End of the first day? Waves can be two, three feet high in the ridges. Old-timers like to say only the foolish ones drown, but I've heard of excellent swimmers getting in trouble in the Cut. Most people know enough to wait a couple of days. The current's still strong enough to be fun then, but it's not so strong you're risking your life. Some people, though, just don't want to wait. That's why the engineers and the pond commissioners, they try to keep it a secret. Which they can, if they're opening it under a new moon. But if the moon is full—well, you can't keep a full moon secret."

Ginger looked out the window and saw it, a daytime moon. "There's a full moon now."

She found the notes under Callie's pillow, two small pieces of paper folded like little origami hats. Both messages were the same. *I want to swim in the Cut.* She ran her finger over the words. Her sister's handwriting was like that of a young child. Ginger whispered, "Be safe."

She joined Mimi and Thomas in the living room—"I found two notes"—and gave a note to each. After Thomas read his, he offered to drive. When they got to his truck, Ginger saw Echo in the driver's seat.

"Why is Echo with you?"

"Sometimes if Callie's going somewhere she thinks Echo won't be happy, she'll drop him off at the house. That dog does not like to be alone, but he does like to lie on my mom's feet." He glanced up at the sky. "Looks like we're going to have a storm."

"Will they postpone the opening if it's raining?" Ginger asked.

"Not usually. But I can make a call. I know the guy who drives the digger. If they're digging today, he'll know where. Location changes, depending on conditions." He stepped away to make the call. "You might want to grab rain gear," he told them. "Or bathing suits. You're probably going to get wet."

By the time Ginger had changed into shorts and a T-shirt with a raincoat over it, Thomas was off the phone.

"No answer," he told them. "That doesn't mean anything. But we should probably get going."

As she got into the truck, Ginger noticed a defib kit in the flatbed and next to it, a rescue board, emergency blankets, and flares. "Why do you have all that equipment?"

"Volunteer paramedic. Always got my gear." He slid behind the wheel. "The pond is big. There's lots of choices where to dig. It may be a bit of a hunt."

"Is there time for a hunt?" Mimi asked.

And Ginger answered, "Yes," because she would not accept any other option.

CHAPTER THIRTY-SEVEN

Sepiessa and Long Point both had public access to the pond, so Thomas stopped there first. But the dredge was not at either location. They headed next to Quansoo. "There's not a lot of public entries," Thomas said. "It's mostly locked beaches. But Callie wouldn't have a problem getting in."

"Why not?" Mimi asked.

Thomas made a turn at the sign for Sheriff's Meadow. "Clients. She's got a bunch who like her to take their dogs to their private beaches for a run. So they give her keys to their gates."

The daytime moon, low in the sky, followed their movements like a malevolent eye. "How much farther?" Ginger asked.

"Almost there." The truck bucked in and out of a ditch, and Thomas apologized for not going faster. "These are private roads and some of the owners, they let them get run-down. To keep people from going fast. Some of the owners, they'd prefer we didn't come here at all."

The rain stopped and now Ginger saw drops glistening on the low grass of the wide meadows that stretched for miles around them, no homes or people in sight. Remote, except for the trees on the side of the road, which leaned in hard, as if they'd been whipped by the wind for so long they were permanently shocked into impossible angles of submission.

As they passed a grove of gnarly oaks, twisted branches testifying to their resolve, the road narrowed further. Thomas had to slow even more. Now, Ginger could make out giant wood hollows in the wide-trunked trees and though she couldn't see them, she could hear the rustling of small creatures. Above a hawk circled. Echo poked his head out the back window and barked, and a cloud of startled butterflies burst up out of the meadow.

"Can't we go any faster?" Ginger asked.

Thomas shook his head. "No. This road likes to eat tires for lunch." He held tight to the wheel as the truck rocked in and then out of a deep rut. "We're almost at the boat launch. Callie's a good swimmer," he added to reassure them.

A few minutes later they reached a parking lot. Thomas pulled his phone out and checked for a signal. "Good. I'm going to go make a call. See whose boat I can borrow." He stepped away.

"Mimi, look." Ginger pointed to a row of trucks, half a dozen parked close together, the pole racks on flatbeds and above the grills all empty. "Fishermen are here."

She and Mimi stepped out of the truck, and before they could stop him, Echo leaped out and took off, his leash doing figure eights in the sandy soil.

Mimi ran after him, calling, "Echo!"

Thomas returned, sliding his phone back in his pocket. "All set."

Together, he and Ginger unloaded the gear. Ginger took the throw blankets and rescue board. Thomas carried the defibrillator. They caught up to Mimi on a path that cut through a meadow. She held Echo tight, by his leash. Together, they hurried on, past high white sea grass, a small cluster of red lilies poking up out of the white like a surprise.

"It's not far," Thomas told them.

Ginger caught a glimpse of the moon disappearing behind gathering clouds. In the distance she could make out water, the same steely gray as the sky. A narrow stream snaked along beside them. A couple paddled by in a kayak, as if it were any afternoon, and Ginger, Mimi, and Thomas were a random group of hikers who just happened to be jogging at a pace befitting an emergency. "Is this the pond?"

"Tidal pools. Hear those paddlers arguing?"

The wind carried over the nagging melody of discord. She nodded and Thomas sped up. He was working hard to keep the conversation going as he hurried, keeping things light, Ginger guessed, so that panic wouldn't set in. "Guarantee," he told her, "when that couple pushed off this morning, they never gave a thought to what the current would be like when they wanted to come back. We call those two-seaters 'divorce kayaks.'"

Ginger turned and saw that despite how hard the couple was paddling, their uncoordinated strokes were confounding any chance of forward movement.

"They'll be fine," Thomas assured them. "They don't have far to go." The path curved and he started running faster. "Neither do we."

A pair of starlings startled out of the meadow, and in a motion that looked choreographed, swooped close together and then separated, so from opposite directions they could dive at a raven to drive it away. "Nest must be nearby," Thomas said.

Ginger and Mimi were full-out running now, to keep up. They hurried past wooden signs stuck into the earth like pickets. "Danger to Swimmers" "Danger: Steep Beaches" "Dangerous Currents" "Danger: Shifting Winds".

Thomas pointed. "This way."

"Walking on Private Shoreline Prohibited" "Horses Prohibited" "Trespassing Prohibited Regardless of Water Level".

Thomas led them down a short staircase. "Here we go." They stepped out onto a wide beach. As Ginger caught her breath, she waited for the first flush of fear, but nothing came.

Echo pulled hard at his leash, and it flew out of Mimi's grasp. She called after him, but this time the dog ignored her, loping into the rough water and paddling out, snout in the air.

"Is he okay to swim in the ocean?" Mimi asked.

Thomas whistled for Echo, but the dog ignored him too. "This is the pond."

The pond. It was easy to understand why Mimi mistook it for the ocean. Sizable waves lapped at the shore, and the air held the smell of a seaweed stew. Ginger tasted salt on her teeth and on her fingers. Small cuts she didn't know she had began to announce themselves. A low fog had set in now, covering everything in a hazy scrim. In the distance, half a dozen sailboats bobbed and then vanished in the clouds. She heard a dim hum, but it was hard to know if it was a hidden boat or a small passing plane. A hard wind skipped off the water and crept in through buttonholes, armholes, neck holes. Her shirt and raincoat billowed like sails.

"The dredge was here. You can see." Thomas pointed and Ginger saw them, tractor tracks on wet sand, disappearing before her eyes, swallowed up as the water raged from the pond toward the sea. "This way." Thomas guided them to his friend's boat. He handed Ginger a life vest and she clipped it shut.

Mimi said, "You stay. I'll go."

"No." Ginger blinked hard to see through the mist.

Thomas whistled again and Ginger saw Echo paddling hard into the wind, trying to get back. They boarded the boat and headed toward the dog. When they got close, Thomas cut the engine. The boat rocked as they idled, and Mimi leaned over, grabbing Echo's rear and heaving him up and in. The dog stumbled, righted himself, shook off the water, and nuzzled Mimi's leg.

Thomas restarted the engine, and the boat moved slowly across the pond. Water blew in from all sides. Though the beach had vanished in the fog, Ginger could make out the current going both ways at once.

"There should be lifeguards," Mimi said. "There should be swim cables. Why aren't the police guarding the shore?"

"There's miles of coastline." Thomas kept the boat on a steady slow course. "We'd need an army. We do the best we can."

The wind kicked up, howling its worry as it whipped them from every angle.

"What if we're too late?" Mimi's voice sounded small.

"We're not," Ginger said. *We can't be,* she thought. She looked up and saw a faint suggestion that beyond the clouds a sun existed. "It's going to blow over." She predicted this even though she couldn't know for sure. "We're going to find her."

Water thrashed the boat and Thomas stood up, knees soft to keep his balance. With a hand shading his eyes, he scanned the horizon. Echo moved next to him, tongue hanging out of the side of his mouth. Ginger rose to join the search.

Mimi held her arm. "Don't."

Ginger pulled away, and like a lighthouse turned, slowly, in a circle, searching in every direction. "Wait." She saw something. "There." She pointed.

Picking up a scent, Echo lurched to the prow of the boat and before anyone could stop him, the dog was overboard, off again, paddling hard toward what they could now see was a small figure in the water.

Ginger cupped her hands. "Callie!"

Thomas grabbed a rope with a small float attached to one end, and tied it to a cleat.

"She's okay," Mimi said. "She's doing the dog paddle. She's okay."

But Ginger saw something else. "She doesn't look okay to me."

Thomas agreed. "She's in trouble." He reached back and threw out the float rope. "Callie!" The wind carried her name away. "She's trying to outswim the rip." He drew the rope back and threw it out again. "She should be swimming perpendicular. She knows that."

"Then why isn't she doing it?" Mimi asked.

"Panic?" Ginger offered. "She looks tired." She dipped her hand into the water. Good. It wasn't cold. "How deep is it here?"

"Not very."

Ginger unbuckled her life jacket, took off her raincoat, and put the jacket back on. She moved to the front of the boat. "Is the ladder the best way in?"

"Don't." Mimi grabbed her arm. "I'll go."

"Whoever's going," Thomas said, "needs to put on the rescue rope now."

"Ginger can't go. She's afraid of the water."

Ginger took the safety rope out of Thomas's hand and attached the snap hook to her life jacket. Thomas adjusted the rope so it was tight to her waist.

"No matter what," he warned her, "do not let go of this rope. And don't let Callie drag you down." As he moved to the cleat, making sure the knot on the throw rope was tight, he told her, "Drowning people do crazy things. Best approach is from behind. If she still manages to grab your neck, just peel her hands off. She puts her hands on your head, you push them away. She pushes you underwater or tries to climb on you, you let go and use the rope to get back to the boat. I'll get you out."

"I can't leave her."

"Then don't go. If she's desperate and you don't let go, we lose you both."

"Please don't go," Mimi begged.

"That won't happen." Ginger started down the ladder.

Thomas tugged on the rope. "When I tug like this, it means I'm asking if you're okay."

Ginger tugged twice in reply. "And I'll tug back so you'll know that I am."

Thomas steered the boat as close as he dared to where Callie was swimming, close enough so that Ginger could see that although her sister's arms were thrashing, her legs were no longer doing any work.

"Go now," Thomas told her. "Stay safe."

Ginger scrambled down the ladder and she was in, in the water, all the way in, except for one hand holding on to the bottom rung. She felt the pull of the water on her weightless body. She let go and went under.

When her head came up she saw Echo ahead of her, back legs hanging loose, paddling fast toward Callie, who was struggling. Propelled by adrenaline, Ginger kicked hard, put her head under the water, came up to breathe, reached her arms over her head and fell into a strong rhythm. Reach, reach, reach, breathe hard, mouth sucking in air, reach, reach, reach, push air out in a rush, reach, reach, reach, and then, one last burst, and she was there, beside her sister.

Immediately, Callie's hands clawed at Ginger's neck and with great purpose, Ginger peeled them off. She repositioned her sister's arms so they wrapped around her waist, but Callie seemed determined to use Ginger's head as a lever to heave herself out of the water and when that didn't work, she tried to make a ladder out of Ginger's torso.

Ginger could feel her sister's feet desperately scrambling to find footing on her shoulders and then on her head. It was just as Thomas had described. Callie was in a full panic, ready to do anything to get air. But Ginger would not push her off. She would not let her sister drown.

The water rushed over them both, and again Callie pushed down on Ginger's head to try and get to air. Down Ginger went, down and further down and then, there was something behind her, Echo behind her, pushing at her back.

Taking advantage of momentum, Ginger forced her body up, her head up, gasping for air. Beside her, she saw Callie staring, wide-eyed and confused.

"Hold this." Ginger tried to force the goose-egg float of the rescue rope into her frightened sister's hand, but Callie flailed. Ginger felt herself tiring. The thought came like a life raft, her mother telling Callie she would not be scared if she sang.

The song came into Ginger's head out of nowhere. "Sing with me, Callie. 'There once was a boy in the north country.' Sing like Mom told you. 'There once was a boy in the north country.' Hold the float, Callie, and sing with me." And she saw it, Callie's hand closing around the small float. The pond water was stinging Ginger's cheeks as she urged her on. "Sing, Callie Claire. Sing."

And head tipped back, water spraying her face, Callie's lips parted and moved. In a quiet voice, she began to sing. "'He had sisters one, two, three.'"

"Keep going, Callie Claire. We're almost there."

"'Love will be true, true to my love. Love will be true to you.'"

Ginger's hand smacked against the side of the boat and then Thomas was pulling Callie in. Thomas and Mimi both were pulling Callie in together, and with her last remaining bit of energy, Ginger heaved herself over the lip of the dinghy and belly flopped onto the deck.

For a moment she lay still beside her sister, both of them breathing hard. When their heads turned toward each other, Ginger saw Callie's eyes open wide, the same bright blue as their mother's.

"Don't ever do that again," Ginger told her in a rush. In that moment, it was as if no one else was there. "Charlie died. Julia left. You cannot get hurt."

Callie turned on her side and spat up the sea. When Ginger heard the sound of crying she thought it was Callie and then realized it was both of them, sobbing together.

The bottom of the boat scraped at the shore of the pond. Ginger sat up. "Where's Echo?"

Callie tried to move, but she was too exhausted. Mimi kneeled beside her and stroked her sister's hair. "Thomas is turning the boat around. He's taking us back. We're going to get Echo now."

CHAPTER
THIRTY-EIGHT

There wasn't a life cycle event that Mimi didn't think could be improved by a theme. It took some brainstorming, but she figured it out. The scattering ceremony theme would be "Cast Party." With Richard, Neil, and the boys—collected from the last ferry of the day—sitting in the living room with Ginger and Callie, Mimi made her pitch. "Imagine a Lifetime Achievement Award after-party kind of thing. Perfect, right?"

Neil and the boys mumbled sounds of consent without looking up from their devices.

"Sounds good to me." Richard sat close beside Ginger on the couch, both of them leaning in to keep their bodies touching at all times, like teenagers. They'd only had a moment in private after the ferry got in, but that was enough time to let each other know they were committed to making things better between them.

Callie pulled a list from her pocket. "This is what Mom wants."

"You're kidding." Mimi grabbed the paper from her. "This better be the last one. There's nothing left to decide after this."

Callie nodded. "Last one."

Of course Glory couldn't anticipate all the particulars Mimi would come up with, but she managed to cover most of the bases. Mimi read aloud: "'I know darling Mimi will want to plan the world's most amazing memorial but don't go crazy with the food. I'll be dead, and you'll be too sad to be hungry. A little something to nibble is enough. Nothing fancy. Nothing messy. And no flowers. All the decorations I need will be right there, by which I mean all of you. Musicians, also no. You want music, use your voices. Callie Claire, remind everyone to project. Gingie, remember your posture. Slumping won't make you less tall. For the boat, I want Captain Lou. Callie, you call him. Tell him you need the big boat. On the big boat everyone will fit—the originals, the husbands, the boys, Julia.'" Mimi shot Ginger a look.

Ginger met her eyes. "I never got a chance to tell Glory about Julia."

Mimi quickly barreled on. "'Also, Callie, call Thomas. He'll bring Evelyn and Casper. Richard and Neil, you'll have to help Thomas and Captain Lou put Casper's wheelchair on the boat. Neil, try not to strain anything.'"

There was no way to argue with the dead, so Mimi got busy, canceling the bagpiper, the banquet tables, the galvanized tubs, the champagne and flowers, and the catered beach supper.

It was in the bright light of the noonday sun that Ginger finally saw Casper Diggans. His eyes had sunk deeper into his long face and his hands, curled into knots, lay limp in his lap. He sat, listing slightly, in his wheelchair, his understanding of the occasion unclear. Thomas had told her to expect this, that his uncle was in a state of genial befuddlement, happy to go along in good humor even when he didn't know what it was he was going along with.

When Casper saw Callie at the dock, his face brightened, but when he called out, "Hello," Ginger was struck by how weak his voice was, and how devoid of authority. He glanced at Echo, who had a cone over his head, and asked, "Well, well, who have we here?"

"That's my dog, Echo," Callie reminded him. "He has to wear a cone till his eye heals. It got injured at the pond. Remember, I told you? How your friend Bo helped rescue him?" Casper's forehead remained furrowed. "Bo," Callie prompted him. "Commissioner of Clams."

"Ah, yes. Bo." Casper smiled, but a moment later he lost the plot and nodded toward Echo, asking, "Well, well, who have we here?"

Evelyn laid a hand on Callie's shoulder, as if to reassure her there was nothing she could do, and then she moved and stood beside her brother. "Casper, I want you to meet Mimi's boys." She wheeled him over to the boys, and Ginger watched as he offered each of them a shy wave. Another wave went to Mimi, which Mimi returned, though Ginger thought it looked begrudging. After that, Evelyn wheeled him to where Thomas and the other men stood, talking to Captain Lou.

The men gathered round to admire Casper's new motorized wheel-chair, but now and then, Ginger saw Casper steal a glance in her direction. She had no idea what memory she'd evoked, but it was clear, when he looked her way, his agitation increased.

She found it hard not to stare. She was sorting it out, how to reconcile the threatening stranger her father had mistrusted on first sight, with the sunken-eyed befuddled man listing in his wheelchair. As to whether Casper Diggans had done anything to earn her own disdain, she could no longer say.

The captain dropped anchor at three nautical miles, the legal distance for a scattering at sea. The boat rocked for a moment and then steadied, but Ginger and Richard, standing together in the middle of the deck, still grabbed each other's arms as if they needed to hold on to keep balance. At the bow, Callie and Mimi stood together, Mimi busy wrangling the boys out of an argument over who would hold the urn, who would toss it, and who would read the short speech they'd written together. Glory had somehow neglected to leave a list about whether she did or did not want a speech.

As she tried to defuse the situation, Mimi fussed, organizing the boys for photographs, making them stand in size order, and after Wallace tried to cover Hunter's face with his baseball cap, grabbing Neil and inserting him like a human shield between the middle and eldest boys. When Troy looked over at his mother, she smiled and gently touched his cheek, and when Wallace's face collapsed into a sulk, she leaned in and gave him a light kiss on his head. There was something in her movements that reminded Ginger of a cat managing a litter. Light touches here, quick nudges there, a mild but firm assertion of power all conveying love.

Ginger closed her eyes and pictured Julia when she was five, the year she discovered soccer and announced she loved to sweat, and when she was eleven and ran into the kitchen like it was an emergency to say she needed to learn how to cook eggs, and when she was thirteen, moved to tears in a department store dressing room because the saleswoman announced in a loud voice that she didn't fill out her dress, and when she was seventeen in the parking lot at Mount Washington, refusing to get out of the car.

There was a moment that afternoon on the mountaintop when the wind went suddenly still and the sun burned hot on their necks. Julia could have made a sarcastic remark about the weather—Ginger would now say she deserved it—but instead she'd just tugged her mother's arm and took her hand. It was an unexpected and surprising gesture of grace—but Ginger was stuck in the argument, stuck feeling hurt, so her hand stayed limp, a dead fish in her daughter's hot palm. It didn't take more than a moment for her to cast her pique aside, but by then, by the time she finally grabbed Julia's smooth soft hand, it was too late. *Too tight*, Julia told her, the melody of her words like a curse as she pulled her hand away.

"No running." Captain Lou was losing his temper with the boys, and Mimi stood with arms akimbo, contemplating the best intervention.

"Captain Lou," Ginger called. "Any chance you know where Lillian Hellman lived?"

"Yup."

Wallace, grateful for the distraction, mouthed *thank you* and Ginger smiled, happy to have helped. She turned to the captain. "Could we possibly do the scattering there?"

"Can't get closer than three miles out," he reminded her. "Three miles is the law."

"Three miles from Lillian Hellman's house would be great. My mother was a fan. If there's added expense, we'll cover it, right, Mimi?"

Mimi nodded and the captain agreed. It was all the same to him.

The boat slowly turned around and then speeded on, and the boys ran over and thanked Ginger for saving them from more lectures. Then they stood, three boys and their aunt, faces tipped toward the sun.

Ten minutes later, Captain Lou called out, "House is just ahead," and dropped anchor. "This is as close as I can get."

"Come on, boys." Mimi called them over to the side of the boat. "Come on, everyone."

Thomas hung back with Evelyn and Casper, and Captain Lou stayed at the helm. The rest of them gathered at the stern where, in a rare moment of brotherly kindness, Wallace insisted Troy be the one to hold the turquoise shell urn while he and Hunter rested their hands on top.

In the distance, a steamship ferry pulled away from the dock. Its horn blared. Captain Lou's boat heaved in the wake. The turquoise shell slipped out of Troy's hands. They all watched as it fell with an unceremonious plop, into the sea.

Ginger let out a laugh of surprise, but then noticed Troy was crying. Hunter shoved him and told him to stop being a baby. Ginger glanced over the side of the boat. "Boys," she called. "Come over here. You have to see this."

Troy, first to see it, shouted to the others. "Grandma Glory refuses to sink."

"Typical," Mimi said as she joined her boys at the side of the boat and they all watched Glory float, refusing to sink, until, without warning, the sea swallowed her in a giant gulp and she was gone.

Captain Lou let them off in Vineyard Haven. In the parking lot, Casper Diggans held his hand up in a stiff wave and Evelyn, standing behind him, put her hand in front of her mouth. But whether she was blowing a kiss or holding back a cry, Ginger couldn't tell.

CHAPTER THIRTY-NINE

Thomas joined them for dinner: lobsters Richard had picked up, steamed, from a fish market in Menemsha. They ate on the back deck, Wallace and Hunter sucking lobster tentacles soaked in butter and dipping wet fingers into empty bags of chips to get the last of the salt. Troy stayed with Callie, running in circles on the back lawn, struggling to control a kite she'd bought as a gift, the kite now threatening to crash in the gusty wind.

"More string," Callie told Troy. "Let out more string."

The kite lifted off and Troy let the spindle turn in his hands, yelling with delight as the kite darted this way and that, drawing an erratic course across the sky.

"Keep letting it out," Callie shouted. "But don't let go. No matter what."

Ginger watched them, Callie guiding Troy, both of them giddy as they ran from one end of the wide lawn to the other, the kite rising above the tree line, putting on a show.

Thomas broke the silence. "So, I'm guessing Julia is away at college."

Hunter, who hadn't developed his poker face yet, went wide-eyed. Richard moved closer to Ginger. Wallace spoke up. "We don't talk about that."

"Isn't the sky spectacular?" Mimi marveled. "Look at the colors."

"It's okay, Wallace," Ginger said. "We can talk about Julia."

"I'm sorry," Thomas said. "I didn't know—I don't know—I'm sorry."

"Nothing to apologize for. Julia's fine."

"I think this is actually the most beautiful sunset I've ever seen," Mimi said. "Have you ever seen a sky this gorgeous?"

"You don't have to change the subject," Ginger told her. "Boys, if there's anything you want to know about Julia, just ask me. I *want* to talk about her."

Wallace shrugged. "We don't have any questions. We know what happened. Some kid at school started a rumor she ran away, but I told him she's at boarding school and he should butt out."

"Watch the kite," Mimi called to Troy. "Callie, it's getting too close to the trees."

"Mimi, did you tell the boys Julia's at boarding school?"

Mimi slumped. "Sorry, Gingie." A moment later she straightened. "Neil, go take the kite." She called to Troy, "Give the kite to your father and come here. I need to talk to you. Callie, can you come too?" She turned to her husband. "Neil."

Busy searching through a pile of discarded lobster pickings for anything that still had meat, Neil didn't look up.

"Hey," Richard said. "Neil."

His brother-in-law stopped his search. "Yeah?"

"Our wives want us to go fly a kite." Richard turned to Thomas. "Care to join us?"

"Sure."

Happy to disappear into a kite-skills competition, the three men jogged over and relieved Troy and Callie of their toy.

Troy returned to the bench and sat down. Callie sat beside him and draped her arm around his narrow shoulders. When Echo tried to insert himself between the two of them, they laughed and let him in. Wallace moved closer to Ginger. Hunter inched toward his mother. Everyone waited. Finally, Mimi spoke.

"Boys, I made a mistake. I'm sorry. Julia is not at boarding school. I told you that because I didn't want you to worry about her. The truth is your cousin Julia went away. With a friend."

"Why?" Troy asked.

"Remember when you were little and I used to tell you how important it is to pick carefully? Like with apples, you shouldn't pick the ones with fingernail marks, and how it's the same with friends. You have to be careful not to pick a bad one?"

Ginger interrupted. "Julia didn't pick bad friends."

"You're defending the boy now?"

"This is not about the boy. Julia went away," she told her nephews, "because she needed to figure herself out. Most of the time, practically all the time, people can do that right at home. I'm sure that's what all of you are going to do. But every once in a while, someone can't manage to do that at home. So they go away." She looked at Callie, who offered her an unexpected smile. "Want to know the best thing to do when that happens?"

The boys nodded.

"Talk about it. Talk about the person. Talk about them all the time. Can we do that? Can we talk about Julia? Because I bet if Julia was here, she'd have a lot of funny stories about Grandma. Like the year you all went trick-or-treating and Julia dressed up as a movie star and Grandma thought she was dressed up as *her*?"

Wallace remembered that. "Grandma Glory thanked her and Julia got so mad."

"But she let Grandma think it," Hunter added. "Even though Julia was mad, she told Grandma, *You're welcome.* She wasn't even snotty when she said it."

Troy smiled, remembering. "And Grandma liked her costume so much, she gave Julia an extra Hershey bar. The big size. And Julia gave it to me."

"That's not fair," Wallace grumbled. "How come Grandma always gave Julia extra stuff?"

"No more reminiscing. Forward march. We need to be sure—"

Ginger interrupted. "We need to be sure not to confuse marching forward with forgetting."

They were throwing away paper plates, cups, and lobster carcasses when Callie announced her news. "I found Charlie yesterday."

Ginger put down the stack of cups she'd been carrying. "How could you find him?" She met Callie's eyes and spoke the words slowly. "Charlie died, Callie. A long time ago."

Callie stared back, unfazed. "I can take you to see him. Do you want to come with me?"

While Ginger struggled to figure out how to answer, Mimi said, "That is crazy talk, Callie. We—"

Ginger cut her off. "We do. The answer is yes." She hooked her arm through Mimi's elbow. "We'll go wherever you want."

They were twenty minutes from the house when Callie pulled the car onto a grassy shoulder. "He's right through there." Ginger turned and saw the rough-hewn gate of a cemetery.

As they walked through the gate, Callie explained. "Whenever Mom visited me, she went to see Charlie. But she never let me come along. She said it would upset me to think about him. I told her I thought about him anyway, every day. But she still said no. I started looking for him the day I got back. There's more seminaries on the island than you would think."

"Cemeteries," Ginger corrected her.

Callie nodded. "Yesterday, I found him." She stopped. "Here." She squatted in front of a small footstone. Her sisters kneeled beside her.

Ginger read the inscription: "Charlie Tangle. Beloved son and brother."

"We need some rocks," Mimi said. "There's got to be rocks around here." She got up and searched the grass between the plots, looking for stones to lay atop the grave.

Ginger turned to Callie. "I had no idea you lived here. You know that, right?"

Callie nodded. "We kept it a secret. Because, *separate the troublemakers.* That's what the school said. Together, we were trouble. Separated, we were okay. It worked." She smiled. "We're all right."

Mimi returned, her hands clutching rocks which she then shared with her sisters. She kept the largest, a flat one, and put it on the top of the footstone. Ginger laid hers on top of Mimi's. Callie crowned the pile with a third. There was one stone left in Mimi's hand, and Callie took it and placed that one on the top of the tiny tower.

"There," she said. "Now it's four. All the originals." She leaned over and let her hand hover above the pile of rocks. Mimi placed her hand on top of Callie's, and Ginger placed her hand on top of them all. Then, hands stacked, one atop the other, muscle memory took over and as if they were once again thirteen and ten and six, Callie pulled her hand out from the bottom and put it on top, and Mimi did the same, and so did Ginger until, hands moving fast and then faster, they became a muddle, impossible to tell one from the next.

Someone's hand, Ginger couldn't tell whose, hit a rock and the pile tumbled. Mimi put the stones back, carefully rebuilding their tower.

Just as Mimi finished, her cell phone buzzed. "At least someone in the family lives where there's good cell service." She read her text.

"Neil's thirsty. He wants to know, can we stop and pick up beer. Do you mind?" Ginger's phone buzzed and Mimi joked, "Guess all the men are thirsty."

But Ginger's text was from an unknown number.

Mimi looked over and saw the text was just a link. "Don't you hate that? Isn't cell phone spam the worst?"

But Ginger couldn't be sure it was spam. She touched the link and a video came up. Her sisters leaned in close to watch as she turned up the volume and pressed Play.

She saw the girl first, a girl in a long sundress, Julia. Not someone who looked like Julia but really, Julia. She saw Nick next. Nick in his Salvation Army uniform. He was sitting on a chair with a cello between his knees. Had Julia ever mentioned that Nick played the cello?

They were on a stage, she saw now. Not exactly a stage, she realized. Their chairs were on a sheet they were using to mark off the area as if it were a stage. Julia was holding something. A marionette. A marionette made out of a doll. It was one of Julia's old dolls. The American Girl doll with red hair, the one they bought because Julia said it looked like her. The doll was wearing a dress, which Ginger saw was made from a Salvation Army uniform; the doll's clothes matched Nick's.

Nick called out, "Can you hear me?" and the answer was a shout from a crowd, "Yes!"

Then Julia spoke. "I'm dedicating this song to my grandma 'cause she taught it to me."

It was hard to make out all the details on the phone screen, but Ginger could see that Julia was operating the American Girl doll marionette. The marionette, she now noticed, had a toy cello and a chair, and was moving in concert with Nick. Ginger was still thinking what a surprise it was to discover Nick was a good cello player when she realized the melancholy sound she was hearing came not only from the cello. Her daughter was singing. Julia had a beautiful voice.

"'There once was a boy in the north country. He had sisters one, two, three. Love will be true, true to my love. Love will be true to you.'" The screen froze. Ginger waited, but that was it. The video was over. There was no more.

"Look." Callie pointed up to the sky where a pair of birds was circling and chattering loudly. "They like Julia's song so much they're singing along."

"That's not a song," Mimi said. "That's a warning. There's a hawk. See?" She pointed.

"Maybe." Callie turned to Ginger and took her hand. "Julia will be back." Then she closed her eyes. "If you keep your eyes closed and you don't see the hawk, it sounds like a song. Like a happy song."

Ginger held on tight to Callie. And when she closed her eyes, she heard the joy.

ACKNOWLEDGMENTS

First, a huge thank-you to the people who generously shared their expertise on a number of subjects: Linsey Lee, oral history curator at the Martha's Vineyard Museum, and Dana Costanza Street, assistant librarian at the museum, for helping me better understand life on the Island in the seventies (Linsey Lee's fine *Vineyard Voices: Words, Faces and Voices of Island People* gave me a wonderful view into the Vineyard of the past); Seth Wakeman and Kent Healy, for telling captivating stories about the origin and engineering of the opening of the Cut; Tom Kilroy and Lauren Carlton, for teaching me what it means to be a law guardian; Dr. Sylvia Olarte, for deepening my understanding of "as ifs" and "imposters," as well as for countless other brilliant insights; Dr. Alexander Mauskop, for sharing knowledge of brain injuries, PTSD, and all things headache; Sheryl Horowitz; Rich Finkelstein; and the late Stan Hugill, for his important collection, *Shanties from the Seven Seas.*

My heartfelt thanks go to an esteemed group of early and perceptive readers: Marlene Adelstein, Valerie Block, Susan Dalsimer, Alice Elliott Dark, Lisa Gornick, Jill Smolowe—as well as early champions: Cindy Handler, Christina Baker Kline, Jillian Medoff, Jayne Pliner, Dale

Russakoff, Pam Satran, and Laura Schenone. To the very wise women of the Montclair Writers Group: I am lucky to have your unending support and kinship. To Margot Sage-El, the lovely and indefatigable owner of Watchung Booksellers: thank you for being such a great friend to all the writers in our town.

Gratitude forever goes to: Elizabeth Winick Rubinstein, my insightful, delightful, and supersmart agent, and the wonderful Amelia Appel; Jodi Warshaw, whose careful reading, wise suggestions, deep support, and keen commitment make her this writer's dream of an editor; Marianna Baer, whose sharp eye and fierce determination to make everything better actually did make everything better; and the supergreat powerhouse team of Dennelle Catlett, Kathleen Zrelak, and Jeff Umbro.

Not to be forgotten is my dear Fremily and all the friends—too many to mention by name—who have been stalwart champions and nurturers of soul during this long and solitary enterprise.

Above all, there is family. Thanks go to: my dear sister, Jane, who always remembers things I forgot; my wise and bighearted children—Izzy, Lizzy, and Peter—I love you all beyond words; and my cherished husband, Larry, who never stopped cheering me on, never doubted the result, never refused to read another draft, and sweetly fed me, body and soul, on all the long days when I disappeared into my work. You make everyone and everything around you better.

SISTERS ONE, TWO, THREE

BOOK CLUB READING GUIDE

1. In the prologue, we learn that Ginger has kept a big secret from her daughter. Later, Ginger learns others have kept secrets from her. Do you think these characters are keeping secrets to protect someone else or are they keeping secrets to protect themselves? Does it make a difference? Are secrets ever okay to keep?

2. Glory Tangle makes some questionable decisions. Given the circumstances, do you think her decisions are understandable or unforgivable? Were they made out of love, desperation, or something else? Do you think her parenting style was typical for the time? Did your opinion about Glory change by the end of the book?

3. Being a worrier affects every part of Ginger's life, from her choice of profession to her ability to mother. Do you think she was like this before the family tragedy? How much did the tragedy change her? If Ginger had grown

up in a family with Glory and Solly as parents but *without* that terrible day at the beach, how might she have been different?

4. Mimi thinks Ginger was Glory's favorite. Ginger thinks Callie was Glory's favorite. Do you think Glory had a favorite? If so, who was it? Among the three sisters— Ginger, Mimi, and Callie—did you have a favorite? By the end of the book, had your opinion about any of them changed? How?

5. The story moves back and forth, in time and place. How did this affect your reading experience? How do you think the experience would have been different if the story had been told in two parts, the past first and then the present day?

6. Ginger and Julia have a difficult relationship. If you had been in Ginger's position, what would you have done about Julia and Nick? What parallels do you see between the conflict Ginger faces with Julia and the conflicts Glory faced with her daughters? Which do you think is more damaging: holding on too tightly or letting go too soon?

7. When Charlie shows off his ant farm to Thomas, Thomas asks him, "How can that many ants share one measly drop of water?" Think about this as a metaphor for the Tangle children. Did you find Glory and Solly to be stingy with their love? What adaptations do you think the four Tangle children had to make to thrive in their childhood home?

8. At the end of the book, Ginger wonders whether Casper Diggans was really a threat or whether, as a young teenager, she'd perceived things that weren't really there. What do you think? What made her mistrust him? Does

Casper have any responsibility for what happened to Ginger's family? Evelyn says people think she has responsibility. Do you?

9. Discuss the character of Callie. What turned out right for her? What turned out wrong?

10. Let's look into the future: Do you think Callie will move back to be close to her sisters? What kind of relationship do you think the Tangle sisters will have? How long do you think Julia will be away? How do you think her relationship with Ginger will change when she returns?

A CONVERSATION WITH NANCY STAR

1) Where did the idea for this book come from?

Like many writers, I find the process of how stories come to life to be somewhat mysterious. Often the things I write about have been on my mind, in one way or another, for some time. For this book, family secrets was one of several themes that drew me in. As it turns out, there was a specific moment when it first struck me that this would be an intriguing subject to explore in a novel. It occurred at a dinner party in the home of someone I barely knew. The host was telling a story about something that happened in her first marriage. At the sound of footsteps coming down the stairs, she suddenly dropped her story and in a hushed voice warned us not to say a word about it. "My daughter," she explained, "doesn't know I was married before." Her daughter was a teenager. I was practically a stranger. This made me so curious. Why had this mother's benign story, casually told while I ate my salad of mixed greens, been withheld from her teenage daughter? Since then, I've heard many similar and much more dramatic stories of family secrets. What interests me is not only *why* secrets are kept but also the struggle people face as they try to figure out *if* and *when* to reveal them. What seems clear is that waiting to tell can make it harder. This made me wonder: Is there a moment beyond which it's *too* late? The Tangle family is the result of these musings.

2) Why did you choose to tell this story in two time periods?

I've always been drawn to exploring characters before and after something big happens. It really boils down to the age-old question of how we become who we are. I loved the prospect of meeting Ginger when she's at the cusp of adulthood, of seeing that early snapshot of her as she is coming into herself but not yet fully formed. Later, when we meet her as an adult in the present-day story, we get to observe how the events of her life, particularly her family's calamity, have changed her. The same is true for the other characters. Some are more profoundly changed than others. But no one gets by without the events of their lives changing them to some degree.

3) Martha's Vineyard is like a character in your book, and the Vineyard in the seventies seems like a magical place. Were you there?

That would have been fun! But no, I wasn't. I had to research my way back in time. Which was also fun! I am a seasonal resident of the island, but I do not lay any claim to knowing the Vineyard as a native or year-rounder. The island we meet in the book is very much one seen through the eyes of an outsider. Like any real place, life on the Vineyard is a mix of wonderful and hard and complicated—but with an extra-large serving of great physical beauty. To me the island seems to accept "otherness" more than most places I've been. Maybe this has to do with being an island. No matter how much time you spend alone on beautiful walking trails or at the shore, at the end of the day you're going to see everyone you know in the supermarket, so maybe people try a little harder to get along. All I know for sure is I love the place and the people I've met there. It's possible that comes through in the book!

4) There are many unique and original characters in this book. Who did you find easiest to write? Who was hardest?

My feelings about the characters changed in the writing in the same way they change for a reader in the reading. In this book there were characters I knew well immediately. Others were harder to fully understand. And it doesn't always relate to "page time." Solly and Casper, for example, have little time on the page, but I knew them right away. Glory wrote herself. She's still here if you'd like to talk to her. Callie was probably hardest. Just as she's hard for her sisters to know, she was hard for me to know in the beginning. But I am a mother with no favorites! Once I understand the characters and why they do the things they do, I love them all.

5) This book made me cry. But there's also much that's funny. Are you some-one who sees humor in tragedy? Is your first inclination to cry or laugh?

Ask my family! If I cry, it barely gets noticed because, unlike Ginger and her sisters, I'm an easy weeper. But yes, I also love to laugh. I guess you could say that I see the world through a split lens—the funny and the tragic often come to me in the same moment. I will add, though, that even when I *see the funny*, I take this writing thing very seriously. Whether tragic or humorous, my mission is to work as hard as I can to find the truth in my *characters* and in how they view their own lives.

6) Memories play a big part in this book. Different characters remember different things. Some memories are false. Some are only partly true. When you hear someone share a memory, what's your first impulse? Take it as it's offered, or with some measure of disbelief?

I would never judge someone else's memories! If you tell me something happened to you, I will totally believe you! On the other hand, I don't completely trust my own mem-ories. I won't go into the science here, but I think it's pretty well documented that memories are slippery; they change over time, and it can be hard to know what's a real truth and what's a "felt" truth. Have you ever experienced this in your family? Different members remembering different versions of the same event? My guess is it happens in most families. This is why bringing up a discussion of a past event over Thanksgiving dinner can be so thrilling! If you haven't yet, give it a try!

ABOUT THE AUTHOR

Nancy Star is the author of four previous novels: *Carpool Diem*, *Up Next*, *Now This*, and *Buried Lives*. Her nonfiction writing has appeared in the *New York Times*, *Family Circle*, *Diversion* magazine, and on the web. Before embarking on her writing career, Nancy worked for more than a decade as a movie executive in the film business, dividing her time between New York and London. She has two grown daughters and a son-in-law and now lives in New Jersey with her husband.